HEARTS ON LOCK

A Modern Day Love Story

Olivia E. L. Scotland

Manufactured in the United States of America

ISBN: 978-0-615-47237-9

HEARTS ON LOCK

"JUST BECAUSE I DON'T HAVE A MAN... DOESN'T MEAN I DON'T WANT ONE!"

Audria is a thirty-eight year old woman who finds herself uttering this line over and over to her nagging Mother who keeps insisting something must be wrong with her to still be single and with no prospects at her age. But it's not her fault all the fine, eligible, healthy, sane, and financially stable Brothas are ignoring the fact she exists. They just weren't beating her door down for dates. And they didn't seem to care much that The World Class Nagger had already picked out the perfect Mother-of-the-Bride wedding dress, had the minister on standby and the reception hall paid for.

What was a girl to do under all that pressure?

Exactly what Audria keeps doing – ignoring her nutty Momma and enjoying her life as much as possible.

Then, on a whim, she begins a pen-pal friendship with Michael, a man in prison. He's fine, eligible, healthy as far as she knows, and seems sane in his conversation. And an extra plus? He's tall, dark and handsome. But he's far from perfect. He is a flawed, often angry man who battles personal demons and his memories of a time when he lived without conscience. He has never had time for love. Never, before Audria.

The more they talk, the deeper they fall. Michael touches emotions inside her that have long been buried, and before she knows it, Audria shares her most intimate secret with this man that she has kept hidden from everyone all her life. It is something from her past. Deep, dark, and disturbing, it has hovered over her and threatens to destroy any happiness that comes her way.

Unless she faces it.

This is a story about two people's willingness to step away from society's hang-ups, dictates, and their own personal fears. They bring light and happiness to dark spaces, warmth and healing to hurt places. They embrace each other and the love they find together as they discover what it feels like for the first time to have their **Hearts On Lock.**

"Love awaits the brave."
                    - Markus Pierson

FOR DADDY...
I feel you often!

one
Looks Like WYSIWIG

"JUST BECAUSE I DON'T HAVE A MAN DOESN'T MEAN I DON'T WANT ONE!"

My Momma sure could get under my skin whenever she had a mind to, and it looked like she was of a mind to right now. She was standing there with that look on her face. The one she got when she was getting ready to needle me about one thing or the next. This time, looked like it was gon' be her favorite thing to needle me over, the lack of a man in my life.

If it was anybody else, that look wouldn't bother me, not in the least lil' bit, but my Momma? Ain't like anybody else. Nobody needles like my Momma. I mean, nobody. She's a world class champion needler and Sweet Lord Jesus, help whoever happens to be on the receiving end of her needling tongue when she gets cranking. Which, in most instances, happens to be me, since I'm her only 'still unmarried' girl child, and the only one who can't ever bring myself to cuss her out and tell her to mind her business, I'm grown.

I know exactly what her problem is too. She doesn't listen. It doesn't matter what I say and how much I try to explain to her that my single status is not by choice. I mean, it's not like we have any control over fate, right? You don't map out your life and decide you want to still be single at thirty-eight. I mean, nobody would be that crazy. But, does she listen when I try to say all that? Nooooooo. That would be too much like right. She just gets that look on her face, wags a well-manicured finger at me and tells me that what her problem is is that she's the only one in her bridge, bingo and bowling clubs with a grown-ass daughter pushing forty and still single. Then she has to go and remind me that not only am I pushing forty and still single, but that's pushing forty and still single *with no prospects*.

Okay, I gotta give her that. My man prospects are about as dry as the driest spot in the Mojave desert, and that's pretty damn dry however you look at it, but it's *still* not my fault. Seriously? -- and I know this might sound stupid -- but if I'm gonna lay blame at anybody's feet, it would have to rest squarely in front of Daddy's size thirteens. And he's been passed on now for the last ten years, so I can't say that too loudly or he might decide to borrow one of St. Peters' lightning bolts up there where he is and take aim at my ample backside for slandering his good name.

Although Daddy should know, before he takes aim, that in this instance it's not really slander, and blaming him for my situation is not necessarily a bad thing. It's just that Daddy knew how to love him some Momma. She was the sun, moon and stars in his eyes and he loved her more than he loved himself, I thought sometimes. When you bare witness to that kind of love, it makes you want the same for yourself. And everything that comes along that isn't Daddy's special kind of love pales in comparison and feels like a colossal waste of your time. It wasn't my fault that God didn't make another one of Daddy to double as my long-awaited man.

But try telling that to Momma. She wasn't feeling me on that. In her mind, I had to be doing *something* wrong to keep attracting the kinds of losers that seemed to be following some spotlight beacon in the sky that pointed them directly to my doorstep. Seemed like every emotionally unavailable decrepit, commitment phobe, relationship escape artist, cheating spouse, and unambitious, lazy good-for-nothing so-and-so would eventually cross my path. And me Miss I've-Got-To-Love-With-My-Whole-Heart-Or-Not-At-All would fall for the bullshit lines and sob stories every time. And sooner or later, I'd find myself wrapped up in some mess that usually involved a whole lot of tears, self-berating, and the occasional restraining order to get out of. Damn, can a sistah just find her a good man without all the unnecessary, unwanted drama?

See, the thing is... it's not that I can't find a man. That's not my trouble at all. Shoot, I find them quick as some women change footwear. My problem is the ones I do find, or should I say the ones that find me, always got something wrong with 'em. And not just a lil' wrong something. Oh no, they got a rack of issues, lots of 'em. It just takes me longer than everybody else to figure out that spells trouble for Audria. And trouble with a capital T.

Audria. That's me. Audria Christine Hope. My Momma named me after her own Momma who, God rest her soul, died two days before I was born. And she took my middle name from my Daddy's Momma who died a week after I was born. She was all the time saying she thinks one of the reasons she and Daddy's love got as strong as it did so early in their marriage, is because they both lost their Mommas within a week of each other. Whether she's right or wrong, I don't know, but I can't argue that their love was some kinda strong.

Not in a zillion years would I ever admit this to Momma, but sometimes I find myself wondering whether she's right. Is something *wrong* with me? Do I have some subconscious wish, embedded deep down in my psyche, to sabotage my future's happiness by gravitating to men who ain't about nothing? I don't think so, but what do I know, right? This from the woman who carried on a two-year affair with a married man and actually believed him when he said he was going to leave his wife? Obviously, I'm not to be trusted with matters of the heart.

But I can't trust my Momma either. The last time she got on this kick about finding me a man, she started dropping by my house unannounced all hours of the day or night with some man cowering behind her that she wanted to introduce to me. She would usually introduce the cowerer as 'this nice boy' and insist we have coffee, although she knew damn well I didn't drink coffee and more importantly, that I wasn't big on inviting strangers into my home.

Because I had such a hard time saying no to her, I would make nice, serve up tea and something or other for the three of us, *yes, she would stay*, engage in a little small talk, and then send Robert, Tony, Ben or Jerry on their way with promises to call. Half the time, the business card or piece of paper with scribbled phone number would be discovering the bottom of my trashcan as its new home before Mister even reached the end of my driveway. I know Momma means well an' all, but there's just something innately icky about your own mother trying to set you up. That is sooooooo not happening.

"Look Audria. Don't you think your Momma deserves to have some grandchildren, or at least *one* to ooh and ahh over and spoil like that ole no-good braggin' Sylvia Hendricks? She up to number four now, Audria. Four." She held up her fingers in my face like I didn't know how to count. "And the way her daughter Vie and that buck-toothed, no-neck husband of hers are all loosey goosey with their planned parenthood, they'll be working on baby number five in the next few months. And here I have none. None."

Here we go. I rolled my eyes at her and just waved her off. We had this conversation at least once a week, and I wasn't going there with her.

She was all the time calling me or just busting through my front door with some new designer wedding dress catalog she wanted me to look at, or pictures of some brand spanking new ballroom that Sister so-and-so could get us a good discount at, or better yet, like was her latest thing -- loading me down with brochure after brochure for the perfect honeymoon. Never mind the obvious -- that I had to find a man first, before we got to all that.

So Momma does her thing and I do mine. She gets under my skin like a Brazilian jungle parasite, but what Momma doesn't get under her daughter's skin from time to time. I'ma love her regardless. *That* is non-negotiable.

So don't ask me where and when this idea just popped into my head. Well, okay, you can go on and ask me. It was about two weeks ago and it was around 10 o'clock on a Tuesday night. I was sitting in my bedroom kinda peripherally watching Lingo on the Game Show Network. I know, I know, but I like word games and will pick that any day over some of the other mess on the box.

So, I'm sitting there watching Chuck Woolery with his fine White ass, romancing them game show contestants. Every time I'd quit watching Chuck, I'd find myself looking at my computer. So eventually, I tuned out Chuck and got on there to surf around and see what I'd see. Went into a couple of them chat rooms, but after about fifteen minutes dealing with Punjab and his cousins an'em trying to private message me for online humping, I got tired of that and came outta there.

Then I get this bright idea about checking out penpals. I go to Google and type in the word 'Penpal', hit GO, and sit back to let the search engine do its thing. Couple seconds later, the first hit that pops up says 'Prison Penpals'. I roll my eyes until I feel like they're gon' stay stuck up in the back of my head if I don't stop. Lawd, just what I need, to start messing around with *that* kinda madness. But something makes me go on and click on the link and it tells me to 'Click here to read hundreds of ads from inmates all over the country.' I go on and click on the new link and a line with the alphabet pops up. What's this? When I check it out, I see the way this thing works is they have all these inmate ads set up according to the last name of the inmate. Big help there. I mean, what am I supposed to do with that? This could take all night.

Anyway, since my keyboard is in front of me and my fingers are resting on the 'home' keys getting ready to type, I think, 'why not try looking at everybody under A-S-D-F first and then if nothing jumps out at you there, you can move on to L-K-J, holding the semicolon. So I click on the A's and start reading. Half hour later, I'm rolling my eyes even harder. Wasn't nobody under the A's that I would even *begin* to consider writing to. So, I click on the S's and start reading. I'm already starting to feel bored, so I decide to start reading from the bottom of the ads instead of the top.

Szubrowski, Arthur. Loser.
Symonds, Anthony. Loser.

Sweeney, George. White guy. Nothing against White folks but I'm not trying to look at that behind closed doors nor next to me in bed.

Swanson, Calvin. Looks short. Don't like no short-short man. Might be short in other ways.

Sundaram, Adi-somebody-or-the-other. No picture, but he sure enough sounds like another Punjab to me and I can't even pronounce his first name. Whats am gon' do with a man whose first name I need a language specialist to learn how to pronounce?

Sullivan, Kenneth. Nice looking, tall, light-skinned. And damn, look at the body on him. But nah, ain't trying to fight with no man for the mirror. Just too damn pretty.

Stuckey, Ronald. He look just like his name. Stuck. Like he's always gon' be stuck on stupid and always gon' be stuck being a criminal.

Strong, Michael. Hmm, like the name. Both of 'em. Like the last name – Strong. And he looks it too. Kinda like WYSIWIG. What you see is what you get? Plus Michael has always been my favorite name for a man. Don't know why. Just seems manly like. And baby boy ain't hardly bad on the eyes, okay? Matter of fact, he's kinda a cutie, but in a strong, confident kinda way. Let me read this profile. And I was off and running with this Michael guy.

He was listed as African American. I could see that, so a plus. His birthday was given as February 14th – Valentine's Day. Not like I could ever forget that date, and it said he was born in 1971. Damn, that made him 40, just two years older than me, so right age. Then I get to the scary part. His profile says he's in jail for a bunch of stuff. Armed robbery. Possession of firearms. Possession of a controlled substance. Sale of a controlled substance. Conspiracy. And some more mess that I couldn't even follow. Lawd, this man is some kinda Billy badass. Don't know if I want to be messing around with that.

I'm all set to click on the next guy, but something keeps me reading. I click on the part of the page that lets me see what he has to say. His ad's short, a lot shorter than some of the others. I go on and read it.

> *Peace, I'm Michael.*
> *The past is exactly that - the past. I want to focus on my future and I'm looking for someone who can help me do that while focusing on theirs. And if we're lucky, maybe eventually we might start focusing on the same thing. I only ask one thing of whoever responds - come with truth or don't bother.*

That was it? Brotha man didn't mince words, did he? Said what he needed to say and was out. I read his ad over again a couple times, and felt myself liking it, liking the tone of it. This Michael guy sounded like he was . . . what? I thought about it for a little bit. Real. He felt REAL to me, solid, like he was exactly what his surname was – *strong*. Before I even started hunting around for something to write down the address and his information, I already knew I was going to write him. Didn't know what the hell I was going to say to some guy in prison, but it didn't matter. I was writing him and that's all there was to it. When I got to the actual letter, I'd think of something *appropriate* to say.

two
Hello

After four days of walking around with this man's ad and the address for the penpal thing in my purse, stealing looks at the words and of him from time to time, I finally decided to piss or get off the pot. Lawd, my mouth could be so crass sometimes. Just anything would fall out of my head from time to time. I really needed to do something about all this cussing. It sure wasn't lady-like, but guess I had to be me. Love me or leave me, right?

Unbeknownst to him, Mister Michael Strong had been all over the place with me. Had been to work, to church, to the grocery store, to that hole-in-the-wall nail shop I went to for them Asian women to jack up my nails a little more by putting on more of that gel crap. I *really* needed to take that mess off my nails and let my nails do their own thing, but what can I say, I like the polished look. What was I supposed to do with stubs for nails? Which is exactly what my nails would look like if I took off the gel acrylic.

But anyway, I was saying, this brotha had already been more places with me than if he was really my man. Hmm, My Man. Wish I could... Okay Audria, you're not going there. You're just not. Those kinds of thoughts usually took me in only one direction, and it wasn't a good one, so I let that go and whipped out the picture to look at it and him again.

The picture was kinda grainy looking, but still clear enough that the details were already imprinted on my brain. Tall. Looked to be about 6'2" or 6'3". Damn. Liked the way he was standing in the picture too. Casual, hands in his pockets, but strong all the way from the bottom of his sneaks to the top of his bald head. I loved me a bald-head brotha. Not all of them could wear it, but this Michael guy was wearing it and wearing it well. He had on casual clothes in the picture, nothing but some sweats, but I could see the definition of his thighs through his pants, although they weren't tight on him.

He was standing kinda angled to the side like, with his legs farther apart than most men would feel comfortable with, but on him, it made him look confident, like he could handle his business; whatever his business was. His left leg was thrust out in front and the way he was standing made him look slightly bowlegged. Another plus. Don't know what it is, but I've always been a sucka for a slightly bowlegged brotha. Don't get me wrong. I'm not trying to be able to wheel a shopping cart through their legs or nothing, but it was just one of those things that bumped up things a notch on the attraction scale.

Looking at the picture, I felt something turn over somewhere in the pit of my stomach. I liked this man's look. Liked his chest area. It looked strong. Liked how his arms looked and how broad his shoulders were. Everything about him screamed *strength* to me, like I would have nothing to worry about being held by him.

And let's not talk about his face. Like I said, he was easy on the eyes. Had a strong, *why couldn't I stop using that word,* handsome face. Not like some pretty boy, but strong like Morgan Freeman, Sidney Poitier, and Denzel kinda strong. Strong like Ice Cube kinda strong. Strong like The Rock kinda strong. Like Mekhi Pfeiffer, DMX, Fifty Cent, The Game, Luda, Bussa Buss, and Terence Howard all rolled into one. He just looked like he wasn't about no game playing, like he was straight up WYSIWIG – what you see is what you get. And I was curious to see what I'd get, so I knew it was time to get busy writing my hello letter.

Poured me a glass of Merlot, turned on some Luther – *Luther knew how to set him some mood, didn't he? Missed him so much,* - got the gas fireplace going with the remote so I could feel some warmth on my toes, and curled up on a nearby sofa to start writing.

Lawd, what was I gon' say to this man? I couldn't very well tell him what I really wanted to say – that I liked the fact that he *looked* like his name and that the simplicity of his words are what made me want to say hey. I mean, he would probably find that all schoolgirlish or something. But that's what I really wanted to say. Took a sip of the wine and nibbled on the tip of the pen I was holding poised above the writing pad. Michael's ad was sitting on the couch next to me. I looked over at it and my eyes fell on his last sentence: "I only ask one thing of whoever responds – come with truth or don't bother." That made up my mind for me and I started writing.

> *Sat. 4/14 - 8:40 p.m.*
> *Hello and Peace to you too, Michael.*
> *My name's Audria. This is my first time doing anything like this. Writing an inmate, I mean. I'm not sure exactly why I'm writing you, except that I liked what you had to say. It was simple and seemed sincere.*

Okay, did I want to get into this whole thing about what he looks like? If I do, he might think I'm all about the physical and I don't want him thinking that I'm just some desperate, horny woman trying to get laid. Woman, you are tripping. Just go on and finish this letter. Let's see, where was I? Right. Simple and seemed sincere.

> *...I like your name. Actually, I like both your names. Michael has always been my favorite name for a man and your surname seems to fit you somehow, like you're really STRONG all the way through. Okay anyway, some details about me. I'm 38. African American. I was born in the D.C. area but my people are originally from North Carolina. I think I'm a fun person. Like to do a lot. Concerts. The Theatre. Travel. And I believe in helping people who need it where I can.*

God, I'm groaning here. That stuff sounds so freaking weak. Your people are originally from North Carolina? Who are you?

Moses? Leading your people, the Children of Israel, out of Egypt? And a 'fun' person? Are you trying to bore him to death? And what's with the I'm Miss Goody-Two-Shoes thing about helping people when you can? Okay so it's true, but did you have to tell *him* that? It's going to sound phony to him. Whatever. Whatever. Just go on and finish the damn letter.

> *...Like you, I believe that the past is the past, but many times, we need to look at our past before we can look at or to our future. And the present is another part of that trio which people often ignore, but I'm not trying to get all existential on you. Just saying hello. Okay, I'm not sure what else to say. I'm not really big on the physical thing, at least not from my angle, so if you want any details about what I look like etc., please ask for them. That's it for now, I guess. I hope I'll hear from you soon. Take good care of yourself.*
>
> *Audria.*

'I'm not trying to get all existential on you?' So now we're in Psych class? And why couldn't you just tell the man what the hell you look like? You know he's probably gon' think you're a dog or something. And 'take good care of yourself?' Who the hell else is going to take care of him other than himself? Audria, you are such a flake. Ain't no way in hell that man's gon' write you back. No way in hell.

Whether he would write back or not was a question that had gone unanswered, 'cuz the letter was still stuck down in the bottom of my purse a week later. Folded it up, put a stamp on it, even put it in an envelope and wrote his name and the address on the outside.

Michael Strong #03579-212
Blasenburg Federal Penitentiary
15038 Victory Way
Pittsburgh, PA 15219

Pittsburgh? Damn, he's close by. I roll up that way sometimes to visit my girl Rose. Okay Audria, stop tripping. You don't even know if this guy's gon' write you back and you're already thinking about geography? Plus, how's he gon' write you back and you haven't even mailed the damn letter yet? Chicken. Oh shut it. I'll mail it. Mail it when I get good 'n ready.

So I kept playing these little games with myself, doing the back and forth thing about mailing the letter, until someone made the decision for me.

There I was at work. I work as a legal secretary for this hella' big law firm in D.C. Have been doing this kind of work for longer than anybody needs to be doing it. I hate it. Hate everything about it. I think it's the servile aspect of it that gets under my skin the most. Hate having to deal with condescending assholes all the live long day. "Is that my phone Audria? Get that." "Was that the mail cart going by? Why isn't my mail opened already?" Here, type this hundred page document that I've spent the last two weeks making edits to, but could you turn it around in 15 minutes. "Oh Audria, you don't look busy. Whyn't you run grab me lunch so I can take this conference call?" *But I'm really gon' be gabbing it up on the phone with my mistress.*

It was all the same crap. Taking bullshit off idiots who were usually way younger than me and had about zero experience in the School of Hard Knocks. Most of them had Momma and Daddy in back of them handing them life on a silver platter. Ivy League schools all their lives. Loans or outright gifts to go to Law School. Buying them their dream car. Downpayment on their first house. Floating them a couple hundred thou here and there whenever they decided they needed to go get laid by somebody other than their Ivy League girlfriend, running down to Jamaica or the Virgin Islands. I hated it and hated them. Didn't want to be doing this crap any more than I wanted to be a two dollar 'ho sellin' my tail on Georgia Ave, but it paid the bills. Actually, paid them quite nicely, thank you very much, and it was one of the only non-degreed professions in this far too political city that you could make decent money at.

Anyway, so there I was at work, minding my own business. I get a phone call from the Mailroom that confuses the hell out of me. It's Dean calling to tell me he put the envelope in with the rest of the outgoing mail. What envelope, I ask him. Then he tells me that there was an envelope on the floor next to my desk when he was passing with the mail cart and since it already had a stamp on it, he scooped it up and threw it in with the rest of the mail.

I slam the phone down on Dean without even thinking about it and start digging through my pocketbook like a mad woman 'cuz I'm thinking, NO, NO, NO, I wasn't ready yet. I wasn't ready to send it yet. And sure enough, NO envelope addressed to Michael Strong, so it's gone. Out of my hands. Guess I'll just have to wait now to see if I hear back from him. I frown up my face, throw a hand on my hip and glare at the little pissant attorney picking that particular moment to pass by my desk. I want to throw my stapler at his frigging head. This was the one thing that could rankle me even more than Momma. I despise waiting. But that's exactly what I was gon' have to do if I wanted to hear back from Michael Strong.

three
Hello Yourself

"STRONG. MAIL."

Michael looked sideways through the partially open cell door at the dude standing there holding out an envelope to him. He didn't even feel like moving. Ever since putting that ad up on the prison's penpal website, he kept getting bothered by a bunch of horny housewives, mostly White ones, who had nothing but surfacey conversation to offer up, wanting him to give them graphic details about what position he would put them in first before he started pounding away. Wished he could take it down, but the guy who ran the whole penpal thing was an asshole who believed in doing everything by the book. You asked that your ad run for a year, and he was running it for a year and not a day less. But assholes made the world go round too, so whatever. He would just keep doing what he'd been doing with the last bunch of letters that came in – chuck them to the side and keep rollin'.

He nodded slightly at dude by the door, telling him with a subtle tilt of his head to drop the letter on the bed and shuffle on with his cart. He wasn't trying to move right now. He was tired. Tired of working like a slave, real work, and receiving chump change for it at the end of every month. Tired of living like and feeling like a caged animal. With the amount of time he had already served up in here and the rest of his bid still looking at, one would think he would have gotten used to this by now, but prison was the kind of hell nobody could understand until they lived it. He was tired of being around so much testosterone, like that's all there was on the planet. Was no softness, no kindness, no real warmth. Just Niggaz doing time, trying to make peace with their individual demons. Some did, some didn't, but whether they did or didn't, *everybody* did time.

He rolled over on his back, and started staring at the same spot in the ceiling he had been staring at for the last 4,669 days. This was a game he had started playing after about two years behind these man-made walls, adding up the days and keeping track of them instead of the years. He knew what the years meant. Didn't need a calendar to keep track of them steadily rolling by, but counting the days, focusing on the big numbers, kept him from thinking about how many years had passed with him here and how many were still to pass.

Michael stretched his neck muscles, tilting his head sharply against one collarbone then the next, waiting for the crack. He liked these moments that came few and far between when his cellie was off somewhere else. He understood the way this prison thing worked. It was big business for White America. They crammed as many prisoners into a spot as they could, and it wasn't good business practice to have a cell without two cellies, or roommates, in it, so he had to share an 8 x 10 foot space with another grown ass man, a man who only had something like twenty-two months to do on his bid, but didn't a night go by that he didn't cry his bitch ass to sleep.

Michael wasn't knocking him or his tears. If that was dude's thing to deal with his pain and his demons, then that was his thing, but he just wasn't comfortable with weakness in a man, especially another brotha, and he had seen this dude back down from enough confrontations to know his weakness went far deeper than the tears he spilled every night. It was just a matter of time before his weakness resulted in that shit being brought to his own doorstep, and that he wasn't having. He backed down from *no* man.

He went to turn over and his hand came in contact with the letter laying there. Damn. He grabbed it up to throw it in the corner, but found himself looking at the return address. It was some kind of law firm. That much was obvious from the LLP. He didn't know who would be writing him from a law firm, considering that it was some asshole at a law firm that made the case against him to send him to this living hell. He ripped it open.

> *Sat. 4/14 - 8:40 p.m.*
> *Peace to you too, Michael.*
> *My name's Audria... This is my first time doing anything like this. Writing an inmate, I mean...*

Twenty minutes later he was re-reading the letter for the third time. Damn. A sistah writing him? And with a nice name too. Audria. It sounded kinda exotic, but cool like, sophisticated. And she sounded real. Sincere. Like she was really nervous because this was her first time writing an inmate, not saying it because she'd figured out this is what every inmate wants to hear – that he's her first. Dangling like a ball of yarn to a cat the chance to pop a mental cherry.

He sat up, balanced his tall frame on the side of the bed and read it again. She sounded sweet. Kinda what she said about him in her letter. Simple. Easy. And not in no wanting to bust drawerz kinda way. He looked at the date on the letter. April 14th. Damn, that's how long mail took to reach just from D.C.? It was almost two weeks old. Well, that was cool. Didn't matter none. He had already decided he was writing her back.

Reaching over to the tiny in-wall desk he and his cellie had to share, he grabbed a legal pad and a pen, got comfortable and started his scribe.

> *Fri. 4/27*
> *Hello yourself, Ms. Audria, and bringing you Peace again.*
> *It was a nice surprise to receive your letter. I don't get many letters from Sistahs, so it was nice to get yours. I'm glad you decided to write, even though you weren't exactly sure why you did. I too, found what you said simple and sincere. Thank you for the compliment on my names. My Mother always reminded me of the meaning of my name. Michael means one*

who is like God. Can't say I'm anything like God. Hell, look at me where I am, but that was her choice. Plus she got a kick out of telling me that she named me after an angel - the Guardian Archangel of the Jews in the Old Testament. And Strong? Yeah, not to brag or nothing, but that's me. Always been, always will be.

So, you're 38. Two years younger than me. Nice age for a nice lady. At least you sound like a nice lady. And you're from D.C. In days gone by, D.C. used to be a stomping ground of mine, but I would never be there long enough to really appreciate the city and all it probably has to offer. I'm originally from New York, the Boogie-Down Bronx, but some of my peoples are from North Carolina too. The Elizabeth City area, Northeastern side near Virginia Beach, right near the water. You'll have to tell me where yours are from and whether you ever visited my side of town. Who knows, we might have crossed paths before.

You sound like a fun person. Can't say I see many concerts, go to the theatre or do much traveling in my present circumstances, but it's all good. Nothing lasts forever. I'm glad you're able to do those things and to have fun doing them. Maybe you can give me a blow-by-blow on one of those things in your next letter. Truth be told, although I've been to concerts in the past, I wasn't really there for the same reason most everybody else was there for. Same deal with traveling. I been to a lot of places, but they were just that - places. I would be there for a purpose, handle that, and then leave. I wasn't there to see the sights like everybody else. And whether you believe this or not, I've never been to the theatre. The way you spell it, make me know you're talking about theatre, like to see a play or symphony or something, and not the movies. I think it's something I'd like to do some day.

Michael sat up, put the letter to one side, and scrubbed at the side of his face with a less-than-soft hand. This wasn't like him to start talking about something he wanted to do *someday*. It wasn't like that *someday* was just around the corner. And he wasn't usually this fast and free with personal information about himself either, talking about his Moms and his name. But okay, whatever. Obviously, there was something about this woman's vibe that was making him go there, so he would just keep writing.

Audria, I like what you said about helping people who need it where you can. That's one of the problems with us (Black folks). Not enough of us understand what it means to give back and do our part to help our younguns come up with their coming up, you know? It's important, so I'm glad you take the time out of all your funning to give that some energy.

Now what you said about looking at the past before we can look to our future? I'm with you on this in some ways, but not really all the way there in another way. Let me explain. I'm gon' use ME as an example of the first thing. I know where I been, know the kind of person I was, a dude I'm happy to tell you is in my past. So, I've done all the looking at my past I want to do. I'm not gon' forget it, but I'm using it as a reminder that I don't ever want to go back there, and that's the thing that makes me want to look at my future now. That's one example in favor of why looking at your past shouldn't always be a focus. Now, for the next example, I'm gon' use Black folks. I love my people, can you tell? But anyway, Black folks. The majority of Black folks get stuck looking at their past so much that they can't see their future. Like somebody who can't see the forest for the trees. They make themselves stay back there in The Middle Passage and on the plantation so much that they can't be bothered with trying to find ways to lift Our Race from the rut we're stuck in. Okay, so you done got me started. Didn't mean to say all that, but I needed to explain my thinking on this particular thing.

And yeah, you're right, we can't ignore the present either. That's where we live, ain't it? Now. In the moment. Sometimes, for us to think to the future or our past, we have to make sure we're all the way right in the present. Does that make sense to you? Listen Audria, you used a word that I'm not familiar with. Existential. Don't know what that is and I don't have access right this minute to a dictionary to look it up. I will though, so next time you write me, I'll know what it is.

Alright, I been rambling enough here. Don't want to monopolize your time, so let me wrap things up. Oh, before I forget. Yeah, I'm curious about what you look like, but something's telling me to fall back on asking you too much about the physical just yet, so I'm gon' listen to that something. We'll get to it, right? No rush. I mean, I ain't going nowhere and neither are you, right? We'll get to it.

Well, you take care of yourself, Audria. By the way, that's a very pretty name. I imagine a pretty name for a pretty lady. Peace.

Michael

He was sticking the letter in an envelope when his pain-in-the-ass cellie came bouncing in from wherever.

"What up, Cuz?"

Dude was a straight up fool sometimes. Michael looked at him sideways, making sure his face showed a slight trace of annoyance.

"Name's Strong, or Michael, not 'Cuz'." He'd done told this Negro more than enough times not to call him no Cuz, but did he ever listen? That was his problem right there. He didn't listen for shit, and that not listening was what would eventually get him fucked up by somebody tired of having to repeat themselves over and over to him.

He ignored Pain-in-the-ass and read over his letter again, still feeling some surprise at how much personal information he was giving up to this woman, but he wasn't tempted to withhold it by not sending the letter though. This was a woman he wanted to have repeated conversations with. He could only hope his letter would find its way to her and that she would write him back.

He wasn't deluding himself on the way the world looked at inmates. It was easier for them to marginalize you and write you off as less than human, not worth the time to rehabilitate or reshape into productive citizens. They gave it lip service and all, *saying* out of one side of their neck that's what they wanted, but it was bullshit. If they really meant it, the government would be sinking more money into after-school programs for young people and finding positive ways to keep them off the streets, rather than building more penitentiaries. But whatever. Right now, he just wanted Audria to get this letter and to write him back. Guess he just added another thing to his list of things to wait on. Damn, that felt like a dirty word in his mouth. He hated waiting.

<u>four</u>
Fallback

Audria sat at her desk fuming. *Why* did she, a grown ass woman, have to put up with this kinda nonsense? This man had been standing at her freaking ledge now for a good half hour marking up some document. Just acting like he didn't have his own office which was practically the size of her master bedroom at home. It didn't make a bit of sense how people could just disregard your need for privacy. What? He thought she liked him breathing his stank coffee breath all up in her space, listening to her phone conversations, and trying to read every e-mail she got? Didn't make a bit of sense. She rolled her eyes, loudly cleared her throat, grabbed her purse, and headed off to the Ladies' room with attitude. Hopefully, he would learn how to take a hint and be gone by the time she got back.

She had been edgy all week, feeling out of sorts and ugly, like anybody saying the slightest wrong thing to her would wind up holding their chopped off head. She knew what it was, although she didn't understand it, but she had finally figured it out when she found herself calling the mailroom for the third time in one morning asking them if any new mail had been delivered from the

Post Office. She was actually waiting to hear back from that Michael guy.

Ridiculous. She wasn't waiting on any... *convict*. That wasn't for her and she needed to just face that. What could she possibly want with some loser behind bars? Whether he sounded sincere or not. A lot of people sounded sincere but that didn't stop them from turning out to be straight up criminals or crazy. Look at Charles Manson, Jeffrey Dahmer and even that loon Jim Jones who talked all them people into drinking his special mixed-up batch of poison Kool-aid. She was sure all them folks guzzling that mess believed he was sincere and look what they got for their belief. She needed to just put this guy out of her mind and go back to trying to find a man the regular, old-fashioned way.

A picture of her mother popped up in her head and she groaned aloud inside the bathroom stall. No, anything but that. She loved her mother dearly, but she was not subjecting herself to even one more fixer-upper blind date her Momma brought around. She just didn't have the energy or patience to deal with that kinda madness. Maybe she could start going to church again. She hadn't gone in a long time. Didn't church always have good, strong eligible men here and there looking to make an honest woman out of somebody? She would have to dust off her Sunday best and make arrangements to go.

She stepped out of the stall, made a point to ignore the stringy-haired blonde attorney standing two sinks down from her, and pulled out her tube to apply fresh lipstick. The woman left the bathroom and Audria took a moment to check herself out in the mirror.

She wasn't drop dead gorgeous like a Halle, Beyoncé or J-Lo type, but she knew she was fine. She had a fairly decent figure, a little on the thick side, but thickness ran in her family, 'specially on her Momma's side. She thought she carried it well on her 5'8" frame that featured curvy hips and a firm, deliciously round backside, despite the little stomach she couldn't seem to get rid of despite all her work on the Ab Roller. She had nice thighs, beautifully shaped calves, and slightly large feet, but from the waist up though, she knew that's where her biggest strengths lay as far as physical attributes went. Her breasts were nice. Large but not saggy, and they were the perfect complement to her well defined arms and shoulders, a fairly long neck, and a soft, oval-shaped face.

She really liked her features. Her nose was slightly larger than she liked, but it was her's and she was thankful to the Universe for all her gifts. Her cheekbones weren't particularly high, but her face tapered to full, thick lips and a strong chin. Her eyes were expressive. Someone way back when had called them haunting even. Call them what you wanted, she liked them.

She poked her lips out in an Angelina Jolie kinda puffy pout, stuck her tongue out at her reflection, and laughed a little at her silliness. See? She could be nice and not all crazy edgy. She needed to find her center again and stop acting all weird over a letter from some guy who was probably not thinking about her in the least lil' bit. She applied the candy apple red lipstick, lined her lips with a chocolate brown liner that contrasted nicely with the red color, fluffed her Kinky Twist African braids, and headed back to her desk. She hoped Mr. I'm-Gonna-Invade-Your-Private-Space-Just-'Cuz-I-Can had gone back to his office. She came around the corner, got happy when she saw he was gone, but felt a weight drop down in the pit of her stomach. Dean was standing at her desk with his mail cart holding up a bundle of mail.

"Okay, Miss Thang. You owe me an apology for slamming the phone in my ear the other day and not bothering to call me back to apologize. What's up wid' dat?"

She rolled her eyes at him. She liked him and all, but he was such a queen most days. She didn't know why she was drawn to him with all his drama, but she loved his big-head ass.

She waved him off. "Whatchu got for me, Daddy-O? You got anything good?"

He nodded, pursed his lips like only a gay man can, rolled his oversize eyes back at her, and got all hush hush. "Audie, you ain't nevah tole me you got family in lock-up. Who you got writing you from the pen in P-A?"

Audria felt the breath catch in her throat. *Michael.* He'd written her back. Oh God. She didn't know what to say to Dean. She was embarrassed. She hadn't been crazy about the idea of using the Firm's address to get mail, but she didn't think it would be safe using her home address for something like this. She mumbled something unintelligible to Dean. She knew it was by the weird look he gave her, but he handed her the mail, gave one of his signature queenly snaps, and pushed his cart on down the hall.

As soon as he and his cart were around the corner, she sat down and started rifling through the stack of mail he had handed her. She didn't understand why she was feeling so nervous and overheated, and her stomach was doing mad flip-flops like a thousand butterflies had been set loose inside there.

Throwing everything else to the side, she grabbed up the envelope and just stared at it for some moments. He had such a neat handwriting, but with bold strokes, kinda like his name – strong. She looked at the postage date on the envelope. April 27th. Her eyes flitted to the calendar on her desk. That was last Friday. Here it was a week later. So, it took his letter all this while to get to her? Gawd, this wasn't good. This waiting thing.

Audria was all set to rip open the envelope when Asshole Attorney decided to take up residence at her ledge again. This time he was bringing her work, and lots of it. Michael and his letter would have to wait until later. Damn.

Later didn't come until almost 8:30 when she was finally released for the day from the concrete plantation. She knew she needed to put these attorneys she worked for in check. Just because she didn't have a husband and some kids, they looked like they always made the incorrect assumption that she had no life or didn't want one. They were always bringing her work five minutes before it was time for her to go home, and it was never anything easy or quick. Most of the time, their 'one last little thing' usually turned into about ten big things that meant her staying an hour or two or three past her quitting time. She wasn't complaining too hard though. Her birthday was coming up in July and come hell or high water, she had promised herself to go away someplace nice, so all this overtime money was right on time.

Traffic in and around D.C. didn't make a bit of sense. Even as late as 8:30 at night, there were a ton of cars on the road and people were still hustling about on the streets. She thought that for a city where countless politicians resided or at least came through on the regular, it was interesting that they didn't come up with a way to eliminate or at least lessen this kind of inconvenience, but whatever. You dealt with the madness and kept rolling.

Her rolling was done in a two-year old Honda Pilot that she had scrimped and saved just to get, 'cuz she liked sitting up kinda high in a vehicle and plus she couldn't deal with the press of all the bodies when you rode the train. All them strangers pushing and shoving into your personal space made her feel claustrophobic and uneasy, and rather than subject herself to that, she just drove in.

The commute from Waldorf, Maryland was a long one, damn near an hour or more into the city, and fighting to drive up Branch Avenue with everybody else coming out of Waldorf was no picnic, but give her the solace of her own car, some easy listening tunes on that Jazz Station 105.9, maybe a cup of herbal tea, and she was good to go.

Audria looked across to her passenger seat where the letter was laying, still unopened. She reached for it. Knew she shouldn't do this in traffic, but she was going nowhere fast. Wasn't like they were even moving. She would just take a little peek. Pulling the letter flap open, she slid the yellow folded-up pages out onto her lap, and opened them up.

> *Fri. 4/27*
> *Late P.M.; not sure exactly what time it is*
> *Hello yourself, Ms. Audria, and bringing you Peace*
> *again...*

The breath caught in her throat again, and before she knew it, she was swinging her car into a parking space on the side. She was just too curious and she wasn't trying to run into somebody's rear and wreck her car trying to read this man's letter. 'Sides, she was kinda hungry. She could kill two birds with one stone. She could go get something to eat and read the letter over dinner. Grabbing her purse and a stationery pad out the glove compartment, she headed for Luigi's. She was in the mood for some fine Italian dining and not too many places topped Luigi's in the city.

Because of the late hour, she didn't have long to wait for a table, and in short order, she was sipping on a chilled glass of Chardonnay and munching on cheese encrusted French bread dipped in a mixture of oil, garlic pepper, chopped tomatoes and eggplant. Stuff was to die for. She crossed her legs under the table, got comfortable, and pulled out the letter. She picked up where she'd left off in the car.

> *...It was a nice surprise to receive your letter. I don't get many letters from Sistahs, so it was nice to get yours...*

What's he mean he doesn't get many letters from Sistahs? Who's writing him then, White women? Ugh, why they always trying to snatch up our men, and why our men always seem so damn ready to *be* snatched up? Lawd Audria, there you go. Just read the man's letter. It's not like he's telling you he's about to get married to some White woman. He just said ain't a lot of Sistahs writing him.

> *...I'm glad you decided to write, even though you weren't exactly sure why you did. I too, found what you said simple and sincere...*

She read on some more until she got to his last sentence talking about his name:

> *...And Strong? Yeah, not to brag or nothing, but that's me. Always been, always will be...*

Something about that made her feel light-headed. It was obvious he was just stating facts. She didn't feel any arrogance or the ugly big-head with that. What she *did* feel was a sense of unshakeable confidence from him. Again, like he could and would always handle his business. She went back to the letter, reading over the parts about him visiting D.C. in days gone past. So he was from New York, the Bronx. She wondered what his voice sounded like, whether he would have that strong – *there was that word again* – New York accent. And his peoples coming from North Carolina too? It was a different area to hers, but she would have to remember to ask him if he ever got over to the Rocky Mount or Pine Tops area.

Audria took a sip from her glass, took a bite of the swordfish in white wine butter sauce over angel hair pasta she'd ordered, and continued reading. She felt a kind of whimsical longing coming off the page when Michael talked about not seeing many concerts, going to the theatre or traveling in his present circumstances. His 'but it's all good. Nothing lasts forever' comment made her sigh. She would have to watch being fast and free with information that threw up her freedom in his face while reminding him he had none. She kept reading.

Was this man trying to tell her he had been so wrapped up in his life of crime that he didn't pay attention to the places he'd been? She found that sad. And the fact that he'd never been to the theatre? Well, she had just the thing to share with him. She couldn't wait to start her reply letter to him.

Feeling like she could barely tear her eyes from the page to take bites of food here and there, Audria kept reading. The more she read, the more confused she got and the more conflicted she felt. She thought men in jail were supposed to be all rough and tough, with that whole criminal mindset. Nothing about this brotha made her feel like he should be in that category or that he even belonged in jail. For Christ sake, he was talking about helping younguns come up, and about learning lessons from your past and using those lessons to help you look forward to the future. She felt so attracted to his strength and character, but she wasn't supposed to be attracted to a man behind bars, was she? It was like going there with a loser although you knew from out the gate you were dealing with a loser. So when you wound up losing out 'cuz you went on and messed around with a loser, who did you have to blame but your own damn self?

She quickly scanned over the rest of what he had to say, feeling a twinge of something when he called her name pretty, but she had already made up her mind. Some word he used when he talked about not asking for her picture yet, was trying to find its way to the surface of her consciousness. She started looking for it in the letter as confirmation. Yeah, there it was - fallback. That's exactly what she was going to do. Fall back. She was gon' fall wayyyyyy the hell back. So far back that he would have to forget her.

Audria folded up the letter, stuffed it back in the envelope and shoved it deep down into the nether regions of her purse. She wasn't trying to be involved with some convict that she didn't know nothing about. For all she knew, he had written her back probably because he recognized the name of her law firm on the envelope, thought she was a lawyer, and wanted to use her to try to get out of jail early or something. She was *not* the one. Michael Strong was nothing more than a letter to her, and everybody knew not every letter had to be answered. Fall back? Yeah, that had her picture all over it, 'cuz that was *exactly* what she was gon' do. She had too many problems of her own and other more important things to think about. As a matter of fact, it was about time she found herself something to get into to take her mind off all this mess. To hell with Michael Strong.

five
Getting Into Something

The woman rounded a blind corner, passed a small dirt parking lot jammed solid with foreign-made expensive looking cars, and headed for a tiny, hole-in-the-wall opening set at an angle in a nondescript, dirty-looking warehouse.

Wasn't the kind of neighborhood or the kind of building a woman like her would necessarily want to be hanging around, especially this late at night. And you could easily drive past the place, missing it completely, unless you knew about it. But the sistah obviously knew about it and knew where she was headed, despite the tensed hunch of her shoulders and the nervous look on her face.

With a furtive glance backward, she slipped into the tiny doorway, past two men roughly groping at each other in the dark, and headed up a couple flights of creaky wooden stairs that sucked the tips of her high-heeled boots down into some gooey mess with almost every other step.

As she walked up, cresting each landing, it was like watching a transformation take place. The uneasy furtiveness and nervous tension seemed to melt off her, replaced by an arrogant, bad-ass strut and an overconfident smirk on her face. She threw back the black, caul-like hood on her head, revealing a shock of fiery red hair that was obviously a wig. A slender hand reached up and unbuttoned the knee-length lightweight Gharani Strok coat that opened up to reveal a seriously risqué outfit straight off a Fredericks of Hollywood catalog page.

She was dressed all in black – a short, tight patent leather mini skirt with silver-buckled slits on either side that hugged thick hips in all the right places. That was topped by a matching patent-leather, strapless zip-up bustier, also with silver buckles on each side, that cinched in her waist and made her creamy cleavage holler for attention.

When she got to the top of the last landing, she tipped her head at the bouncer standing outside the wooden, barn-style doors, slipped two dubs to the bored-looking attendant inside a grimy-looking glass cage off to one side, slowly put her hands on her hips, spread her legs wide, and waited for the bouncer to pat her down.

"Cain't bring no guns, knives, razors, bottles, needles, pins, cameras, phones or none a' that otha' shit in heah," he growled at her, as he ran rough, calloused hands all up and underneath her unbuttoned coat, obviously checking for any of the items on his list. "You carryin'?"

"Unless you count these as contraband," she responded sarcastically, pointing at her breasts, "then I guess I'm not *carryin'*." She deliberately rolled her eyes at him, making sure he saw it, and started tapping a foot, waiting for the rest of his schpiel. She had heard it enough times that she could probably recite word for word along with him, but she let him meet the requirements of his lil' nine dollar an hour moonlighting gig, so they could both go about their business.

"DCPD's on premises. Undercover. That means no fuckin', no solicitin' and no drugs. You gotta ask if you want in on a scene, and if you hear no, no means NO! No grabbin' or touchin' anybody if you ain't invited to grab or touch." He hitched up his pants, cracked his neck muscles, and kept on in his bored monotone.

"Don't touch no equipment that ain't yours 'less you ask. If you just watchin', keep your distance from people in the scene. If you playin', pick a safe word and make sure you give that to your scene partner 'fore you get started or get one from him or her. We ain't liable for if you get cut, burned, or fucked up in any other way, and if you cut, burn or fuck up anybody else, we ain't liable for that shit neither. You enterin' these doors at yo' own risk." He tilted his head at her. "You unnerstan' e'rything I just got done sayin'?"

She nodded at him, rolled her eyes again, and waited for him to push back the heavy barn doors so she could go in. She thought she heard him mutter "fuckin' freaks" under his breath, but didn't give two shits. She wasn't about to be judged by some over-sized, pumped-up-on-steroids flashlight cop. She was here to relieve some stress, and wasn't nobody spoiling this for her tonight.

As she strutted into the dimly lit warehouse, she could feel the cautious side of her trying to raise some objection, asking her what in the hell she thought she was doing. Although she didn't consider herself anybody's prude, this was far more risqué than made any kinda sense.

An image of her mother's disapproving face popped up in her head and she just about stopped dead in her tracks. Her mother and anybody else who knew her would shit a ton of bricks if they could see her up in this place and dressed the way she was.

She hesitated for a minute more, giving in to the tug-of-war happening in her mind, but then shook it off. She *needed* this. Call it sick, dirty, twisted, freakish or whatever else, but this was the only place she could come to and escape all the mess inside her head.

All around her, people were indulging in scenes of sadomasochism, dominance and submission. It was wicked debauchery to the highest, but something about it instantly got her blood boiling. Her eyes flicked here and there, lighting on one scene then flitting to the next, taking it all in.

In one corner, a woman was being trussed up with what looked like electrical cords that appeared to be cutting off her circulation, if not her air supply. Right beside her, a man's high-pitched squealing drew her attention as his partner viciously stomped on his erect penis and nuts with wicked looking stiletto heels. Despite his obvious pain, after each scream, he would nod his head vigorously, lick his lips like he were tasting candy, and shout "more, more", egging on his partner.

Two stations down, a woman was having six-inch needles thrust through her nipples and clitoris simultaneously, double-teamed by identical twin brothers who were obviously masters of pain. The woman wasn't making a sound, just lying there staring up at them with dead eyes. Across from her, flabby ass cheeks of pale white flesh humped rapidly back and forth, and as she watched, she recoiled gently when she realized that urine was steaming out of the man's itty bitty penis into the eager, waiting mouth of his male partner. She didn't know what it was with white folks and their water sports, but that was just taking shit a little too far for her taste.

She walked past all of it, heading for a corner she had become intimately familiar with over the last few months, and began setting up her station. Ten minutes later, her first scene partner approached, timid in his nakedness, and it was on and popping. *This* is what she had come here for.

"Get your ass on the table," she ordered him, pulling on some thick latex gloves. Immediately, she began wrapping silk cords around his hands and legs, binding him face down to the stainless steel surface. Other people opted for leather furniture, but she wasn't into providing these people with comfort. If it's pain they wanted, then she was here to provide just that.

"You get a 40-minute session or until you can't take anymore," she purred in his ear, warming up to her role as his dominatrix. "Little bad boys like you deserve to be punished, and I'm here to do exactly that. Now, here's how I work."

She broke everything down to him, making sure he understood what he was getting himself into. When she was finished, she walked directly in front of him, stooping to make eye contact.

"You still want to do this?" she demanded, fake venom dripping from her voice.

"Yes Mistress," he responded, in a way too eager voice, sounding all breathless with anticipation, like a kid in a candy store.

She nodded. "Okay then. Tell me your safe word."

When he had given it to her, she walked around to her instrument table on the side, picked up a nail-studded paddle and ran the tips of her fingers across the surface. She looked at him coyly over one shoulder, as she held the paddle, studded side down over the open flame of a kerosene lantern, waiting for the nails to glow red. When she was satisfied, she moved back to the table, slowly running the points of the nails just above the sunken surface of his fleshy ass. She saw him flinch slightly, then clench his fists, and his pale white butt tensed up, waiting for her.

Raising the paddle high above her head, she fixed an image in her mind of the person she hated with almost every breath she breathed, the one who had brought her more pain than she could ever begin to inflict on all the pain seekers in the world. She imagined that it was his naked ass lying defenseless before her, imagined this was her moment to get her some get-back. With that image firmly in place, Audria brought the paddle down... HARD!

six
Hello #2

Hello again, Ms. Audria. Peace.

So when I didn't hear back from you, I thought at first it was the slowness of the mail. But it's almost a month and a half later, so it's obvious that's not it. Two things. It's either you didn't get my letter or for some reason, you decided not to write back. Don't know what it is, but something's telling me it's the back half of that - that you decided not to write back. I started to just let it go, chalk it up to a friendship not meant to be, and I still might do that, but for some reason, before I walk down that road, I need to tell you some things.

The first is this. Don't let my incarceration fool you into thinking that all I am is some prisoner. I'm far more than that. There was a time when that's all I was, but things change and so can people. You said in your letter to me that my words were simple and sincere. Ask yourself how you REALLY feel about what I'm saying now.

Second thing on the docket, and I'm not even sure why I want to touch on this. It seems kinda trivial, but my gut's telling me to mention it, so I'm going to, 'cuz I always trust my instinct. I noticed from your return address that you obviously work at a law firm. I don't know whether that means you're a lawyer, paralegal or something else there, but let me say this. That's not what this is about. Remember, you wrote me first. I don't need a lawyer or a law firm. My situation is a done deal and I've made my peace with that. I'm doing my bid (time) 'cuz that's the punishment that I got for my crimes. So if you were

> *thinking I had some plans for you just because of your affiliation*
> *with a law firm, please leave that thought behind.*
>
> *Audria look, I don't want nothing from you, except like*
> *I said in my ad, somebody who can help me focus on my future,*
> *while focusing on your own. Meaning, a friend. Is that so hard*
> *to get with? A genuine offer of friendship? If you think it is,*
> *then okay, this wasn't meant to be nothing but a passing hello.*
> *But if you're cool with us having a friendship, then please write*
> *me back. I hope to hear from you soon.*
> *Michael Strong*

Michael propped himself up against the bleachers next to the B-ball court, kinda absentmindedly watching the game. He read over the letter. Didn't know whether it was too harsh in some places or not. That was one of the things he struggled with doing time. Being around the male aspect 24-7 had a way of dulling the sense and sensibilities and making you forget the pleasantries the rest of the world took for granted in human interaction. Prisoners weren't trying to be nice. They didn't say 'please' and 'thank you' for shit. If somebody wanted something, they took it, and if you didn't want them to have it, you handled your business, stopped them from taking it, and moved on. Beefing in some way, shape or form was as much a part of a prisoner's existence as the walls, gates and barbed wire fences that were fixtures of every facility. You understood that and worked around it the best you could to focus on doing your time and on whatever future you would make for yourself.

He looked at the letter again, folded it up, and stuck it in a pocket. He would mail it out the next day. Whether it was too harsh or not, he had to be real with this woman and anyone else he wanted in his cipher. People spent so much energy playing games and not saying what they were really feeling, but that just wasn't him. Never had been. Even when he was slanging shit and with that whole past life, he was always true about his feelings. His word was bond and wasn't a man or woman alive could argue that fact. Shit, it was the only thing he had that he could give somebody and be all the way real with it. He had never been a liar or somebody to step lightly around the truth and he wasn't about to start now, for Audria or nobody else.

Audria. Michael wasn't sure exactly why he couldn't just walk away from this woman. It's not like they had exchanged a whole bunch of letters or something. There had only been the one from her, but there was something about the connection there that made him want to hear more from her, find out all about her, see where her head was at with things.

The day after mailing his first letter to her, he had spent a little time in the library looking up the word 'Existential'. He was surprised to find it meant of or relating to existence, based on experience. That was funny because so much of what he had been talking about in responding to her seemed straight up existential. He had some light moments with that.

But maybe that was it. Maybe she was some big shot lawyer or something that thought his conversation too weak, maybe figured he wasn't educated enough to roll in her league. Whatever. He wasn't even gonna go there. Besides, she was the one who decided to write. It's not like she didn't know from jump that she was writing to a man in prison. Not that that should make her automatically assume he was stupid. He had finished high school and done a year and a half at the Bronx Community College before deciding to focus all his attention on selling product, so he wasn't like some of the other men in here who couldn't name the Vice President of the country and who thought Canada was a northern U.S. state where the people just talked funny. Whatever. He wasn't going to second guess himself over some woman he barely knew. He had a good mind to just toss the letter and let the whole damn thing be, but his gut was hammering at him not to fallback in this instance, so he was gon' send it and see if she would answer.

He roused himself, did some calisthenics for about 30 minutes, hit the weights for an hour or so, then headed for the showers. Rounding the corner into the dormitory style shower room, he saw his cellie surrounded by about five Chicanos who looked ready to whup his punk ass. Michael went over to the urinals and started doing his thing, careful to look front and center. He wasn't trying to get into the middle of no bullshit that would mean time in the hole or worse, time added to his bid.

He could feel eyes on him, waiting to see if he would do something. He was willing them to stay over there and do what the hell they were doing and not bring him into the madness, but that wasn't gon' happen, obviously. The biggest of the Chicanos walked up behind him and stabbed a finger hard in his shoulder blade.

"Yo man, your cellie got money for us he can't seem to find nowhere. Whatchu gon' do 'bout it?"

Michael put away his shit, washed his hands, and stepped back, looking sideways at dude. "Ain't my problem."

"Yeah? Well, we making it your problem."

He cracked his neck muscles, smiled a thin smile, and looked at the no-neck bulging muscles freak standing in front of him dead in his eyes. "Naw, you ain't. Can't nobody make nothing my problem 'cept me, and this ain't my problem."

He went to leave and dude stepped to the right cutting him off. Michael was tired of the nonsense and just dropped him. Didn't waste a whole lot of time with it either. Just a sharp chop to his neck and dude was down on the floor gasping for air. The rest started to swarm him like a pack of rabid dogs, eager to draw first blood. He got in a fighting stance, waiting for any one of them to make the first move. But they must have seen something in his eyes that told them this would not end well. They eyed him warily and backed off for the open doorway, leaving their partner still on his knees gagging, trying to suck in air.

He stepped around dude, ignored his whimpering cellie, bitch ass that he was, and backed into a shower stall. He stripped off his clothes, carefully hung them on the hook outside the stall, and began to wash himself, keeping both eyes on the opening to the bathroom. Just like he thought. This Niggah had brought shit to his doorstep because of his weakness. Well, wasn't like it was the first time. First time for this particular cellie, but not the first time trouble had come knocking. He would handle it and keep rolling, 'cuz that's what men did. You handled your business, took your stripes like a soldier, and kept shit moving.

This prison crap wasn't no easy cakewalk. You had to constantly watch your back and sleep with one eye open, 'cuz you never knew who was the snake lying in wait for your ass. It forced you to always be in a defensive posture, never trusting any damn body, but that was like first nature to him. It was the code of the streets, so to extend it behind walls wasn't a stretch. What bothered him was the fact that lately, everything inside him seemed to be rejecting this. He didn't want to consider a lifetime of not being able to trust anyone. Although it was such a part of him, both past and present, it didn't feel 'natural' to him to live like this.

Audria. There she was again, just surfacing, popping up in his thoughts at the strangest possible times. He didn't understand it. Other women had written before and had even gotten into letter sex, giving him graphic scenarios to think about. Some moved him and some didn't, but even the ones that moved him, only did so on a physical level and that shit was dangerous to a man who had been behind walls for as long as he had, and who was still facing some years yet left on his bid. But with Audria, it wasn't a sexual thing. Hell, he didn't even know what she looked like. She could turn out to be a 400 pound hefty chick with fucked up teeth, bad hair, and a mole the size of Long Island on her top lip. Although he doubted it. She *sounded* pretty. He just felt a connection with her that he hadn't felt with anybody else before, and he didn't want this to be it. He wanted to hear from her again. Yeah, he wasn't giving up on Ms. Audria just yet. He was hoping his letter would stir something in her and make her write him back.

<u>seven</u>
Nothing More, Nothing Less

"Audria, we KNOW you in there. Open up this door. Right this minute."

She groaned, hid her face in a cushion and kicked her legs fast at the air in frustration. Why wouldn't they go away and leave her in peace to her misery? Didn't they know all she wanted to do was just be alone? Why was everybody and their cousin all of a sudden so concerned with how she was doing?

Audria sat up on the sofa where she had been laying since Thursday night, all of Friday, all of Saturday and a little bit of Sunday. She hated when she got like this, but felt almost powerless to prevent it. Sometimes she got in these slumps, what she called her 'dark days'. For more than a month and a half she had been fighting it, but finally gave in and conceded defeat a few days before. She had barely been able to function the Thursday at work, kept screwing things up left and right and having to suffer through more than the usual condescension. Finally, when it was obvious she needed to either get the hell out of there or risk getting fired if she dropped the ball on one more thing, she went into the partner she worked with the most, lied to his face about eating something bad for lunch, and hauled ass to the parking garage to get her car.

It was all she could do to drive in a straight line on the way home. She just felt drained, worn out, like she had gone eight rounds with Mike Tyson. Well, maybe more like four rounds minus the ear biting shit. She couldn't wait to get into her own space, to the solitude and solace of her own house, surrounded by the familiar. She shucked off the zoot suit she had on, threw it and her pumps across the room, and put on a big ass t-shirt that hung down almost to her ankles. She tied up her braids, washed the makeup off her face, got munchies, and hunkered down on the sofa to watch anything and everything on the tube. And that's where she had stayed from Thursday night, all the way through this minute.

The only things that moved her from her spot were the few and far between trips to the bathroom, to rummage around in the kitchen for more munchies, and to sign for two separate orders of Chinese Food from the Golden China Inn two streets over from her house. She was a lazy ass sometimes. She could have walked over there and picked the food up herself, but she didn't feel like being bothered with having to wash her face, brush her teeth and taking a bath. She knew she looked a hot mess, but she could look like a hot mess in the privacy of her own house all she wanted. That lil' Asian boy who looked sweet as a sugar pie cream puff to her didn't have to see the crust in her eyes. She cracked the door both times he came by, shoved a coupla twenties at him, grabbed the bag, and that was the full extent of their transaction.

First it had been her mother with call after call after call, and her threats to stop by. She had gotten rid of her every time, thankfully. Now, here was Angela and Vanessa pounding on her door like the hounds of hell were nipping at their heels and were going to get them if she didn't let them in. Well, they would just have to deal with ate up heels, 'cuz she wasn't getting up to let them or nobody else in. She lay back down and rolled over, burying her face deep in the sofa cushions. Finally, she heard footsteps going down her front steps and knew they were leaving.

She knew her friends meant well. She worked with both of them. Actually, Angela sat around the corner three carrels down from hers, and Vanessa worked for another law firm but in the same building as theirs. They had been friends for almost six years, and would frequently go out to lunch, do girls nights out and usually had a standing appointment for Sunday brunch. That's probably why they had come looking for her, 'cuz she had stood them up. She just couldn't face them today though.

Angela was the main one. She had been married for almost ten years to a fine ass man who, lazy eye and all, loved her more than life itself. It hurt her to be around them 'cuz she wanted what they had so bad that it sometimes set her to grinding her teeth 'til she thought she would start choking on tooth powder. They made her jealous as shit.

And Vanessa? She was another story entirely. According to her, she didn't want no man. She had men. Plural. She was so materialistic, by her own admission, that she needed to keep four and five brothas on the hook at a time, just to get everything she wanted. So, she didn't really count as any kind of love or relationship role model. That chile had some serious issues, but whatever. She was just glad they had gone.

Audria went to get up to go get a glass of water, but ducked when she heard footsteps coming back up the steps. Lawd, they were coming back. She stayed right where she was and kept quiet. Eventually, she heard something slide under her door and Angela's loud mouth sang out. "I know you in there hiding and can hear my ass, but it's cool. You'll come out when you get good 'n ready. Just letting you know I swung by your desk and picked up your mail. You got two pieces – something from the Paris office and some letter from somebody in Pittsburgh. We *need* to talk about that, so don't try to dodge me whenever you decide to bring your ass back to work. Lo' you girl. Holleratcha later."

Before Angela could reach her bottom step, Audria was scrambling for the front door to snatch up the mail laying there. Pittsburgh? Michael? He had sent her another letter? Ohmigawd. She snatched it up, threw the interoffice mail from Paris off to one side, and plopped down on the sofa to read it. She felt her hands shaking as she tore open the envelope flap.

Sat. 6/16

The week before.

43

> *Hello again, Ms. Audria. Peace.*
> *So when I didn't hear back from you, I thought at first*
> *that it was the slowness of the mail. But now that it's almost a*
> *month and a half later, it's obvious that's not it...*

She tried to swallow the guilty lump that sprang up in her throat at that, but it wasn't going nowhere. Trying to quiet her breathing some, she kept on.

> *...So it's either you didn't get my letter or for some reason, you*
> *decided not to write back. Don't know what it is, but*
> *something's telling me it's the back half of that - that you*
> *decided not to write back.*

She started talking out loud to the room. "Boy, that *something* ain't telling you no lie. I just couldn't do it." Shushing her own self, she went back to the letter.

> *...I started to just let it go, chalk it up to a friendship not meant*
> *to be, and I still might do that, but for some reason, before I*
> *walk down that road, I need to tell you some things.*
> "What things?" Talking out loud again.
> *...The first is this. Don't let my incarceration fool you*
> *into thinking that all I am is some prisoner. I'm far more than*
> *that. There was a time when that's all I was, but things change*
> *and so can people. You said in your letter to me that my words*
> *were simple and sincere. Ask yourself how you REALLY feel*
> *about what I'm saying now.*

Audria felt her mouth drop open. How could he know she had been thinking that, about him being just some prisoner? This was unreal, eerie. She propped a leg under her, clutched the letter tighter and kept going. When she got to the part about her working for a law firm and him not needing a lawyer or a law firm, she had to set it down. Just felt like she couldn't hold it anymore. It was like this man had crawled inside her head. She couldn't believe the words she was reading, but as unbelievable as it all seemed to her, she *knew* deep down inside, in a place where people didn't often allow themselves to look, that this man was coming to her with nothing but truth. It made her feel ashamed that she had doubted him, thinking he had some ulterior motive for wanting to communicate with her.

It was obvious he was as true as his words, and that he only wanted to offer and receive genuine friendship. So what was the big deal with that? She could offer him that, couldn't she? It's not like she didn't have male friends. Well, she didn't have a whole lot of them, because they were mostly always trying to get in her pants, and although Dean was male, he was more of a queen and a diva than she was, so he didn't count. But whatever, she was getting sidetracked. She could offer Michael friendship without feeling all weird about it. It's not like he would be all up in her space. As a matter of fact, this was the perfect, safest way for her to offer a man friendship without feeling like she had to constantly fight some physical battle. He wasn't here and wouldn't be for... hey, she didn't even know how long he was going to be in prison, or even how long he had been in there. She would have to ask him in her reply letter to him, and she *was* replying. Of that she had no doubt.

Audria got up from the sofa, sniffed at her armpits and made a face. She stunk. To high heaven. Didn't make no sense for a grown woman to sit around for three damn days and not wash her ass. Was time to do something about that. Already feeling lighter in her spirit, she headed for the bathroom to run herself a bath. Might as well make this a nice luxuriating one, she thought, so she lit some candles, put on a Will Downing CD and turned on the bathroom speakers. Testing the water with her toes, she climbed in and settled herself down among the suds.

The water felt soothing to her body and Will was doing his thing, crooning in his sensually sexy way. Sump'n about that brotha made her think he swung both ways, but whatever, she could care less. As long as he kept singing them sexy ballads, he was a friend to her.

Friend. Michael. Didn't take her mind no time to work her way back to him, did it? But if she was honest with herself, and she wanted to be, he hadn't been far from her thoughts over the last month and a half. She didn't know why, but she would think about him when she least expected it, and it made her feel like somebody had punched her in the gut when she thought about not hearing from him again. But still, she couldn't bring herself to write.

She had to admit. Men scared her. Well, not every man, because it wasn't something she felt all the time. But men like *this* man scared her. Although she was drawn to them for their strength and confidence, she felt like it was those same sides to them that made her want to back off and head for the hills. She knew that all this went back to that thing that had happened to her when she was thirteen, something she tried not to think about whenever it tried to surface, like now, but she wasn't going to let it.

Maybe that's why none of her relationships really lasted, or why she kept gravitating to losers. It wasn't clear exactly, but all she knew was that she was drawn to men that seemed to embody all the qualities this Michael guy did, but when she got up-close and personal with it, they made her afraid to open herself to it and to them. She would have to be careful. But hey, the man wasn't asking her to be his girlfriend or nothing. He had asked for friendship and that's what she would give him. Nothing more, nothing less.

An hour later, she stepped out of the tub, applied some Neutrogena Jojoba oil to her still damp skin and towel blotted herself dry. In the bedroom, she put on deodorant, dusted herself lightly with some Healing Gardens powder, sprayed some Anais Anais on her wrists and behind her ears, and pulled on her favorite silk lounging robe. Picking a different spot to sit in the living room *– she would probably need to fumigate that sofa before she sat there again –* she pulled out a writing pad and started her reply letter to her new friend.

Sun. 6/24 - 2:17 p.m.

Hi Michael.

It's me -- Audria. Peace to you. I got your letter today. Somebody brought it to me at home. Look, I can lie and tell you that I've been busy, or traveling, or any number of things, but you asked me to come with truth or not at all, so here I am. The truth is that I was doing exactly what you suspected I was doing, which was allowing your incarceration to make me think of you in a certain way, in a not very good way. I don't like to judge people, but if I'm to be truthful here, it's obvious that I did exactly that with you. I'm sorry.

The second point you made about where I work? Strange, that was also part of what caused me not to write you back. I started thinking that maybe where I work had something to do with why you wanted to communicate with me, but you're right, I was the one that first made contact with you, so that

---

should never have come into play. Thanks for trusting your instincts and mentioning it.

Okay, you say that you really don't want anything from me - just making an offer of a genuine friendship. I believe you. So, I'm going to take you up on your offer and make you one of my own. I'd like us to have a friendship. Nothing more, nothing less. If you're cool with that, then in the words of Marvin Gaye, "Let's Get It On." The friendship, I mean, okay?

Okay. Moving on. Since I never responded to your first letter, I wanted to take some time to touch on a few things here from that letter. In that letter you said that you don't get many letters from Sistahs. I'm just curious. Who do you get many letters from then?

Thanks for the information on your name. You talked about your first name, but didn't really say much about your last name, other than to admit that it speaks to your personality. I was just curious about your surname and where it comes from.

And you're from New York? I've visited a few times, mainly just to check out the theatre scene (that again) and like on day shopping trips, etc. but I haven't been up that way in years. It's so noisy and dirty, but I guess that's what one should expect from a city that never sleeps, right? I was wondering whether you have a New York accent or not. Just something I'm curious about. Why don't you tell me what you think. Do you have a New York accent?

So, your peoples are from Elizabeth City? Mine are from Rocky Mount, opposite side of the state, I guess. Just curious as to whether you ever got over to my side of town much. I used to go down there every Summer from when I was about five or six right up 'til I was thirteen, and then I stopped going back after that. Who knows, we may have run into each other at some point, if you can stretch your mind that far back to remember your VERY distant childhood. ☺ Sorry, couldn't resist.

Okay, moving on. I have to tell you that I was surprised to hear someone in prison talk about giving back to the young ones coming up. It's like you think: if this person really believes that, WHY would he allow himself to be locked away and become just another bad role model for our youth, but like you said, things change and so do people. Maybe that's something you weren't in a position to think about back in your past, but now, it's become important to you? I'm glad you feel this way, because the young ones really are our future, and if we don't nurture them and help guide their steps, then we won't have much of a future to speak of. I'm sorry I stereotyped you as just another prisoner. It's obvious you're so much more than that.

Alright, I'm already up to almost 3 full pages, and I don't want to talk your ear off, but just a few more things, okay? First, 'Existential'. Did you have the chance to look it up yet? I know you probably got a good laugh over that, didn't you? Just about everything you were saying to me was from the school of existential thought. It's funny how sometimes our spirits know things but we may not know the appropriate name for what resonates inside us. Don't you think that's strange?

Secondly, I agree with you and it makes perfect sense that people should spend more time getting themselves right in the present so they can solidify their futures, but that can be hard. If one hasn't faced up to something in their past, it makes it kinda difficult to be 100% right in the present and to put the right amount of energy and focus to the future that you should. But,

I guess it's all a process. You live and learn and hopefully, learn not to make the same mistakes over and over again. Okay, that's all I wanted to say on that.

Oh, one final thing. Can you do something for me? Close your eyes. Okay, well not your physical eyes, but your mind's eye. Go on, close them. Picture some powerful Black Sistahs working their way onto a stage. Women that remind you of the Mothers and Nanas of yesteryear. Some are dancing, some are clapping, some are rolling their hips, some have their hands thrown up, seven of them, but they're all smiling; big, bright, beautiful smiles from the depths of their souls. They're dressed colorfully. Bright reds, oranges, yellows, royal purples, forest greens, brown earth tones. Some are holding instruments, cha-chas, cowbells, tambourines, African drums and gourds. They sit and they make music, they become music, their voices, that is. They sing acappella, their voices sounding rich and alive, warm like the life blood of Africa. They tell stories in their songs of slavery but of victory; of hatred but of love; of suffering but of the joy of redemption. They rock you with lyrical notes and soothe your spirit with the warmth of their syncopated rhythm. Think Blues, think spirituals, think traditional and non-traditional gospel hymns, think rap, think reggae, African chants, Hip Hop, ancient lullabies, jazz improvisation. They make you FEEL their music, put you inside their music, uplift you to another world with their music. They are called Sweet Honey In The Rock. Okay, that's it. You can open your eyes again. Did I do good? You asked me to give you a blow-by-blow of a trip to the theatre, so I thought this might be nice. I went to see them back a couple months ago at one of the local theatres in D.C., and I try to go see them every chance I get when they come through town. It's an awesome experience.

Okay, well, I've already taken up much more of your time than I probably should, so I'll say bye for now. You take care of yourself, Sir. Until we speak (or write) again.

Your New Friend,
Audria

P.S. This is kinda one of those weird, awkward things, but I'm curious, so I'm gonna ask. I didn't see anywhere on the ad where it talked about how much time your sentence is. Can you tell me how long you've been in prison and also how much longer you have? Hope it doesn't make you feel weird me asking you that, but I'm curious. Okay, talk to you soon, I hope. Bye.

<u>eight</u>
My Future

Michael was standing in his 8 x 10 foot cell. Still. Quiet. He didn't want to move. Felt like he couldn't. He had put his cellie out a half hour before with just one word, "Move," spoken barely above a whisper but with such intensity that it couldn't be ignored. And still he hadn't moved from the same spot he'd been in after dude hustled off.

He could remember feeling like this only three other times in his life. The first time he got cornered in a deal gone south and knew he was 'bout to be shot even before the little weasel who shot him pulled out his gat. The second time was the night he got busted. Knew they were coming for him, though nobody told him. Even knew who had given him up, but couldn't do nothing about none of it, but wait. And the final time was the night his mother breathed her last breath and left him.

Them three things didn't have nothing to do with each other, not really, 'cept for him being present at all three, but what they all had in common, like now, was this foreknowledge swimming in his head like a premonition, that they were gon' happen. This woman, this Audria, was gon' be his future, his wife.

He didn't know *how* he knew this thing. Didn't understand it. It didn't make any logical sense. She hadn't said nothing to him like that in her letter. Matter of fact, he could feel caution coming off the page at him like a stink, but something turned over inside him in the exact same way it had on three separate occasions at other moments in his life, and as he read every word of her letter, he knew it, could feel the truth of it, as much as he could feel the breath passing through his nostrils and down into his lungs.

It scared the shit outta him. This wasn't no time to be trying to cultivate no relationship, with him doing bid. Plus, this woman sounded like she genuinely needed somebody to be there for her. *There.* One hundred percent. Not sixty or eighty. One hundred percent there. In every way. Heart, mind, soul, spirit, *and* body. What was he supposed to do with this knowledge that had already started up a beat in the back of his chest somewhere?

Damn. Life sure could be strange. When he was walking free, women were all over him like flies on shit. Couldn't turn one way or the next without bumping into some fine honey trying to give him some, but he dismissed every one of them, 'cuz he had already made a commitment to one person and when it came to women, he did one thing at a time. Besides, most of the time, his woman was the streets and the relationship he gave his energy to was making money and moving product.

He had never been in love, at least he recognized that now, and didn't think all that highly of something that would shake him from his game and get all up in his chest plate, causing him to lose focus. Yet, here he was, feeling like he was on the threshold of some never-before-felt feeling. But he wasn't running from it. He wasn't no punk. He didn't back down from no man and nothing, and he wasn't gon' back down from this.

So it wasn't the right time, but *when* would be the right time? He could do his bid, walk outta here in some years and get hit by a fucking bus crossing the street to head home. Naw, he wasn't gon' fallback, not in the least lil' bit. He just had to be about his business, and be as truthful with this woman as she needed him to be. And he could handle that. Wasn't no doubt in his mind about *that*.

What he had doubt about was whether she would haul ass in the opposite direction soon as she got the picture he was gonna start painting for her. With her 'nothing more, nothing less' thing.

He would make damn sure the word 'less' had nothing to do with the vocabulary he would create between them.

Audria. He said her name out loud in the quiet of his cell. The name of his wife. His future.

The work undertaken in the year had brightened the
the very many ... small changes ... sick beds.
Therefore ... had been spent for him in the expected his roads. He
seemed more ... he bore.

nine
More; Not Less

Thurs. 7/5

Peace Audria.

Can't tell you how good it was to hear from you. Was starting to get kinda worried there, but you didn't disappoint. I got your letter today. Guess there was a little delay because of the Fourth of July holiday, and although I don't much celebrate this particular holiday, I'm hoping you're spending a good one.

Alright, let's get into this thing. First things first. This real wise cat I did time with a few years back used to always say to me that if you pay close enough attention to the words a person speaks, that it constitutes 1/3 of the actual science of mind reading. So, I applied that to your letter and came up with some things. The first and only one I'll touch on here is that I don't think your P.S. was meant to be a P.S. I think you wanted to ask that before you asked me any other question, so let's talk about my time. This is my 13th year, yeah, 13. Your eyes ain't playing tricks on you. And I have almost four years left. This wasn't my original sentence, but when you're young, you tend to have a hard head and think you know everything. That got me a few more years than I came in with. I hope this answers your question, but if you want to know anything else on this subject, just ask me.

Okay, into the meat of your letter. Gotta tell you, Sweetheart (and I hope you don't mind me calling you by this and other pet names? If you do, I won't do it), but Sweetheart, I gotta tell you that what you did telling me the truth behind you not writing me back wasn't no easy thing. I know that had to take a lot of courage, but it didn't surprise me none. You seem to me to be a strong sistah who's not afraid to say when she's wrong. It means a lot to me that you owned up to that. Like I said, I deal in truth and being real. If you can't bring that to me EVERY time, then just don't say nothing 'til you can, okay? And you know what else? In all my 40 years, my instincts ain't never steered me wrong. I see they didn't fail me yet another time. That whole deal with where you work. I didn't even know why that was in front of me strong as it was. Almost dismissed it, but something kept at me to mention it, so I did. Glad I did now. Audria, don't never think that I have some kinda ulterior motive dealing with you, alright. I got nothing but good intentions to you, so relax okay? Ain't nothing here for you to be worrying your pretty head over.

So, we're 'bout to be down with Marvin? Let's Get It On? Let's do that, Beautiful. Bet you're wondering why I'm calling you Beautiful. Ain't seen you, but guess what? You FEEL beautiful to me, so I can call you beautiful all I want 'cuz you're beautiful in my mind's eye.

And BabyGirl, speaking about my mind's eye. WHAT a picture you painted me with them sistahs - Sweet Honey In The Rock, you called them? Man, if that ain't something to want to experience, then I don't know what would be. That was an awesome picture you brought me. Thank you for that. Makes me want to ask you for one of those a letter, but I don't want you to think I'm greedy or nothing. I'll just let you do what you do whenever you feel like it, but just understand that a brotha likes. And I gotta ask this, and if I'm getting too personal, feel free to tell me to slam on the brakes, but do you write for a living? If you ain't, you need to be, 'cuz you got a way with words. Ain't no joke. Talk about painting a picture on paper. You got you a gift, Ms. Audria. Of course, you already know this, I'm sure.

Now, you asked me a question that sounded kinda.... I don't know what exactly to call this, so I'll just call it like how it sounded - jealous? Lemme find out that Pretty Audria is a jealous somebody. ☺ Couldn't resist. So look, you asked me who I get many letters from, so I'll tell you. The ad you responded to been up for about 7 months. Not sure why I put it up there, especially after all these years. Guess I just wanted to see what kinda response I would get. Anyway, the group of people that I mostly DIDN'T want to hear from is the exact group of people that's been writing mostly, and that's White women. That might work for some brothas, but I'm not one of them kinda brothas. I love my Nubian Queens. Hope this answers that question. So White women write and after awhile, they get tired. The minimum amount of time the ad can run is a year, so it's gon' be up there for the next 5 months, then it comes down.

Next thing you asked me about was my last name - Strong, and where it comes from. It belonged to the dude that got my mother pregnant. Can't really call him father or none of that, 'cuz he wasn't nothing to me.

Alright Lady, no talking bad 'bout my city. Nobody but nobody talks bad 'bout The Apple, got that? Just playing. I know it's dirty and all that, but New York is so much more than people think it is, or better yet, everything they may think it is, multiply that about 100 times going in either direction - good or bad, and THAT'S New York. Love that place, Audria, and what I love... So how about I let you finish that sentence?

And you want to know whether I have a New York accent? Growing up, I always thought that everybody else not from New York was the ones with the accent, but you ask any New Yorker the same thing, and they'll tell you that. Guess the only way you can have that question answered is to hear me for yourself, then you can decide.

So you got jokes about my age, do you? Listen, you're only 2 years younger than me, so don't be too fast and free with the insults, joking or otherwise. You playing catch-up yourself, don't forget that.

Your folks are from Rocky Mountain, huh? I never really hung in that area, although I passed through a couple times here and there to drop off something. Was always just a lil' too country and a lil' too White for me, but then what part of North Carolina ain't the latter? Now, like you, I'm curious about something. You said you used to go down that way from when you were about five or six up until thirteen, then you stopped. What happened? Your peoples moved or something? I'm curious.

Got to speak on this topic about giving back to the young bloods coming up, but before I get into all that, I gotta tell you this again. Despite your apology, that comment you made about being surprised to hear someone in prison talk about giving back, scratched some skin off my ass. I know you gon' be tempted from time to time, but stop trying to define me as some prisoner. Don't get caught up with what society might want you to believe about everybody doing time. I ain't 'everybody' and I ain't 'some prisoner,' so open your mind to who I tell you I am 'cuz my word is my bond and when I say something, It's not to hear myself talk or to pass time or none of that. Alright, that's all I need to say on that. Moving on to giving back. There's a school of thought that says we not only learn from our mistakes but we pay for them. Guess what? I made plenty of them - mistakes, I mean, during my early years. Some of my mistakes I made over and over again. That's why the person I am today tries to make sure I don't make the same mistake twice. So, I learned some lessons from my mistakes, still learning, but I recognize I gotta pay for my mistakes too. My bid (time in prison - served and serving) is part of that payment, but I gotta pay a damn sight more than that. My actions in the past destroyed lives, ruined families and devastated whole neighborhoods. And yeah, neighborhoods of

<u>our</u> people. And you're absolutely right. At the time I couldn't see past my desire to be a big shot and to line my pockets, so I wasn't thinking about there being repercussions to my actions. So every instance of me providing a negative role model to a young brotha coming up watching me sport the rimmed out Lex or Nav, flashing gold and platinum, spending ill gotten money off the misery of people with the addiction monkey on their backs, and thinking he had to be like me, <u>I</u> gotta pay for that. Nobody else can bear that burden but me. And I could go the same route some brothas go and try to absolve myself from responsibility, falsely believing that he was just assuming the role left him by a society closed to the Black Man's success and so he started selling the government's product. Make no mistake about this. It is the government's product. Ain't no brotha got the kind of connections required to bring product into this country in large quantities like they come, but at the end of the day, the government didn't hold a gun to my head and make me hit the streets with the vengeance I did to convert product into green to put in my pockets. <u>I</u> did that, so <u>I</u> gotta pay for that. So yeah, <u>I</u> gotta give back. In whatever capacity I can, I gotta return to the streets to try to repair some of the damage my actions caused. Alright, I'll stop here on this subject. Feel like I'm saying so much and that's not usually my way. Matter of fact, with some things, I believe less is more, but for some reason, that doesn't quite fly in my dealings with you, Ms. Audria. Damn, I'm suddenly feeling this need to see what you look like, but take your time with that. Handle it when you're ready. Cool? Alright, moving on.

Just some minor things. Yeah, I had me a laugh over the word 'existential'. I was surprised to see that all my talk was really on an 'existential' level. It was a little strange, I agree. And yeah, I think our spirits know things that other parts of us (the brain or mind) might not yet be able to comprehend. I had me one of those moments when I finished reading your letter. Does that happen to you sometimes too?

Okay, I was gonna close here, but something's telling me not to fallback just yet. This is on the time people spend getting themselves right in the present in order to solidify their futures. And let's not forget that looking to the past plays a role in all that. Yeah, it's not always an easy road. It is a process, but that's not really my point. To be honest, not really sure I know what my point is. Guess I wanted to ask you if there is something in your past that you haven't faced up to. Alright, for some strange reason I'm feeling like I just crossed a line with that question, so now it's time to fallback.

But, one final thing before I go. Two, actually. The first is simply this. Nobody, least of all me, is dictating how long your letters should be. When you write me, don't think you taking up more of my time than you should. Let me worry about my time. I want to hear from you. Hell, right now that *feels like a <u>need</u>, so stop thinking you got to count pages. I'm not when I write you. That's the first thing. Next.*

Earlier in this letter there was a point when I said less is more, but I also said that I believe that only applies to some things. This is not one of them. Please listen carefully, Audria. I am rejecting your offer of friendship the way you gave it. Friendship, like love, can't be contained or qualified. The way you offer friendship is like somebody offering a fat kid cake with one hand and then covering it with the other so he can't get to it. Now look, I ain't fat - you know this, you seen my picture, but I want my cake. You can't offer me friendship and then try to define the offering with your 'nothing more, nothing less' thing tacked on the end. In fact, Audria, I want more from you, not less, but I think maybe you're not ready to hear all that, so I'm gonna fallback on this too. For now.

Oh, for the record, just some information you need to file away for future reference. Don't ever ask me a question if you think you might not be ready to hear the answer. I deal only in truth. I'm not one of these kinds of brothas who's gon' tell you what I think you want to hear. If you ask me a question, expect the truth and don't get all twisted if it's not the answer you expected to hear and didn't want to hear, Alright? Don't say I didn't warn you.

Okay young lady, it's been my joy and pleasure spending time with you. Thanks for writing me back, even if it took you a little while, but it's more important that you did, not <u>when</u> you did. Well, you take care and be safe out there. Write me soon. Bye Beautiful.

Peace,
Michael

P.S. When's your birthday?

ten

I'm Scared

Hi Michael.

Yes, today is my birthday. July 14th, Bastille Day. It's France's Independence Day. Anyway, I was planning on treating myself to a get-away trip for my birthday, but I changed my mind. None of my girlfriends could go with me and although sometimes I'm cool being alone, I just wasn't really feeling the idea of being on a beach somewhere by myself for my birthday, so here I am. I got up early today. I decided I'm going to treat myself to a pamper-me day, so after I finish this letter to you and mail it, I'm going to the spa to get the works. Hair, nails, toes, body massage etc., then my two best girlfriends, Angela and Vanessa, are supposed to take me out tonight to celebrate, so it's going to be a full day. Michael, I'll tell you, I can't believe I'm actually 39 today. I don't know what I'm going to feel like next year when I turn 40, but I guess I'll cross that bridge when I come to it.

I got your letter on Thursday at work and I've been going back and forth with it since then. I barely know what to say and how to begin. There were so many parts of it that outright disturbed me on levels deeper than I feel I can even talk about, or at least not yet. You are really <u>so</u> very different than anyone I have ever talked to, whether in person or on paper. I'm feeling some things that are making me afraid and I don't know what to do about that, so I guess I'll just put that to the side and respond to your letter. First though, I need to tell you that there are some parts in your letter that I don't think I *can respond to. Not because I don't want to, but because I feel like I <u>can't</u> just yet. Maybe I won't be able to for a long while, don't know, but I'm mentioning this because I want you to understand that I'm not just ignoring things or your questions, okay? Okay then, I'll turn my attention to your letter now.*

I thought it was kinda interesting that you said you don't celebrate 4th of July. I don't either. I feel the same way about Columbus Day and Thanksgiving Day. I just have a serious problem celebrating days that commemorate a country where its founding fathers stole land from people who were already here. It's like, how can you show up and say you're discovering a place when people have been living there for hundreds of years already? Anyway, let me not get started with that. I just thought it was interesting that we have that in common, although I don't know what your reasons are for not celebrating 4th of July, but I won't be surprised if you tell me they're the same.

Michael, I know I said that I was going to get into responding to your letter, but I can't just yet. You ask me to bring you truth when I come to you, so I have to do that here. I'm so scared. I'm feeling you so deeply, more than I've ever felt anyone, and that's what's scaring me. I know it's not about you being a prisoner. Well, that's true and it's not. I'm past the point of feeling like you're just some stereotype of who a prisoner is. I understand and believe that you're sooo much more than that. What I'm having a hard time with is the time. 13 years? And counting? I can't even begin to wrap my mind around being behind anybody's walls for 13 years. I don't think I could ever deal with being locked up like that, but this is not about me. Well, it is and it isn't. Lawd, I'm not doing a very good job of saying what I want to say here, am I? I guess what I'm trying to say is that because of how I'm starting to feel about you, it's making me even more scared. Okay, so I'm single, yes, but that doesn't mean it's my choice to be alone, okay? I want to have somebody who's just for me, but I don't want to make compromises on how I believe I should be loved just for the sake of having a man. I'm better off by myself if I'm gonna do that. But here's the thing, Michael, I can't begin to imagine waiting four years to be with somebody I care about. It seems like forever, and I hate waiting. I'm just afraid, so afraid that I'm gonna get caught up feeling all of what I'm feeling and then not be able to handle what comes next. I know I'm a strong woman but in matters of the heart I don't feel strong at all. Okay, I'm gonna let this go, because I don't really know how to make you understand all of what I'm feeling, and I might be making a damn fool of myself telling you all this, so I'll just leave it alone and go back to responding to your letter.

You asked whether I mind you calling me Sweetheart or any other pet names? No, I don't mind. As a matter of fact, I like it. Strange too, that you wound up calling me Babygirl. It's always been my favorite term of endearment. It makes me feel special and cared for, protected, so no I don't mind.

As far as where I work, Michael? I want to share this with you, and I know I don't have to, but I want to. I'm a legal secretary at this law firm. Actually, one of the largest law firms in D.C. I despise my job. Seriously. Guess maybe it's because I know I was meant to do so much more with my life, specifically writing, but somehow I got off track and haven't been able to figure out how to turn things around. I know before too long I'll have to figure it out though, because I don't want to be a legal secretary for the rest of my life. Okay, moving past that.

So you liked envisioning Sweet Honey In The Rock? ~~I can't wait~~ I hope you get to experience them live and in person one day. They really are incredible, and in a way that I could never be able to explain to you. It's something that everyone has to experience for themselves to truly understand and appreciate.

Me? Sound jealous? You gotta be kidding! I don't have a jealous bone in my body. Okay, I need to just stop the madness right here and right now. That is so not true. You're right. I guess I felt a pang of something when I thought about other women writing you, especially if it was White women, which you confirmed. I don't know what it is, but it bugs me when I see them (White women) pushing up on Brothas, and I think it bothers me even more when I see Brothas reciprocating, especially when there are beautiful Brown-skinned Sistahs like me who are left to warm our own beds at night and who want to be in a caring, committed relationship with a Brotha, but whatever. I know I can't change the way all that enfolds. People go where they feel love, I guess, and sometimes because of circumstances and so many years of having to hold things down on her own, many Sistahs build up these walls that give Brothas the wrong impression. They think we're hard and unapproachable and that we don't know how to love, so when a White woman comes along who serves them up the very thing or things they've been looking to the Sistahs for, they accept it and ride off into the sunset with their Sheena Queen of the Jungle, when their Nefertiti is standing right there ready to give them their every heart's desire. But that's how things go sometimes, I guess. I'm glad you love your Nubian Queens.

Damn Michael. You sound like you have some issues with, how did you put it? The dude who got your mother pregnant? I know that not every family works the way families are supposed to work, but I guess I've never really encountered anyone who feels like you about their father. My father was always so much more than a father to me. I guess that's why I call him Daddy, because he was so real to me and embodied everything a father is supposed to embody in that word. I miss him everyday I wake up breathing. I can't fathom feeling the kind of disconnect that I feel you do with yours, but once again, that's the way things go sometimes, is it not? We don't live in a perfect world.

And hey, I wasn't talking bad about New York City. At least I didn't think I was. Just thought I was stating the facts. It is dirty and noisy, but I know it's a great place. I'd like you to I think it would be nice to have somebody who knows the city show it to me one day. Michael, I don't think I know you well enough to finish that sentence 'what you love'. Why would you ask me that? Very strange. Anyway, I don't know you like that, so I don't think I can finish that sentence for you.

So you think Rocky Mount is too country and too White, huh? I understand what you mean. Look, this is one of the things I can't talk about, okay? Hope you understand.

Michael, I need to tell you how proud I am of you that you've decided, on your own, that you need to do something to repair some of the damage you've done within your community by selling drugs. That is so commendable, and speaks so highly of your character, the kind of person you are. I wish more Brothas could accept responsibility for their actions the way you are. It would go a long way to making our neighborhoods whole again, making our people feel good about their lives and their contributions to the big picture of who we are as a people, but once again (feel like this is the theme in this letter), we don't live in a perfect world, so that is as it is.

I want to ask you this next question, but I'm back to feeling scared. I didn't miss the part of your letter where you told me point blank not to ask you anything that I wasn't prepared to hear an answer to. Believe me, I didn't miss that. It feels like it's imprinted on my brain, but I'm curious and I guess my curiosity in this instance outweighs my fear? So, I'm gonna ask it. You talked about our spirits knowing things that other parts of us (the brain or mind) not yet being able to comprehend. And then you talked about having one of those moments when you finished reading my letter. Can you explain that?

Skipping over the next thing in your letter, okay? This is where you ask me if there is something in my past that I haven't faced up to. To be honest, Michael, I think you did step over a line with that. You don't know me like that to ask me something so personal, so thank you for falling back where that's concerned. Moving on.

I've got to tell you that the next paragraph in your letter was probably the one I've spent the most time reading over and over again. You're rejecting my offer of friendship because you didn't like my trying to define it with 'nothing more, nothing less'. Okay, that's fair, I understand it. But I guess what's puzzling is your last sentence where you say you want more from me, not less. What does this mean? I mean, it sounds kinda straightforward, but it almost feels like there's some hidden meaning there too that I'm not understanding. And then you say that you think maybe I'm not ready to hear all that. You don't know what I'm ready or not ready to hear, okay? You don't know me, so don't assume you do, please.

Alright, that's about all I have to say. Oh, before I go, I want to thank you for calling me beautiful. You're so kind. I guess one of these days, I'll send you a picture so you can see whether you're right or not, but I'm gon' make you wait a little while longer. I don't want to be too fast and free with the picture sharing thing just yet. You might turn out to be some psycho and who wants to know they've handed over their picture to a psycho. Hee-hee. Just playing. And Michael, if you're very, very good, I may give you my phone number one day too, so you can call me and I get to hear for myself whether or not I think you have a New York accent, but you're gonna have to wait for that too.

Okay My Friend (in a friendship that will stay unqualified and not contained), let me run along and get my day started. Wish me Happy Birthday? Although this will get to you long past today, would you send me a birthday wish anyway? Look, I just thought about something. What's it like in there? I don't know much about prison except what I've seen on that old HBO series Oz (or was it Showtime), a coupla episodes of Prison Break and other bad prison movies. Do you have light moments? Do you ever smile? If you do, would you allow a smile to bless your lips for me when you receive this? Who knows, the Universe may let me know that you're sending me one. So smile for me, okay? Stay strong. But then you <u>always</u> are, with your name as a constant reminder. Well, gotta go. I'm off to the spa to get pretty. I'll be thinking about you.

Bye for now.

Audria

eleven
Is You Crazy?

"Girl, you done bumped your fool head hard and must be sufferin' from a concussion. IS YOU CRAZY?"

Audria rolled her eyes, took a sip of Moet and sat back in the booth, crossing her legs sideways under the table. She knew she should've kept her mouth shut about Michael with these two. They wouldn't understand. Shit. She and her big mouth.

Angela and Vanessa were looking at her like she was some six-legged yellow and green freak thing from another planet that had just crash landed its space ship in the middle of the restaurant and had taken over her body. Angela especially was acting like she thought Audria was supposed to answer her 'Is you crazy' question. She wasn't hardly trying to have this conversation with them, especially not on her birthday. They were supposed to be having a nice dinner, not discussing her choice in men.

See? That right there? She had been doing that a lot. It felt like she was laying claim to Michael already, and it bothered her. A lot. It's not like she had any permission to start thinking about him as if he were hers. She didn't even know if he was interested or not. Okay, so there was definitely a certain vibe she had picked up from him in his last letter, but that might not mean a damn thing other than the man was just glad that a sistah had taken the time to write him. It didn't make a bit of sense that she was feeling this . . . this . . . ownership of him. She knew she needed to stop, but it was already happening without her even thinking about it. Like now.

After her day of pampering at Body & Soul, a Black-owned day spa in D.C., she had checked in to her suite for the night at The Mayflower Hotel, spent some luxuriating moments enjoying the opulence of her surroundings, ordered her some champagne from Room Service, had Housekeeping come scour the tub so she could watch them do it, then ran herself a bath. Okay, so she wasn't off on a beach somewhere for her birthday, but she could damn sure treat herself to a night of finery at one of D.C.'s oldest and most well-respected hotels. She would go have dinner with her girls, then come back here, get pissy drunk on champagne and take her happy ass to bed in her $500 a night suite. Shoot, she deserved it. Why the hell not.

So, she ran her bath, luxuriated in her expensive bubbles, both the ones she was laying in and the ones she was sipping on, got out and leisurely began getting dressed.

As she pulled on the fiery red fiesta Dolce & Gabana mini dress her Mom had gotten her as a birthday gift, she checked herself out in the mirror and found herself touching parts of her body and wondering what it would feel like to have Michael's hands on her. Wondering if he would be soft with her, gentle, or would he be all rough and anxious. Not that the thought of some urgency to lovemaking bothered her. It had been way too long for her since she had been with anybody, and she could feel the familiar wanting starting to make its presence known. Mmm Michael.

Audria put the thought aside, applied her makeup, and gave herself a final glance in the mirror, feeling sexy, Black and FOINE, but somehow owned. She walked out the door still feeling it, felt it all the way down in the elevator, all the way through the hotel lobby and out to her waiting car that the valet had brought around. She even felt it on the short drive over to the restaurant they were at – Georgia Brown's. Now though, it, along with the nice buzz she had started to feel from the champagne, was quite rapidly drying up under the disapproving glare from her girls.

"What?" she barked at the both of them, throwing up her hands in exasperation. "I thought this was *supposed* to be a birthday dinner to toast my survival of another year, not a roast-Audria alive 'cuz you don't agree with a choice I'm making." She rolled her eyes again.

Angela rolled hers right back and leaned over. "Audria, you *know* damn well that we got your back, always have, always will, but one of the reasons why we all been friends as long as we have is cause we don't bullshit each other. A friend who says only what the other person wants them to hear ain't no real friend. You can't be serious about getting with some dude on lockdown. You just can't."

Vanessa chimed in with her two cents. "Yeah Audie. 'Sides, what that Negro gon' do for you up behind barbed wire fences? Not a damn thing is what. He gon' just bring you down and be trying to get you to send him money and shit for commissary. I mean, not that I would know from personal experience or nothing, but that's what I done heard." She took a quick gulp of champagne and Audria looked at her sideways.

"'Nessa, you done been with somebody in jail? Tell me the truth. Girl, I can tell when your ass is lying."

Vanessa started smoothing down the sides of her baby-soft layered hair, raking her 3-inch nails through the folds of her fresh haircut. Audria knew for sure now she was trying to hide something. And so could Angela.

"V, *you* been with somebody on lockdown? When and how? You better give it up."

Soon, they were both messing with their girl so hard, forcing her to tell them about a man she used to see years before that wound up doing 18 months for jacking somebody's Volvo. Vanessa even admitted she had visited him a few times in prison, and had even tried to wait for him for some months, but it got too hard for her and she quit him and stopped accepting his collect calls. Audria was just beginning to relax, thinking the pressure was off her, when Angela turned the conversation right back around to the topic of Michael.

"Audria, don't you get too happy crackin' on V. We ain't forgot not in the least lil' bit about your jailbird. How long all this been going on, is what I wanna know, and the question of the century is whether your Momma know."

Audria's mouth dropped open. She hadn't even thought about her mother, although they had talked earlier on her cell phone while she was at the spa.

She could barely get her tongue working, but knew she had to set some things straight with Angela and Vanessa before it went any further. "First of all, Michael and I are *just* friends." She started to say 'nothing more, nothing less' but caught herself. "We've been writing each other since April. Well, that's when I wrote my first letter." She could see Angela getting ready to interrupt, probably to comment on the fact that she began the whole thing, but she wasn't about to let her butt in. "Like I said, we're *just* friends. I won't lie and say I'm not feeling him and feeling a kinda vibe with him and from him, but y'all, the man's been in jail for 13 damn years and got 4 more left to go. I couldn't let myself 'go there' even if I wanted to, okay?"

"THIRTEEN years, as in a 1 and a 3? Goddamn, what he do, kill somebody?" That was Vanessa with her eyes wide like saucers.

Audria shook her head at her. "No, he didn't kill anybody. He used to sell drugs and from what he says, he didn't go in there with as long a sentence as what he's ended up with. I guess time got added on for other stuff he did maybe when he first went in."

She took another sip of the Moet champagne and nibbled on a garlicky breadstick.

"But look, getting back to this thing about my Moms. NO, she doesn't know about him and neither one of you gon' say nothing, right?" They just looked at her with dumb looks on their faces and she yelled it out even louder. "RIGHT?"

Angela waved her off. "Yeah, yeah, whatever. We ain't gon' tell your Mommy on you. But what I want to know is when are *you* gon' tell her?"

Audria looked at her all crazy. "And just why exactly you think I'ma hurry up and throw myself under the wheels of that particular bus?"

She watched Angela and Vanessa exchange some knowing look between them, then Angela slowly took a sip from her own glass of champagne, then reached for her napkin to wipe the corners of her mouth. Audria grabbed her elbow hard and shook it. "Woman, you better start talking."

Angela smiled at her, then got serious after a beat. "Audria look, I been knowing you for damn near seven years, okay? In all my time knowing you, I ain't *nevah* seen you like this, even when you were messing around with that triflin' married man Rod or Rob, whatever his name was. Don't get me wrong. You're a beautiful woman and that always shows, but when you walked in this restaurant tonight, both me and V took one look at you, and you can ask her. V, didn't I turn to you and say Audria look like she in love? Tell me if I didn't."

Audria watched her other friend nod her head yes in agreement, then turned back to Angela as she continued. "You got this... this... glow about you, like you know something nobody else but you know, and it's all over you. So you can try to tell me and V all you want how you and this Michael guy ain't nothing but friends, but you lying to yourself. The sooner you start telling yourself the truth, the easier your conversation with your Momma's gon' be, 'cuz let me tell you somethin', the next time Ms. Viola see your ass, she gon' know before you even open your mouth, so it's either you gon' start avoiding your own Momma, which we *all* know is damn near impossible to do, or you better start owning up to some shit right here and now."

Audria looked at her friends, tried to breathe because all the air had suddenly been sucked out of her lungs, and then burst into tears. What a way to celebrate her 39th birthday.

twelve
I Got You!

Fri. 7/20

Peace Baby Girl.

First things first. Happy Belated Birthday, Beautiful. Hope it was a special one for you. I'm sorry I missed knowing about it before the actual day. That won't happen again.

It's funny you asked me at the end of your letter whether I have light moments in here, whether I ever smile. If somebody had asked that a few months ago, my answer would have been 'naw, not really'. I'm mostly a serious kinda brotha. You can't be too friendly around what you walk next to up in here, 'cuz people tend to mistake smiles for weakness. But like I said, it's funny you would ask, 'cuz a smile did bless my lips soon as I saw your name and the return address on the envelope, so you got what you asked for. Did the Universe let you know that I sent you a smile? As a matter of fact, many? Hope so.

Okay, let's get into this thing. You with me? Cool. Let's go for a ride. Speaking about riding, that was something I used to like to do before I started my bid. Loved to get on the hog (a Harley low-rider) and just ride. Sometimes I would be in another state before I even knew it. It's one of the things I miss, but let's not go there. We might be here all day talking about the things I miss. So you with me? Let's go.

Right off the bat, I gotta say this to you. I don't make promises often, Audria. Don't like to, never did, 'cuz if I find myself in a position where I'm not able to keep a promise, it eats at me like a parasite chewing on my lower intestines, but I'm making you one here, and you can believe that my word is bond, always. I got you. Babygirl, stop being afraid of whatever it is you're feeling, and stop thinking you're alone with it - the _feeling_ I'm talking about, not the fear. I'm right there with you. And in case you're wondering, yeah I feel fear, but I'm so quick to challenge it, that it doesn't hang around long. Audria, as time passes, things will come clear to you, but in the meantime? Relax, lay back, enjoy the ride, Pretty. I got you. Ain't gon' let nothing happen to you, Babygirl. Damn, I'm finding myself wishing for a day when I can put the word 'my' in front of 'Babygirl', but that's something only you can decide. Until you do that though, trust me. I got you. Cool?

Alright, I'm gonna focus on your letter now. First, the age thing. I think this might be the second or third time you mentioned your age and approaching 40. You know, everybody on this planet eventually starts feeling time creeping up their ass. It's as inevitable as the need to eat, sleep and go to the bathroom, but I always look at it like attitude is the thing that makes it easier or harder to deal with. Make yourself forget it. If you find that getting hung up on the day itself and its approach and all that, is the thing that's adding to your stress, find something else to get into around that time and focus your energy elsewhere. I guarantee you that number will lose whatever power you been giving it. Just try it and see what you think. Of course, you might decide you want to try that _after_ your 40th birthday, 'cuz your friends may have plans for you to celebrate the big one. Don't know.

Gotta tell you. When I think about you, I like the picture I get, so it bugs me a little bit to hear that parts of my letter outright disturbed you. Understand that wasn't my intent and never will be with you. I'm not in this thing to try to bring you worry or angst (I learned this word a couple days ago; trying to teach myself some new words). But anyway, I was saying, I don't want to think that I'm bringing worry to your life, but stick with me Babygirl, I'll try to calm the waters after the storm, no matter how big the storm is, alright?

Now, I don't know exactly what it is you're feeling that's disturbing you. I mean, I got some general ideas, but you gotta be specific when you talk to me, okay? I think from some things you said that you're feeling something for me, and there ain't enough words in the English language to tell you how _that_ makes me feel, but you're not alone. I know that things seem like they're moving kinda quick and I know how people can get sometimes thinking they have to follow society's guidelines on how fast or slow to move. I don't live by society's rules. Never have, never will. That's one of the reasons I ended up in here, but despite that, I understand that I can choose not to live by society's rules, and still be legal about that choice, so don't start thinking you gotta worry about me going back to the old me. That dude's dead and buried. I just want you to know that we don't have to follow anybody's rulebook on how shit (sorry, *gotta learn how to talk without cussing) unfolds between us. You with me?*

And don't think I don't understand and feel your fear about my time. Yeah, 13 years is a long time. Before getting arrested, I used to say that I could never tolerate being locked up either, but here I am in my 13th year and I'm still here, handling what I need to handle, so that's a testament to never saying never. I know it seems foreign to you, like something you can't comprehend, and I understand that, but never say never to nothing. And I know hearing I got 4 years left wasn't what you expected or might have wanted to hear either, but that is what it is. Can't do nothing about that, but I'm just asking you not to say never with me, okay? If you can't give me nothing else I ask for, please give me that.

Alright, was ready to move on, but don't think I'm done with this subject yet. So, there's the obvious - the issue about my time as it relates to what you're feeling for me. This is one of the things that's causing you to worry your beautiful head. But I think it's also the other thing that you can't talk about yet. Look Audria, you can't tie my hands with you like this, okay? I gotta be who I am with you, or this friendship, this thing between us can't work. I'm not trying to get all in your business. NO, NO, that's not true. Yes, I am. I am trying to get all in your business. I don't know what this 'thing' is that you won't talk about. Something inside me tells me it's something big, like the kind of shit a brotha would need to sit down behind, but let me tell you something right now. I don't care what it is. Whatever it is won't make me feel any different about you. Don't think there's a whole lot that could do that right now, 'cepting you tell me you was really born as Adrian and you had a sex change to make you Audria. Now, we would have to have a discussion behind that. ☺ Seriously though, I just want you to know that I'm here for you, Babygirl. Whenever you're ready to talk about whatever it is, you got you an ear, okay? I hope it's soon though, 'cuz anything that brings you pain, I'm not liking, and we gotta hurry up and address it so we can move on to other things. Remember we said to really look to the future, we got to face our past, then get whole in our present. So maybe it's time for you to face your past. What you think? Alright, moving on.

Your job. I hear you about feeling like you got off track from where you wanted to be or go. Me, more than a whole lot of other people, understand that getting off track deal, but the first part of that is recognizing that you went off track, which you do recognize, and then you can start taking steps to getting back on track. And nobody's telling you it's gon' happen overnight. Sometimes stuff just don't work like that, but so long as you recognize that you want to be doing something else with your life, then you can start doing little things to make that happen for you. I got faith in you. I know you can do this. Just from the letters you write me and the

Sweet Honey In The Rock concert picture you painted me, I know you can do this, Babygirl. Just come with your coming, whether fast or slow, but come with your coming. It's gon' happen for you. See it, feel it, start to breathe it and it's gon' happen for you. Alright? Cool.

Look, something else I gotta say. A lil' something that scratched skin off my ass again while reading your letter. Two places in your letter I noticed you scratched something out in the beginning of a sentence and changed it to something else. Usually, somebody's penmanship don't bother me none, but I told you before that if you pay close enough attention to the words a person speaks, that it constitutes 1/3 of the actual science of mind reading. Them scratch-outs are still your words and they're your heart's desire. The first thing was when you started to say that you can't wait to maybe see me experience Sweet Honey In the Rock? And you changed that to something safe, talking about you hope I get to experience them live and in person some day. Then the next thing was where you were talking about New York City. I could feel you getting ready to say that you'd like me to show you around the city one day, but you switched that up too and made it safe. Stop doing that with me. I want to taste your heart's desire, Audria, drink it like some good Remy, so stop hiding from me. I told you, I GOT YOU! I can handle you and anything you bring me, if you let me. Alright, falling back on that.

Woman, you had me laughing when you talked about feeling 'a pang of something' when you thought about other women writing me. If jealousy had a color, my hands woulda been covered in it just from holding your letter. I told you you were jealous, but does a brotha get any credit for pointing out the obvious? Naw, don't look like it, but it's cool. I'ma have to figure out a way to get me some getback, maybe turn you over my knee or tickle you 'til you scream or something, but that comes later.

Seriously Audria, I want to say something here. Yeah, I had my days of running game and trying to be up in a different woman every day of the week, thinking that made me a man, but that shit passed early on, back in my teens. And long before I started doing my bid, my attitude about and to women had changed. Never been the type to lay with women just because they're available to me for laying, you understand? When I call a woman My Woman, you best believe she can ALWAYS rest easy that I'm her man and no one else's. I don't play with that. And ain't a White woman in the world can EVER say she been on the receiving end of nothing named Strong. Me. I don't float boats in them kinda waters. And speaking of floating boats in strange waters, I know you might be curious about what I'm doing in here about sex. I know some of them prison shows you talked about watching, Oz and Prison Break and all that, might paint this picture of rapes and more shit going down, but let me assure you I ain't never been on the front or back end of none of that. I'm not telling you that I don't think about sex from time to time, but you kinda have to put some things out of your mind when they come to you. And when they persist in coming, then I Hand(le) my business, get it? Meaning, I masturbate. Alright, moving on.

Oh, almost forgot to mention this. Woulda been pissed too. Guess who I got a picture of tattooed on my left bicep? You give up? It's a picture of Nefertiti, yeah. Strange that you would mention her in your scribe. About four years ago, I got this dude to do it for me. There are two words that go with her, one above her and one below. Respect. Protect. That's what I offer to My Woman, when I have one. I respect her with everything inside me and I protect her with my life, if it ever comes to that.

Ain't gonna spend a lot of time on this, but I wanted to tell you that for the first time, I got this feeling of envy when you talked about your father and what he meant to you. Sounds like y'all had a real special relationship. If you feel like it, maybe you can share some more about him, just whenever you want to, if you want to, alright?

And the sentence I asked you to finish for me? What I love? I asked you because I know you can. You might not want to do it, but you can, so save that for whenever you feel ready to finish it. Wish you would stop saying you don't know me either. 'I don't know you. I don't know you.' I aint' buying that; Feds took my money. Babygirl, close your eyes, take a deep breath, two, then exhale slowly, listen to your heart. If you're listening right, your heart will tell you you know me. If it doesn't, then you never will.

So, your curiosity is outweighing your fear? I'm liking that. Tells me we can eventually get rid of your fear altogether, which for me, would be a very good thing. So, let me answer your question. You want to know what my spirit knew that other parts of me hadn't figured out yet after I finished reading your letter? You sure you ready to hear this, 'cuz I'm not hiding from you, Miss Audria, although you seem determined to hide from me. My spirit had already figured out that you are everything I could ever want and hope to have in a woman. My Woman. Listen, let me tell you something that might seem strange to you. I have NEVER been in love before. My focus was in other places and on other things, and when I did turn my attention to a woman, it was mostly to try to find somebody to be with for comfort and for sex within the confines of a committed relationship. But even with that and with feeling things that are brand new to me, I'm not running from any of this. I ain't no coward, love coward or otherwise. My spirit did its thing, figured out that you're what I've been looking for although I didn't have a clue that I was even looking for something. And now that my brain and my mind are on board too, I'm a force to be reckoned with, Audria. Let me tell you something else about me. When I focus on something, I'm there, I'm giving that thing all of me, so I'm with you. 100% with you. The rest is on you, Babygirl, but just like I told you with the pictures I asked for, take your time with that. Handle it when you're ready, but understand I'm gon' be here waiting for you. Like you, I don't like waiting, but I think I could learn to like waiting if you're the reward I get on the back end. And in case you ain't figured it out yet, this is what I was talking about when I said I want more from you, not less.

Alright Beautiful (and NO, I'm not just trying to be kind when I call you Beautiful; you are beautiful to me), but look, I gotta bounce. Need to turn my attention to some things, but I'll be thinking about you and waiting to hear back from you, so try to write me soon as you can, alright?

Be good, Babygirl. Peace Audria.

Michael

P.S. Isn't it funny how you can hear certain songs all your life and they don't mean a damn thing to you and then all of a sudden, you're feeling something different in your heart and a song comes on the radio and blows your mind? I heard this song halfway through writing you. It's something by somebody named Patti Austin. I don't know who she is, but I liked her voice. The song made me think of you though. It said something like:

"Please be strong, life's not too long at all.
Life will pass you by before you know it.
If you feel it deep inside, you better show it, girl."

Alright Babygirl, that was it. Sound like this Patti Austin woman know what she's talking 'bout, huh? Okay, I'm gone. Later.

P.P.S. Not sure why, but I actually opened up this letter to put this in for you. Here's the original picture from the ad. I want you to have It. Oh, the part that's cut out on the left (my right in the picture) is one of my partners in here. Okay, that's it. Hope you like it. Peace.

thirteen
Facing My Past

Hi Michael.

I don't know whether you've gotten my letter yet - the one I wrote you on my birthday (July 14*th*). I've been going back and forth with myself saying I should wait to hear back from you first before I write you again, but I want to say some things. Your last letter has been almost a constant companion to me. I even found myself laying it next to my pillow one night. I know that probably sounds crazy to you, but it gave me comfort. I keep feeling like I want to look at you, see your face. I have the picture from the ad, but it's just what I printed off after reading your ad and my printer was messing up at the time, so it's all grainy and the color is off, and it's small. I can't really see your eyes the way I want to see them. Anyway, would you send me a picture of you sometime? I think I'd really like that.

Okay Michael, like I said, I've been carrying around your last letter to me and have been reading it over and over again. I'm still concerned about some things - the time thing and dealing with that, but it's not going to change, so it's either I find some way to deal with it or I'm going to drive myself crazy. I think I'm falling in love with you. I don't know if it's true or if it's that I just want to fall in love, period, was ripe for it, and so I'm convincing myself that's what's happening. But here's why I think it's not just some desire to fall in love and that it's about YOU. If I simply wanted to fall in love, why wouldn't I just pick somebody out here who's walking around free and who's readily accessible to me? Why would I be feeling these things that I'm feeling for a man who's been in prison for

13 years and who has 4 more years to go on his sentence? It doesn't make sense, does it? That's what lets me know this is real and not something I'm imagining.

It's so scary to me, because I don't feel like I'm strong enough to deal with loving somebody who's not here. See, I'm a needy somebody. Even though I don't have a man and haven't had a man in a long time, I _feel_ like I need a lot. I need a lot of attention, need to feel desired, wanted, wrapped up, loved, and I'm worried about all that need and how to deal with that with you being where you are. I'm worried about whether you will feel even half of what I'm feeling, and worried about whether you can handle all of what I'm feeling and whether you'll be able to make me feel like... I don't know... like you have it all under control, like you have me, US. Lawd Michael, I'm tripping, aren't I? WHY am I talking like there's already an US. I don't even know if you feel the same way I do. I mean, I know that in your letter you said you want more from me, not less, but that doesn't really tell me what you're feeling, so I guess I'm stepping out on faith here and hoping that you're feeling the same way I am.

Okay, I'm going to put all that aside, not because it's not important to me, but because something else is even more important right now. You asked me a question in your letter that I've spent a lot of time with over the last week. You asked me whether there was something in my past that I haven't faced up to. In my response letter to you, the one I wrote you on my birthday (have you gotten it yet? Hope so), I basically told you that yes, you were crossing a line with asking me that. I'm sorry for saying that to you, because I know you care or you wouldn't ask the question. That was just me running from facing this thing that I feel like I've been running from all my life. Well, just like I'm trying to face and deal with these feelings I'm having for you, I think it's time for me to deal with this thing from my past.

Michael, again, I don't know if you will even want any of this or whether you will be in a position to handle it. I guess what I'm banking on is what you said earlier on about being like your last name - Strong. I'm hoping you can be that for me in this instance, even if for nothing else.

In my letter before the last, I painted you a picture, a beautiful one I think you'll agree, of Sweet Honey In The Rock. There's another picture I need to paint you now, but there's nothing beautiful about it. In fact, it's ugly and dirty and is something that you won't want to see, but I'm asking you to see it, because I'm finally seeing it, facing it, but I feel like I can't do it alone and I need somebody strong with me, kinda holding my hand while I do it, so please be with me.

I was 13. Every Summer, my Momma and Daddy would let me go down to Rocky Mount to visit with my Momma's side of the family - my Aunt Sissy and her husband, Uncle Carl. I used to love visiting them down there. Their place was almost *like a farm with cows out back, goats, chickens and this old tire hanging from a weeping willow tree I used to swing on. It's just something about the country I used to like back then. Messing with the cows, chasing the baby goats and chickens, playing under the weeping willow, or going for long walks down to the nearby creek. Sometimes I'd ride with Aunt Sissy to go clean the church, to the Piggly Wiggly or sometimes we'd just pick up food from Gardeners or Abrams, these soul food restaurants that were in town. Their food was sooooo good. I can remember licking my fingers after eating some of that good country fried chicken.*

I guess going down there just gave me a chance to get out from under Momma and Daddy and away from the sweltering D.C. heat and be in a different place. Daddy would take me down to the Greyhound bus station, talk to the driver, and my designated seat would be in back of him the entire way until he turned me over to Aunt Sissy on the other end.

Uncle Carl, Aunt Sissy's husband was this tall, big guy with a deep, deep voice. I remember thinking he looked like a mountain the first time I met him. He went on and on, stretching into forever, like his head was bumping up against the sky. I liked how he felt, how he smelled, and I liked the way he made me feel every time he would pick me up and twirl me around and then throw me in the air. That all felt good, but what felt the best was when he would catch me. He had huge arms that felt solid and safe to me, made me feel warm and protected, like nothing bad could get me when I was with him.

I don't know when things changed between me and Uncle Carl. No, I shouldn't say that, because nothing changed for me. Something changed for him. I don't know if it changed before that year when I turned 13, like if it was a gradual leading up to it, or whether everything changed for him that year, but it doesn't much matter. Something changed in him that made him get some new 'awareness' of me, and whatever was inside him that he couldn't fight against any longer, made him do something that's been with me since then.

Close your eyes, Michael. Your mind's eyes. Picture a little girl, 13, at play. I wasn't into boys or any of that yet, like how 13 year olds are these days. I was a straight A student in school, my nose always in a book, but I was still into dolls and warm fuzzy things like teddy bears and other stuffed animals. Close your eyes. Picture me playing, keeping myself company because the neighborhood kids were at some camp. I had gotten there too late to sign up. Aunt Sissy was down at the Church. She was one of the ladies who volunteered to clean the church every Saturday to get it ready for Sunday services. Uncle Carl was on the porch watching me play. I could feel his eyes boring into my back, watching my every move. That's the first year I can remember feeling his eyes on me like that, but maybe that's just when I became aware of him too, the same way he became aware of me.

I could feel him watching me, but I was more intent on combing my dollbaby's hair, changing her clothes. All of a sudden, he calls to me, tells me to 'come here.' There's something in his voice that sounds slimy to me, some shaky, unsure thing that instantly tells me he's thinking nasty thoughts, but I can't say NO to him, scream it the way I want to, because my Momma and Daddy have always told me to mind my manners and do what adults tell me to do, so I go to him. He looks at me, not in the eyes, but all up and down on my body, and his darting gaze makes my skin pucker and begin to crawl, but I stand there anyway.

He sends me in the house to get him some lemonade. I haven't gone three steps through the front door before I hear him behind me and hear the door close and lock. Before I can turn around to put a hand out, he's on me. I can feel his breath hot on my face. I can feel the scratchiness of his beard against my arms, my chest, my neck, my stomach. I feel dwarfed by the size of him. I feel little and weak and insignificant. In my struggles, a hand touches the eager hardness between his legs and he cries out, something guttural and needy, and I know without even seeing the confirmation in his eyes, that this touch has sent him over the edge, has made him say yes to whatever demon's driving him to take, take, take.

He pulls my panties down, scraping my thighs with dirty fingernails and calloused hands, and he's thrusting inside me, ignoring my attempts to clamp my legs shut and the cries that seem stuck in my throat. He burrows inside me, ruts, fucks, sweats his dirty sweat into my open, terror-filled eyes, and spews his stinking, smelly semen on my stomach as he drags himself out of me. I look down and I can see my blood on his penis and I just go away in my head.

I don't know how else to explain that. I feel myself go away and it's like a part of me is somewhere else watching me laying there with that dirty, stinking, smelly man on top of me still breathing fast from all his exertions. I want to stay away, because it's calm, peaceful where I am, and I know it would be easier for me, and maybe easier for everybody if I stayed away, but he looks down at my body lying there and he starts calling my name and shaking me, "Audria, Audria. Get up, Child. Get up." So I go back. He wants to help me, because he's feeling the guilt. I can feel it when it flies into his body and he doubles over with the force of it, like he can't absorb it, and he tries to help me, but I won't let him. He will never touch me again.

I pick myself up. I pick up my torn panties that have fallen halfway into the blood that puddled under me. I use them to wipe away the stickiness on my stomach and then I wipe between my legs with them. I walk slowly to the kitchen and I get a dish towel and I clean up the mess he's made. Wipe away my blood and his sweat. I wash the spot over and over again until there's nothing there, then I dry it. I wash the towel the same way, over and over again at the sink, then I go upstairs, bury the blood stained panties in the bottom of my suitcase and I wash myself over and over again until my skin feels raw from so much scrubbing. I go to bed and when Aunt Sissy comes home, I pretend that I have a fever and allow her to coddle me like she would her own daughter, if she had one. She makes a fuss over me and all the while, the beast is hovering in the background with an anxious look on his face for he thinks I'll tell her what he did. I know I won't, but he doesn't know that, so he hovers.

The rest of the Summer he hovers and threatens, cajoles and begs, trying to elicit assurances from me that I won't turn him in for the evil he's brought to me. I don't give him what he wants, even though I can, but I want him to suffer. I want him to always wonder whether I'll tell. I want him to feel fear jump up in his heart every time the phone rings, every time he hears my Momma or my Daddy call, every time he sees a police car coming his way. I want him to suffer the way he made a 13 year old child suffer. I want him to die the way I feel like I died inside when he violated me, taking from me the one thing that a woman should have as hers to give freely and willingly to whatever boy or man she loves and feels is deserving of it.

Before we left in Aunt Sissy's car for the Greyhound station, I hunted for the buried panties in my suitcase and making sure she and the beast were outside, I put them under the beast's pillow as a parting gift for him to find that night. On the ride back to D.C., I grew up, or maybe it happened before then. I met my Momma and Daddy at the bus station, gave them hugs, and chitchatted with them like all was fine in my world, leaving them secure in theirs. But when the topic of what I would do with my Summer came up again the next year, I told them I wanted to go to camp, something local in Maryland, and they just assumed their babygirl had grown up and now had other interests. I've never been back to North Carolina, not even for Aunt Sissy's funeral. She passed a couple years before my Dad did. My folks thought it was rude that I didn't want to go, but they didn't push the issue. It was obvious I wasn't changing my mind.

Okay Michael. That's the thing. That's what I didn't want to face from my past. I'm facing it now. I've tried facing it in other maybe not-so-positive ways before, things that I'm kind of ashamed to talk about right this minute, but maybe in time I will. It hurts more than I can tell you bringing all this back, but I'm doing it because I feel like I'm at this crossroads in my life where I want to begin a new journey, maybe a new journey with you, if you'll have me. Don't know if you will, but I want you to, and if I'm really going to begin a new journey, then I have to face my past, relegate it to the place where it needs to be, and use whatever fuel I get from that to help me look to my future. Hopefully, OUR future.

I know I've brought you a lot to deal with here, a lot of pain. I hope this is not a mistake being so open with you, but something's telling me that I can be this way with you and that I need to do this, so here I am.

Alright Michael, I'm gonna close now. Before I go, I wanted to give you some things. The first is a picture of me. You said that you wanted to see what I look like, and since I just asked you earlier in the letter for a picture of you, I think it's only fair for me to send you one of me. To be honest, I don't usually like pictures of myself, but this is a decent one, I think. The other things I need to give you are my phone numbers. I don't know how this will work, because to be honest, I've never communicated with anyone in prison, so I don't know if you can call me direct or if you have to call me collect or whatever. It doesn't matter. I would like to hear your voice, please. Guess it's time for me to decide if you really have a New York accent or not. Anyway, here are all three of my numbers:

(301) 885-1111 (home)

(301) 367-0123 (cell)

(202) 887-9876 (work). If you call me at work, please don't call me collect because that might get me in a little trouble, but you're welcome to call me collect on any of the other two numbers. The final thing I have for you is my home address. It is:

Audria C. Hope

11011 Destiny Place

Waldorf, MD 20602

Okay, that's all for now, Michael. I really hope I hear from you soon. This waiting around for letters from you is driving me crazy, but I guess we can't change that. Hope to talk to you soon.

Thinking of you,

Audria

P.S. By the way, the 'C' in my middle name is for Christine.

fourteen
Handling My Business

Peace Audria.

Wrote you a letter last week Friday - 7/20. Don't know if you got that yet, but I'm discovering that a new word has jumped up in my vocabulary since then - CAN'T. Woman, I <u>can't</u> keep you off my mind. Can't stop thinking about you. I think about you all day, every day. It's like you've decided to take up residence inside me and are just camping out. And don't get me wrong, I like it. Have no problem with it, not in the least lil' bit. It's just strange to me. So I kept sitting, kept waiting and wanting to hear from you, and I feel like I will soon, but I need to say some things to you even before I hear from you.

Audria, I know that you're an intelligent woman. I know that you read between the lines of what I tell you, and so I know you understand that I get letters from other women. The majority of the women who write me are White women. Told you that. But they're not the only ones that write me. I've communicated with a few sistahs during my bid, and I've even had one or two relationships over these 13 years, but I wasn't in love with any of the women.

Damn, I feel like I'm stalling. Look Audria, I've never asked a woman to wait for me while I do time. That's not my style. Matter of fact, I've managed to run most of them off if anything. I don't want to hang that kinda weight around nobody's neck 'cuz when somebody starts feeling obligated to do a thing, most times that means they're not really doing it *from their heart, and that's not coming with truth, you feel me? Still stalling, but I'm gon' get this out one way or the next.*

I know I said I would leave some things up to you to decide, but I need for you to recognize where I am in my head. Sorta give you some information so you can have the necessary tools you need to make a final decision one way or the next. I love you. Naw, that's like what I'd tell my Mother when she was alive. I'M IN LOVE WITH YOU. Yeah, you heard me. I, Michael Strong, am in love with you, Audria Hope. What's your middle name? As crazy as it is to me, I feel it and because I make myself deal only in truth, I recognize what truth feels like inside me, and I recognize that I'm in love with you.

I don't know if I'm jumping the gun here telling you how I feel about you. My biggest fear right now, and I told you I don't feel fear often, or it doesn't hang around long with me, but my biggest fear is that you gon' haul ass out of my life hearing this, but like I do with everything else, I gotta bring you this truth.

Audria, for the first time, I'm feeling HOPE. Yeah, not just feeling you, but I'm feeling everything your last name means or should mean to me or to anybody. I'm feeling HOPEful that I have a chance to give myself to the only woman I've ever been in love with, the only woman alive that I want and need to show myself to.

I know that the time I got left in this place might be the thing that runs you up outta my life, but I still got to try. I got to tell you that we can do this thing, you and me. I feel like with you, not behind me but beside me, that we can move mountains together, tilt the world on its axis and let love be the crazy glue that keeps us together forever.

I want and need you in my life, not just as my friend, but as <u>My Woman</u>. I told you that when I have a woman she has no doubt in her mind that she's My Woman and I'm her man. I want to give you that, as I want to give you all of me. Again, I ain't never asked a woman to wait for me while I do time, and I'm not going to start now, but I need you to know the way I feel about you, and leave it in your hands to follow what your heart tells you to do.

Something else that I need to mention here, and we haven't really talked a lot about other family type stuff between us, so this may come as a surprise to you. I got a son, Aud. Don't know why I keep wanting to call you Aud. Is that cool? If not, tell me not to and I won't. Anyway, I got a son. He's 15. Yeah, that meant he was still just a lil' boy when I got busted. He's with his Mother in the Bronx. She's been raising him. I'm in contact with him and have been all his life.

Look Babygirl, I know this might make you feel a kinda way, but it shouldn't. Having a son (his name is Michael, Jr.) doesn't take nothing off the way I feel for you and what I hope you and me will have someday.

Two years ago, I asked my son's mother, my wife (yeah wife) for a divorce and she flipped out on me. I don't know why, 'cuz she ain't nothing to me, ain't been nothing to me in more than a decade. We ain't been nothing to each other, so I don't know why she had that reaction. Still don't. But that is what it is. I guess what I'm trying to tell you here is that matters that were of no importance to me just a few short months ago are now of importance. I'm handling my business, so that when I walk free from behind these walls, I can walk to you and offer you ALL of me. You understand? I hope you do, Babygirl, 'cuz I don't like surprises and this feels to me like I'm gon' be bringing you some surprises that mightn't be too pleasant, but I gotta bring you truth. Like I said, it's the only way I roll.

Alright, ain't gon' take up no more of your time. Just wanted you to know the way I feel and that I'm handling my business so you can rest easy with that and with me, if that's your choice, okay? I hope it is. Okay Babygirl, you take care. I'll wait to hear from you. Hope I get a letter from you tomorrow or the next day. It's been almost a week since I responded to your last one, so I think I'm due. Alright Beautiful Audria, I'm out.

Love you,
Michael

fifteen
The Past Haunts

"Why did you do it?"

Audria whispered into the phone, voice tortured and low, the tears flowing freely, streaming miniature rivers down her cheeks. Since writing her last letter to Michael, it seemed like she hadn't stopped crying. Telling him about her childhood violations had punctured a fissure somewhere in the dam of her emotions and it seemed like she couldn't go five minutes without crying.

After exhausting all her sick leave at work -- the miserly 7 days a year the Firm gave them, two of which she had used earlier in the year, she finally called the law partner she worked with and told him the truth. She hated telling him her business or anybody else for that matter, but nobody had to drop a boulder on her head to convince her she was skating on thin ice with her job. It was either she told him the truth or as close to it as she could get, or she wouldn't have a damn job before too long. So she called, told him that she was having a personal crisis that she wasn't handling so good and that she needed him and the firm to work with her a little while longer and give her some time and understanding.

Like almost all White men she knew, he was uncomfortable dealing with anybody Black, so he hurried up with the call, told her to take all the time she needed, without pay, of course, and to give him a call when she was ready to come back to work. Biting back the 'I ain't nevah coming back' that was tickling the inside of her mouth to spring out, Audria thanked him for his understanding, hung up, and dialed the number from heart.

She hadn't used this number in over a quarter of a century, but it was still with her and she knew, through her Mother, that it was the same it had always been. When the voice answered, she asked her tortured question then hung up, not waiting for any response. This was her seventeenth time calling. She would stop at #25. One call for every year she had lived with this thing since age 13.

Hang up. Redial. Wait for the frustrated voice to answer. Ask her question. #18.

Hang up. Redial. Wait for the really frustrated, borderline pissed voice to answer. Ask her question. #19.

Hang up. Redial. Busy tone.

Wait. Try again. Busy tone.

Wait. Try again. Cautious answer. Ask her question. #20.

Hang up. Redial. Busy tone again.

Wait. Try again. Busy tone. Wait 10 minutes. Try again. Busy tone again. Wait 10 more minutes. Cautious answer. Ask her question. #21. Four more to go.

Hang up. Redial. Ignore the shaky 'Who this? Audria?' Ask her question again. #22.

Hang up. Redial. Ignore the shaky 'You ain't tole nobody, is you?' Ask her question. #23.

Hang up. Redial. Blah blah blah blah blah. I ain't listening to them fake ass tears, old man. Asking my question. #24.

Hang up. Redial. "WHY DID YOU DO IT? WHY DID YOU FUCKING HURT ME, YOU SICK SON-OF-A-BITCH? I WAS ONLY 13, ONLY 13."

Hang up. Lose it. Utterly and completely. Lose it.

Why did this man do this to me? He robbed me like some dirty thief. Took my youth and innocence and spit in the face of my future, of my happiness. I didn't deserve that kind of hurt. Nobody does. NOBODY DOES. I hate him. I hate him. I hate him. I hate him. And he's only crying his old ass now 'cuz he's STILL scared after all these years that I'm going to tell and he'll die a miserable death in jail, some shriveled, old, unloved thing. I HATE HIM!!!

Audria was on her knees, crawling across her bedroom floor. She felt a burning, a searing inside her chest that felt like somebody slowly pouring a vial of acid down her throat and into her lungs. She felt like she couldn't catch her breath, felt like there wasn't enough, would never be enough air on the entire planet to make her take a clean, full breath again. She suddenly felt dirty, soiled, nasty, almost like she was reliving the day when the beast had listened to his inner demons and despoiled her, ruined her, took from her the one thing that no man should take, should have it offered willingly to him.

She crawled into her bathroom, still on her hands and knees and dragged herself up and into the tub, turning on the showerhead. As the cold water pounded down on her head, wetting her braids, drenching her, soaking through her clothes, stinging her skin, she screamed aloud over and over and over again, her voice sounding ragged and hoarse, like a stranger's, sounds she barely recognized as coming from her. "WHY? WHY? WHY? WHY? WHY DID YOU DO IT TO ME? TO ME? WHY?"

An image of her father flashed in her mind and she screamed for him, missing him intensely, like she had every day since he left her. Some detached part of her couldn't believe she was behaving like this, losing it so completely. She had always prided herself on how *together* a person she was, how well she handled things, how she rolled with the punches, but this was something that was outside her ability to control. Wasn't no handling this and wasn't no rolling with these punches. She felt like she had been k.o.'d, was flat on her fucking face in the middle of life's boxing ring with the force of these blows.

She turned her face upward, feeling the water sting her face, starting to choke her as droplets spattered up her nose, trickling down her throat, but she didn't care. She pounded her fist repeatedly across her chest, hard, feeling the thuds reverberating deep inside her. She screamed aloud again, feeling wild and out of control, like she was tottering on the edge of madness, like she was two steps shy from going away in her head again. But this time, she knew there would be no coming back.

* * * * * *

Michael was on the balls of his feet. Couldn't sit still. Couldn't sit at all. He had been pacing for the last three hours. Feeling... he didn't know what the hell he was feeling. It didn't make sense to him. He was generally calm, easy, relaxed, but nothing inside him felt calm, easy or relaxed right this minute. In fact, it was exactly the opposite.

He wasn't sure when it had started exactly. Seemed to remember that it had begun as just a general feeling of uneasiness, but with every minute that passed, it got worse. Now, his stomach was tied in knots and his head was throbbing like somebody was slamming a sledgehammer upside his temples with maniacal force. He couldn't remember the last time he had felt nauseous in thirteen years, but now he did. That, along with some kind of burning in his chest that made him feel like he couldn't catch a breath.

His cellie was coming at him waving some piece of paper, probably with some more of his whiny bullshit, but Michael put a hand in his face, stopped him in his tracks, and went back to bouncing on the balls of his feet again. He needed to figure out what this shit was. Was something getting ready to jump off and this was some kinda internal warning thing? Naw, that didn't feel right either. This didn't feel like anything else he had ever felt. It didn't even feel like his own shit.

He spun around and looked at the half cut mirror over his desk, his eyes narrowing into tiny slits. Was that it? Could this be coming from somebody else? Audria maybe? He leaned forward, his muscular arms falling on either side of the mirror, his knuckles balancing the rest of his body. Was she in trouble? Hurt or something? His eyes met the eyes of his mirrored reflection, and he felt something turn over deep inside him that he recognized as the familiarity of truth. It was her. She was hurt, in a lot of pain, and he couldn't do a damn thing about it. This was so fucked up not being able to *do* something. And because he could think of nothing else that would remove the worry that had him tied up in knots now, he went back to bouncing on the balls of his feet and staring at his haunted, reflected eyes in the mirror.

* * * * * *

Mommas have impeccable timing. Whether for the good or bad of it, nobody could beat a Momma's clock. Leave it to them and they could mess up a good buzz, interrupt some heated lovemaking, or feel their child's pain and come running. Her Momma is who saved her.

Audria's gaze had just fallen on her shaving razor sitting on the side of her tub, the blade shiny and seeming to beckon her enticingly when her Mother's frame filled the doorway and then threw itself at her, arms wide.

"Baby, what's the matter? What's the matter with you? Lawd Audria, Jesus, tell me what's wrong. *WHO HURT YOU?*"

Audria couldn't talk, couldn't face the anxiety and anguish rolling off her mother in maternal waves, so she buried her face in her hands and bawled like she had never bawled in front of her Mother before. She let her Momma do for her what mothers the world over did for hurting daughters. She let her hold her to her bosom, speak soft, soothing words in her ear, and eventually she let herself be coaxed out of the tub and to her bed.

She surrendered to her mother's ministrations, allowing her to remove the soggy clothes hanging on her body, then drying her and dressing her in her warmest flannel nightgown, and putting socks on her feet. She cried some more as her mother towel-dried braid after braid, made then fed her tea with honey and lemon, all the while whispering comforting reassurances in her ear. Eventually, the tears subsided into hiccupping sobs, and pretty soon her head was lolling to the side as she began to drift off to sleep from emotional exhaustion. Just before she slipped into a fitful sleep, her mother holding her head in her lap the very way she had as a child, Audria spoke the name of the man who seemed never to be far from her thoughts now. *"Michael."*

* * * * * *

"*Audria.*" Michael spoke her name aloud. He was shaking where he sat. He had never felt weak in his life, but his legs felt like they would buckle when he finished reading her letter, and he immediately had to sit down. He couldn't believe she had been living with this kind of pain for damn near twenty some years and was sharing all this with him.

He looked at the picture she had sent him, contemplating the woman he desired to be his future, his everything. She was beautiful. In the picture, she was sitting cross-legged Indian style on a purple chaise lounge, wearing a red robe that looked silk and holding a brown, fuzzy-looking stuffed bear. Her eyes were smiling at the picture taker. *This* was the woman he was in love with.

She looked like an African Princess to him. Beautifully defined features, caramel-colored skin, nice cheekbones, full, very kissable lips and a defiant tilt to her chin. Her eyes though were something else. Expressive wasn't the word. They seemed to connect, look deep within him to his soul, and his spirit shed tears for her pain.

Tearing his eyes away from the picture but refusing to let go of it, Michael looked at the letter again, his eyes starting and stopping at various points, taking in words that seemed unbelievable to him.

...Close your eyes, Michael. Your mind's eyes. Picture a little girl, 13, at play...
...I could feel him watching me, but I was more intent on combing my dollbaby's hair, changing her clothes...
...He looks at me, not in the eyes, but all up and down on my body, and his darting gaze makes my skin pucker and begin to crawl...
...He pulls my panties down, scraping my thighs with dirty fingernails and calloused hands, and he's thrusting inside me...
...He burrows inside me, ruts, fucks, sweats his dirty sweat into my open, terror-filled eyes...

He couldn't take any more. Had to stop. *Made* himself stop reading. He felt the rage building inside him that made him a walking, breathing danger to himself and to anyone within a stone's throw. He looked over at his cellie watching him warily and the only thing that saved dude from getting his head bashed in for daring to breathe air in the same room as him was the fact that he had brought him Audria's letter, the very thing he had been trying to hand him earlier.

Earlier. This letter had to be somehow related to what he had been feeling earlier, all that pain and anxiety deep inside that almost made him crazy. He picked up the letter again. He had to talk to her. Had to hear her voice and assure her that he was here for her, would help her work her way through all this. She had given him her phone numbers, hadn't she? He would call her.

Forty-five long minutes later, when he was 'bout to come out his skin from all the delays waiting for the phone, he breathed relief with a ragged sigh as the call was placed for him. He waited through the call announcement letting the party on the other end know that the call was coming in from a federal penitentiary. The call wasn't collect, but whoever answered would have to press 5 to accept the call or 1 to reject it. He waited, occasionally looking at the picture he was still holding, barely able to breathe and anxious to hear her voice.

On the other end of the line, Audria's mother was looking at the phone like it had turned into a vile and slithering two-headed snake in her hands. Federal Penitentiary? Michael Strong? She didn't know no Michael Strong and Audria had damn sure never told her about knowing anybody in a federal penitentiary. Her daughter had obviously been keeping things from her, but whether she was or not, she wasn't in any shape to talk to anybody right now anyway.

'Sides, it was probably this Michael Strong person who was responsible for her being in the state she was in right now. She didn't think twice. She pressed 1 on the telephone keypad and dropped the phone back in its cradle. Maybe that would give this Michael Strong the message he needed. Back off and leave my daughter alone. Audria was too precious to be messing 'round with no inmate. She didn't need that kind of madness in her life. Smoothing the worry lines that had appeared over her daughter's brow in sleep, she looked down at her child lovingly. What she didn't know could never hurt her. She had already made up her mind not to even tell her about the call.

sixteen
Heart Ears Ain't Listening

Didn't understand why Momma was hanging 'round, fussing over every little damn thing there was to fuss over, but *not* asking me any questions. Hell, it's not like I hadn't just had a mini nervous breakdown in front of her, and it's not like she wasn't the world's nosiest, needlingest momma, so why wasn't she asking me what the hell was going on with me?

I looked over at her, sitting on the purple chaise with her legs up and sipping on my good Lemon Zinger tea that I always tried hiding from her but that she always managed to find. "What's up with you, Momma? Why aren't you asking me about earlier?"

She looked at me over the rim of the huge earthenware, sunflower yellow mug, sipped some tea, and smacked her gums like she was 80 instead of her sprightly 62. For some reason, I started doing the math in my head. My Mother would have been a year younger than I was now at the time of my rape.

It's funny how when you were young, anybody over 30 seemed like they were two steps away from social security or the grave. Now that I was a year older than what she would have been the year I was violated, and the more I contemplated it, I understood that time just passed and it's either you learned how to adapt to the passing of it, or you would drive yourself crazy trying to hold on to your fleeting youth. After all, none of us were promised the next day, so it was up to us to just live in the moment as much as possible and try to enjoy the life we'd been given. Of course, I recognized all of this on a very basic level, but the challenge was making it real to me and learning how not to struggle against it.

I looked at Momma and raised my eyebrows waiting on an answer. She looked like she was contemplating something, making some decision, and then she spoke in a harsher tone of voice than I was expecting.

"Audria, you grown, ain'tchu? I know I'm your mother, but I also know that not because I'm your mother means you gon' tell me everything 'bout your life. The way I figure it is when you ready to tell me what this is about, you'll tell me. Until then, I ain't trying to *force* you to tell me nothin' you don't want to tell me."

Remembering what Angela had said to me over my birthday dinner about my Mom being able to figure out I was in love, I wondered whether to tell her about Michael. It was obvious she hadn't figured it out, despite what Angela had said. But then I realized that if I told her about Michael, it would mean she would still be left wondering why I had been crying my soul out, and that was a discussion I knew I never wanted to have with my mother. What she didn't know couldn't hurt her, and I wasn't trying to hurt her over something that had happened such a long time ago. I would work through it as best I could, hopefully with Michael's help, and move on to a future with him, if he would have me.

The doorbell rang and I waved Mom back into her seat and turned to go get it. Figured a three-hour nervous breakdown and another three hours sleeping qualified me to rejoin the rest of the world who had to concern itself with answering ringing doorbells, hugging best girlfriends and snatching offered mail.

"What up, 'Ho?" Angela breezed by me, bringing a waft of Red Door perfume into the house with her. Vanessa was right behind her, sporting an even shorter haircut than I remembered seeing her with just two weeks before. I shushed up Angela, pointing to the next room and mouthing 'Moms' to let her know I wasn't alone. We giggled behind that and she pulled me close, whispering in my ear that there was a letter from Michael in the stack she had just handed me. My heart immediately started fluttering and it seemed like an eternity suffering through all the bullshit small talk and back-and-forth between my girlz and my Mom, but eventually I got them all out the house and sat down to read the letter from the man who had me feeling wide open.

> *Thurs. 7/26*
>
> *Peace Audria.*
> *Wrote you a letter last week Friday - 7/20. Don't know if you got that yet...*

7/20? What letter? I only have one letter from you. She rifled through the stack of mail trying to find something else from him, but knew there was no other letter.

> *...I'm discovering that a new word has jumped up in my vocabulary since then - CAN'T. Woman, I* can't *keep you off my mind. Can't stop thinking about you. I think about you all day, every day.*

"Me too, Michael. Me too. I'm thinking about you all day, every day too." She whispered it aloud to the room and kept reading.

> *...Damn, I feel like I'm stalling. Look Audria, I've never asked a woman to wait for me while I do time. That's not my style. Matter of fact, I've managed to run most of them off if anything.   I don't want to hang this kinda weight around nobody's neck 'cuz when somebody starts feeling obligated to do a thing, most times that means they're not really doing it from their heart, and that's not coming with truth, you feel me?*

"I feel you, Baby, I really do, but what the hell are you trying to tell me? You are stalling. Damn, this is nerve wracking." Audria didn't understand what he was trying to get at. He sure was bold and didn't beat around the bush. He was moving way faster than what she was expecting, but she guessed it was okay. After all, it's not like she hadn't written him and moved kinda fast her damn self.

> *... I know I said I would leave some things up to you to decide, but I need for you to recognize where I am in my head. Sorta*

> give you some information so you can have the necessary tools
> you need to make a final decision one way or the next. I love
> you. Naw, that's like what I'd tell my Mother when she was
> alive. I'M IN LOVE WITH YOU. Yeah, you heard me. I, Michael
> Strong, am in love with you, Audria Hope.

"In love with me? Oh God, he's IN LOVE WITH ME?"
Audria put the letter down, closed her eyes and leaned her head
back in the chair, contemplating the miracle of what she had just
read. He was feeling the same way for her? She started
murmuring a silent prayer. "Oh God, are you *finally* going to give
me my heart's desire? Have you sent me a love all my own?" Her
heart felt light and giddy and she felt like it was probably a good
thing she was sitting or she knew her knees would be buckling. He
loves me. He loves me. Her heart was singing. She went back to
the letter.

> ...My biggest fear right now, and I told you I don't feel fear
> often, or it doesn't hang around long with me, but my biggest
> fear is that you gon' haul ass out of my life hearing this...

"Me? Run from you? Boy, you best own you some heavy
equipment 'cuz that's the only way I'm moving. I ain't going
nowhere, you hear me? Nowhere."

> ...I know that the time I got left in this place might be the thing
> that runs you up outta my life, but I still got to try. I got to tell
> you that we can do this thing, you and me. I feel like with you,
> not behind me but beside me, that we can move mountains
> together, tilt the world on its axis and let love be the crazy glue
> that keeps us together forever.

"And I'm gon' run from you with you saying all this to me?
I'd have to be crazy. We'll deal with the time issue, Baby. We will."

Five minutes later when she turned the page and saw what
was waiting for her on the other side, Audria felt like screaming
aloud in the room. What she was feeling felt eerily reminiscent to
how she had felt earlier. Fate had just played a horrible trick on her
and her heart felt twice as heavy as it had before. Even with the
misery she felt deep in her spirit like a ten-ton weight, she went in

search of pen and paper to write him the last letter she felt she would ever write him.

Fri. 8/10 - 9:11 p.m.

Michael,

    I'm so disappointed. I feel like my heart and soul are just shriveling in on themselves right now. Just feel cold. The thing that I least expected to happen relative to you and the way I think about you has happened. I feel like you've been reduced in my eyes, and I hate that!!!

    I just finished reading your letter. First of all, I'm not understanding, because it's dated 7/26 and I know I wrote you my last letter on 7/20, but your letter doesn't respond to <u>anything</u> I shared with you in my last letter, so it's either you chose to ignore all of what I shared with you, and it was a whole lot, meaning that none of what matters to me is important to you in your scheme of things. And you speak about some other letter you wrote to me but there is no other letter. At least I don't have it so I have to go on what's in front of me.

    So I get your letter. I've been going through a whole lot lately, took some time off work, and my girlfriend Angela just brought it to me. I'm reading and my heart's singing because you're saying so much of what I want or thought I wanted to hear from you. You're saying that you can't stop thinking about me and don't want to. You're saying that although you've had relationships with other women during the last 13 years in prison, that you weren't in love with any of them. And then, incredibly, you say the thing, the one thing that I've been craving and dreaming about hearing you say - that you love me. Even said that you're IN LOVE with me. I even had this moment of eerie déjàvu but in a good way when you called me 'Aud', because only my Dad ever called me Aud, so I found it so special that you would call me by the same pet name he used for me. But I want you to listen very carefully, Michael, you don't get to call me Aud. As a matter of fact, you get to call me NOTHING!!!

    I'm reading all these nice words from you and feeling you and your words so deeply until I get to the sentence: "Two years ago, I asked my son's mother, my wife (yeah wife) for a divorce and she flipped out on me." I had to put your letter down and literally backed away from it, because it suddenly felt greasy in my hands and it felt like maybe if I didn't put it down, it would transform into some venomous snake and bite me, spreading poison through my veins. WHAT am I supposed to do with that enlightening bit of information, Michael? Can you hear me screaming at you? Is this what you do? Is it? You make someone - ME - start falling in love with you, you stir these feelings of intensity and passion and raw emotion, you make me feel like I can share my past hurts with you, things that I've NEVER shared with another living soul, you make me start *hoping and dreaming and believing that maybe I <u>can</u> do this waiting thing after all, because after all, what's four years to wait if I can look forward to maybe someday having the awesome pleasure of calling this man who I feel is my soulmate MY HUSBAND? You wait for me to go there in my head, but mostly in my heart, and <u>then</u> you pull the whole freaking carpet out from under me to tell me that more than likely I won't have it, because of some woman somewhere who wants to hold on to something you <u>say</u> is over? Maybe it's not really. Whatever. You know, even with feeling as cold as I do and with the anger that's crept in, I can't hate her although I want to, because I know that she's perhaps just reluctant to let go of her prize. Right now, it's you that I... No, I won't say that. I won't voice that much anger, because I know I don't hate you. And if I speak it, all it'll do is reduce me, reduce you, reduce whatever potential for an US even more than has already happened. Oh, fuck this trying to be proper shit. I love you. I've NEVER felt like this before. I've never wanted anything or anyone as much as I feel all in and through my spirit that I want and need you. I've <u>never</u> <u>ever</u> moved this quickly with anyone or anything, but somehow I've thrown caution so far to the wind with you that it's probably scattered to the four corners of the earth by now. I feel like a fool to have put myself in this position, and it makes me feel like I really haven't the first clue who I'm communicating with. What could I have been thinking? Well, obviously, I haven't been thinking, just feeling. All that stops right now.*

This is feeling so strongly to me like it's some kinda goodbye letter. That terrifies me more than I can possibly express with words, because I already can't begin to imagine my life without you in it, Michael. Is that not insane? I've never met you, never laid eyes on you except for that grainy ad photo I have of you and that doesn't count, yet I feel like we've shared so much already, and I feel like I've been waiting my whole life for <u>you</u> to come to me. I guess all that says is that I'm not a good judge of bullshit. I seem to take bullshit and twist and turn it every which way I can until I turn it into something that looks and smells like flowers, but underneath my clouded vision because I sooooooo want to be in love and have somebody love me, it's still just bullshit.

I feel so cold and numb and just want to go to bed. I wish I hadn't given you my numbers or my address now and if you've tried calling by now and I haven't made myself available for your call, then you'll understand why. Although I know this is going to hurt and hurt for a very long time, I'll just go ahead and say goodbye now.

Audria

seventeen
I Know You Love Me!

"You silly, silly goose. Stop hidin' back there and come give your Auntie Audie a huggie."

Audria chased her little 3-year old play nephew Isaiah and pulled him out from in back of the giant indoor palm he was hiding behind. She covered his face with kisses. This was her girlfriend Gina's boy. Although he was no relation to her, she had adopted him as her play nephew and ever since he learned how to form words, he had started calling her Auntie Audie. He was such a good little boy, the kind of cool, affectionate dude she had always envisioned calling her own one day. Pushing aside the hurt she still felt deep inside her, she allowed Isaiah to pull her into his little boy world.

Today was her first time venturing out of the house since posting her last letter to Michael almost a week before. She hadn't been right since, fluctuating between a crippling pain deep in her nether regions that made her feel like she wanted to walk doubled over, and an emptiness to her days that felt endless. There was no doubt in her mind that she was in love with that man, but the same way she fell in love with him, she would eventually fall out of love with him. Time was the greatest equalizer and she would simply allow it to do its thing.

With Isaiah holding her hand, his fingers feeling tiny intertwined with hers, she went off to find Gina and Silas, her friends who had invited her to their twice-a-month Sunday barbecue. They had a bomb diggity house on about four acres of prime real estate in La Plata, Maryland, and loved having people over as often as they could.

Gina was a Psych professor at Howard University and Silas owned his own landscaping company. They were such an odd couple. Gina with her polished, well spoken, Prada wearing bourgie self and Silas with his down home, cigar smoking, drinking moonshine in the garage country ass, but they loved each other and they made their marriage work; had been making it work for the last seven years.

They called Isaiah their love child, 'cuz they had been trying their entire marriage to have children, going to a ton of fertility specialists, reproductive experts, herbalists and even a hypno-therapist. They had spent a small fortune trying to make something happen, but soon as they gave all that up and relaxed with each other, their miracle happened and Isaiah came bumping along. Audria was so happy for them.

She found Gina making apple martinis in the kitchen for the seven or eight people who had already arrived and were out back.

"Hey Pretty Lady. How you doing?" She hugged her friend.

Gina licked some spilled martini off her fingers and hugged Audria hard. She pulled away and looked at her closely. "Dear heart, I'm the one who should be asking how *you're* doing. Are you okay? You look... I don't know... like you're going through it. Something."

Not trusting herself to speak, Audria just nodded her head and hugged her friend again, harder this time. Gina hugged her back, then handed her a martini. "Well, you're doing the right thing in coming out, Precious. It's good to be among friends and not sitting at home facing whatever you're facing alone. You know I'm here for you in *any* capacity you need me. If you need to talk to me from a professional standpoint, I'm here, and if you just want to talk to me girlfriend to girlfriend, just say the word, 'kay? Love you, Babygirl."

Audria blanched at the use of the familiar word, something she had most recently heard from Michael. She turned away pretending to take a sip of the martini, but really to hide the tears that suddenly sprang up in her eyes. *Lawd, how am I ever going to get over this man? HOW?*

She excused herself and went in search of the half bathroom in the foyer to get it together. She pulled open the door, looking forward to a few moments alone to quiet her emotions, and saw a man standing there using the toilet. When it finally filtered through that she was staring at exposed flesh that she had no business seeing, she slammed the door, horrified, and headed back to the kitchen and Gina.

Oh God. How utterly embarrassing. She didn't know whether she should leave or not. It wouldn't be the most comforting feeling meeting whoever that was at some point during the afternoon knowing she had just seen him holding his ding-a-ling in the restroom. And she sure as hell wasn't gonna be shaking his hand. Eww.

Giggling to herself, she took a sip of the apple martini and started helping Gina take trays of food and drinks out to the deck in back. She said hey to the couples enjoying the sunshine and good music, found her a lounger and chilled for some minutes. Isaiah found her again and she enjoyed having him sit close to her, drinking his apple juice from a Blues Clues sippy cup while she sipped on her apple martini. She pulled on his locked hair and he pulled back on one of her braids and they shared one of their special bonding moments reserved only for them. She loved this little boy so much that it hurt somewhere deep inside.

She was just about to go get them some hot dogs and potato salad, when a shadow fell in front of her and she looked up to see Mr. Don't-Know-How-To-Lock-A-Bathroom-Door coming over. Lawd, what was she gon' say to this man? She wasn't about to make small talk with some man whose Johnson she had just gotten a good look at.

"Hi, I'm Al. I just wanted to apologize for that bathroom thing. I didn't think anyone was in the house except for Gina, but that's no excuse, I should have locked the door."

Audria folded her hands, practically jamming them up under her armpits, although she didn't see him making any moves to extend his for a shake. She looked him over. He was alright looking in a kinda supporting actor kinda way. Nice face but nothing really memorable. Clean shaven, low hair cut, nice eyes, nice mouth, decent body, but nothing spectacular, except maybe for his lower extremities she had gotten a look at.

"I'm Audria," she said, introducing herself, then turned to her little sidekick. "And this is Isaiah, one of the masters of the house." She tickled him under his chin and they giggled.

"Yeah, I know Isaiah," the voice came again. "We're good buds, ain't we Zi?" Audria was surprised when Isaiah went over to the stranger and reached up to smack five in his outstretched palm. She felt less than special. Isaiah usually went to no one but her. She walked away from them feeling slightly pissed and headed for the food table.

"Can I refresh your drink while you're fixing your plate?" The Al person had followed her and was holding onto Isaiah who seemed way too content sitting atop his shoulders. Audria looked at him, annoyed at his familiarity with her little baby. "No, I can refresh my own drink, thank you." She turned away.

"Are you always this rude to people who forget to lock the bathroom door after them, or is it me?" He obviously wasn't going to leave her alone.

Audria wasn't trying to be nice to him or any other man. Matter of fact, she wasn't feeling men right about now and she would prefer if he just went away and left her the hell alone. She was all set to tell him exactly that when she heard her favorite song come on the radio. She went around him with some serious speed, and was down in front of the stereo system listening with everything inside her. She loved her some Patti Austin.

"Please be strong, life's not too long at all.
Life will pass you by before you know it.
If you feel it deep inside, you better show it, girl."

Audria listened to the whole song with her eyes closed, down to the "whoo-whoo-whoo" at the very end, then got up, dusting off her jeans. Everybody was looking at her when she turned around and she felt embarrassed at being the center of attention. That was so not her style, except when she was erotic scene playing, and *that* was a whole other story. She hurried up, got the plate of food she was after to begin with, and found her another apple martini.

On her second bite of Gina's famous potato salad, a blinding white light erupted behind her eyes followed by a piercing pain somewhere deep inside her and she felt a howling begin, some primal bellow that came blasting at her from somewhere within. The plate of food fell out of her hand, splattering her jeans and sneakers, and she was down on her knees, potato salad, baked beans and hotdogs squishy beneath her knees. She was powerless to control whatever this was she was feeling.

Oh God, Oh God, Oh God, Oh God.

Audria didn't know what to do. She kept trying to wring her hands and moved rapidly from doing that to grabbing at her stomach that was doubling her over in fiery spasms that felt like somebody was dragging her insides through a power wringer.

Oh God, Oh God, Help me, somebody help me.

Gina and Silas were down at her side, crouched on the deck, trying to hold her, asking what was wrong, and Audria could feel people gathering around, thought she glimpsed anxious faces, little Isaiah's even, but she was helpless, powerless, didn't know what to say, how to respond to them. Couldn't.

Noooooooooooooooooooooooooooooooooooooooo. She heard the word rip through her like somebody was shouting in her ears, and she looked around, confused, trying to see where it was coming from, but other than Gina and Silas offering to help, no one had spoken. She doubled over in a spasm of pain again, clutching her hands to her midsection, then she heard her name, loud, in the same bellow as before. *Audriaaaaaaaaaaaaaaaaaaaaaaaaaaaaaa.*

She knew then, in an instant, that it was him. It had to be Michael. He must have gotten her letter. *Oh God.* He was reading her letter and feeling some kind of misery in his soul that was transferring to her. Had she made a mistake ending things with him? She pushed away from Gina and the rest of the hovering crowd, and started talking to him aloud, not caring if they thought she was crazy. They probably already did, but she didn't care.

"It's okay Michael. It's okay. Everything's going to be okay. I can feel you. I know you're hurt, Baby. I know you're feeling pain, but it's okay. We'll work it out. I don't know how, but we'll work it out. I think I made a mistake about you, but I'm here. I'm right here for you. Everything's going to be okay."

She got up, walked inside and started cleaning the food off her jeans and shoes with paper towel, still talking to him aloud. "I'm just scared of everything I've been feeling, but I'm going to work my way past it. Anybody who can transmit their feelings to me in this way *has* to love me. I know you love me. I don't know how this has happened, but I don't care. I know you love me and I know I love you, so everything's going to be okay, Baby. I promise you. Just give me a chance to fix it, okay? Please Michael, please calm down, Baby. It's going to be okay. Just calm yourself and know that I'm here for you. I'm right here for you. Please."

Gina came up behind her and tried to hug her. "Audria Baby, you're not well. I think you need to see somebody."

Audria turned and pushed away, smiling a sad little smile at her friend. "Gina, I know you love me and I love you, but don't pull your psychologist psychobabble bullshit on me. I don't need to see a shrink. I'm fine. For the first time in my entire life, I'm fine. I know you don't understand, you can't, but trust me when I tell you, I'm gonna be okay." She reached out, touched her arm reassuringly, then walked to the front door, back to whispering assurances to her man.

When she pulled the door open, Dean from her job was standing there with his latest flavor of the month, getting ready to ring the doorbell. He and Gina had been friends for years. His mouth fell open when he caught sight of the hot mess Audria knew she was.

"Damn woman, you look like the dog, the cat *and* the freaking hamster done throwed up all over your ass. You're supposed to eat the barbecue, not wear it?"

She smiled at him and hugged him, glad to see him since she hadn't seen him in a few weeks. He introduced her to his friend Phillip. Audria smiled at Phillip and turned to go. "Hope you guys have a good time, but I've gotta get going."

She was a few steps from her car when Dean came jogging up. "Audie, Audie, wait girl. I almost forgot. I been holding on to this letter for you that came in from that guy in Pittsburgh some weeks back. Strong? I didn't know if you'd be here today, but I brought it with me just in case."

Audria turned, gave him the strangest look, and then kissed him full on his big, pouty lips. "Dean, you just saved my life, you beautiful Queen. I love you. You just saved my life." She took the letter out of his hands, kissed it, and headed for home.

eighteen
Time Will Tell

Jab, Hook, Jab. Jab, Hook, Jab. Straight right, left cross. Feint. Bob, weave. Jab, Hook, Uppercut. Jab, Hook, Jab. Jab, Hook, Jab. Jab, Hook, Uppercut. Feint left. Feint right. Bob, weave. Start over.

Michael was pounding the seven-foot black vinyl punching bag. Hard. Had been punching it solidly for almost two hours. Although he had stopped long enough in the beginning to wrap his hands, he could feel the wet stickiness every time his knuckles connected with the leather, knew he was bleeding, but he wasn't stopping. This... this physical pain he was inflicting on himself was the *only* thing keeping him from taking off somebody's head, and he wasn't trying to go out like that.

Seeing the murderous look in his eyes, the other inmates using the gym were staying the hell away from him, making sure they kept him in sight so they could know what to expect, but nobody was venturing close. He didn't give a fuck about them, didn't give a fuck about nothing right now. The one thing, the one person he cared about had just walked out of his life, so what the fuck was left.

This shit made him feel like he wanted to step back to the same cold-blooded mufucka who used to murder niggaz in his way, just blow holes through them wid' his nine, then go get sump'n to eat afterwards, with no backwards thought. This is what happened when you let your guard down, let people get too close, get inside your chest plate an' shit.

He knew it though. Knew it would happen. Had even said it to her. His biggest fear was now a reality. She was hauling ass. But what could he expect? It's not like he was no prize. Yeah, he was true to his word, and yeah, he had some solid plans on things to do when he walked out of this stinking hellhole, but he would be a convict for the rest of his life in the eyes of society, and wasn't nobody trying to give no convict a break.

He knew he would be fighting an uphill battle every step of the way, but he wasn't running from it, from none of it. Was even looking forward to the challenge, but lately he had started thinking that with somebody like Audria by his side, things would be so much easier for him. Not that he was trying to use her or nothing, 'cuz he didn't take nothing off no woman. He could and would always handle his own, but he just felt with her love, things could be so much easier. But whatever. Was out of his hands now. Wasn't a damn thing he could do about her walking off, so he would just let the shit go and keep getting up.

He went back to pounding the bag, hammering it, trying to batter what he was feeling out of his heart, but he knew it was useless. Now he understood why some people didn't want nothing to do with this love thing. If it worked right and you got what you wanted, it made you feel like a fucking giant, but the way he was feeling right now was like some cold trash.

He didn't understand some things from her letter either. It was obvious she hadn't gotten one of his letters, the *most* important one where he told her point blank the way he felt about her. So, of course, she would get the wrong impression with the things he had said in this last letter, or might think he was trying to run game on her. But *how* could she think he would just ignore all the things she had shared with him about the violations in her past? That would make him some kind of animal to just ignore all the hurt she had poured out. People could say whatever they wanted about inmates, but it was a serious mistake to think that the majority of inmates were unfeeling and uncaring, selfish monsters who looked out only for themselves. That was a crock of shit, but that was society for you. People believed what the media fed them most times and didn't bother trying to find out the truth for themselves.

He pounded the bag hard a few more times, more from a dogged determination not to quit punishing himself just yet than for any other reason. He eventually left it though and headed for the showers. He could feel several pairs of wary eyes on him as he passed by and a skinhead sitting off to one side said something about his hand dripping blood, but Michael ignored him and kept walking.

He showered absentmindedly, watching the water run pink down the floor drain as it hit his hands. He tried to block out the stinging pain but knew this was just the beginning. It would be a bitch to deal with the next day, but he wasn't afraid of it. Matter of fact, he welcomed it, because the physical pain would be a distraction from the pain he felt deep inside. After showering, he dressed, wrapped his hands with fresh cloths and tried resting. He gave that up in mere minutes, knowing there would be no rest for him until he did what he needed to do. Okay, she had walked away from him, but he wasn't nobody's quitter. He would tell her what he felt in his heart to say and then let the shit go. He sat up and reached for his pad and paper. Only time would tell how this thing between them would end up.

* * * * * *

Audria was looking at a picture of the man she wanted with her whole heart to be hers. He was FOINE. She couldn't believe this man was in love with her, and that she had almost walked away from him. She loved everything about him, thought they complimented each other in a way she had never felt with anyone else. She liked the way he just said what was on his mind to say. Loved the way he stepped up and wanted to be a strong support for her. Her eyes were still wet with tears from reading the part of his letter where he said that he had her. She looked at it again.

> *...Right off the bat, I gotta say this to you. I don't make promises often, Audria. Don't like to, never did, 'cuz if I find myself in a position where I'm not able to keep a promise, it eats at me like a parasite chewing on my lower intestines, but I'm making you one here, and you can believe that my word is bond, always. I got you. Babygirl, stop being afraid of whatever it is you're feeling, and stop thinking you're alone with it - the <u>feeling</u> I'm talking about, not the fear. I'm right there with you...*

She found it so curious that they had started thinking the same things around the same time. She had started wanting to be for him, and it was obvious that he had started feeling and thinking the same thing. But although he felt what he felt and thought what he thought, he was chivalrous to the core, leaving it up to her to determine how fast or slow they moved, wanting her to be the one to decide.

> *...Damn, I'm finding myself wishing for a day when I can put the word 'my' in front of 'Babygirl', but that's something only you can decide. Until you do that though, trust me. I got you. Cool?...*

It was eerie how so much of what he said seemed like he had crawled inside her head, like he could read and taste her fears about how quickly things were unfolding between them.

> *...I know that things seem like they're moving kinda quick and I know how people can get sometimes thinking they have to follow society's guidelines on how fast or slow to move. I don't live by society's rules. Never have, never will. That's one of the reasons I ended up in here, but despite that, I understand that I can choose not to live by society's rules, and still be legal about that choice, so don't start thinking you gotta worry about me going back to the old me. That dude's dead and buried. I just want you to know that we don't have to follow anybody's rulebook on how shit (sorry, gotta learn how to talk without cussing) unfolds between us. You with me?...*

He had even talked specifically about his time in prison and acknowledged knowing it would scare her, but asked her not to say never to him or to the idea of them being together.

> *...And don't think I don't understand and feel your fear about my time. Yeah, 13 years is a long time. Before getting arrested, I used to say that I could never tolerate being locked up either, but here I am in my 13th year and I'm still here, handling what I need to handle, so that's a testament to never saying never. I know it seems foreign to you, like something you can't comprehend, and I understand that, but never say never to nothing. And I know hearing that I have 4 years left wasn't what you expected or might have wanted to hear either, but that is what it is. Can't do nothing about that, but I'm just asking you not to say never with me, okay? If you can't give me nothing else I ask for, please give me that....*

And although it was obvious that he hadn't yet gotten her letter telling him about her past, he had talked on that peripherally, letting her know that he would be there for her in whatever way she allowed him to be and encouraging her to face the thing that haunted her the most.

> *...Look Audria, you can't tie my hands with you like this, okay? I gotta be who I am with you, or this friendship, this thing between us can't work. I'm not trying to get all in your business. NO, NO, that's not true. Yes, I am. I am trying to get all in your business. I don't know what this 'thing' is that you won't talk about. Something inside me tells me it's something big, like the kind of shit a brotha would need to sit down behind, but let me tell you something right now. I don't care what it is. Whatever it is won't make me feel any different about you....*
>
> *...Seriously though, I just want you to know that I'm here for you, Babygirl. Whenever you're ready to talk about whatever it is, you got you an ear, okay? I hope it's soon though, 'cuz anything that brings you pain, I'm not liking, and we gotta hurry up and address it so we can move on to other things. Remember we said to really look to the future, we got to face our past, then get whole in our present. So maybe it's time for you to face your past. What you think?...*

Audria read Michael's letter again for the umpteenth time from start to finish. She couldn't believe she had been ready to walk out of this man's life. Her soulmate. Her intended. She felt a shiver of fates avoided run up and down her spine, shook her head to cast the negative vibe aside, and went in search of her writing pad and pen. She had to write him to let him know exactly the way she felt about him. Maybe she was already too late. Maybe he had already said to hell with it and was figuring that they weren't meant to be, but she was banking on his love for her being as strong as he was. Ultimately though, only time would tell what happened between them.

nineteen
I Need You!

Peace Audria,

Don't know where to begin. Don't really know what to say to you. Don't even know why I'm bothering, 'cuz it's not like you weren't clear in your letter to me, but I ain't never been one to walk away from nothing. I like to finish what I start, so I gotta say some things.

I got your letter today. Was some kinda mix-up with the mail delivery on Saturday and it didn't get to me until today. People around here know me and know that I just do my time, try to steer clear of trouble, but your letter made me have to leave these buildings before I find myself having to spend more time than I'm supposed to up in these buildings.

Let me tell you first off that you're something else, Lady. Like no one I ever met. In just four months, you by yourself, have made me feel things that I ain't never felt my whole life. This is my first time being in love and this is my first time getting my heart broken by having somebody walk away from me. But I'm not trying to blame you or nothing. You're just feeling what you're feeling and following what your mind tells you, but I need to set you straight on a few things.

Gonna just respond to things in your letter as they jump out at me, but before I do that, let me just say that I don't feel pain often, Audria. Maybe this is something from my past where I keep shit at a distance and try not to let too much emotion flow through me, but I'm feeling pain now like I didn't know I could feel. Not just because you're doing the one thing I was afraid of - walking away from me, but I'm feeling pain *because you're feeling pain. And I'm not just talking about what you're feeling right now 'cuz you say I've been reduced in your eyes. What I'm talking about is all the other pain you been holding inside you for so many years. That's why I called you, so I could talk to you and let you hear my voice and tell you that I'm here for you, can help you get through this if you let me. Didn't think writing you some letter could say all the things I wanted to say to you, but you didn't accept my call. Let me tell you something, Woman. Tears ain't my thing. Haven't cried in about twenty years, but that shit right there and you saying that you wish you hadn't given me your phone number and address, made my soul cry. But that's life, right? Okay, moving on.*

Yeah Audria, I'm married. That is a fact I can't change right this minute, but did you really read my letter and understand what I was saying to you before you let your anger get the best of you? For the record, yeah I could hear you screaming at me. I know anger. It's been a part of my life for a long time, and I also know danger, Audria, a place where you're treading by allowing your anger to rule you. You need to check yourself with that. But look, when I talked about handling my business and making matters that were of no importance a few short months ago of importance now, that was me telling you that I was going to take care of all that. Don't know if you know the way this thing works, and from your reaction it's obvious to me you don't, but in the State of New York, it's considered abandonment if either spouse has been away from the marriage for more than one year. My thirteen years being in here means that my marriage is considered abandoned, and it's as easy as signing some papers to have it all dissolved.

Then something else I didn't mention to you 'cuz it really didn't have nothing to do with you and me, but my wife (really my 'nothing') has another boy who's eight years old. You do the math. That should tell you he ain't mine, so what does that mean? This is another reason why it's as easy as signing some papers to be free. Alright, I can go back and forth with that all day long and still feel like I ain't accomplishing nothing, so I'm just gon' say the rest of what I gotta say.

You ain't the only one feeling what you're feeling. I've never felt like this before either. I've never wanted or needed anybody the way I feel like I want and need you. Audria, I NEED you in my life. In this short while, you've become a lifeline for me. I haven't lied to you, PLEASE believe me. I know you feel like you've been made a fool of, but that's just because you're not listening to your heart. See, this is what happens when we start listening to our minds instead of our hearts. Remember that wise cat I told you about that I did time with at one point? Something else he used to always tell me is that our mind's job is to play devil's advocate. It's like your heart will be feeling something and here come your mind trying to step in and doing the 'what if this/what if that' thing.

Woman, listen to your heart and see if it tells you that I'm lying to you. If you tell me yes, then I'll walk away and leave you alone, but until then, I'm not going nowhere. You hear me? I know you're scared, but I told you this before. I got you. I don't want nothing from you except your love, Audria, and I know you love me. Even before you said it in the middle of all your anger, I could feel it coming. Babygirl, just relax, calm yourself, and let me do what I know I can do, which is love you back.

Audria, you can still have me if you want me. Heart, soul, mind, body, and yes, on paper. Look, I've told you that I don't feel fear often, and even when I do, it don't hang around long 'cuz I'm so quick to challenge it, but that goodbye shit in your letter scared the hell out of me. But I'm challenging it, Audria. I'm not accepting that from you right now. I can't. Love you too much to just walk away like you don't mean nothing to me when you mean everything to me, alright? Besides, my Moms used to always say to me that every goodbye ain't gone. So, here's what I'm gon' do. I'm gon' wait. Hate waiting, but I'm gon' wait. Gon' wait for this mail to do its thing and for this to get to you, then I want to hear from you. Even if you write me just a one-word letter -- NO or YES, please write me back.

Okay Babygirl, that's all I gotta say right now. Remember, I love and need you. I'm gon' be waiting to hear back from you. Until then. I'll be thinking about you.
                    Michael

* * * * * *

Sun. 8/18 - 5:12 p.m.
Hi Michael,
I don't know where to start, so I guess I'll just say what's in my heart to say. The very first thing I've got to tell you is that I love you. Do you hear me? I love you. Love you so much that it feels almost like it hurts on the inside, but I've always heard that love doesn't hurt, so I guess this is some kind of exquisite achy feeling associated with the love I feel for you.

I don't know how this has happened, and it's so scary to me to be feeling all of what I'm feeling, especially this quickly, but like you said in your letter (the one I just got today), I'm not running from it. So I hope you meant what you said about having me (I sooooo like that -- your 'I got you' promise), because I'm gonna need you to really have me. Gonna need you to be every bit as strong and supportive as you talked about being, maybe even more, because I need you.

Words can't begin to describe how much I feel I need you. Yes, I've had other men in my life, but I have never felt with any of them what I feel with you, and that's so crazy to me, because you and I haven't even defined what it is we have. I mean, we haven't made anything official yet other than to say that we love each other. So I'd like to show you how I'm facing my fear by laying claim to you. Yes, you heard me right. I'm laying claim to you as My Man. I hope you're okay with that because I feel really fragile these days. Don't think I could take a rejection from you, even though I just did the same thing to you. I'm so very sorry about that, Michael, really I am. I feel awful saying the things I said to you and allowing my anger to get the best of me, talking as harshly as I did to you. Yes, I was angry and hurt, but nothing excuses rudeness, so please forgive me. But Michael, please understand, I didn't have all the information I needed to have from you. Your first letter - the one you wrote on 7/20 didn't get to me until today, so it threw me off guard to get that other letter and hear you talk about being married and having a son and all that. It made me think I might not get what I desire, which is to have you -- ALL of you.

I may still never get to be with you in the way I truly want to, but I KNOW you love me, and that's all that's important to me right now. We'll face everything else later, but I need you to know that I love you and that I want to be for you if you'll have me, and I'd like you to be for me. Please be for me.

Michael, I just said that I KNOW you love me. Do you want to know how I know, with such assurance? I'll tell you. I felt you today. I don't know how else to say it. It's like you climbed inside my head and I FELT your pain, FELT this awful, primal scream from you. You got my letter today, didn't you? You don't even need to confirm that if you don't want to, but I think it has to be that. If it's not, then you're hurt in some other way, but I don't think that's it. I've never had this kind of connection before with anyone else. It's like this deep down primal need to have you, to be with you, and I think you feel the same way I do. It's incredible to me to hear you say that this is your first time being in love, yet you're allowing your heart to lead you. Thank you for loving me. I feel so special to have found something and someone so unique and all mine. I can't begin to tell you how that makes me feel.

Okay Baby, just a few more things then I'm going to go. I'm feeling worn out all of a sudden. I've been going through it here lately and have been feeling so much pain. I know I need to get a handle on all these emotions running through me, but that's often easier said than done, you know? I'm hoping by now you got my letter sharing that thing from my past with you. That wasn't easy to share, and I still don't know exactly why I felt comfortable enough to share it with you because I've never shared that with anyone else, but I guess it's because I love you and don't wish to hide anything about my life from you. I think I really want to talk about it with you, but it's a little hard to do that just through letters, but I'll try. Maybe little by little I can talk about it with you and work through all the hurt I feel. Maybe we can work on it together? I don't know why, but I think you can help me through this; maybe through anything, so we'll see.

Thanks for sending me your picture. And can I just tell you that you are FINE to me. You seem so solid and strong, like the kind of man I have always wanted and always been attracted to. Not just physically, although there's that, but you just look like a picture of strength to me, and I need that in my life right now in a huge way. I'm so happy that you're here and that I have your love. I want to make you happy in whatever way I can, Baby. I'm so sorry for our misunderstanding. After all, I'm not supposed to make your life more complicated by being in it. I'm supposed to bring you love, light and warm smiles like honey buttered, fresh-from-the-oven cornbread Momma used to make. Well, not my Momma 'cuz she doesn't go anywhere near a kitchen these days unless she can help it, but you know what I mean. I want to be a calm place for you to go to whenever you need to escape your surroundings. You haven't said much about the way things are for you, but something tells me it's not an easy road you walk. So I want to make things as easy for you as I possibly can. Will you let me?

Want to hear something funny? Patti Austin is one of my all-time favorite female vocalists. There's something about her energy that I really, really like and the lyrics to just about every song she sings are deep. The same song you talked about in your letter, I heard today, was actually grooving to it, shortly before I felt you. Strange how things are unfolding between us, isn't it?

Alright Michael. One last thing before I go. A few letters ago you asked me to finish a sentence for you. You said to finish the sentence 'what you love.' I'd like to do that now, if it's okay with you, so here goes: What Michael loves, he respects to the utmost and protects with his life. What Michael loves he cherishes like the world's most valuable treasure, puts it in a fixed position in his mind and never wavers from that place. What Michael loves he carries close to his chest, his heart, gives it a place of importance like nothing else. What Michael loves he never leaves. What Michael loves is me. Okay, how did I do? Was that fine? I hope you like it.

God, this is the hard part. Leaving you and then having to wait to hear back from you. I hate waiting, but since I have no choice in the matter, I have to wait. Please write me soon, Michael. I so want to hear from you. Want to sit in your presence and taste your essence. And speaking about sitting in your presence, would you please let me know how you feel about me coming to visit you? We can write letters to each other as often as we wish, but nothing beats being able to physically look into the eyes of the one you love. So when you write me back, would you tell me what you think? Okay Baby, gonna go now. Hope to hear from you soon. Remember that I love and need you in my life. Please be there for me.

Your Babygirl, Audria

twenty
I'll Walk Through Fire

"VIOLA, YOU HAD NO RIGHT TO DO THAT. NONE!!!"

Audria was standing in her mother's kitchen, hands on her hips, breathing hard, her face all twisted in anger. She couldn't remember any other time in her life ever raising her voice at her mother nor calling her by her first name, and she could see the shock reflected in the woman's eyes, but there was a first time for everything.

She had read Michael's letter over and over again, felt her heart crumple at the pain she felt in his words as he considered her walking away from him, but she knew it was all something that would be fixed between them, just as soon as he got her letter. And judging by the date on his, which was the same day she had written hers -- *these coincidences between them continued to amaze her* -- she knew he had either already received hers or would be receiving it very soon.

She spent a long time with his letter, absorbing every little detail of it, taking in everything he said to her and making it sink into places she had never allowed words to go before. He seemed like an extraordinary person to her, in so many ways a contradiction. Here was a man who admittedly had never been in love before, had never laid eyes on her except for the one picture she had sent him, but yet he was challenging the fear of his feelings and wasn't allowing the tough exterior he obviously had surrounded himself with for most of his life to prevent him from listening to the softer interior voice of his heart that told him he loved her.

Audria felt so overwhelmed thinking about him and what he had come to mean to her in such a short time. What they had discovered between them seemed almost like God Himself had reached down and, with His hand of fate, had made them find each other, so she wasn't about to go second-guessing her feelings or Michael's. All the doubt she had been feeling was behind her. She would give herself heart, body, mind and soul to this man and leave the rest to God to work out.

But the more she read his letter, the more puzzled she got at his reference to calling her. She kept reading it over and over again, especially the part about her not accepting his call, and then it hit her like a shotgun blast. It had to be her freaking Mother.

Audria was up and out the house in a flash and was pulling up in her mother's driveway in no time. She didn't even bother ringing the doorbell, just let herself in and went in search of her meddling mother to have it out with her. She found her in the kitchen rummaging in the sideboard for something or other, and pounced on her like a lion on prey.

"WHY did you do that, Viola? You had NO right to speak for me like that. None!" Her voice sounded far louder and her tone much more accusatory than she had meant it to, but she wasn't backing down from what she already knew was going to be a knock-down, drag-out fight. "Why didn't you accept Michael's call?"

Her Mother slowly let the drawer close, turned and reached for the cup of coffee she had sitting on the center island, took a sip and looked at Audria dead on. Shaking her head slightly, she set the mug down, then got up close in Audria's face. "You'se my child, Audria, and I understand you upset and we gon' deal with that soon enough, but let's just get one damn thing clear right here and now, I brought you in this world and I can damn sure take you out. Don't you *ever* cross the line between Mother and daughter and think you can come up in my own house and howl at me like some lil' untrained alley cat, you hear me?"

Audria just looked at her mother, stubbornly refusing to speak, but her mother wasn't backing down either. She stuck her face even closer up in Audria's and got as loud as Audria had before. "I know you're not going to stand there acting like I didn't raise you better than this. Do you hear me, yes or no?"

Audria relented in the face of her mother's anger and backed down. "Yes Ma'am, I hear you," she said grudgingly, folding her arms defensively across her chest. But she wasn't about to let the issue slide. Taking a deep breath, she tried to keep from gritting her teeth and took another approach. "Mother, I need for you to explain why you decided not to accept Michael's call."

Viola stepped back and took up her coffee mug again, taking her time about it too. Blowing into the hot liquid, she looked at Audria over the cup's rim. "Oh, I guess you're talking 'bout that jailbird you done got involved with." Her blasé, off-the-cuffness burrowed under Audria's skin, and she found herself pissed off all over again.

"He's NOT a jailbird, Mother, but why would I expect you to understand."

"Expect me to understand? I'm not the one keeping secrets, Miss Keep Shit to Herself, okay?" Her mother slammed an arm on her hip. "Did you even bother trying to come explain your life to me?"

Audria looked at her incredulously. "Explain my life to you? Explain my life to you? That's a laugh, Mother. I can barely explain my life to my own self, let alone explain it to you or anybody else. And judging from the way you're so quick to dismiss somebody I care about as a jailbird, why *would* I want to explain anything to you?"

The two of them looked at each other, neither one giving any ground. Audria found herself looking at her mother's face, barely unlined still at 62 and wondered if she would be so lucky when she got to be the same age. Her mother was looking at her appraisingly.

"Okay, if you care so much about this jailbi-... this *person*, how come you were bawling like you was trying to win some bawling competition just a few short weeks ago? You gon' tell me all that hurt and misery you were feeling wasn't because of this Michael guy?"

Audria couldn't meet her mother's eyes. Damn, she wished she had considered this before rushing over here to have it out with her. She really had to get a handle on her anger. Now just how was she supposed to respond to this question. If she said that Michael wasn't responsible for how upset she had been, her Mother would want to know what else had made her so miserable. But if she lied and told her he had made her upset, she knew her Mother well enough to know that she would *never* forgive him for that, whether he was really responsible for her pain or not. And that was not a place she wanted her mother to go to. It was bad enough they were fighting against whatever preconceived notions she and the rest of the world had about men in prison. She wasn't trying to add another reason to the mix of reasons why her mother would never trust this man she loved. She took a deep breath and just blurted out the first thing that came to her mind.

"Momma, it's complicated, okay? I can't really explain it to you, but Michael wasn't really responsible for making me hurt. He asked me some kinda hard questions about my life and it kinda hurt me, but he..."

"*Kinda* hurt you?" her mother interrupted. "Audria, you got some kind of memory loss gene that you inherited from your daddy's side of the family or something, God rest his precious soul? 'Cuz lemme tell you, my memory's working just fine and wasn't no little bit o' hurt you was feeling, so you need to cut the crap and tell me what that son-of-a-gun did to you."

Audria threw up her hands. "See? That's what I mean. You don't listen. You *never* listen. I'm telling you that he didn't hurt me, and you're just stuck where you are thinking that he had to be the one who hurt me. Why do you do that?"

"I ain't doing a damn thing. You're the one who's messing 'round with some convict and in denial about the kind of hurt them kinda people gon' always bring to you and anybody else stupid enough to mess wid' 'em.

Audria looked at her mother with eyes as hard and steely as diamonds. "Thank you very much, Mother. Thank you for calling me stupid and thank you for letting me see just how prejudice you really are. It's not like I didn't always know it, but somehow you get to thinking that when it comes to you, the child, the same rules won't apply. Thank you for showing me how wrong I was about you, my own mother."

She turned to go, but her Mother's arm snagged hers.

"Lawd Audria, I don't know what to say to you. Don't you understand that I just care about you? I don't want to see you hurt. I want nothing but the best for you. That's all me and your daddy ever wanted was the best for you. He probably turning over in his grave seeing the way you acting."

Audria snatched her arm away with some serious force and looked at her mother bitterly. "Don't you dare talk about him that way, don't you *dare*. Wherever Daddy is, he's looking down and he's feeling happy for me because I'm happy, you hear me? For the first time in my life, I'm happy, because God has sent me a man and a love all my own, so don't talk to me about daddy."

"Oh, that's right. I cain't say nothin' 'bout your precious Daddy. You think you got some monopoly on your love for that man? You think your daddy was perfect just 'cuz he was *your* daddy? Well, he was *my* husband 'fore he ever got to be *your* daddy, and NO Audria, he wasn't perfect. He had shit wid' him just like every other man and woman walking this planet."

Audria's eyes bugged out at the words her mother was spitting at her. She wanted to clap her hands over her ears and stop this, stop her from saying something she would regret, but all she could do was stand there and stare at her mother.

"Your daddy wasn't always the daddy you think he was, you hear me? He used to run around on me, all the time up in some heifer's house like he didn't wants no part of house and home, leaving me to love and care for you by my damn self. But what thanks do I get? Jes' 'cuz he decided to stop running the streets right when you mighta figured out what mess he was into, all you see is perfect Daddy. Daddy who's 'bout family, Daddy who's 'bout wife and child, Daddy who's 'bout work and home and providing. You don't know shit, Audria. I been a good mother to you all these years, but do I get any thanks for what I do for you? No, what I get is to live in the shadow of your precious daddy and feel like I ain't no parent to you."

Audria looked at her mother disbelievingly. She was shocked at how bitter the woman sounded. All these years and she would never have guessed her mother felt this way. She didn't know what to say and she felt twice as bad when she realized tears were streaming silent rivers down her mother's turned-away face.

She reached for the woman that had mostly been a nag to her in recent years, but who she loved despite all the anger moving through her. "Momma, I didn't know. I didn't know you felt like this. You have to know that I love you and that I appreciate everything you've done for me. You *have* to know that, don't you?"

Her mother's shoulders shuddered under her touch and Audria felt a huge lump form at the base of her throat at the thought that she had caused her mother, the woman who bore her for nine months, this much pain. She was just a regular ol' bringer of pain to people she cared about these days, wasn't she?

Viola had never been overly affectionate with Audria over the years, and crying or not, she wasn't one to cotton much to change. After a beat, she moved herself away from her daughter's reaching embrace, cleared her throat uncomfortably and spoke without looking at her child.

"I'm just trying to save you from yourself, Audria. I don't know how long you been talking to this Michael person. I don't think it's been all that long or I woulda heard somethin' 'bout him by now, but if he has the ability to hurt you the way I done seen you hurt that day, Lawd, I'm scared of what might come later on when you *really* get all wrapped up in it so deep that you cain't do nothing but walk through fire."

Audria tried to no avail to get her mother to look at her, then gave it up, talking to her the same way she had been spoken to, without eyes connecting. "Momma, I know you don't want to hear me because it's easier for you not to, but I'm asking you to please hear me. Michael didn't hurt me. I can't explain it to you any more than that, but what I can tell you is that I'm already wrapped up in it and I'm willing to walk through fire, as long as he's walking next to me."

She saw her mother getting ready to interject some other negative thought, but she was through listening to any more slandering of her man's name, and as much as she was through with that, she was through with this conversation. But before she turned to go, she wanted to say one more thing. "Momma, you're doing the exact same thing I did with him in the beginning – doubting him and doubting his character just because of geography. I can't change your mind about him and I'm not going to try to. All I can do as your daughter is ask you to be happy for me. Can you give me that at least?"

She saw her mother purse her lips and knew she wouldn't hear what she most wanted to from her, not this day, but she tried again anyway. "Please Mommy, can you not be happy for me?"

Hearing no reply, Audria turned with tears in her eyes and headed for the door. Okay, so that's how it was going to go down? Well, fine. Guess she would have to walk alone with her man then. She wasn't afraid. With Michael by her side, she felt she could walk through a forest fire if she had to. Ten thousand forest fires. To hell with her Momma and the rest of the world if they wanted to sit in judgment of her new love. She knew exactly who would have the last laugh. She went out and closed her mother's door softly behind her.

<u>twenty-one</u>
Got Me A Woman

I got a woman way over town,
She's good to me, Oh yeah!
Well, I got a woman way over town,
She's good to me, Oh yeah!
Now she's my dreamboat, oh yes indeed,
She's just the kind of girl I need,
I found a woman way over town, She's good to me, Yeah!

I save my kisses and all my huggin' just for her, Oh yeah!
I save my kisses and all my huggin' just for her, Oh yeah!
When I say baby please take my hand
She holds me tight, She's my lover girl
I found a woman way over town,
She's good to me, Oh yeah!

She always answers my beck and call,
Ever lovin' mama, Mama tree top tall.
I feel so proud walkin' by her side,
Couldn't get a better girl, No matter how hard I tried.

I got a woman way over town,
She's good to me, Oh yeah!
Someday we'll marry, way over town,
She's good to me, Oh yeah!
Someday we'll marry, don't you understand
Cause she's my only lover girl
I found a woman way over town,
She's good to me, Oh yeah!

"I Got A Woman" Lyrics
- Ray Charles

"Nigga, you bettah get out my face wid' that bullshit."

"Nah, nah, I'm tellin' you. Paco was smilin' all up in her face like he wanted to sop her up wid' a biscuit."

"Oh yeah? Well, look like me and my shank gon' be havin' a discussion wid' Paco."

Michael pretended like he wasn't hearing the conversation at the table next to his, but he was shaking his head on the inside. His bitch ass cellie again. The lil' fuck didn't know how to keep his mouth shut and his ass out of trouble, seemed like. All the time stirring up some shit. Here he was whispering in some other inmate's ear about the man's woman who had come to visit him the day before. Okay, so it was common knowledge in Blasenburg that the trick in question muscle hopped, moving from inmate to inmate and discarding them after she got bored. The more muscle a guy flexed, the more interested she got. This particular muscle head she had recently set her sights on looked like a Black Lou Ferrigno and like he could bench press a baby Hummer, so Michael suspected the trick would give dude at least the next couple months. But none of that shoulda been his cellie's concern, but here he was tryin' to meddle in shit that didn't have a damn thing to do with him. Well, that was on him. He would make damn sure he stayed away from him as much as possible, 'cuz he knew it was just a matter of time before somebody knifed him for talking too damn much.

Wasn't no simple thing the lil' punk was doing. Inmates didn't play. He had seen brothas get stabbed up, damn near split open from limb to limb over much less than this. You tell a man that some other dude's looking at his woman too hard, that's like telling him that man's spitting in the face of his relationship, thinks his woman's easy, a bitch for the taking, whether or not she was. And it didn't matter to geography. You did that anywhere and you might as well start pulling on the boxing gloves, 'cuz a fight was bound to come behind that shit. But in here, with as much testosterone as was walking the walk next to each other, it was probably five times as bad as anywhere else.

Michael looked over at his punk-ass cellmate still whispering in dude's ear and disgustedly picked up his tray to leave. As he walked out of the dining quarters, his hand automatically went up to check his breast pocket to make sure the letter was still there. It was. He released his breath in a silent exhale. He wasn't the kind of man that really stopped to consider his happiness most times, just did what he had to do and kept getting up, but for the first time, he felt himself thinking that somebody else was now responsible for much of his happiness. Audria. *His woman.* Damn. He couldn't believe he had actually found a woman like her and a love as intense as he was feeling for her.

He found himself a quiet corner and folded the letter open again. Damn. She loved him. Him. It's not like he thought he was a bad person. He had made some bad choices earlier in his life, but he knew he had painstakingly worked to transform himself into the kind of man that in no way resembled the one he used to be, but still, he found himself in awe that she actually loved him.

And she was counting on him to be strong and supportive to her? Hell, that alone put her in a class all by herself. These days Black women weren't trying to admit that they needed a damn soul for shit. *I Can Do What I Need To Do For And By My Damn Self.* That's the kinda shit you heard from them every time you tried to have a meaningful conversation. Was no wonder so many of the men turned around and said, "To hell with you then. I'll go find me a White woman who's as needy as the day is long. Maybe she will make me feel like I'm a man and like I'm doing something."

He recognized it as a vicious cycle hard to break out of. The Black woman was as independent as she was because she felt the Brothas weren't stepping up to the plate and taking care of their business. But the flip side of that was the Brothas failed to take care of their business 'cuz they felt that the Sistahs didn't give them half a chance to step up. Both sides seemed to do nothing but point the collective finger, and in the meantime, nothing got done and no progress got made. He wasn't about to let himself become some Black Man statistic. If his woman, *damn he still couldn't believe she was his*, was woman enough to admit she needed him, needed his strength and support, he would damn sure step up and keep stepping up to give her every bit of what she needed to do her thing.

Damn, he wished he could see her, hold her, tell her everything he wanted and needed to tell her, make promises to her that he would put his life on the line to keep. Well, he knew he couldn't get everything he was wishing for right this minute, but he could write her and tell her what he had in his heart to say. He went in search of pen and paper.

Fri. 8/24

Peace Audria,

So, you're laying claim to me? Damn Babygirl, you sound like you been walking in the world I used to walk in. Excuse me for saying this, Audria, but THAT IS GANGSTA! I think I'm going to try to burn those words into my memory, so that years down the road I can tease you about the day you came riding up into my world, my pretty Black Gangsta Cowgirl with your spurs on, stetson tipped down over your braids, guns blazing, to lay claim to my heart. Woman, you're incredible to me. You make me do something I ain't really done in years -- you make me smile. Got to watch that. Wouldn't want none of these brothas up in here to think I'm smiling at them. Might give them the wrong idea, you know what I mean?

Okay, let's get into this thing. I hear you, Audria. You're laying claim to me, and that's a good thing. Naw, that's a great thing. Though I don't talk much, especially in here, I ain't never been the kinda brotha who can't find words to express himself, but that right there left me not really knowing what to say. Your laying claim makes me feel like somebody just handed me a pot of gold, you know? Thanks for stepping up and laying claim to me, Babygirl, but the man in me needs to honor you by asking you to be My Woman. Now, I know this is almost like a rhetorical question, especially since you stepped up, but understand I need to do this to show you how much I respect and honor you. So Audria, please be My Woman. Yeah, I can hear your answer even now. Damn Babygirl, I'm wanting to hear your voice. Okay, chillin' on that. Don't know what your phone situation is right now and remember I told you, I try never to make the same mistake twice. Until you tell me it's cool to call you again, I'm not calling.

Audria, I got to be straight up with you. One of the biggest reasons why I would wind up running off the few sistahs that got interested in me over the years is 'cuz I know the limitations of 'being there' for somebody who asks you to be there for them. Ain't no little thing to me when I have a woman. I want and need to be a man to her in every way a man can be a man to a woman, and in my present circumstances, I can't be everything to you that you might need me to be. I just need to lay that on the line, be clear with that so you understand. I'm in here doing my bid and you're out there. I

---

can't physically watch out for you the way I would if I was walking the streets. I can't protect you from the harm that might come to you. And even if I'm walking streets, harm can still come to you, but I think you know what I mean. A man wants to think if he's physically present for his woman, he can protect her from any harm that might come to her. So when you ask me to be there for you, I need you to understand that I'm gon' be there for you in _every_ way I can, considering my situation. Beyond that, Babygirl, all I can do is make you a promise that one day, you'll have the fullest protection and support I can give you. And for now, you know I got you in the ways that you and me both know are more important than any physical protection.

Babygirl, I don't really know what to say about the way your uncle violated you. If he's still breathing air, that bastard needs to pay. I ain't one to bring violence to another man's doorstep, but to think that he's walking free and been walking free for all these years and that he basically 'got away' with raping a little girl? And family too? Ain't happening.

Audria, I know you don't really know why you felt comfortable enough to share this violation with me. I don't understand it either, 'though I'm glad you did, 'cuz you don't need to be walking alone with this kinda pain. But look, what I can tell you is this. I may or may not be the right person for you to tell. The right person, yeah, 'cuz I wasn't playing when I made you a promise to help you get past this thing. I'm with you and you can count on my support. But Audria, I might have been the wrong person to tell, 'cuz I don't play with shit like this. When I say that I protect My Woman, I ain't just flapping gums. The Man upstairs must know why He got me on lock right now hearing this, 'cuz trust me when I tell you, if I was walking free, that old goat in N.C. would wake up to a slit throat some morning. That might sound harsh to you, but that's exactly the way I feel right now. But I'ma fallback on that and try to move myself away from feeling the kinda anger I'm feeling right now. You don't need that.

Babygirl, I need to ask you some questions about this though, and I recognize they might be hard questions for you to deal with, but if we gon' face this thing together, then you gotta understand why I'm doing this.

First off, I need to ask you how come you never told anybody. I mean, I understand maybe you not wanting to tell your folks, although I don't know how a 13 year old could keep something so big and life changing to herself, but why didn't you tell?

Next thing is this. Do you think you up to telling at some point? Now, don't go getting all crazy with that question, Audria. We gon' move as slow as you need to move with all this, but I need to know where your head is when it comes to facing this. Are you facing it to just work through your pain and try to put it behind you? Or are we facing it to right this wrong, get some closure for you, and <u>then</u> put it behind you? Gotta tell you, and I'm sure working where you work you probably already know this. Ain't no statute of limitations on rape, especially the rape of a minor, so whether it's the day you get this or 10 years from now, if you decide to make your monster pay, that dog will eventually get his day, you hear me? Promise you that!

Last question. And I already know the way this might make you think of me, but that's a chance I gotta take. It's so you understand and make no mistake about the love I feel for you. You're at a fixed place in my heart and in my mind, Babygirl, so there's <u>no</u> hesitation to ask you this. My question is this. When I say 'pay' relative to your monster, which way you want to go with that? You're a big girl. Know you can read between the lines and understand I can't say everything I might want to say here, but you know where I used to live. When it comes to protecting mine, I got no problem going back for a minute. When the time comes, you say two words to me, just two: "Go Back" and it's done.

Now something else just came to me. In your letter you talked about trying to face your past in other 'not-so-positive ways' (your words). Even said you were kinda ashamed to talk about that. I gotta know. Need you to share all of it, Babygirl. That's the only way I can really be there for you 100 percent.

Okay, moving on. You made me an apology in your letter for allowing your anger to rule you. I know this might sound strange to you, but I don't get hung up on apologies, Audria. That shit makes liars out of people. Want to know how? It leads to us making promises we can't keep, 'cuz we ain't perfect. It's like you'll say 'I'm sorry I did this thing, I won't ever do it again.' So what happens when you do it again? You've made a liar out of yourself and out of me if I believed you when you made your impossible promise. So, no apologies Babygirl. Look, both of us gon' mess up, maybe even a lot, not that I want that to happen, but that's just life. If we can just remember when that happens though, to approach it with a no regrets/no apologies theme. Let's just put the issue on the table, deal with it, and keep moving on. That sound cool to you? Alright, let's do this thing, Beautiful.

So, you think I'm fine? Woman, I probably ain't never blushed in my whole life, but that made me feel all schoolboyish and shit. You know how to stroke a man's ego, don't you? Thanks for the compliments, Baby, but let me reciprocate. I've been walking around with your picture. In fact, it's right in front of me as I write to you, so every now and then I look up and stare into your pretty eyes. You're beautiful, Babygirl. I never really liked lipstick. Don't think I like the idea of it getting all over my face if you kissed me, but you wear it well. Think I could even come to like it, as long as you're the one wearing it and you're the one kissing me. Mmm, let me chill on that. Them kinda thoughts are dangerous for a man in *my position to be having too often, and ever since I got your picture, I been having them more and more.*

Okay, gonna try to wrap this thing pretty soon. Before I go though, I want to give you your props for finally finishing my sentence. I see you listened to your heart and let it speak to you. That's My Girl. You did an awesome job with that. Did me proud. Everything you said in that sentence are things I've said to you at some point either in this letter or in others. I especially love the part about what Michael loves he never leaves. Can you handle that? Knowing I ain't going nowhere? Better invest in some heavy machinery if you want me gone, 'cuz that's about all that's gon' move me. Damn, I'm feeling you, Audria. Loving you hard.

Alright, Babygirl, it's official. You're My Woman and I'm Your Man. Sound good to you? I know it 'sure nuff' sound good to me, like my Moms used to say. Well, I could keep writing you forever, but I'm not trying to wear out your pretty eyes, so I better go. But although I'm leaving you on paper, hope you know I'm always with you. Every time you close your eyes, I'm right there with you. Feel me?

Peace Babygirl.
<u>*YOUR*</u> *MAN,*
Michael

P.S. I know you asked about coming to see me, but we need to talk about that. Look, I'm not trying to be reduced anymore in my woman's eyes, so I'm not sure that should be our focus right now. I ain't going nowhere, Audria, and like I told you, my love for you is in a fixed place, so let's keep the fast songs on minimum and do US a slow grind, Babygirl. No need to hurry, okay? Talk to you soon.

twenty-two
Temptation Begins

"Daaaaaaaammmmmmmnnnnnnnnn, that's a big dingaling!"

Audria busted out laughing, along with all the other sistahs in the room, at Vanessa's loud squeal. They were having a hell of a time at the Waiting to Exhale Adult Toy Party that a girlfriend of Angela's had organized. These women didn't make a bit of sense. All afternoon they had been oohing and aahing over one battery operated toy or the next and having them some serious fun doing it.

She had started to say no to the invitation, 'cuz sex and anything surrounding it was something she was trying to put out of her mind as much as possible, especially considering where her man was and for how long, but Angela and Vanessa wouldn't let her back out. They came and got her with their loud asses, even picking out the outfit they wanted her to wear, and then the three of them piled into Angela's SUV and headed into D.C. to the party.

Angela's new buddy Yvonne, was a Vice President at some local bank, but when she wasn't handling things at her 'day job', she organized these adult toy parties in her spare time and hosted out of her English Stone Tudor home on Sixteenth Street. This was Audria and Vanessa's first time going, but Angela had been to one already and warned them to expect the unexpected. Yvonne's requirement to all invitees was you had to wear something sexy, come with an open mind, and bring along cash, credit cards, your checkbook, or all three depending on how much freaky shit you decided to buy.

When they pulled up outside the house, Audria was amused as she watched Vanessa's mouth fall open looking around at the dazzling array of expensive, latest model cars parked in the open three-car garage, in the driveway and on the street. There were Porsches, drop-top Mercedes', some Beemers, a shiny gold Lexus, a Bentley, a Ferrari Coupe, and two Escalades that looked like the kind of equipment men would sport with tinted windows, polished chrome on every available surface, and spinners.

"Damn Angela, you done stepped up. Rolling with the big dogs, ain't you? Where you say you done met this Yvonne woman again?"

"Girl, it pays to go get pedicures at upscale Black-owned businesses, I keep telling your ass, wid' your crusty feet," Angela giggled. "Yvonne was sitting in the chair next to me at Body & Soul a coupla months ago getting her feet done, and we just struck up a conversation. She's cool people."

"Yeah, and rich as all get-out too," whispered Vanessa, craning her neck back to look up at the massive house. Audria rolled her eyes at her friend's materialistic nature.

A half hour later, they had met Yvonne and about eighteen other women, none of whose names Audria knew she would remember. Yvonne gave them the grand tour of her place, pointing out the indoor splash pool, a dual-partitioned infrared sauna that featured dry heat on the wooden side and steam on the tiled side, a hot tub that could easily seat twelve, and a Master Bedroom that looked like something out of Architectural Digest.

Later, sipping on some Perrier-Jouet champagne, Audria watched Vanessa work the room, cozying up to several of the women, and kissing some serious ass in the way only Vanessa could. Vanessa was a grand master at ingratiating herself without seeming to, and Audria knew her girl wasn't about to walk away from this little shindig without some new friends of her own. She shook her head and smiled. That was Vanessa for you. Her motto was, if you wanted money, you had to go where money was. She was obviously taking her own advice every chance she got.

Yvonne didn't just own a fine home, but was a fine hostess as well. A sumptuous spread with all kinds of finger foods and other delicacies was laid out on two long tables. Swedish meatballs. Barbecued chicken wingettes. Beef, mushroom and green peppers brochettes. Crab balls. Jumbo shrimp with sauce. Smoked salmon with capers. Pigs-in-a-blanket. Sweet rolls. Little tuna fish and cheese sandwich squares. Peppered turkey wraps. Julienne veggies. Deviled eggs. Some spicy Indian dishes that looked like a mix of eggplant and buttered Korma chicken. And there was another side table filled with nothing but desserts. Cakes, pies, cookies, pudding and other decadent delights. And if that wasn't enough, Yvonne had hired a bartender for the afternoon. Judging from the little Audria could see, there wasn't a drink missing from the fully stocked collection on the bar.

But the real festivities began an hour later when Yvonne clapped her hands and asked the women to move into the den. It was a huge space with two stone-work fireplaces on opposite ends of the room, period furniture, and high gloss hardwood floors. A little dark in décor for Audria's taste with all the heavy velvet drapery, mahogany wood paneling and what not, but to each his own. It was obvious Yvonne had gone to some lengths to make the space as warm and inviting as it could be. There were huge vanilla and rose scented candles in groupings of three and four all over the room, Khush incense burning in vertical incense holders, and over-sized comfy cushions for people to recline on if they preferred to sit low. Audria grabbed a seat on the floor in between Angela and Vanessa and took a sip of her second glass of champagne while munching on a strawberry.

A minute later, some smooth jazz mood music started playing, and the party really got started. One by one, a line-up of beautiful sistahs came gliding through modeling some unique pieces of lingerie and lounge wear. Yvonne acted as Emcee, describing each piece as the girls strutted their stuff in various stages of undress, and shushing the ladies here and there when they got loud talking about who was going to sport which outfit for hubby or boyfriend at home.

Looking at a silky black, body stocking-like outfit with cutouts in the breast and crotch area, Audria's mind began to wonder and before she knew it she was indulging in a waking fantasy of wearing something like that for Michael. She wondered what he would be like in bed. Wondered whether he would be an attentive lover or not, whether he would know how to make her body sing the same way he made her heart sing. More importantly though, she found herself wondering whether she would be able to please him the way he would want and need to be pleased.

She knew she was a decent lover but because of the selfishness of most of the men she had been with in the past, sometimes she got lazy in bed. Plus, there was that thing, the violation from her past, that seemed always to be there, like some invisible third body in the bed between her and her lover. Very often, it kept her from relaxing completely and truly enjoying herself. Sometimes, unexpectedly, she froze up. Whenever that happened, she would just close her eyes and allow whoever she was with at the time to get his. He would roll off eventually, oblivious to the pain she was feeling, and she would be careful to keep that part of herself hidden. It wasn't difficult. People saw what they wanted to see, and most times, their sight didn't include someone else's hurt.

Audria shook her head, trying to pull herself away from the dark thoughts that had sprung up in her head. The lingerie show had ended and Yvonne was introducing Beverly who explained that the pieces they had just seen modeled was part of a collection called Bedroom & Beyond Wear that was specifically designed for the African American woman who had a little more junk in the trunk and a little more upstairs cushion for the pushin' than "them Sistah-wannabes." Most of the women laughed at that and Beverly handed out business cards and catalogs, letting everyone know she would be available afterwards to take orders.

A few minutes later, the lingerie models began filing back in holding baskets and trays filled with all kinds of adult toys and goodies. Several pairs of eyes, along with Audria's, got huge looking at all the stuff. There were all sizes and shapes, devices that were eerie in their life-like resemblance to penises, to still others that looked like they were straight out of a medieval torture chamber. There were vibrators, dildos, anal plugs, clit stimulators, erection arousers, penis extensions, benwa balls, g-spot finders, pressure spot ticklers, leather harnesses, oils, gels, and a whole lot more.

The women started oohing and ahhing, picking up this thing and the next and laughing out loud about the fun they were going to have trying out all the new products. Audria joined in for a little while, making fun of Angela who was checking out some device called a Lover's Triad, which was a combination vibrating ring for the man and a clitoral stimulator for the woman. But pretty soon, it started feeling like a huge waste of time to her. Yeah, she had a man, *it still thrilled her to think that she had found love with Michael,* but unlike every other woman in this room, she couldn't just go home to hers and rock his world with new goodies. Audria was on her feet and moving to the front door before she had even processed the thought. She ignored Angela's 'what's wrong' question thrown at her back and walked out. She needed to get away from all this sex stuff and get her some air.

She headed down a side street walking briskly and trying to suck as much air into her lungs as she could in an effort to clear her head. She went to cross in front of a long white-walled driveway when a large gray Suburban started backing up fast. Seeing the truck coming right for her, Audria screamed and tried to jump out of the way. She fell, scraping her left knee on the sidewalk, but heard the screech of brakes and knew the idiot driving must have seen her just in time to stop.

"You Jackass! Who the hell comes backing out of a driveway going ninety miles an hour like that?" She marched around to the driver's side of the truck, brushing off her knees as she went, and ready to give somebody a good tongue cutting. She was expecting to hear a spluttering apology from some White asshole late for his golf game. She got something way different from that.

"What kind of airhead just walks into a driveway without looking where the hell she's going?"

Audria's head snapped up. "What?" She was shocked to see the person standing there. He looked vaguely familiar.

"Aren't you?"

"Aren't you?"

Both of them asked the question at the same time. Then it dawned on Audria this was the same guy from Gina's cookout, the one who had forgotten to lock the bathroom door behind him.

"You're Audria, right?"

She nodded her head, a little embarrassed that she had been ready to cuss him out.

"I'm Al. Sorry I called you an airhead. I guess I wasn't paying attention to how fast I was backing up."

"No, you weren't," Audria replied, agreeing with him. She wasn't about to let him off the hook that easy. He had been going way too fast.

He was looking down at her knee. "Damn, now I *really* feel bad. You're bleeding."

She looked down at her knee, surprised to see a trickle of blood in the place of what she thought had been just a scratch. She reached down to wipe it away, but he stopped her.

"Look, why don't you come inside and let me at least clean that and get you fixed up with a band-aid or something?"

"Oh, you live here?" Audria asked, surprised.

"Yeah, but it's a well-kept secret, so don't tell anybody, okay?"

Audria smiled and allowed him to lead her up a few steps into the house. He showed her into the kitchen. The place was huge, nicely furnished, but she could tell that it was definitely a man's home. It was missing some of the extra touches that a woman would have given it.

"How long have you lived here?" she asked him, and was surprised when he told her a little over three years. He explained how he and another buddy of his had put together and bought the house, since neither of them could have afforded to get it on their own. Unfortunately, his friend's job had moved him to another city a few months before, and he was now stuck with the house by himself. His buddy was being pretty patient, and was giving him time to buy out his half of the property.

"What about finding a roommate or something to help with the mortgage payments?" Audria asked him.

"Yeah, I thought about that, but I don't really live well with people."

Audria nodded her head. "I know exactly what you mean."

She winced as he swabbed the scratch with some disinfectant then applied the band-aid. His hands were huge, with fingers that felt like miniature sausages brushing up against her skin, but soft. She felt a shiver of something run through her, racing from the small of her back up along her spine, and an image flashed through her mind of one of those fingers sliding up into the slick wetness of her centerspot. She was on her feet and backing up before he was barely finished.

This feeling felt traitorous to her. How could she say she was in love with Michael and be feeling some kind of excitement at another man's very innocent touch.

"I gotta go," she said, anxiously looking past his shoulder at the front door.

"What's the matter?" Al asked her, with a puzzled look on his face. "Did I hurt you or something?"

"No, no," Audria stammered. "It's just that I've been gone for awhile and my friends might be looking for me."

"What friends? You have friends around here?"

"Me and my girlfriends are at this party over at this woman named Yvonne's place."

"Oh, one of those," Al smiled, with a knowing look on his face. "One of Yvonne's Waiting to Exhale parties, huh? Did you buy anything?"

She looked at him and raised her chin defiantly. "As if that's any business of yours."

"Hell, ain't no business of mine, but the way you're acting like you're wound tighter than a Seventies jheri curl, I'd say you shoulda got you something if you didn't."

Audria wasn't about to even dignify that comment with a response. She just brushed past him and headed for the door. "Thanks for the band-aid," she threw over her shoulder.

"Anytime," he threw back, then raised his voice. "Please don't slam the door."

She made good and sure she slammed it as hard as she could behind her. She hoped it fell off its freaking hinges. It would serve him right for his rudeness. Tighter than a Seventies jheri curl, my ass. She wasn't tight. She didn't know what the hell he was talking about. She was just fine.

Walking up the street though, Audria knew she was lying to herself like a big dog. She *was* tight, and she was going to have to address this issue with Michael before long. She couldn't wait to get home so she could start a letter to her man.

twenty-three
Do What You Gotta Do

Hey Babygirl,

What's up with you? Hoping everything's cool in your world right now. Was banking on a letter from you at least by today, but guess the mail's doing it's thing, and we just gotta keep doing ours. So, I'm here thinking that maybe I need to wait until I hear back from you, but damn woman, you gotta be some kinda tired 'cuz you keep hotfooting it through my mind. I know, I know, corny as hell, right? But it's true.

So look Audria, it's not that I got a whole lot to say, but there's one thing in particular on my mind. For some reason every time I look at your picture, especially when I look in your eyes, I get this feeling that's hard for me to explain. I'm not trying to be forward with you or nothing, hope you understand that, but there's something about you that tells me that when you say you're needy, that it goes deeper than just the kind of emotional need that makes you ask me to be there for you. It's almost like I'm picking up on this sexual erotic kinda energy from you. I could be wrong, could be way off the mark with that, but I don't think so.

Babygirl listen, I ain't no expert on the kind of violations you been through, alright, but a lot of what I do in here is read, and for some reason, most of what I read stays with me, you know? Some years back, I read this article about the effects of rape (damn, it's hard for me to use that word, especially thinking about it with you), but I read this article and it talked about how some females who been through what you been through go in different directions. Some of them don't want nothing to do with men and they either turn lesbian or they just freeze up and don't have nothing to do with sex, period. But on the flip side of that, some females get this kinda hypersexual awareness and so a lot of their focus is on sex.

Damn, I don't know why I'm finding it so hard to just say what I want to say here. Audria, Sweetheart, outside of what you shared with me about what your uncle did, we never really talked about nothing on the lines of sex. I mean, I told you that you don't have to worry about me floating boats in strange waters up in here, but that's not really talking about you and me and the way we feel about sex, is it?

Need to say some things to you here. Kinda plain speaking, alright? I don't have no illusions about what you might need or want as a woman. You're 39. All the supposed experts say that a woman gets to her sexual peak right around 40. Knowing that, I should be shaking in my boots and worrying about what that's gon' mean for me, but I'm cool. Like I told you, I got you, and now I know you love me, I'm really cool. Look Babygirl, all I'm saying is you do what you gotta do, alright? Audria, so long as I know I got your heart, I'm cool. And you know you don't need to worry about mine. Remember, it's in a fixed place when it comes to you.

Alright, that's all I gotta say. I know you're a big girl and know how to handle things and I know you ain't gon' be swinging no wild sex parties or nothing like that. Look Audria, for the record, I'm telling you to handle your business, but don't ever think that means I want or need to know about some other dude sampling what's mine, alright? Gon' fallback right here. Not really liking my energy right now and I'm not trying to bring that to you, so talk to you later. Peace.

Michael

twenty-four
Want!

Hi Michael,

God, I don't know where to begin. This is kinda hard for me to say, okay, so please bear with me. Baby, I'm not trying to upset you, but I need to talk about something with you. Michael, I'm feeling so hot right now, like I'm on fire. I need you. I'm sorry for being so open like this, but I'm not trying to hide any part of me from you, okay? You promised to be there for me, so please be there for me with this too?

I went to this party today with my girlfriends Angela and Vanessa. I told you about them before, remember? Anyway, this new friend of Angela's had this adult toy party. Baby, it was nice. It was at this really awesome place in Tenleytown, D.C. That's one of the richest sections in the District. Yvonne, the woman who hosted the party has this huge stone Tudor house that's laid like you wouldn't believe. I'm not really into material stuff like that, but you should've seen my friend Vanessa. She's so materialistic, Michael, it ain't funny.

Anyway, there were something like 25 plus women at the party, including some really pretty models who came out wearing all this sexy lingerie, and then there were all these adult toys that the hostess passed around for everybody to look at and decide whether you wanted to buy something or not.

It started out like fun, you know? But after awhile, I found myself just feeling sad, Michael. It's like everybody there kept talking about going home to their man or their husband, and how they were going to try out this thing or the next thing on him, and I got to thinking about you so much. Michael, I'm so afraid that I can't do this waiting thing. I know I love you. I have no doubt in my mind about the way I feel for you. It's kinda like you said to me about your heart being in a fixed place when it comes to me? That's the same way I feel now. But it's just that I feel so freaking needy right now, and I'm not talking just on an emotional level or wanting to be held, although there is all of that and I do need that. What I'm talking about is sex. You know, ever since that thing happened with Uncle Carl, it seemed like after a couple years, I just got so interested in sex. I hate to even say this to you, Michael, but again I'm not hiding anything from you. I got a little promiscuous from like around 16 into my early 20s, and then thankfully, I slowed down with all that, but this focus I have on sex has never gone away. Sometimes it seems like sex is all I can think about.

And I'm kinda into some things that I've never told anybody about, not another living soul. I have membership in this S&M club, and I do erotic scenes with people. They're all strangers. Sometimes I use paddles to spank people or actual whips. Sometimes I use candles and pour wax all over them. And sometimes I just watch. Nobody ever touches me. I don't allow that, but I just feel this need deep inside me that regular sex doesn't fill. It's like I need to bring pain, or to watch it. Maybe it's because of my past . . . no, I KNOW it's because of my past, but it's a part of me now and since I promised to share everything with you, I'm sharing this too.

But with all that said Michael, one of the reasons I KNOW without any doubt in my mind that I'm in love with you is because the way I am about sex. I feel sometimes like it's an almost physical need for me to be with somebody. So knowing that, why would I pick somebody behind walls to give my heart to? I guess it really is true how the old saying goes about us not picking who we fall in love with?

I don't know what I'm trying to say to you. I guess I'm a little scattered all over the place and maybe just want to hear your thoughts on all this. Kinda see where your head is. I'm not trying to frustrate you or have you thinking about something that you might not want to think about or can't even do anything about. Please don't misunderstand, okay? It's just that I'm feeling the way I'm feeling, and you're such a comfort to me that you're the only person I could think to share this with. I love you, Baby, and I would never do anything to hurt you, please believe that. I just needed to tell you how I'm feeling right now.

Your Babygirl,
Audria

P.S. So, you're never gonna believe this, but I almost got run down by this fool driving this great big ol' Suburban truck. Let me tell you what happened. I left the party and went for a walk. I think all that sex stuff was getting to me and so I decided to go get some fresh air. I'm fast walking down the *street minding my business and this truck starts backing up fast out of a driveway. Your baby almost got turned into road kill. It was crazy. Anyway, come to find out that it was this guy Al. Remember I told you that I <u>felt</u> you that Sunday when you got that awful goodbye letter from me? Well, when all that happened, I was over at my friend Gina's place at this cookout she gives a couple times a month. I met this Al guy there in a kinda weird way. Anyway, it was him driving the truck that almost ran me down. We had some words. But Baby, can you believe that man had the nerve to tell me I was 'tight'? I couldn't believe he was that bold and brazen. In any event, I had to admit (later on, of course) that he was right. Your baby's wound kinda tight, Michael. Whatchu gon' do about it? I got some ideas in my mind. What about you? ☺ Just playing, Baby. Loving you. Hope I get a letter from you soon.*

P.P.S. Michael, I almost forgot to say this. I know from what you told me in the last letter I have from you, that you tried to call me once already. I'm sorry about that. My Mother was over here and she didn't accept the call. I know what I said to you in my angry letter about not taking your call and how that must've looked like to you, but I only said those things because I was angry and didn't understand what you were saying to me at the time. Baby, I want to hear your voice. It's almost like craving the air I breathe. I want you to feel comfortable calling me whenever you can, okay? Want to see you as soon as we can arrange it too. So if you ever feel like calling me, please don't hesitate. I'm here for you. I can't wait to hear My Man's New York accent, so call me soon. Love you and thinking about you.

twenty-five
A NEW FRIEND

"Look, all I'm saying is that people put wayyyy too much pressure on each other in relationships, and ninety-nine point nine percent of the time, all that winds up being is a formula for failure instead of success."

Audria didn't understand what this woman was going on about with all this talk about failure and success relationship formulas, but she was trying to keep an open mind. She had always believed that you could find truth in any number of places, even when you weren't looking for it, so she was following the discussion intently.

She and Angela were squeezed in next to each other and two hefty sistahs on a sofa a tiny bit bigger than a love seat in the dimly lit space of Heart & Soul II café off Capitol Hill. It was Thursday night and Audria would have been quite content heading home to spend time writing to Michael, but Angela wasn't having it. It was Love Talk and Relationships night for Sisters hosted by some fierce exotic poetess named X-taci, and when Angela made up her mind she was gonna have company to do something she wanted to do, you might as well just ask when and where to show up 'cuz there was no getting out of it. Like it or not, Audria had been designated Angela's *company* for the evening.

Despite their plan to arrive early to snag some *good* seats at the restaurant slash nightclub, they had barely made it in time to join the mad stampede of sistahs angling for a place to plant their derrieres during the two-hour discussion. She and Angela practically had to beat down four other sistahs for their spot and two minutes later were still forced to play people sandwich when hefty and heftier decided to squeeze their massive rumps onto the sofa despite the obvious fact that it could barely hold two people, let alone four. Audria rolled her eyes in the general direction of heftier. The woman cut her eyes at her and wiggled her huge backside further back onto the sofa. Didn't make no kinda sense.

She and Angela took turns holding each other's seats while the other went for drinks, to the ladies' room, and to hit the buffet line. Audria took a bite from the plate of appetizers and closed her eyes, savoring the tangy flavor on her tongue. Just like the original Heart & Soul Café that had closed down some years back, H&S II knew how to cook them up some buffalo wings and deep-fried catfish nuggets. Audria nudged Angela in the ribs to silence her friend's smacking. The woman was just as bad as Vanessa sometimes with her ghetto behavior.

Audria had already asked Angela why Vanessa wasn't joining them. Seemed like girlie had snagged herself some new fella who was so overcome with her charms, he was falling all over himself to lace her with anything and everything her greedy lil' heart desired. Audria shook her head at this news. Vanessa would never change.

For the last forty minutes, they had been content listening to the open discussion where the women brave enough to stand up and address the circle, talked about their love and relationship troubles and looked to the wiser ones in the group to share the wisdom of the aged, she supposed. She and Angela had been taking turns exchanging looks and elbowing each other as the discussion progressed from one relationship topic to the next.

They listened to one woman talk about not feeling appreciated at home because her husband was a throwback to the fifties and sixties where the man was king of the castle and thought of his wife as the person whose only purpose was making sure he stayed well fed, well taken care of in bed, and did everything in his power to keep her barefoot and pregnant. The woman herself admitted that the six children she had already given her husband, all before she hit thirty, resembled a step ladder when you looked at them.

"Thirty?" Angela barked in Audria's ear, sarcasm lacing her voice. "That heifer look not a day under fifty and if I'm lying I'm dying by way of drowning in a pile of my own stinkin' shit, I swear, my hand to God."

Audria poked her hard in the ribs and hissed at her to behave. They turned their attention back to the discussion. Next came a mousy looking woman who surprised them both and most likely every other woman in the joint when she started talking about her boyfriend using her like some kind of sex slave to participate in twosomes, threesomes, foursomes and a whole bunch of other nasty 'somes' whenever the mood struck him.

"So why you putting up with that shit, unless you like it, huh?" somebody hollered out from way in the back.

Miss Mousy peered off into the dimly lit space like she was trying to determine which direction the voice had come from. After a beat, she shook her head and said in a much smaller voice than the one she had started out with. "That's just it, I *don't* like it, but I love him. I don't want him to leave me."

The loud, brassy voice spoke up again from the back. "See? That's the problem right there. You actin' like that's the only man in the whole wide world. Is people like you putting up with that kinda shit that's making it hard on sistahs like me who just want to find normal. When you don't learn how to say no to them dogs, they go and tell they' boys what a good lil' freak they have at home, and then all the others start expecting to find them a good lil' freak too. Grow a friggin' backbone. You make me sick, you lil' whiny..."

The discussion host cut off the rest of the comment with a loud clearing of her throat into the microphone and asked the ladies to show respect. It was too late for Miss Mousy. The last Audria saw was the woman's departing back heading in the direction of the ladies room, and she could swear she saw the sistah's shoulders heaving like she had already turned on the waterworks. Not that she disagreed with the comments Loudmouth had made from in back, but she certainly wouldn't have lit into a total stranger the way the other woman had. Some people needed to learn how to be more sensitive to other people's feelings, but she recognized that the world was full of all types. It was part of what made it go 'round, so who was she to judge.

Next up was a bitter tirade by a woman who left everybody trying to figure out whether she had been dumped by a man, woman or both. She swapped 'he' for 'she' and 'she' for 'he' so many times during the telling of her tale, that by the time she finished her story with a squeaky 'you know?' on the end of it, people just looked around at each other, scratched their heads and waited for the next daring soul to step to the mike. Even the emcee did a little 'alrighty then', took a sip of her Cosmo and handed the mike to the next person.

Audria perked up when she saw the sistah who was stepping to the mike. Several times during the evening, she had found her eyes wandering over to the woman, drawn perhaps by the air of confidence and peaceful energy the sistah exuded. She was what one would definitely call Afrocentric. She had on an ankle length form-fitting African print skirt with masks imprinted on it, a white painter's shirt with loose, blousy sleeves, and her curly-locked hair was swept off her shoulders in an up-do, a pair of ivory decorative chopsticks holding it in place. Her jewelry looked like authentic African pieces. High glaze wooden bangles, gold neck rings, ivory stones and several anklets, and she was wearing a pair of leather and gold heelless slippers on her feet. Before the woman even opened her mouth, Audria knew she would hear something profound.

"What you people know of love, eh?" That last word sounded like a cross between a deep-throated hum and a derisive laugh. Her voice was a soft, lilting sound, with a hint of the Islands in it, but with undertones of a British accent as well. She tilted her chin upwards indicating the crowd, but in an arrogant way.

"I'm sure you gon' school us, Sistah Souljah?" Miss Loudmouth again.

Audria held her breath waiting for the woman to respond to the rudeness with something dismissive, but she acted like she hadn't heard the loud comment.

"If all you listen to each otha, the answer is right in front you, but is hard work gettin' people to take a break from hearing theyself talk, is it not?" Audria could swear she saw the woman sniff the air in front of her, her nostrils expanding slightly like a dog tasting the air with its olfactory senses. "What's de one t'ing everybody in here find theyself wantin'?" She waited, piercing eyes scanning the room. "Nobody gon' tell me?"

Audria found herself lifting a hand before she was even aware of it, and felt an electric tingle run through her when the eyes found hers.

"Yes, Pretty lady with 'de braids, over by 'de sofa 'dere. Go on, stan' up. What's yo' answer?"

Ignoring Angela's poke in the ribs, Audria rose to her feet. "Well, I guess everybody wants love. They want their relationship to work. They want to be happy, right?"

She felt herself being pulled in, charmed by the woman's smile. She had never seen such pretty, white teeth on another individual. Sistah girl was smiling a wide smile, so Audria figured she must've given her the answer she had been looking for.

"Yah man, you right, Queen. Thas' what mos' everybody lookin' for. But guess what?"

Audria was loving the dips and inflections of that voice. It soothed her in a way she couldn't begin to explain even if she tried. "What?" she found herself asking.

"Therein lies everybody's problem." The woman pronounced the word 'problem' the way Jamaicans did when they said "no problem, mon'". She found herself smiling back and warming to their exchange.

"How is that a problem? It's natural for us to want love, isn't it? To want to be loved? To want to be cherished and want to be special? To want to be happy and to want to build something with another person who makes us happy and who wants to be with us. That's all natural, isn't it? So how can any of that be a problem?"

155

The woman looked around the room again, her smile widening even more. She started snapping her fingers slowly next to the microphone and began counting. "One. Two. T'ree. Four. Five. Six. Seven." She looked at Audria again, her gaze direct, smile still steady. "You want to know what I'm counting, Queen?"

Audria nodded.

"From one queen to anotha', I'm counting de numbah of times you said 'dis one word in your very short sentences. Now, you gon' ask me which word 'dat, right?"

Audria nodded again.

The woman looked away, making eye contact with someone else briefly, then found her eyes again. "It's 'de word '*want*'. You said 'de word '*want*' seven times."

"So what's wrong with that?" Audria asked her, feeling a little annoyed with the woman for drawing things out.

"What's wrong with 'dat, Pretty Lady, is 'dat *want* don't have nuthin' to do wit' love."

The room erupted into a loud murmuring swell after that and the emcee had her hands full for some long minutes trying to give everyone a turn who wanted to respond. She finally cut off the commentary, nodding her head like she had just achieved a moment's clarity herself.

"I think you're right, Sistah. Everybody *wants* so much that they forget about the other side."

"What other side?" somebody hollered out off to the left. "Would you make some sense, please?"

The hair locked, Afrocentric sistah spoke up again, nodding her head to X-taci for permission to take the floor. "In my book, 'dere ain't no otha side. Is just one side. Love don't have not'ing to do wid' want and want don't have not'ing to do wid' love. Once people understan' 'dis, all go smooth."

The same loud brassy voice from earlier barked. "So If I tell my man I want him to keep loving me, you tellin' me that ain't got nothing to do wid' love? What kinda shit you been smoking?"

Audria wanted to shush the crowd so she wouldn't miss a word spoken. She was hanging on every word. "Look people, all I'm sayin' to all you is 'dat people, especially women, put wayyy too much pressure on each otha' in relationships, an' ninety-nine point nine percent of 'de time, all 'dat wind up makin' for you is a formula for failure; not success."

The room erupted again and sistahs on every side of her were getting to their feet. Audria struggled to keep her eyes on the woman. She didn't know how or why, but she knew she wasn't letting this woman leave without talking to her some more. She suffered through the rest of the discussion, shooed off Angela in the direction of the bar to refresh their drinks, and elbowed past a line of sisters waiting for the ladies' room. She finally spotted the ivory chopsticks in the distance and angled for her.

When she got closer, she realized the woman was in the middle of a conversation, so Audria stood back patiently waiting her turn. The woman was obviously well known, and Audria found herself waiting far longer than she had anticipated, watching sistah after sistah say hello, kiss cheeks and exchange hugs. Eventually though, the woman turned her way.

"Ah, Miss Pretty Lady who wants and wants and wants." They laughed at that and Audria suddenly found herself feeling awkward. She wasn't sure what to say, but didn't want to come across as a dummy, so she blurted out the first thing that came to her mind.

"You seem so wise and I was thinking maybe you might be somebody who I'd... I'd want to get to know more. Maybe have a friendship with?" Her voice sounded shaky and squeaky and all weird to her ears, but the woman just smiled at her, eyes dark and strangely unreadable.

"'Dere you go again wid' yo' wanting." She wagged a finger at Audria, and they laughed again, but the woman's smile didn't last long. She took a few steps into Audria's space, far closer than she would consider a comfortable distance if one was of a mind to respect someone else's safe zone. Suddenly, the woman's mouth was to her ear and she was speaking softly, in that same lilting accent, but for Audria's ears only. She could smell some incensey fragrance on the woman.

"I don't have many friends, so when you talk of friendship to me, be careful. But we gon' see wid' 'dat. Time tells all, yes?"

Audria felt warm breath on her earlobes and the woman continued in the same low lilt. "But 'dat's not what's impo'tant right now. You have the look of love in yo' eyes, Queen, but 'dere's somet'ing else 'dere too. You been hurt, bad, and you lookin' to some man to heal 'dat hurt fo' you, but you puttin' too much on yo' man's shoulders. You keep walkin' down 'dat road, gal, you gon' hurt him and he gon' hurt you; maybe a kinda hurt you won't neva' recover from."

Audria jerked away and stepped backward like the woman had just said something dirty to her. How could she know any of this? How could she possibly know any of these things? She didn't want to look at the woman, look into those knowing eyes, but knew she didn't have a choice. They were standing much too close to one another to avoid it, so she looked.

"How...?" The word died on her lips as the other woman shook her head at her slightly.

"Is a road I been down myself, Cherie, and although people can walk with you on de side, even help you find de road again when you lose your way, they can't walk de road wid' you. Only you get to step 'dere."

Audria could feel the tightness in the back of her throat and the sting of tears welling in her eyes. "I'm not strong like other people. I don't know how to..."

"Ah, fear will make us t'ink we walking the road of failure *every* time, Cherie, but guess what?"

Audria looked at her questioningly, eyes bright and shiny with the tears she knew would come later. She could barely get the word out. "What?"

"All Queens are stronga' than they t'ink, gyal," the woman smiled at her, a warm hand rubbing the small of her back somewhat intimately.

Audria snorted almost derisively. "Me? Strong?" In her mind, she couldn't help but think of Michael and what he and his name had already come to mean to her. He was the strong one; not her.

"Yes, you. Listen Pretty Lady, let me bless yo' ears wid' somet'ing powerful you need to 'member, hear? It's said that 'de strongest people in 'de world aren't those most protected; they're 'de ones that must struggle against adversity and obstacles, learn to surmount them, and survive."

Audria looked at her, still fighting to blink back the tears that she felt would come any minute.

"Is all inside you, you know?" The woman smiled at her again and Audria found her mind drifting, wondering a strange thought - - what toothpaste could somebody use to make their teeth get such a startling shade of white.

"What's inside me?" she asked, her voice sounding even shakier than before.

"'De answers to fix whatever's wrong wid' you. You just have to look for 'dem."

Audria had just opened her mouth to say something else when Angela poked her from behind. "You ready?"

She didn't want the conversation to be over, but knew Angela wouldn't be patient enough to wait. She turned back to the still smiling face.

"Can we talk again? Please?"

"Of course," came the voice, with a hint of teasing behind it. "Talk is free. Everyt'ing else you pay for."

Audria smiled at her and put her hand out to shake. "My name's Audria. Audria Hope?"

Her hand was ignored and after a few seconds of it hanging out there like a dead branch, she let it drop to her side.

"Queen Audria, my name is Nadira Zawadi. Those in my inner circle all call me Zawadi, but you can call me Nadira for now."

Audria couldn't help herself. She gave the woman a *'no she didn't* kinda look, but reined it in when she felt Angela poke her in the small of her back again.

"Okay, Nadira it is. How can I get in contact with you?"

"I will call you," the woman countered again, giving her a pointed look. Audria felt that mild frustration again. This was not at all going the way she had expected it to go. Angela was poking her almost non-stop now and people were crowding in on them from all sides. She started digging in her purse to find a piece of paper and a pen. Scribbling her contact information quickly, she handed the paper across to the waiting, outstretched palm, noticing that the woman's skin was flawless. She looked up at that interesting face again, realizing she had no clue how old this woman was. She could usually guess another sistah's age, and be pretty close with her guess, but this was the first time she felt like she hadn't a clue. Nadira's eyes hadn't left hers yet.

"All right, Miss Wanting Audria. Yo' friend there look like she gettin' ready to bore a hole in yo' back wid' her urgent little finger, so I'll let you go 'long now. I'll call you soon."

Audria wanted to ask when, when could she expect a call, but instead she allowed herself to be rudely pulled in the opposite direction by her impatient friend. She knew she was going to have to have a little conversation with Angela about her rudeness, but that would come later. For now, she was content throwing a backwards glance over her shoulder at her newest friend. Well, *maybe* friend. She had a feeling Nadira had a lot to teach her.

twenty-six
Smooth

It was Friday, first day of her long Labor Day holiday weekend and Audria was more than ready to get it started. Although Labor Day fell on Wednesday, middle-of-the-week, she had taken off the Monday and Tuesday, so she was all set to have five glorious days away from the corporate plantation, and she was so looking forward to her time off. And since all the attorneys she worked with were on travel, Audria had decided to sneak out of the office around noon to get her weekend started early.

Before leaving the City, she had changed into the sneaks she kept in the trunk of her car and gone for a long, brisk walk around Hains Point in D.C. It was one of her favorite walking spots. As she came around the point, she felt momentary sadness at the empty spot that used to house the gigantic half buried statue of a giant called The Awakening. It had been moved a few years back over to the National Harbor, but she still missed it every time she passed its old home. The sculpted work of art, done in cast aluminum, always made her think of the movie Planet of the Apes for some reason, maybe because it resembled some long forgotten relic of a far distant time when imagined prehistoric giants ruled the earth. It was creepy but beautiful all at the same time.

With practically every step she took on her walk, Audria found herself thinking of Michael. She had never experienced anything this intense before with any of the men she had been with. She thought about him almost all the time. When she woke up, while she showered, eating breakfast, driving to work, while she was working, at lunch, on the way home, hanging out with her friends, getting ready for bed, while she was in bed. At the strangest times and in the strangest places, she would find herself wondering how he was, whether he was thinking about her as often as she was him. She would never have thought it possible to think about someone this much and want to be with them even more, but the fact that she was living it, was proof that it could happen.

When she wasn't actually writing to Michael, she was thinking about writing him, or hoping to get a letter from him. She couldn't wait to get home to see if he had written her. Their conversation seemed so free, like they could talk about anything and everything. From their lives growing up to bad choices they had both made, his life on the streets and his life of crime, to existential topics to politics to Black history, all of it. She had never felt this degree of freedom before to express herself and her innermost thoughts with anyone.

She still felt a little weird about her last letter to him, bringing up the sex thing and her membership at the S&M club, her first time doing that outside of what she had shared with him before, but she would have to wait and see how he responded. She didn't know why exactly, but something told her that her man might be a little bit jealous, and the same way she didn't want to be fast and free to throw up her freedom in his face, she would have to watch how much she shared with him about things she was feeling. See? That was just it though. She didn't want to start feeling like she had to hide things from him. That felt dishonest to her and she wasn't trying to start playing games like that with the person she loved.

Audria finished up her walk, stopped to watch some teenagers feed a paddling of ducks squawking around in the murky waters of the Potomac, and headed for home.

She stopped long enough to grab the mail, noticing the now familiar return address from Michael, *yes, her man had written her,* quickly changed into shorts, a tank top and slippers, poured herself some iced-tea and headed out back. She slumped down onto an Adirondack chaise lounger under the trellis-covered partially enclosed patio, took a sip from her glass of iced tea, and took a moment to breathe in deeply of the Tuberose scented fresh air.

Audria looked over at the double beds of fragrant white flower spikes her mother had spent long hours planting for her some months before, and felt a familiar tightness at the back of her throat. It had been weeks since that last awful conversation between them, the longest she had ever gone without talking to her mother, but although she missed her terribly Audria was adamant she wasn't going to call first. All she was asking for was a little support on this choice she had made to follow her heart, and her mother was acting like she had just signed away her soul to the devil or something. If she didn't stand firm on this, she knew her mother would never respect her decision, nor would she respect Michael, if and when she finally met him. She pushed aside the depressing thought and the ache she felt in the pit of her stomach because of her mother's unusual silence and ripped open Michael's letter.

> *Fri. 8/24*
>
> *Peace Audria,*
> *So, you're laying claim to me? Damn Babygirl, you sound like you been walking in the world I used to walk in. Excuse me for saying this, Audria, but THAT IS GANGSTA!...*

She found herself giggling as she read more, especially the parts where he talked about teasing her. The man was crazy. Calling her a Black Gangsta Cowgirl with spurs on, stetson tipped down over her braids, guns blazing, laying claim to his heart? Certifiable. But she couldn't help smiling. He just did that to her.

She kept reading some more and felt herself start to swoon – *damn, did Sistahs swoon* – when he talked about needing to respect and honor her by asking her to be his woman. See? That was exactly what she was talking about. He was so different. She didn't really know how to explain it, but it was almost like he was this olden days gallant knight type in the body of a modern day man. None of the men she dated had ever really asked her to be their woman, at least not that she could remember. It was more like you started dating casually, then kinda just fell into an unspoken exclusivity that seemed to mean for both people that you then had the right to start making demands on each other. It made her feel so special that her man seemed to understand how important it was to ask this question. She wished she could hear his voice right this minute so she could give him his answer. Her heart felt like it was overloaded with feeling for him.

Taking another sip of her iced tea, she set the glass down, let the lounger back all the way down and flipped over onto her stomach to keep reading. She had just found her place again in the letter where he was talking about running off all the other sistahs who had shown interest in him before, when the phone started chirping in the kitchen. Audria was tempted to ignore it, but knew it might be Angela. She and Vanessa were supposed to be swinging by early Saturday morning to pick her up to go work their buns out at some new Zumba class over at the local gym. She set the letter down and hurried inside to get the cordless.

"Hello."

There were a series of odd connecting clicks in her ear and Audria said hello again, louder this time, wondering if some kid was playing on the line.

A disembodied, slightly mechanical-sounding voice came back at her with a whine of static. "This call is being placed from a Federal Correctional Institution from Michael Strong. You will not be billed for this call. To accept the call, please press 5 on your telephone keypad, or to reject the call, please press 1."

Michael? It was Michael calling her? Audria could feel her heart begin an erratic dance in her chest, and she clutched the phone in a vise grip. Oh God. He was actually calling her? What would she say to him? How would he sound? Would she like his voice? Would he like hers? She tried to calm herself, but it wasn't working and she could feel her hands shaking as she gripped the phone like it would grow wings and fly away from her. The numbers on the phone keypad all started blurring in front of her eyes and she found herself having to blink a few times to bring them back into focus. She hit 5 to accept the call and held her breath.

"May I talk to Audria?" His voice sounded smooth, like hickory-flavored coffee, butterscotch toffee and expensive bourbon all rolled into one big ball of smoothness. She couldn't find her voice, felt like all the air had been sucked out of her chest, and his came again.

"Hello, may I talk to Audria?" He said 'talk' the way all New Yorkers the world over had always said 'talk' and would be saying 'talk' until the end of time, with emphasis on the middle, almost like they were saying the word 'torque'.

Her brain finally decided to fire off a message releasing her tongue, and she spoke, her voice sounding whispery soft, like a Jennifer Tilly wanna-be. "Hi Michael. It's me. It's Audria."

There was a brief silence between them and then they both began together, the same sentence. "I can't believe..." They stopped at the same time, then that sweet, smooth voice came at her again.

"Ladies first."

"I can't believe I'm actually talking to you, hearing your voice. You sound so sweet, Michael."

"Sweet? That ain't exactly the kind of word a man often hears as a descriptive for his voice. Smooth, yeah. Manly, yeah, but sweet?" Audria could hear him smiling at her through the teasing.

"You know what I mean, Michael. Smooth was actually the first word that came to my mind when I heard your voice, but I'm not trying to give you the big head or nothing." Audria stopped, not wanting to waste time with trivial playfulness. "There's so much I want to say to you, so much we need to talk about. Did you get my letter?"

"Take a breath, Miss Audria. Remember what I told you? What I've *been* telling you from the jump, when we realized that what we were feeling is mutual? I got you. No need to rush, Babygirl."

Audria felt her heart jump when he called her 'babygirl'.

"I know, Michael. I know you keep telling me to slow down, but don't you realize that maybe time means something different for both of us? I can't help what I'm feeling. I've never felt anything this intense for anybody..."

He cut her off. "Shhh, Beautiful. You ain't alone. I'm feeling everything you're feeling, maybe more. People sometimes think that women got this lock on emotion, like they feel things so much deeper than men, but you know what I think? Men just know how to hide their emotions better. It's the only way they know how to feel the things they feel and still hold on to their masculinity. But Babygirl, I got you. That's all I need for you to understand. We'll figure out the rest as we go, a'ight?"

"Yes, Michael."

Audria could hear him choke back something that made his voice waver momentarily, then he continued. "I just need for you to get me on this, Audria, and this is about the letter you're talking about, the one dated last Sunday. First off, understand this. You can talk to me about anything you want to, everything. No subject is off limits between me and you. I got to have honesty from my woman, okay? And I promise you get that from me. As long as me and you respect each other, deal only in truth, the rest is gravy, feel me? Now, you talked to me in that letter about some things you were feeling. I hear you, a'ight? Even understand it. But the one thing about all that I ain't cool with is that club scene. Kinda understand the need for it, but that don't sound safe to me, and it's my job to make sure my woman's safe. So handle that."

There was a brief silence on the line, then... "Is funny how this thing's moving between us, ain't it, 'cuz I wrote you a letter the day before yours that spoke on the same subject. You got that yet?"

Audria shook her head like he could see her through the phone and smiled at her silliness. "No, I don't think I have that. I was actually in the middle of reading the one you sent me dated Friday, 8/24. Seriously, I was in the middle of reading it and had just gotten this thought about wanting to hear your voice and then the phone rang."

"Hmm, well, the other letter will be along soon enough, right? Then you'll see what I mean. Wait for it, a'ight? Want you and me to be on the same page, Babygirl."

Audria sighed softly. "That's kinda hard sometimes with this mail thing the way it is." She listened for his voice again.

"Yeah, I know, but is just a thing, ain't it? We can work around that, right?"

She could suddenly hear a hint of questioning in his voice, like he was unsure, maybe not of himself but of her. She hastened to reassure him. "Of course we can work around it, Michael. It's just a... a thing, right?" She made sure he heard her smiling at him through the phone. There was a beat of silence between them, then his voice came at her again.

"This thing between us is... is some kinda... let's see, lemme use your word, 'sweet', ain't it?"

"I like intense better in this instance," Audria said, feeling flirty.

"Oh, you like intense?"

"Yeah, I like intense."

"And can you handle intense, Miss Audria?"

"I can handle *anything* you bring me, Mister Strong."

"Oh, you sound real confident-like with that. You sure?"

"Very sure," Audria whispered into the phone playfully, feeling a tingling begin in her nipples. She couldn't believe she was actually talking to this man. Her man. Teasing with him.

She was just about to say that to him again, when the same disembodied voice that had announced the call in the beginning, cut in with some recording saying that the call was originating from a federal penitentiary.

"They gon' cut us off in a little bit, Baby."

"Oh no," Audria cried out, not caring how needy she sounded. "Please don't go. Don't go yet, Michael. We just started talking."

"Gotta go, Beautiful, but we'll talk again soon, and in the meantime, we'll keep writing each other, a'ight?"

She felt like pouting, but didn't want to end the call on a negative note. "Okay," she agreed. Then, "Michael?"

"What, Babygirl?" came her man's smooth voice in her ear.

"Will you ask me the question before you go? Make it real for me?" She could hear him smile on the other end of the line and he cleared his voice briefly. She held her breath.

"Audria, you wrote me your letter laying claim to me, and I'm cool with that. That makes me *your* man. We agree on that, right?"

"Right," she whispered back at him, feeling chills crawl up and down her spine, especially at the way he emphasized the word *your*.

"So I'd be honored if you'd please be *my* woman. Whatchu say?"

She closed her eyes, breathed deeply, trying to hold onto this moment she already knew she would be replaying over and over in her mind for years to come.

"Yes Michael, I'm yours. I'm your woman."

He gave a short laugh in her ear that made her long for the day when she could climb atop him and actually watch his mouth make that very sound.

"A'ight then, let's do this thing."

Before either of them could utter the same three words that were on both their lips to be spoken, the call disconnected. In the quiet of her kitchen, leaning against granite countertops, feeling soft, sexy and owned, Audria whispered them anyway, knowing her man was sending them right back.

I love you.

twenty-seven
Dark and Dangerous

Is this man saying he'll kill for me?

Audria was back sitting on the Adirondack lounger, gripping one side of it with one hand to steady herself. The other was holding on to Michael's letter. Even now, after reading it for the fifth time, she could see the pages fluttering, belying the fact that her hands were still shaking.

She had been so excited to hear his voice, to actually talk to him for the first time. She could still hardly believe they had just finished a conversation. It felt weird to her, kinda like having a chance encounter with some actor you had gotten used to seeing in movies or on TV and then here you were meeting them in real life. Somehow, experiences like those almost always added another dimension to that person for you. That's how she felt now that she'd had a chance to talk to Michael. Not that she hadn't felt he was real before, she had all his letters to prove that, but he seemed twice as real to her now.

After talking with Michael, she had spent some long moments in the kitchen replaying the conversation over and over in her mind, at least the parts of it she could remember. She started growing frustrated with herself that she was having difficulty remembering their talk word for word. It's not like they had spoken a week or days before, for Chrissake. They had just spoken minutes before and already the short term memory was playing dirty tricks on her.

She finally gave up and focused on replaying the lines that seemed burnt into her memory forever.

"Michael?"

"What, Babygirl?"

"Will you ask me the question before you go? Make it real for me?"

"Audria, you wrote me your letter laying claim to me, and I'm cool with that. That makes me your man. We agree on that, right?"

"Right."

"So I'd be honored if you'd please be my woman. Whatchu say?"

"Yes Michael, I'm yours. I'm your woman."

"A'ight then, let's do this thing."

She pulled out his picture from her pocket, brought it as close to her face as she could get it without distorting the image, and looked deep in his eyes. The picture was never far from reach. She felt silly and schoolgirlish, not at all the 39 she now was, but she put her lips against it anyway, pretending she was kissing him, the real person. After some minutes, she walked back outside and picked up his letter. She could barely contain herself. She wanted to write him, to share with him all she was feeling for him, but she decided to finish reading his letter to her first. Almost an hour later, she was still sitting there trying to understand exactly what it was Michael seemed to be saying.

She felt cold chilly tingles baby-stepping back and forth along her spine. She knew he had said he wanted to protect her from harm, understood that he seemed to feel very deeply some emotion connected to her violation, but this blackly dark, barely controlled anger that she could almost taste coming off the pages from him was something she had never encountered before. Even thinking back to the pain her uncle had inflicted on her as a child, all she had felt from him then was a dirty lustfulness, some nasty unclean spirit that had overtaken him, causing him to think only to his own sexual gratification. But this anger coming from the man she loved scared the hell out of her. It made her suddenly feel like she didn't know nearly enough about him.

Audria slammed her hand against the chair in frustration. She so wished she could talk to somebody, especially to her Mom about all this. It's not like she had any real misgivings about Michael. She knew she loved him and knew he loved her. It's just that the intensity she had just talked about with him so playfully an hour before, now seemed like it had ratcheted up a hundred notches higher on the scale.

She didn't have a clue what to do or who to talk to. She felt like she couldn't call her Mother, not about this. Audria was sure all that would do was add fuel to the fire and give the woman cause to say 'I told you so', in her loudest, most overbearing tone. She'd be damned if she was going to have to listen to that. And although she, Angela and Vanessa were close, she just didn't feel the kind of connection with them she needed to on this. Neither one of them were saying so, but Audria could feel them waiting for the day when she would tell them that Michael had turned out to be nothing but a convict with excellent letter-writing skills. She couldn't go to them either.

She found herself thinking of Nadira, the earthy Sistah she had met at Heart & Soul II Café. Nobody had to tell her the woman was wise. That was obvious. She felt like it was somebody like this she needed to talk to, lay everything on the line, and get some serious advice from. But it wasn't like she had a phone number for the woman. She would just have to wait until Nadira decided to call her. Audria thought some more, reading through the letter from start to finish for the sixth time. Hadn't Michael just reminded her again on the phone that he always wanted them to be honest with each other? So, if she couldn't talk to anybody else about this, she would just have to talk to him and tell him the way she was feeling. She hopped up off the lounger and headed inside to refresh her iced tea and to find pen and paper.

Fri. 8/31 - 6:11 p.m.

Hi Michael,
We just talked a few hours ago. I can't begin to tell you how special it was for me to actually hear your voice, I guess, put some sound bytes to all these letters. Thanks for calling me. I hope it was as good for you as it was for me. ☺

Baby, I have some concerns. I don't like that I have to bring them to you now, especially so soon after hearing your voice, hearing us laugh together and all that, but I just finished reading your letter and it's changed my mood in a really big way. To be honest (which you've asked me to be with you), I really wanted to talk about all this with somebody else, kinda like an objective party, you know? But there's really nobody else I can think to talk about this with, except for this one person, and I don't really have a way of reaching that person right now, so I have to tell you how I feel.

Okay, I'm not going to beat around the bush too much with this, because it's really important, and I don't know any easy way to say it, so I'll just say it. A lot of what you said in your letter scared me. Not scared me in the sense that I think you'd ever hurt me, because I don't at all think that, please understand, but it scares me because there's like this darkness in you that I don't understand and that worries me.

Michael, you said you've left behind the person you used to be, that bad boy drug dealer type that didn't care about anyone or anything except getting money. You promised me that man was dead and buried, behind you, yet here you are talking about violence in a way that leaves nothing to my imagination. I get the picture, okay? I know <u>exactly</u> what you're proposing and I don't know what to say. What do you think I'd say to that? You think I'd sanction you to do something that could potentially mean you being taken away from me to spend even more years behind bars than what you're already serving? Maybe life even? Are you crazy?

I mean, I think I understand some of this. You love me. I know that. I feel it in a way I can't explain to you or anyone else, feel it almost like a palpable, breathing thing. And you've explained to me how important it is to you to protect your woman. I also feel that and welcome it. It makes me feel safe and wrapped up, like you're this impenetrable cloak and shield surrounding me. But every woman wants to feel that way about her man, doesn't she? Wants to feel that he can step up and have her back always, but what you're proposing is something that seems to me to go far beyond that. When I read certain parts of your letter, it sent chills all through me, and as much as I hate to admit this to you, it caused me to think that there's a side of you that's as dark as the rest of you is light and that's a side of you that I don't think I want to know or even contemplate its existence.

Look, I'm not trying to climb up on the back of some judgmental horse with you, okay? Like my Momma likes to say often, we all have shit with us. I have days when I feel bitter and ugly and don't want to be bothered, when I'm really not a very likable person. I can be moody and fifty paces past bitchy when I can't get my way, but those things are personality quirks that everybody has, and they may be here one minute and gone the next. This thing in you that you've given me a glimpse of seems dark and dangerous and threatening and I don't like it. I'd really like you to spend some time with this, Michael, please. Please share your thoughts with me and let's see if we can't find a way to reach some solution, okay?

In the meantime, you asked me some specific questions that I'll try to answer here.

First, you asked why I never told anyone. Who could I tell? Aunt Sissy was my mother's only remaining sister. Two older ones had passed some years before. They were close, real close. It would have put a rift in the family that nobody would ever have recovered from. Even at thirteen, I could see the way Aunt Sissy worshipped that monster. She loved him, Michael. And she might have felt some obligation to stand by her man, no matter what, and that would have meant severing ties with her sister, my Mom, forever. I couldn't put that on either one of them.

Then there was my Dad to think about. I don't claim to know a lot about men, but I think I know enough now to be glad I never told. Him, especially. He would never have gotten over it. To consider his only child, the apple of his eye, violated in such a brutal way? Baby, there are some things I found out about my Dad recently that kinda opened my eyes a little bit to the real him as opposed to the way I wanted to see him, but even despite all that, I don't think my father could ever really have been categorized as a violent man, but something like that might have sent him in that direction, and then perhaps all our lives would have been changed forever. And not in a good way either.

And so Baby, once I'd decided I wasn't going to tell my parents, then nobody else got told either. I've thought about maybe going for rape or crisis counseling or something over the years, but I'm not really big on the idea of sitting on some shrink's couch, having him recommend some psychosomatic medication for me that's gonna have me walking around like a zombie, or worse yet, trying to drag out therapy sessions into some ten-year emotional journey that just lines his pockets and bleeds me dry in more ways than one. That's just not for me.

Now, this leads me to some of your next questions. I don't know whether I'm up to telling at some point or not. I kinda feel like I want to. You know, I never really got a chance to talk to you about this, because so much has happened between us in such a short time. I got that letter from you telling me about you being married and I misunderstood and you know the rest from there, but the day you called me when my mother refused your call, I was in so much pain. I can't even begin to describe to you how much pain I was feeling. Michael, I even had thoughts of hurting myself to make the pain just stop. I think it started right after I told you about the rape. It was like some dam broke loose inside me and everything I had been trying so hard to keep in check for years and years just came pouring out.

I think I want to confront this in some way, but I know I'm going to have to go slow with it, because it hurts too much to try to handle all at once. You're asking some hard questions, Baby. Do I want to face it, work through my pain and put it behind me, or do I want to have the wrong righted? I don't know. One side of me wants to have the wrong righted, in a court of law, where I get to see him pay for the way he hurt me, but that would mean telling my mother after all these years, and I know that would hurt her. Things aren't quite right between us at this time, and that would only make it worse, I think. Just don't know. Maybe little by little, as we talk about it, we can figure it out together, okay? But for right now, I don't have any solid answers for you.

Okay Michael, I'm gonna go now. I feel sad and feel like crying. I guess things are starting to surface, and the energy I got from you in your letter isn't helping. I know you talked about some other things in your letter, but I guess I'll cover them another time. I love you. Talk to you later.

Audria

twenty-eight
Motivation

Day 4,795 of his bid. Michael was counting again. It's something he had gotten used to doing over the years, recognizing the number of days he was up to. Time didn't mean the same thing for the incarcerated that it did for people on the outside, he recognized that, but ever since Audria had come into his life, he had started feeling a restlessness he had never really felt before.

It wasn't like he lacked motivation. If nothing else, the greedy bastards who masterminded the prison industry had grown adept at recognizing it was to their benefit to provide proper motivation and incentives to inmates. The majority of the prison population had options. Limited yeah, but still options. Most were forced to work for mere pennies per hour at the same types of jobs that skilled laborers, union and non-union alike on the outside, were paid $20 and $30 to handle. But they had the opportunity to learn and become accomplished in select areas and at various industries. Options were available to them to seek higher education, whether academically or vocationally, and there were workshops and other courses that provided them with ongoing training on how to successfully reintegrate into society when that time came.

In his thirteen years, he had taken advantage of as much of it as he could handle, challenging himself and expanding his mind beyond the limitations of his surroundings. Some brothers would occasionally seek him out, wanting advice on this thing or the next, and he never turned them away. But for the most part, he rolled alone. It wasn't that he didn't like people, but he had lived long enough to recognize the true nature of people. They were basically selfish to the core, wanting whatever they wanted, and if you happened to be standing in their way, then you could kiss your ass goodbye 'cuz they would go through you to get at whatever their pot of gold was. Sometimes they recognized they were going through you, and would make a conscious choice to keep coming, but other times, they would go through you anyway, not even thinking about it, 'cuz you happened to be in the wrong place at the wrong time. When you recognized this very basic behavior in people, it made you want to stay out of their way as much as possible.

For some reason, he didn't feel that way with Audria. The woman made him feel things he had never felt before. Without realizing it, she challenged him in ways he had never considered before to really think about who he was, and more and more here lately, what he wanted to do with his life when he walked free. He didn't think he was a bad person. Matter of fact, he had worked hard over the years to transform himself into the kind of man who he could be proud of, who *anybody* could be proud of, but still, he found himself wanting to be a better man for her.

Although he had some things in mind, angles he could pursue on the outside, he hadn't really spent a whole lot of time thinking about that, but now he wanted to. He wanted to have a solid plan that would think not just to his own future, but to theirs. He loved New York, it was his home, but outside of his son who he loved sometimes more than life itself, it wasn't like he had anything keeping him there. His mother was gone now. He knew he didn't have to go back to New York if he chose not to, but he wasn't trying to make any assumptions about building a future with Audria either. He knew the way society thought about inmates. They viewed them as liars and manipulators whose grand design was to set themselves up with a place to live and some woman to ride when they finished their bid. This was not the way he wanted his woman to perceive him. He knew it would take a lot of work, and wind up maybe being more of a struggle than doing time, but his motivation was a woman that had captured his heart.

Michael knew Audria probably wouldn't understand the way he thought about this, but it wasn't for her to understand. That's just the way it was. He had already decided that he would do anything for her. *Anything.* Including giving his life or taking one.

twenty-nine
Whatchu Know

"Hello?"

"Yeah."

"Who is this?"

"Look chile, don't play games wid' me. I know you know good 'n damn well who this is 'cuz you looking at that there caller i.d. you got on your phone. You know who this is."

Angela cleared her throat to hide her discomfort. "Yes, Miss Viola."

"And you can drop the Miss Viola crap. This ain't a social call inviting you to tea. This is one woman talkin' to another."

Angela looked at the phone like she was imagining the conversation. She didn't trust her mouth to respond, so she kept quiet.

"You prob'ly one of the only friends Audria got that seem to have something other than hot air between your ears, so you was the obvious choice to call."

"Yes?" Angela said tentatively. "Is there something I can help you with?"

"Yeah there's something you can help me with," the too-harsh, raspy voice shot back at her before she could barely finish her sentence. "You can start by tellin' me whatchu know 'bout this jailbird my daughter done got mixed up with."

So, that lil' sneak Audria had been hiding stuff. She hadn't said nothing to her nor Vanessa about her mother finding out. And from the sounds of things, Angela knew Miss Viola wasn't none too happy about her daughter's choice in men. She didn't know what to say.

"Uh, Miss... I mean, Viola, look Audria's my best friend. I don't really feel comfortable talking..."

The woman cut her off. "I could give a rat's dirty ass whether you're comfortable or not. I ain't asking you to tell me nuthin' I ain't gon' find out on my own in time, but I'm not tryin' to wait 'til my daughter gets dragged off to some white padded room over to St. E's 'cuz she done lost her mind over some Casanova in the can." Angela heard a quick exhalation of breath on the other end of the line, then the woman continued. "Look, for whatever reason, Audria done decided she's some expert on people, including jailbirds, and her mind's made up that I'se the enemy jus' 'cuz I don't happen to cotton to snakes. So, my question still stands. Whatchu know?"

Angela could tell there was no getting around the question or this conversation. She might as well come clean with the little she knew. She didn't feel right talking about her friend like this behind her back, whether it was to her momma or not, but she had spent enough time around both Audria and Viola over the years to understand where the phrase 'like mother like daughter' came from. They were like peas in a pod. When either one of them decided they wanted something, the word 'no' was banished from their vocabulary.

She started talking.

"I know his name is Michael Strong and he's in a federal penitentiary in Pittsburgh."

"Which one?" Viola barked at her.

"I think the name's Blasenburg."

"Alright, go 'head. What else?"

"He's been in there for a really long time."

"What's a long time? Two years? Four years? Six years?"

Angela felt awful telling Audria's business like this. "Thirteen years," she mumbled.

"Gal, speak the hell up. Whatchu say?" Viola barked again.

"I said he's been in there for thirteen years," Angela huffed back.

"THIRTEEN damn years? What the hell he do, murder somebody?"

Angela pulled the phone away from her ear as Viola's raspy voice screeched in her ear. She waited for the woman to calm down, then told her the rest of what she knew based on the little Audria had shared with her and Vanessa.

"How long they been knowing each other?" Viola wasn't about to let up on her Gestapo grilling.

"Maybe like four or five months? Something like that," Angela answered. There was a palpable silence on the line. But just when she was about to ask whether Viola was still there, she heard a sniff and a half snort and the grilling began again.

"You tryna tell me Audria only been knowin' this man for four damn months and he already hurtin' her?"

Angela looked at the phone again, like she was hearing things.

"What? What are you talking about?"

Viola bellowed into the phone at her. "Look lil' gal, don't make me have to drive over to where you is. I know where you live. Now, stop playing games and tell me whatchu know 'bout this jailbird hurtin' my baby. People don't just wake up one morning and decide to get in their bathtub with all their clothes on, turn the showerhead on full blast and start screaming like the grim reaper hisself 'bout to bust down their door."

"Miss Viola, I don't know what you talking about. Audria's been happy with Michael. I mean, I'm not crazy about her hooking up with somebody in prison either, especially since he got four more years to go..."

There were all these choking, hiccupping noises on the phone in short starts and stops, and Angela couldn't help but think about Tyler Perry's crazy Madea. That's just what Viola sounded like right now, and she found herself wishing for a speedy end to this conversation before the woman keeled over with a coronary. The choked disbelieving voice bawled at her. "Four more wha--? Four more, WHAT? You tryin' to tell me that negro still got four more years to go on his sentence? And he talking to *my* daughter?"

Angela just hung her head even over the phone and said a quiet "Yes Ma'am" when she thought Viola had calmed down enough to hear her.

"Somebody got to talk some sense into that chile."

"Miss Viola, Audria's a grown woman and..."

The screeching started up in her ear again and Angela could have kicked herself for daring to open her mouth.

"Don't you tell me my daughter is a grown woman. I know good and damn well she grown, but she ain't nevah too grown for me to put my foot up her ass when she actin' the fool. She must done bumped her fool head if she think I done mothered her for thirty-nine damn years to have her throw her life away over some jailbird..."

Angela pulled the phone away from her ear, knowing the pattern. She could probably set it down, go make herself some coffee with cream and sugar, come back, and Miss Viola would just be getting wound up. She was sorry she had even answered the phone to begin with. She suffered through the tirade, waiting for Viola to remember she was still on the line. Eventually the woman calmed down.

"Angela, you still there?"

"Yes Viola."

"Sorry for going on so, but you done got my blood pressure up with all this. You go on, hear?"

"Yes Viola."

Angela was just about to put the phone down, when she heard more squawking that sounded suspiciously like her name being called again. She put the receiver back to her ear. "Miss Viola, you said something else?"

"Yes Chile, I got one more question for you."

"What's that?" Angela asked her.

"You sure Audria ain't said nothing to you 'bout that man hurtin' her in some kinda way?"

"No, Miss Viola, she hasn't said anything like that to me, and you know we tight like that. If he had hurt her, she would've told me something about it by now."

Although Angela was making assurances to Viola, on the inside she found herself wondering if they were really true. She had never known Audria to keep secrets from her before, but it was obvious her friend had decided not to tell her some things. She had hidden the fact that her Mother had found out about her man, and there was also that weird thing Miss Viola had mentioned about Audria being in her bathtub with her clothes on screaming. That didn't even sound like Audria. She knew her friend went through periods of depression from time to time, but what woman didn't? Now, she wasn't sure. This sounded like something a lot more serious than just the occasional blues. Angela couldn't wait to get off the phone so she could call up Vanessa, have them put their heads together and think this thing through. She didn't know how just yet, but they would have to figure out a way to get Audria to open up and tell them *exactly* what the hell was going on.

thirty
Cold Busted

"Shit, I think I done sprained my ankle."

The tinny voice loud-whispered in the darkness of the night. "I'm serious."

"Good fo' your ass," came back a whispered reply. "I tole you not to wear them hella high heels. Now shut the hell up and come on."

Angela jerked Vanessa to her feet from their crouch behind two cars, and shushed her again. "You all loud 'n shit. You almost made us get caught back there."

The two of them had followed their friend all the way from her house in Waldorf to the seediest part of Southwest, in the heart of the industrial warehouse district. Ordinarily, Angela would never do something like this, but the two of them had gone over to Audria's house to confront her about this whole bathtub scene her Momma had let slip. Before they could even get out the car to go ring the doorbell, they had been surprised to see some wigged up slutty-looking woman come tiptoeing out the house. They were all set to jump her to find out who she was sneakin' outta their girl's place, when Angela realized the obvious.

"That's Audie," she said, yanking Vanessa back into the car and ducking down outta sight.

"You lyin'. That ain't Audria," Vanessa argued with her, struggling to sit up.

"I know my girl when I see her," Angela assured her, forcing her head back down as headlights on Audria's Pilot came on, "but I ain't nevah seen her like this."

They looked at each other as the car whipped by in the dark and hollered out simultaneously. "Road trip." And it was on from there.

The woman Angela glimpsed coming out of Audria's house was sporting a platinum colored shoulder-length wig and was wearing a red and brown leopard-print cat suit that showed off her *entire* figure, big butt and all. She didn't even know Audria owned something like that, and she had rifled through her friend's closet often enough looking for cute shit to borrow, that she would've seen that had it been in there. Looks like she had been right. Audria was keeping stuff from them, so it was time to find out just what in the hell was going on.

Vanessa suddenly grabbed her arm, stopping her in her tracks. "Is that two men humping on each other 'gainst that truck?"

Angela looked in the direction where Vanessa was pointing, then turned her head quickly as the two men glanced over at them. She grabbed Miss Nosy's arm and yanked her in the direction of the narrow doorway that Audria had just passed through.

"I think she went up here," she whispered, trying to peer upward in the gloomy light. They started up the stairs, but stopped midway when they heard voices on the top landing. After some minutes, they got up the nerve to keep going. As soon as they got to the top step, a big mountain of a man stepped out in front of them.

"Fee's forty to get in. Pay the woman," he barked at them, pointing to some bored-looking stringy blonde behind a glass cage."

Angela pulled out forty dollars and slid it through the tiny money slot in the glass.

The woman inside activated a scratchy sounding mike that whined at them as she started talking. "Thas' forty a piece," she said, sounding more bored than she looked.

Angela nudged Vanessa in her side, but Vanessa's cheap behind wasn't going for it. "Look, all's I got is fifty on me and that's it to last me the weekend. Ain't you got no more cash on you?"

Angela rolled her eyes and dug around in her purse for some more cash, stuffing it through the slot. She didn't know what kinda club this was charging no forty dollars just to party. She hoped they had some good drinks up in this camp.

A minute later, she started having serious doubts about the kind of club they were going in when the no-neck, muscled-up bouncer started riffing off his rules and regulations.

"Cain't bring no guns, knives, razors, bottles, needles, pins, cameras, phones or none a' that otha' shit in heah." She and Vanessa looked across at each other the same time, their eyes widening, and they both mouthed the same thing. "No guns or knives?"

Vanessa started backing up with a scared look on her face. "I ain't goin' in no place where they gotta tell nobody don't bring no guns or knives."

Angela snatched her back and whispered fiercely in her ear. "Stop being a chickenshit. Every club tells people that mess these days. You know how folks be acting crazy. 'Sides, ain't we here for our girl? Now come the hell on."

Five minutes later, after they had endured the feel-up by the bouncer and were ushered through the huge wooden doors, the two of them just stood at the entrance with their mouths hanging open at the scene in front of them.

Vanessa's head kept whipping back and forth from one place to the next, trying to take it all in as quickly as she could. And Angela wasn't doing much better either. They couldn't believe their eyes as they watched people getting pinched, slapped, kicked, stomped on, paddled, beat down, burned, pierced and all kinds of other deviltry.

"People actually *do* this kinda sick shit to theyself? On purpose? *And* they gotta pay to do it?" Vanessa half-whispered at her, her mouth still hanging open in slack-jawed wonder.

"Apparently," Angela whispered back, staring at a man taking what looked like a dump on the humongous, obviously fake titties of a grossly overweight redhead.

She had to make herself snap out of her amazement, and focus on why they had come in here to begin with. She started scanning the room for their friend, and eventually had to snap her fingers in front of Vanessa's face to remind her to get in on the search too. With the two of them looking, they finally spotted her over in a far corner playing around with what looked like about fifty candles on a table. Angela started marching over there.

"Wait, wait," Vanessa grabbed her arm, pulling her back. "You jus' gon' go over there like that? What you gon' say to her?"

Angela shrugged off the restraining arm. "I'ma ask her what in da heck she doin' up in a place like this, then we gon' take her up outta here."

She started to move forward again, but Vanessa grabbed her a second time. "What if she don't wanna go, and what if she get mad 'cuz we here?"

Angela turned on Vanessa, suddenly furious. "You want to do this or not?" she demanded. "Our friend's in trouble and you standin' there worrying about your damn self and worrying 'bout if she gets mad? What's wrong with you? Now, just come the hell on."

In the face of Angela's courage, Vanessa squared her tiny shoulders and marched behind her friend, trying to keep up. She didn't want to miss nothing.

Angela was the first to get there, but when she finally got to the corner, she looked unsure about what to say, and stood there awkwardly. Behind her, Vanessa wanted to just get the confrontation done and over with, so she cleared her throat loudly.

"So what's it gon' be tonight?" Audria asked without turning around, her voice much harsher than the one they were used to.

Angela and Vanessa looked at each other, then Angela spoke up, her voice getting louder with every word. "I guess it's gon' be you telling us what in da hell you doin' up in a place like this."

Audria turned around fast, stunned, her mouth almost to the floor.

Cold-busted like a cheater caught with dick in hand.

thirty-one
Swear To Me

"OHMIGOD. OHMIGOD. OHMIGOD."

That's all she could say, all she kept saying as she looked at Angela and Vanessa's angry faces. And Lawd, they were mad.

"What the hell is this, Audria? This the kinda cruddy shit you do? Just hide a whole other side of your life from us? What da fuck? Who does that shit?"

Angela was in full blown pissed-off mode now, and she started waving her hands around in the air, and getting loud. Vanessa was pissed too, but still trying to eye the action all around the room.

Audria knew she owed them an explanation, but she'd be damned if she would do it up in this place with everybody starting to look over at them.

"I can explain," she began, trying to calm them down and seeing if she could diffuse the situation long enough so they could leave.

In the meantime, one of her scene partners who she had seen a coupla times before came strolling up, calling her Mistress, and asking if they could have a scene.

Vanessa took off one high-heeled shoe, held it above her head, and started threatening him with it. "If you don't get yo' nasty freaky ass away from here, I'ma give you a scene."

The whole thing would have been funny if she wasn't so embarrassed. Audria knew there was only one way to handle this. She took charge of the situation, letting a little bit of her Dom personality show through.

"I refuse to talk about this or anything else right this minute with the two of you acting crazy. You can leave and wait for me outside until I come out, or we have nothing to say to each other, understand?"

She turned her back on them, not because she really wanted to, but because she was shaking on the inside and thought they might see it if she didn't try to hide it. She didn't know how they had found out, how they even came to be here. Hell, this was supposed to be her last night even scene-playing, 'cuz she had gotten Michael's letter and could tell he wasn't pleased with it, so she had decided to stop coming after tonight. She wondered how Angela and Vanessa had even found this place. Damn, she had a whole lot of explaining to do.

Audria took a quick glance over her shoulder and was actually a little surprised to find they had left. She knew how stubborn they were, especially Angela, and was half expecting to find them still standing there glaring at her. She packed up some things that she wanted to take with her, pulled on a floor length coat, *she was damned if she would stand outside talking to her girls in a catsuit*, and headed for the door.

As soon as she got to the bottom of the stairs, Angela was in her face, arms folded, jaw muscles working, all the ghetto in her front and center. "Start talking."

"Can we at least go to my car so I can put down my things?" she asked, still trying to figure out in her head what she was gonna say.

"No," Angela shouted at her, sounding obstinate. "I know you. You're stalling. Just tryin' to buy time to figure out some bullshit to tell us. You gon' tell us the damn truth right here and right now, or this friendship is over, you hear me? O-V-E-R.

Over."

That's when Audria realized this had gone far enough. She couldn't risk losing her best friends over some story she was going to make up to soften things for them, or for her. It was time to own up, whether they were ready for it or not. She would just have to trust in their friendship and hope that they would still be there for her and not feel any differently about her once they knew.

Right there, on the cobbled street and in front of the dank, dirty alleyway, she spilled her heart out to her girls, telling them the most important parts about what she had experienced as a child, and what it had done to her, all about what she was still dealing with as an adult. When she was finished, they were all crying.

"I don't know why I do this," she gestured at the building behind her. "It's like this need I have inside me to see pain, to be around it, and sometimes even to inflict it. I guess I'm just fucked up."

Angela and Vanessa crowded around her, pushing in close, and they both wrapped their arms around her at the same time. "Nah girl, you not fucked up," Angela whispered, stroking the crazy wig she still had on. "You just went through some bad shit, but it's cool. It's gon' be okay."

Audria pulled away from their embrace at that.

"I don't know that it's gon' be okay. I'm still trying to deal with all of this and make sense of it in my head, and to tell you the truth, I don't think I'm doing a real good job with it lately."

"But you here," Vanessa chimed in, interrupting. "You here, Audie. Don't that count for something?"

She looked at them, then they all smiled. As quickly as the smile came though, it vanished from Audria's face.

"Y'all can't tell! You hear me? You can't tell!" She started feeling panicky inside, knowing that sometimes they talked to her mother and some of her other friends, especially Angela. She couldn't risk anybody finding out her secret, most of all Viola.

They crowded in on her again. "We ain't gon' tell nobody, Audria," Angela promised, looking her dead in the eyes.

"Swear to me," she demanded, looking from one to the next. "You gotta swear to me."

"We swear," they promised again, being serious in the moment.

Then the next thing she knew, Vanessa was snatching the wig off her head and hollering. "Girl, where you get this wig. You know I gotta rock this." Then Angela was waving her off. "Nah, you can't have that wig 'fore I get that cat suit Miss Thing got on. I seen it first and I done laid claim to it, so back the hell off."

Audria just smiled at them, feeling solid in their friendship. These were her girlz!

thirty-two
Dreams

The day was all billowy bright white clouds on a backdrop of blue that looked like the azure blue in an artist's painting. The sun was a big ball of brilliant yellowish orange flame overhead that kissed the face and warmed the skin, making it feel like slowly melting chocolate.

She had on a pale yellow cotton dress with diamond patterned white lace panels decorating the front. Her hair was pulled back into a single ponytail with a bright yellow bobble, the front a little frayed because of her play. She was barefoot and sitting in the dirt holding a brown-skinned doll that looked a little rough around the edges, like it had seen better days. There was a look of concentration in her eyes and her tongue would occasionally dart out of her mouth as she worked at the painfully straight, coarse, synthetic hair of her doll baby, twisting it this way and that into various styles as new inspiration struck.

A gruffly deep voice called to her and she reluctantly turned her head away from her child's work to look over to the wooden porch where a huge mountain of a man sat rocking in an ancient, time scratched rocker. Goose pimples ran up and down the pretty brown skin of her arms as she walked to him, to see what he needed.

"Get me some lemonade." She turns to go into the house. The giant rises and follows close behind, lemonade the last thing on his mind.

Blackness.

Hot foul breath on her face. The uncomfortable prickle of facial hear scraping, scratching against brown skin – arms, chest, neck, stomach. Giant hands on tiny body. Reaching, touching, squeezing, grabbing. She feels small, tiny, like the little boy Jack in *Jack and the Beanstalk*, only smaller and tinier, and this giant is ten times the size of the giant in Jack and the Beanstalk.

She twists this way. Doesn't work. Twists the other way. Doesn't work either. Escape. Escape. Got to get away. Got to run. Got to fly. Got to get away from here. Not happening. Not happening. Don't want this. Don't want this. Touching me. Touching me. Not right. Not right.

She pushes tiny hands against rock, against giant muscle, trying to get away. Fighting to breathe, fighting to think, fighting not to think, fighting not to breathe. Fight. Fight. Struggle. Struggle. Her tiny hand touches stiffness, hardness, male. The giant cries out, a loud, harsh, guttural growl that grows a tongue and learns to speak in an instant. It tells her the giant has become a demon. The demon's name is LUST and it has one purpose. To consume. To take. To own. To own. To destroy. The demon must have this tiny thing, must consume it. It wants her.

Blackness.

Calloused fingers scrape soft skin, drags panties away from tiny bottom. Nails scrape undeveloped thighs. Smells. Stinking. Sweat. Meaty. Foul. Tiny legs roughly spread apart. Bottom against cold wooden floor. Splinters. Thrusting. Thrusting. Thrusting. Ripping. Tearing. Scraping. Scratching. Bleeding. Groaning. Muttering.

Growls. Grunts. Growls. Screams. Screams. Screams. Tiny person. Tiny. Tiny. Tiny.

Blackness.

Michael sat up fast, breathing hard, hands out seeking purchase, seeking balance, seeking, seeking. *What the hell?* He blinked once, twice, looked around, trying to get his bearings. He was drenched in cold sweat, could feel it cool and clammy on his skin – his chest, his arms, running down his back. *What the hell?*

He swung muscled legs off the cot and sat up, bracing his arms against the side of the bed. He could still feel his heart slamming around in his chest from the dream. Hell, if that was a dream, he would be going home tomorrow. That was a nightmare if there ever was one.

Audria.

Nobody had to tell him what had just happened. He knew with surety, without even needing to examine the images still flitting around in his head, that he had somehow received a telepathic glimpse into her past, to witness her violation.

He didn't understand what was happening between them. It was good. Sweet. Or intense like she had called it. But this? This was about a thousand steps past intense. Michael couldn't remember the last dream he'd had, let alone a nightmare, so he recognized how unusual this thing was.

He thought about the huge fleshy face, those lustful, black beady eyes he had seen on her giant. He felt like he could pick the man out of a crowded stadium, the image was that fresh and that imprinted on his mind. He wanted to block the images out but he kept thinking about those hands on her skin, that dirty mouth kissing her flesh, hard male member soiling her, damaging her, ruining her, taking what was his.

Damn, his babygirl. She had said yes to him. *Yes Michael, I'm yours. I'm your woman.* He had to protect her. He felt like she tried to be strong, tried to pretend, for his benefit, that she was stronger than she really was, but he thought maybe she was more fragile than she wanted to admit. He started to feel a panicky feeling inside him, something strange and disquieting. What if something happened to her before he could finish his bid and get to her to offer her all of him? He couldn't stand thinking about not being able to be everything to her in the way she needed him to be. He knew what he had just written to her in one of his last letters, about understanding the limitations in his present position, but this was exactly why he kept most of them other women at a distance in the past. He didn't want to commit to somebody and then feel like less than a man 'cuz he couldn't *do* his job as a man. He knew this would keep gnawing at him.

Michael stood up, popped his neck muscles a couple times, then dropped to the floor as quick as a cat. He was a big man, but over the years he had heard more than a few people express surprise at how fast he moved. Ignoring his cellie's loud snoring, he began a ritual he sometimes used to calm himself – thumb and forefinger pushups. He didn't even bother counting anymore. The last time he had counted was over five years before and back then, he could do 250 easy without breaking a sweat.

Every time his body dipped low, with the standard military rotating drag he had learned from a soldier years before, he flashed on the mental picture of Audria's monster. He didn't know how, but he'd be damned if that old goat was going to keep breathing air on the same planet as his babygirl. Even if he had to make a connection on the outside to handle that, then that's what he'd do. He loved her too much not to do everything in his power to right this wrong for her. She'd just have to understand, wouldn't she? There were some things a man could live with and some things he couldn't. This was one he couldn't live with.

* * * * * *

Daddy?

Audria didn't know whether she was asleep or awake. She felt strange, like she was in a fugue state, moving in and out of a dream world one moment and the real world the next. She knew she had gone to bed, but she remembered getting up and walking outside and then everything changed.

She was back in D.C. at their house in Northeast, sitting on the hood of her daddy's old '56 Chevy junker out back, swinging her feet and letting the sun's rays beat down on her skin. She ignored her Momma's holler for her for the umpteenth time and peeked past the side gate for the umpteenth and one, checking to see whether he was coming. Her daddy had promised to take her down the street to the SugarPack Ice-cream Shack for a cone of rum raisin ice-cream, her favorite. What was keeping him?

Audria looked through the holes in the mottled gate again and jumped down off the rusted hood of the car, smiling at the *bump-thump* sound it made as the dent from her bottom disappeared. There he was. Her daddy.

She started to run to him, but stopped suddenly, her feet skidding slightly on the dirt underfoot. Something seemed wrong about him. He looked different, older like. Like he was her daddy, but wasn't really her daddy. He was still fine though, her daddy.

Daddy? She called out to him, her voice a question, and started walking to the gate again. When she got there, she made to open it up to give him a hug, but his hand held it closed.

"Stay there, Babygirl. You can't come over here right now."

Audria tried to catch a glimpse of his face through the rotting fence boards, but couldn't see all of him the way she wanted. "How come I can't come over there, Daddy? We not going for ice-cream now?"

She almost felt the smile he sent her from the other side of the fence. "It's not time yet."

Audria was all set to ask him just when it would be time, when his strong, beautiful voice spoke to her again.

"Aud, listen now. I got some things to tell you."

"What things, Daddy? Whatchu got to tell me?"

"I want to tell you about love, Audie."

"What about love, Daddy?"

"Well, Babygirl, sometimes people get confused in their mind about what they feel. They think it's love that makes them do things, sometimes even bad things. But guess what?"

"What Daddy?"

"Love is kind, Audie. It doesn't hurt. It doesn't feel anger. It doesn't feel fear. It doesn't feel jealousy. It doesn't make us suffer. It's not selfish. It's patient and it's pure and it lasts forever. You understand?"

"I think so."

"So Babygirl, when somebody you love starts talking about hurting or wanting to hurt somebody else for you, that's not love. That's..."

His voice faded down to a whisper and Audria tried again to catch a glimpse of his face through the fence.

"That's what, Daddy? Tell me." She caught a quick glimpse of his face, could see his lips moving, but she couldn't hear the words.

"I can't hear you, Daddy. Whatchu tryin' to tell me? Say it again, please. Say it again."

She kept trying to look through the fence posts to see him, but now even his image seemed blurry and fading.

"Daddy, don't go yet, please? Please tell me the rest. Say it again. Say it again. Say it again."

Audria bolted up straight as a board in the bed, breathing fast, the words 'Say it again' on her lips and loudly echoing in the room. Her skin felt clammy but hot, fevered, like she was coming down with something. She reached across to the nightstand for the glass of water she kept there and took a long swallow.

She knew she dreamed often. She had always had a very active imagination and most of her dreams were in color, but in the ten years since he had passed, she had never had a dream of her father that she could remember. Never. And now this one.

She could still see clearly that first vision of his face she had gotten through the boards of the wooden fence. She still felt warmed by the smile she had heard in his voice. Still remembered him talking to her about love. Had her father come back from across time and from beyond death to give her some important message or a warning about something he could see?

Audria couldn't help but think about Michael and about his last disturbing letter. Was this what her father was warning her about? God, this was so frustrating. She so wished she could talk to Michael, hear from him about what he was feeling and where his head was with so many things. She didn't know why but she got the feeling he wasn't in a good place mentally, like he was maybe having thoughts and feeling things that were disturbing him, but for some reason, he would hide those things from her. She didn't like to think there was anything he would ever hide from her. She swung her legs off the side of the bed and got up. Grabbing her robe from off a nearby hook, she headed for the living room. She didn't want to over think this and try to talk herself out of what she felt she needed to do right now before any more time passed. Audria grabbed a pen and some paper and began to write.

Sun. 9/2 - 2:01 a.m.

Hi Michael,

It's late, Baby. I just woke from a very strange dream and I had to share this with you. I've talked to you about my Dad. Think I mentioned to you that he passed ten years ago. As a matter of fact, next month October 10th will make it exactly eleven years since he left us. Michael, I've NEVER dreamed about my daddy, at least no dream that I can remember, so this was a first. It was such a disturbing experience. Nice in a way, because it was so vivid and made me feel like he was still here and I was talking to him as though he had never left, you know? But I guess the most disturbing part for me is why now. Why would I have this experience now?

Do you want to know what my Daddy talked to me about in my dream? He talked to me about love. Some of the things he said to me reminded me of this scripture in the Bible. I think it's in Corinthians, maybe 1st Corinthians, something like the 13th or 14th chapter? I can't remember exactly right now, but it's a scripture that talks about what love is. That's how my Daddy talked, like he wanted to remind me what love is. But he also talked to me about what love isn't. He talked about it not being fear, jealousy, anger, selfishness. But Michael, what he said that has stayed with me the most is that when somebody you love starts talking about hurting or wanting to hurt somebody for you, then that's not love. I woke up before he could tell me what it was, and you were the first person I thought about soon as I woke up.

Baby, I know that as I'm writing this, you haven't yet gotten the letter I wrote you on Friday, but I have to say this now anyway. I kinda sorta know but kinda sorta don't what sharing my violation with you has done. I don't think it's put you in a good place, and just going on some of what you said to me in your last letter, it's made this ugly side of you surface. Michael, I don't like it. I love you and I know you love me, and I know it hurts you when you think about what happened to me, because you have such a strong need to protect me, but although my Dad didn't finish his sentence in my dream, I agree with him. I don't think love should make us hurt or want to hurt anybody. I don't know if my daddy came specifically to try to give me a message or some kind of warning about you, but I'm sharing this with you, so that if you're thinking about doing something for me, just because of how my uncle hurt me, please stop.

I love you too much to want to lose you before we've barely started our journey together, okay? Please, Michael. Set it

---

down for me. Put away whatever it is you're feeling and think to our love, please. I just had to say that to you, Baby. I'm going to go back to bed now. I hope you're okay.

Loving you,
Your Babygirl,
Audria

thirty-three
What's Your Name?

"Queen Audria, de Pretty Lady who wants and wants and wants. Come in, come in, Daughta."

Audria stepped into the fascinating space and instantly felt transported to what seemed like a different country. She had never been around such a concentrated grouping of Afrocentricity in her life. Everywhere she looked, there were symbols of the Islands, Mother Africa and Egyptian culture. There were large, small and medium-sized masks on every wall, bold paintings of the human form, male and female, etched on canvas and what looked like ancient tapestries hanging overhead. Earthy face and figure sculptures made out of clay, bronze, wood and ivory leaned against or hung on man height, obelisk-shaped columns.

There were beads and drums covered in animal hides, decorative pillows, draperies and woven mats in soothing colors of rich browns, grays, black and burnt orange. On wooden tables and shelves, there was piece after unique piece of African pottery that Audria could see had been hand carved lovingly by masters and mistresses of the craft. Seascapes that featured the aqua blue waters of the Caribbean and white sandy beaches that seemed to stretch on for miles. Deep varnished coconut shells, beaded cha chas, mud dolls and straw figurines added to the mix. There were Egyptian glyphs, ankhs and hollowed out bronzed masks featuring the somber, slant-eyed stares of Tutankhamen and Isis.

The place smelled musky, like incense burned here twenty-four seven, and as Audria looked around, she could see the tell-tale signs, smoke rising slowly in lazy patterns all around the room.

"Oh, it's so warm here," she breathed deeply, inhaling the headiness of scents she had never smelled before. "What's that you're burning? What kind of incense is it?"

"Thas' somet'ing called Nag Champa. Is Indian. You like it?"

"Love it," Audria breathed in again, feeling a little out of her element. She could hardly believe she was here. She had been sitting home, enjoying a lazy days Sunday, giving herself a pedicure and thinking about her man, when the phone rang. She raced for it, wanting it to be him, although she knew they had just spoken two days before.

"Hello?" she answered, hope the wind beneath her voice.

"This is Nadira Zawadi. Is this Queen Audria?"

Audria smiled and said yes.

They talked briefly, moved past minor acquaintanceship formalities, then Nadira asked. "So you said you *wanted* to talk to me, get to know me, right?"

"Yes," Audria answered.

"Well, how 'bout we start off wid' gettin' to know Queen Audria? You cool wid' dat?"

"I... I guess so," Audria said, fanning at the royal purple nail polish she had just applied to her toes.

"What yo' doin'?" the lilting voice came at her.

"Uh nothing, not really. I just finished painting my toes, but I'm not really doing anything."

"Well, is time for you to do somet'ing. Come an' see me now."

Audria almost choked on hastily swallowed saliva. "Now? Like right now?"

"Daughta, you neva' heard de sayin' dat dere's no time like de present?"

"O-kay," Audria said, feeling strange as she agreed. She had expected them to maybe talk on the phone for a while before being invited to get together. She listened as Nadira gave the directions to her place, a Gothic Revivalist Brownstone a block and a half from the Heart & Soul II Restaurant. Now here she was, actually standing in Nadira's living room.

The woman reached for her hand and Audria felt a shiver of something race through her.

"A little somet'ing I do wid' people in my space for de first time," Nadira lilted. "Come." She drew Audria forward and pulled her down where they sat together on a tightly-woven vee-patterned straw mat, huge brown comfy cushions at their backs. The woman lit a fresh stick of incense, waved it in the air in wide arcing circles over and around Audria's head and body, then held the incense stick in both hands, bowing her head. Audria could see her lips murmuring. She didn't have a clue what to do or if to say something, so she sat quietly, eyes cast down. Some moments later, she felt Nadira squeeze her arm gently letting her know that she had finished whatever ritual she had just performed.

Audria felt uncomfortable. "What was all that about?" she asked.

Nadira looked at her, eyes direct and somehow challenging. "A lot of people come to me fo' answers and advice to t'ings in they life. I ain't no doctor -- witch, bush or otha' wise, an' I don't have any answers 'dat you or de nex' person don't already have, but people come anyway. Thas' a lot of energy, all kinds, to have in yo' space. Some of it is good, but some of it is bad, na'?" She said this like she was asking Audria a question. "I pray to God and to my ancestors to help me absorb the good energy and to make the bad energy leave wid' whoever bring it. You undastan'?"

Audria nodded, cleared her throat softly, then tried to think of where to begin. Nadira solved that problem for her.

"Queen Audria, I know you in a hurry hurry like mos' everybody who come see me here, but your time and my time is two dif'rent t'ings."

Audria's eyes widened and she looked at the woman with surprise in her eyes. "You sound so much like my man," she said softly, remembering how Michael was always talking about going slow.

"I do t'ings dif'rent, so forget about whatevah you t'ink you want and need to tell me, and whatevah problem you t'ink I can help you wid. Open yo' mind, Daughta, hear me?"

Audria nodded.

Tilting her head slightly, Nadira reached for Audria again. "Gimme your hands, palms face up."

Audria stretched her hands out and tried to relax as the woman's soft yet firm grip clasped both her wrists. "Are you going to read my palms or something?"

Nadira laughed, a tinkling bell-like sound that evoked images in Audria's head of swaying palm trees. "Or somet'ing," Nadira answered her, and began tracing a graceful finger back and forth across the life lines in Audria's palms. She did that for a few moments then released Audria's hands and laughed again, a teasing note in her voice.

"An' you say you not strong."

Audria looked up at her, confused. None of this mess made the least bit of sense to her, but she was trying to be patient.

Nadira stood up suddenly, the long off-white caftan she had on billowing around her tiny feet. "You want somet'ing to drink, Audria?"

"Do you have any tea?" Audria asked.

"Cold or hot?"

"Hot, if it's not too much trouble?" Audria answered.

She waited, listening to what sounded like the music of waves and wind chimes coming from a back room. Nadira came back with two cups of tea, something slightly spicy and cinnamony, that they drank in silence.

It was strange to Audria to sit in another person's presence for so long without saying a single thing. She didn't think she could remember any other time she had been silent for so long in somebody else's company. She felt awkward but was trying to go with the flow, because something told her Nadira could help her in a way she couldn't yet absorb.

Out of the quiet, Nadira suddenly spoke. "What you know 'bout history, Queen?"

"History?" Audria replied, feeling confused. "What kind of history?"

Nadira looked like she was contemplating that for a minute, then spoke softly. "De only history dat should matta' to you and me, Daughta. De history of our people."

"I guess I know a little bit," Audria said reflectively.

"Okay, let's talk 'bout history fo' a little while. Ah gon' ask you some questions to make a point. Jus' answer what you know and tell me when you don't know somet'ing, yes?"

Audria nodded again, playing along.

"You read the bible?"

"Sometimes I do," Audria frowned, thinking it strange that she had just mentioned the bible to Michael in her letter to him in the wee hours of the morning.

"What you t'ink was the significance of all dem chapters, verse afta' verse afta' verse in Exodus, Numbahs an' de Chronicles givin' de names of dis person and dat person and talkin' 'bout they lineage?"

She thought about it for a moment. "Well, maybe to show how each generation was connected to the other and to keep track of the line. Like you said, the lineage."

Nadira nodded at her. "So why is dat important you t'ink? To name names and to know lineage?"

"Your name is who you are. It says a lot about you, I would think, right?" Audria asked.

A slight frown appeared on Nadira's face, like she wasn't used to people asking her questions. Audria supposed the woman did most of the asking. After a beat, the frown disappeared and the questioning continued. "You know what a naming ceremony is?"

"I guess it's what it says. It's a ceremony for naming. I think I read something once about Africans having naming ceremonies for their newborn babies."

Nadira nodded again, then began to share information with Audria about the origins of naming ceremonies. She explained that scholars often argued among themselves as to where the practice originated. Some thought it was embedded in Jewish rituals – the *Brit ha Bat*, a ceremony to name a girl child and the *Brit Milah*, a ceremony to name a boy child. Still others thought it came from time honored traditions in Japan and other Far East countries deeply rooted in the principles of Zen Buddhism. Long before Columbus and his ships discovered the New World, North American Indian tribes were performing sacred ceremonies where tribe elders, in rituals that involved smoking the peace pipe in sweat lodges, conferred a new name on ceremony participants. The only significant difference with Native American naming ceremonies is that names given are earned, so the ceremony is usually performed after the person being named has lived some years, sometimes even into young adulthood, and something significant can be attached to the new name.

Audria was trying her best to be attentive, to absorb all the information Nadira was sharing with her, but it was a lot, and her mind kept straying, wondering what relevance any of this could possibly have for her. The woman continued, talking about the Yoruba tribe in Africa, which some people believe account for the greatest percentage of Africans worldwide and slaves brought through the Middle Passage to the United States. She said that the Yoruba people hold to the belief that without a name, one doesn't exist. A naming ceremony to the Yoruba people is one of their most important celebrations.

" Daughta, all dese religions or peoples basically believe de same t'ing. They t'ink dat a person's name describes dat person's true essence, gives them identity, and connects them to their ancestors. Is a way to give dat person power, you undastan?"

Audria nodded her head.

"Now what you t'ink happens when you take away somebody's name?"

"I guess you take away their power?" Audria asked.

Nadira clapped her on the leg and Audria felt the same jolt as before move through her. Nadira looked at her. "Exactly Queen, exactly." She leaned back folding a leg underneath her easily. "So answer me 'dis then. Why you t'ink the White man went out his way to change de name of every single man, woman an' chile dey ripped away from de Motherland?"

Audria's eyes widened as she considered the implication. "To take away their power, our power," she answered emphatically, wondering why she had never thought about this before.

Nadira was looking at her with a strange light in her eyes. "Lesson numba' one. We coverin' some ground, yes?" She smiled at Audria, a wide embracing smile, and Audria couldn't help smiling back.

"Now, let me tell you a little somet'ing. I believe, and 'dis is only *my* belief, that every African – man, woman and child – should have dem an African name. I happened to have a motha' who understood this and gave me two. They special to me, Queen, special. Maybe one day I gon' share de meaning of dem wid' you, but later for dat. For now, let's start wid' you. Your name isn't African, but 'dat's not for everybody. One day you might take you an African name, but for now, let's talk 'bout de name you have."

Audria pointed a finger at her own chest and giggled. "My name?"

Nadira nodded. "Yes, your name." She reached for another incense stick. "You want to know why I laugh when you tell me you not strong?"

Audria raised her eyebrows questioningly, urging Nadira to tell her.

"Like I tole you before, all Queens stronga' than they t'ink, plus your eyes tell me you strong, an' your life lines tell me you strong. You want to know what else?"

Audria nodded her head again.

"Dat t'ing you been livin' wid' for as long as you have, dat hurt dat make you feel like climbin' out yo' own skin some days, dat t'ing tell me you stronga than you t'ink."

The lingering smile faded from her face, and Audria felt the familiar sting at the back of her throat and tried to swallow it down quickly. She shook her head and looked down.

Nadira reached over and put a finger beneath her chin, raising her head and her eyes to meet her own. "Ask me what else, Queen," she spoke softly, her voice a soothing lilt between them.

"What else?" Audria asked, her voice shaky and unsure.

Nadira released her chin and sat back, her eyes silently commanding Audria to continue looking at her. "Your name, Pretty Lady, is a old English word that means strength and nobility." She laughed as Audria's eyes got wide hearing this. "You don' believe me? Go look it up when you get home."

She leaned forward again. "You stronga' than you know, Daughta. Much, much stronga' than you know."

"Then how come I don't *feel* strong?" Audria asked, feeling frustrated with herself.

"'Cuz you need to release what you holdin' and learn to love yourself," Nadira spoke to her earnestly, almost with an urgency to her voice. "You making de same mistake mos' women make."

"What's that?" Audria questioned her.

"You tryin' to look outside yourself for somebody to give you love when you yourself is de very essence of love."

"I don't understand that," Audria said, feeling even more frustrated now.

"Don' worry. Give it time, Queen Audria. Everyt'ing is undastood in time."

thirty-four
Not My Father

You need to do something. Your son is out of control.

Michael was propped on the wooden back of a chair, feet planted on the seat of it, absentmindedly watching a card game between four other inmates. He had so much going through his mind right now. Earlier, he had received a letter from Audria, which hadn't done a whole helluva lot to improve his spirits. Ever since that vivid nightmare he'd had about her monster, he hadn't felt right. Just felt off his game, anxious, like there was something he should be doing that he was missing. Although he kept thinking about her and wanted to write her back, he'd had to put that to the side when he saw the letter from Trina, his son's mother.

He didn't hear from her often, maybe two or three times a year, and it was never good news. He opened the envelope and steeled himself for whatever it would be this time. Trina had never been big on writing and wasn't one to mince words. She didn't disappoint. The letter was less than half a page.

> 09/01
>
> Michael,
>   I know you had been writing to Michael Junior pretty regular because I see the letters when they come and I make sure he gets every one of them. But he ain't heard from you in

> a little while and that ain't like you.   I don't know if
> something's going on with you, but your son need you. He been
> running with some guys from over Spanish Harlem side and been
> staying out all night on the weekends. This past Tuesday, I get
> a call from his school saying he ain't been there in a week and a
> half. I'm scared he going to get in bad trouble soon. Them guys
> he been hanging with run drugs, guns and some more shit.
> Michael, I know you where you at and can't really physically do
> nothing to make Junior do the right thing, but you need to do
> something. Your son is out of control and he not listening to me
> no more. I'm doing my best but it's hard out here. So, I'm
> asking you to please write him and see if you can reach him,
> 'cuz I can't.
>
> Trina

Michael's jaw muscles clenched and unclenched and he found himself grinding his teeth despite being conscious of it. This was one of his biggest frustrations doing time. It didn't matter as much when his son was younger, 'cuz the boy seemed to listen to him, hung on his every word, and actually wrote him letters from time to time that Michael found to be a source of inspiration. In more recent years, though, it was obvious he had started to move in a different direction. The tone of his letters, when he would bother writing, sounded defiant and dismissive, like he didn't think there was anything a man in Michael's position could possibly teach him.

It's not like Michael had some rule book to follow on how to be a father to his son. He didn't have any memory of fathering he could draw from. He never knew his father. When he'd said the man wasn't nothing to him writing Audria, he had meant exactly that. Except for one dog-eared picture his Mother kept in between the pages of her bible of the man, he would never have even known what the man looked like. The bastard had bailed before his mother even got to her third trimester and he never looked back.

Michael knew the life he had led as a young adult wasn't the best. He had made a lot of mistakes and even now, being where he was, many wouldn't consider him a role model, but he tried his best to impart the good things he had learned to his son as often as he could. He wrote to him about the importance of always keeping one's word, of telling the truth, of being a leader and not a follower, being honorable. He spoke to him as plainly as he could about the way life worked, the way people thought and operated, the traps people set for one another, sometimes without even meaning to.

Michael took the time to explain to his flesh and blood that counting the number of women he took to bed didn't make him a man. What did was having the self control and strength of character necessary to commit to one person and be true to what your heart told you about that person.

Obviously, their father and son relationship wasn't a typical one. His son couldn't pick up the phone and call him when there was a problem he needed help working out, and Michael couldn't pick up tickets to the ballgame and have a Sunday outing or day at the park with his boy. Their communication was limited primarily to letters and the occasional phone call.

He knew that society tried to villainize the incarcerated and make everyone think there was nothing there worth salvaging. Those in charge spoke with forked tongues, promoting the idea of rehabilitation so they could secure more and more funding supposedly to benefit inmates and to improve on their quality of life, but it was for nothing more than ensuring the continuation of the cycle. Convicts were thought of as the dregs of society and for young people, this meant one of two things. Either they were viewed as what not to be, what to avoid at all costs, or they were idolized by those younguns too steeped in the ways of violence to recognize there was nothing much to be gained by a life on lockdown.

Unfortunately, most young men living in the inner city thought of prison as some rite of passage. Somehow, they didn't feel like they had truly become a man until they had done some kinda time behind walls. It was fucked up was what it was, but there was nothing Michael felt he could do about it right this minute. What really bugged him was feeling that he had been making progress with his son, and now this letter.

Yeah, he was in prison but he hadn't abandoned the boy. He had stepped up and was constantly trying to step up to do his job as a father, as much as his present circumstances would allow. By no means was he perfect, but he wasn't bailing on his responsibility like his father had done with him. He'd be damned if he would be that kinda man to his boy. He couldn't physically watch over Michael Jr. and make him walk the line, but he could try to talk to him and be nothing but real with him so the boy understood exactly where he was coming from. He pulled out some paper and grabbed a pen.

09/08

Michael,

It's been a minute since my last letter to you. I been building something new and that's where some of my focus has been, but you know how important you are to me, so want you to know I'm always with you, even if you don't hear from me for awhile, alright?

Now Michael, got some things to say. You know I never waste time telling you what's on my mind. You're a man. Young, but a man, so we gon' talk man to man, alright? When I was your age, the only things important to me back then was seeing how much pussy I could get so I could play the notches-in-the-belt game with my boys. I've talked to you about that before, so you know where I stand with that.

The other thing I was into was making money, as much of it as I could. See, people feel that money is status and power in this country, so they do whatever they feel they have to to get it. They lie, cheat, steal and kill to line pockets, and I ain't telling you none of what I ain't done myself to get green. But let me tell you this, money ain't everything, son. Can't take it with you when is your time to go, so what you gon' do? You want to waste the time you got here trying to put notches on your belt and line pockets or you gon' see about doing something to make your life mean something?

Man to man, I ain't perfect, far from it. Made my mistakes, a lot of them, but the one thing I always tell you is that I try never to make the same mistake twice. I been in here for thirteen years, Michael, thirteen. That means you were two when I left you. Except for the pictures I ask your mother to send me of you each year, I haven't seen you in them thirteen years, 'cuz I'm not trying for you to get used to the image of your dad behind nobody's bars.

Because of my love for green, Michael, I made the mistake once that caused me to have to leave you. What did I just say and been saying to you? I try never to make the same mistake twice. Leaving you won't happen again. I'm here for you and gon' be here for you, but you got to do some things too. Kinda like stepping up to the plate. It's your turn to bat, Son. What you gon' do? You gon' choke and strike out or you gon' knock one out the park? I want you to do your thing.

Michael, I can't tell you who to roll with, can't make you choose your friends, but I can tell you that you got to have your own back. Ain't nobody got your back 'cept for the people

---

who love you, like me and your Mother, so think about what you doing. Think hard. Look at your life and decide what's important to you. If you think sex, Benjies, drugs and guns gon' make you a man, then you ain't been listening. And if you ain't been listening, then maybe I'll just lay back and wait 'cuz I'll get to see you after all, but it won't be on the outside, it might just be in here.

That's all I got to say for right now. I want to hear back from you, and you know how I feel about waiting, so get to it, Michael. I trust you to be about your business. Respect yourself and your mother. Look after her and your little brother. You boys are all she got, so do your thing, son, but in all your doing, make sure it's the right thing.

Love,
Your Dad

thirty-five
Take Care of Me

"Michael.

"Oh Michael.

"Michael. I need you so much. So much, Baby."

Audria lay atop cool silken sheets, soft thighs open, bare and exposed. Although the fabric of the sheets was deliciously pliable, cool against her skin, she was anything but cool, twisting and turning, her body writhing with the need she felt.

She moaned softly, an extended whispery murmur in the back of her throat, and squeezed her thighs shut. She wasn't sure how this had started. She had been driving home from work, anxious to see whether there would be a letter from Michael. She hadn't heard from him in longer than usual and found herself feeling irritable and out of sorts.

Out of nowhere, she had a thought of feeling his mouth on hers, and she reached into her purse for his picture. At a stoplight, she lifted it closer, focusing on his face, taking in every detail of his features, his brows, the hard curve of his jaws, the firm tilt of his chin, his eyes, his lips. Then her eyes traveled the length of his body, imagining what it would feel like to lay next to him. By the time she got home, she was overheated beyond even her ability to understand and seeing she had no mail, headed directly for her bedroom.

Audria had never really been into masturbation. Never had a need for it, since she didn't seem to have a problem finding a man. What she had a problem with was finding a *good* man and getting her relationships to last. The last guy she had called boyfriend wound up ignoring her calls for three weeks. When she ran into him going into the post office one morning and confronted him, he embarrassed her by loudly telling her she was too damn needy and he wasn't trying to be all that serious anyway. That had been hard, but because she had this thing about being alone, not too much time had passed before she found another man to take his place. Now, though, thinking about it, she realized this was probably the longest she had ever gone without being with a man. Her last relationship had ended two weeks before Christmas, so that meant she hadn't been with anyone for... damn, Audria couldn't believe it, nine months. She hadn't had sex in nine months? No wonder she was feeling so irritable. And she couldn't really count her trips to the S&M Club. They had filled a need, and were most often erotic, but that didn't take the place of sex. Besides, she hadn't been back since the night Angela and Vanessa had busted her. She was being true to her word and her promise to Michael.

Without really focusing on what she was doing, her fingertips began exploring her body, snaking an invisible yet fiery trail from the base of her neck on down past hardened nipples, her stomach and the gentle mound of partially shaved flesh at the apex of her thighs. Her insides were shaking, mini sensory earthquakes that made her feel like she was on fire, a slow intense burn from the inside out.

She moaned again, deep in her throat, and pressed her thighs together hard, creating a friction wave of pleasure that shot through her, making her feel as though she had just been entered. In her mind, she was focusing on Michael, thinking of him, feeling him, wanting him.

"Mmm, need you so much, Michael. So much."

On the nightstand next to her bed, the phone rang. Audria reached for it, anxious to get rid of whoever was calling and to go back to her sweet fantasy of Michael. "Hello?"

"This call is being placed from a Federal Correctional Institution..."

She bolted upright in the bed, feeling a sense of the surreal. She immediately hit 5 on the keypad and breathed his name. "Michael."

"Audria?"

"Yes, it's me, Baby. God, I need you so much. I'm... I'm feeling so... I'm so hot for you, Baby. Please, I need you so much. Please take care of me." She lay back, putting a hand between her thighs.

There was just silence on the line and Audria sat up again slowly, wondering why he wasn't saying anything.

"Michael, are you there?"

"Yeah, I'm here." He sounded cool and distant though. She didn't understand.

"Did you hear what I said?"

Silence again, then, "Yes, I heard you."

She was having difficulty understanding what was going on. Why had he called her if he wasn't going to talk to her?

"What's wrong, Michael?"

Dead silence.

"Did I say something wrong? Audria pressed. "Should I not tell you the way I'm feeling for you?"

"You gotta go easy, Babygirl. That's a lot to lay on a brotha."

Audria was *really* confused now. "What do you mean?"

Back to the silence again.

"Michael, please talk to me," she pushed, urging him to open up.

After a beat, his voice came at her, tight and far from pleasant. "Woman, what you think that does to me, huh? You think it's easy for me to call you and hear so much need in your voice, and then deal with the reality that there's not a damn thing I can do about it? Do you think that makes me feel like a man, that I can't take care of you the way you need to be taken care of?"

It was like someone dousing her with a bucket of cold water. Audria sat all the way up and swung her legs off the side of the bed. She opened her mouth to say something, but he continued.

"And what's up with these letters you sent me? Remember that bullshit you started back in the beginning with your nothing more nothing less? Didn't I ask you then not to tie my hands with what we got? You doing it again. Audria, you're trying to tell me how to love you and you can't tell somebody how to love you. You just gotta let them love you the way they love you."

It was Audria's turn to be quiet now. She couldn't believe he had actually cussed at her, called what had only been her fear of the relationship and what she had been feeling at the time 'bullshit'. It hurt her, felt like a deep stab to her heart, and she felt anger, bright, white and hot flare through her. She wanted to light him up, but she blinked back the angry tears stinging her eyes.

Michael was on a roll now though, oblivious to how much he was hurting her.

"Do you or do you not want this relationship, Woman? You can't make somebody sign on and then try to dictate to them what that signing on is supposed to mean, just 'cuz they say something or do something that's different from what you expect or different from what you would do."

The tears were streaming down her face now, but he just kept going. "This ain't some soap opera fantasy, a'ight? This is real life and I ain't got time for games. You want me or you don't?"

Audria didn't know what to say to him in the face of that much anger, so she kept silent.

Now there was silence on his end as well, and Audria started feeling a pain deep inside her, something piercing and powerful that simultaneously felt like her own aching, but not quite. She knew she was feeling something from him as well, and tried to put her own emotions aside.

"Michael, I love you. I don't know where all this is coming from, but I love you and I'm here for you. Whatever it is you're feeling, please don't lash out at me, okay? I can handle a lot, but I can't handle you being angry..." She began to cry and momentarily moved the mouthpiece away, not wanting him to hear her tears.

She wanted to remind him that he was the one who had told her he had her and that he wanted to be so much to her, but she choked back all that and tried to think only of him. Somewhere in the back of her mind, she could hear Nadira's lilting accent telling her she was putting too much on her man's shoulders, something she obviously hadn't paid enough attention to.

"I know I've been laying a lot on you, Baby, and I'm sorry. I'm sure things can't be easy for you and I don't need to complicate your life anymore than it already is." She tried to make a smile reach her voice. "I'm your Babygirl, remember? My job is to bring you love and laughter, right? Not complications."

There was still silence on the line and Audria started to worry that the connection had been broken.

"You still there, Michael?"

"Yes, I'm still here."

"Tell me something sweet," she said to him, fighting hard to keep smiling through her tears and trying to keep things light between them. "Tell me something sweet, Baby."

"I love you, Audria."

"Mmm," she murmured, hearing the mechanical voice in the background, cutting in right behind his, and signaling the call was about to end. "Can't get any sweeter than that. That's sweet."

"Nah, you're sweeter," he countered, and she could hear him smile, his first light moment of the call.

"Uh-uh, you're the sweet one," she teased back.

"No, you."

"No, you."

They played with each other like that until the call disconnected. After he was gone, Audria allowed herself a good cry, then got up, washed her face, and went in search of Nadira's phone number. She placed the call and waited. When the woman answered, she didn't waste any time stating her business.

"I need you to help me figure out why I'm so needy."

"Peace to you too, Queen Audria," the lilting voice came back at her, reminding Audria she had forgotten her manners.

"Peace Nadira," she said hurriedly, anxious to get back to her business, but before she could begin again, Nadira beat her to it.

"Need is as need does, Pretty Audria. I gave you your answer already. You jus' not listenin'. An' Audria, *need* an' *want* is de same t'ing. When you undastan' dat you got everyt'ing inside you dat you can want an' *need*, den and only den, you gon' stop feeling so needy needy."

"Here we go again." Audria sighed, rolling her eyes at the phone. Just once she wished she could have a normal conversation with this woman without feeling like she had stepped into the Twilight Zone.

thirty-six
Fly Free

"Daddy, I miss you so much."

Audria sat cross-legged in front of her father's gravestone, her head bowed, speaking to him quietly. This was a yearly ritual she observed on the anniversary of his death. She would come visit him, spending the majority of the day here. She had already cleaned around the plot, picking up fallen leaves and discarding the dead, withered flowers from the year before. She had just finished arranging the bright orange lilies accented with eucalyptus that she had brought for him, said prayers, and was sitting quietly communing with him.

She knew some people thought it strange to spend money on the dead, buying flowers and spending time at a burial site, when it was just a pile of rotting bones in the ground, their souls long gone. Even her mother had stopped coming three years before, saying she was just fine with her memories of the man she'd loved, and didn't need to go to a grave site to bring it all back. Everybody had a different connection to their loved ones, Audria recognized that, but before putting her father in the ground, she had made him a promise that she would never forget him and that she would visit with him in this way every year on the anniversary of his death. She had never missed a year and there had never been a time when she came here that she didn't feel his essence in this place, hovering around her like a protective shield. She always felt him close by and it soothed her like nothing else.

On the drive over to the cemetery, she had already decided in the car that this was the year she would share everything with him.

"Daddy, there's so much I have to tell you," she began, her fingers playing with the miniature leaves of a Shogun Juniper Bonsai tree she had brought for him some years before. Sunlight reflected off the cobalt blue ceramic pot the tree called home and the leaves rustled gently in the breeze. "I'm in love, Daddy. I've met this man named Michael. Michael Strong. Well, it's kinda complicated. We haven't really met yet, like in person, but we're in love, Daddy."

Audria paused, pulling the lilac-colored cape she wore more closely around her to fend off the Autumn chill. "He's in prison, Daddy." She threw her hands up like she could hear her father's objection. "I know, I know, you might think that's not the best thing, but Daddy, he's a good man. He hasn't always been a good man, but people can change, can't they? And he's shown me that he's changed, or at least he's trying to change.

"He's not perfect, Daddy. He's got a temper, and I think he's got some jealousy issues too, and he feels this deep, deep need to protect me, protect what's his, but what man doesn't, right? What's important is that he loves me, Daddy. *He loves me.* I know it. I feel it in a way that I've never felt love from a man before, except maybe from you, Daddy." Audria smiled and brushed back the braids that had fallen over her eyes. She kept talking until she had told her father all about her man, then she reached for the picnic basket she had brought with her. Pulling out half a sandwich and a bottled water, she took some bites, drank some of the water and then poured the rest over the bronzed grave marker.

Her Daddy had always loved her poetry, and each year, Audria brought a brand new piece she would write especially for him. She pulled out the page and read it to him softly, feeling his presence deepen all around her.

Fly free, my Daddy. Fly free.
Soar like wind giving eagles leave to fly.

**Shake from your feathered breast grave's dust
and dance on sun's glow and moon beams.
Send me your love on shooting stars that
race across galaxies and speed through time
just to utter your beautiful, cherished line:
"Let me tell you about love, Aud."
Fly free, my Daddy. Fly free.**

Audria wiped at a tear that had slowly trickled down her face, cleared her throat, and talked some more with her father. Some of her conversation felt like old times with him, reminiscing, almost like she could hear him answering back, laughing and joking with her, teasing.

Some branches rustled nearby and a squirrel shot up a tree, looking back at her querulously as it went, like it wasn't used to interlopers spending this much time in its space. It stared at her, its eyes bold and beady, and Audria felt her stomach turn over, the sandwich she'd eaten before feeling like so much slushy mush. Those beady eyes reminded her that it was time to talk about the thing she had been avoiding for years. She took a deep breath and began.

"Daddy, I need to tell you something that's been with me now for more than double the number of years you've been gone. It's about Uncle Carl."

It was hard for her, but Audria was intent on getting through it. Just from the things Michael had said to her about facing this, as well as what she had learned from Nadira so far, she felt that this was a beginning step to facing her past. She knew her father's physical self couldn't hear her, but she felt that his spirit could and that he would offer her comfort.

She poured out her heart to him, telling him how her uncle had brutalized her, what she had felt, and why she had decided not to tell until now. "I knew what it would do to the family, Daddy, and I didn't want that to happen. Momma and Aunt Sissy were so close, and I couldn't stand the thought of what it might do to them. I didn't want Aunt Sissy to have to choose between her sister and her husband."

Audria took some deep breaths trying to calm herself, and forcing the tears to dry up. "I'm not even sure why I'm telling you all this now, Daddy. Maybe it's because I've met this man and have fallen in love and I feel hopeful like I've never felt before about starting a new life with someone, you know? Really building something with somebody who loves me for real, and that's not just out to see what they can get, I don't know. But I needed to start somewhere as far as facing all this. I already told Michael about it and whether he knows it or not, he's helped me to face up to it."

She twirled a braid through her finger, brushed some dirt off her left shoe and went on. "I'm still scared of it, Daddy. I know Uncle Carl is old now and he can't hurt me anymore, but sometimes he still hurts me in my dreams and in my mind. It's like this thing will just surface at the strangest times and it makes me come undone like nothing else. I want to face it, know I *need* to face it, but I'm afraid of it, you know?"

She went quiet, almost like she thought she would hear her father speak her name and tell her all would be okay, but the place was eerily still. It seemed almost like the wind had decided to blow elsewhere, that the leaves had frozen in time, and the animals were holding their collective breaths. In the silence of the afternoon, Audria heard a single sound at her back, like a ragged inhalation of breath and casually glanced over her shoulder. Her mother was standing there just looking at her.

thirty-seven
Fine Like Strawberry Wine

Audria leapt up to her feet, heart pounding in her chest like it wanted to burst. She wanted to say something but didn't know what to say. Wanted to ask her mother how much she had heard, but couldn't. She must have opened and closed her mouth one... two... three... times, but couldn't get a single, solitary word to come out. She and her mother moved simultaneously, took a step toward each other at the same time, and Audria knew then. It was written all over the woman's face that she had heard all of it.

She tried to speak. "Momma, I... I... I didn't know. I didn't know you were there. Please, I didn't know."

Her mother shook her head violently, like she was having difficulty seeing, then her knees started to buckle. Audria ran to her to prevent her from falling. She helped Viola walk a short way to a nearby bench for visitors and sat her down, instinctively putting an arm around her and sitting close.

She could feel her mother shivering beneath her touch, her whole body shaking, and her lips were moving like she was trying to say something, but no sound was coming out.

"It's okay, Momma. It's okay," Audria comforted her, not knowing what else to say. They sat that way for almost twenty minutes, Audria's arm around the woman, and her mother sitting woodenly, except for the occasional shudder that moved through her.

Eventually, Viola shrugged her shoulders and seemed to gather her emotions about her. She turned to Audria with tears in her eyes. "Audria, *why* didn' you tell us? Why'd you bear so much pain by yourself all these years? Why?" Viola sounded anguished, her voice raspy with feeling.

"I just couldn't, Momma. I couldn't do that to you and to Daddy and to Aunt Sissy. It would've destroyed you, all of you, the family. I didn't want that to happen."

Viola kept shaking her head and began a light pounding on her thigh. "You understand what you done, Audria? This make me feel like some poor excuse for a mother, like I done failed at being a parent, and not jus' a lil' bit neither. You're my only chile, my only chile, and look what you been living with all these years. You right under my nose and I don't know you. Don't know my own daughter."

"Momma, please don't say that. It's not true. You've been nothing but the best mother to me all these years and you *have* tried to get to know me in your own way. I just couldn't bring myself to share this with you." She rubbed her mother lightly on the back. "Sometimes I wanted to tell you, especially after Aunt Sissy passed, but I just thought it would be too painful bringing it all back up, so every time I thought about it, I talked myself out of saying anything until the feeling went away."

Her mother just kept shaking her head, then spoke in a tortured voice, almost like she had just considered something new. "And we sent you down there all them years, kept making you go back over and over and over again. Was it more than once, Audria? Was he messin' wid' you every year you went down there?"

Audria put her arms around her mother again, feeling the closest she had felt to her in a long time. "No Momma, it was just that one time when I was thirteen, and I never went back, remember? I never went back."

Viola looked at her suddenly, eyes going wide. "That time, some months back, that thing in your bathroom. This is what that was about, ain't it? Your man really didn't hurt you, then?"

Audria shook her head. "No Momma, he didn't. That's what I was trying to tell you, but I couldn't really tell you the whole truth. Mommy, he's such a good man. He loves me, and he's the one who's given me the strength to face up to my past."

Viola patted Audria's hand. "And to think I was coming here to fight wid' you again 'bout him. I knew you would be here visiting wid' your daddy and wanted to talk to you in a calm place, wid' your daddy as a witness. I sure nuff didn' expect to get all this."

Audria looked at her mother. "Momma, I can't make you accept Michael. I know the way you feel about him being in prison and all, but he is a good man and he wants the best for me. We love each other. I've never loved anyone the way I love him," Audria confessed, the feeling strong and deep within her.

All of a sudden, it was Viola's turn to do the comforting. She wrapped her arm around her daughter. "We gon' get through this thing, Audria, we is. You me and your... your Michael. Jus' as soon as we get home, we gon' call the police down in Rocky Mount, make a report and get them on the case. We got to..."

Audria eased herself out from under her mother's arm and looked away, over to her father's grave. "Momma, I don't know whether I want to do that or not."

"Whatchu mean?" Viola asked loudly, jumping to her feet. "You cain't be serious. Carl might be ol' and decrepit, Audria, but he gon' be ol' and decrepit in jail, you understand? He ain't getting away wid' molesting my little girl, you hear me?"

Audria stood up and looked her mother dead in the eyes. She spoke slowly because she wanted her mother to understand her completely. "Mother, that's not your decision to make, okay? It's mine. He didn't rape you, he raped me. I'm *trying* my best to deal with all of this, but I can't go at your pace or anybody else's pace, just because you want me to. I need to take my time with this and be sure which way I want to go."

Viola looked at her hard. "So what you saying? That you want to just forget the whole thing and make him think he done got away with it?"

"He didn't get away with nothing, Momma," Audria assured her mother, remembering the tortured voice she had heard on the other end of the line months before, asking her whether she had told. "He's been living with the guilt of what he did to me all these years the same way I've been living with the memory of it."

"Fuck a guilt," Viola shouted, waving her hands and causing a flock of birds to fly out of a nearby tree, startled. She lowered her voice, perhaps suddenly conscious of where she was, but gripped her daughter's arm hard. "Audria, guilt ain't enough of a payback for what he done to you, hear me? He gots to pay and if that mean him seeing the inside of a jail cell the rest of his useless life, then that's what it gotta be."

The two women squared off and Audria found herself getting angry. "See? You're doing it again. You *never* listen," she raised her voice at her mother. "Why do you do that?"

"I ain't doing nothing," Viola said peevishly, but a moment later, she sniffed and nodded her head. "Okay Audria, have it your way. I cain't make you do something you don't want to do. I can only tell you what I think as your mother and leave the rest up to you."

Audria looked at her and smiled. "Thank you," she said, wrapping her arm around her mother and nudging her playfully. "Come on, Momma, come say hey to Daddy."

They walked over to the grave together and Viola looked down at the smiling photo of her husband Audria had brought along with her and propped up against the headstone.

"Daaaammmmmnnnnn, your daddy was foiinnne wasn't he?"

"Fine like strawberry wine," Audria came back, saying the very thing her father would always say when he was alive. She and her Mother fell out, cackling like hens over their family's little inside joke.

As she laughed, Audria felt a gentle breeze sweep up and around them both, and she imagined she could hear her father laughing along with them, as he whispered in her ear. *Everything's going to be just fine, Aud. Just fine.*

* * * * * *

Audria was sitting at her dining room table, tears of happiness streaming down her cheeks. She had just finished reading a letter from her man. She didn't understand how somebody could go for as many years as she had without finding love, *true* love, and then all of a sudden have it in abundance the way she felt like she did now.

After visiting with her Dad, she had followed her mother to her house, let her park, then had treated Viola to dinner at a Japanese steakhouse a few blocks from where they lived. The place was exactly the kind of atmosphere they both needed after the emotional kind of day they'd had. The two of them laughed and joked with each other with an openness that had never been there before. Audria found herself genuinely enjoying her mother's company. Her Mother surprised her by reaching to hug her at the end of the night when Audria dropped her off.

"I know I don't say it nearly enough, Audria, but you know I love you, right?"

Audria nodded. "Yes Momma, I know. I always know, and I love you too."

They hugged again warmly and Audria said goodnight to her, promising to call the next day, and headed for home. The first letter she pulled out of the mailbox was one from Michael.

Fri. 10/5

Peace Babygirl,

Audria, it's been way too long since I had the chance to write you the way I've been wanting to write to you. Feel like I got so much to say and not sure exactly where to begin, so guess I'll begin with the thing that's front and center in my mind right now. Love you, Woman. I been going through some things, feeling some emotions that are new to me. When I told you this was my first time being in love, I wasn't lying to you. It's like you feel this feeling, you know? And it starts getting stronger and stronger as days pass and you know you started out just wanting that, wanting the pureness of it, right? But then all of a sudden, you start feeling all these other things too.

Gotta tell you, I never even thought of myself as a jealous kinda brotha. It's just not something I ever felt before, but when I got that letter from you talking about how you were

---

feeling and you wanting sex and all that, then I called you on the phone and it was more of the same, damn if that didn't make me feel like putting my fist through somebody's wall. I know you probably saying this Nigga's crazy. I mean, I was the one that had just written you this letter talking all big and bad and telling you to handle your business, but Babygirl, you gotta know right here and now, I'm not down for you laying wid' nobody else. I know this is asking you a lot, 'cuz four years is a long time and I understand what you said to me about what you feel, but you know how I'm looking at this thing? If I can do it, you can do it. So we got to be strong for each other with this, alright? I'm not gon' ask you to make me no promise or nothing like that, 'cuz you know how I feel about promises making liars out of people, but I'm just telling you how I feel on this and asking you to let your heart and our love guide you. Alright, chillin' on that. Moving on.

Damn Baby, can't believe it's been over a month since you wrote me this letter, the one I'm looking at right now. Audria, you always make me think with the things you say. It's like a constant challenge to me to reevaluate myself and see how I can be a better man. Sometimes it's hard to face the fact that maybe you ain't as <u>changed</u> as you think you are, you know? Kinda like reality serving you up a backhand that whips you across the jaw and wakes your ass up. Look, guess what I'm trying to say is that you know the things I've shared with you about my past, the kinda man I used to be. Thought I had left that dude behind me back aways, but your letter made me understand that maybe he ain't all the way gone, you know? Wasn't even considering that this need I got to protect you as my woman might make me think about stepping back to that dude again. Got some work to do on myself, Baby. Gotta watch that ol' dead head that's trying to resurrect, 'cuz that ain't nothing but trouble, and I'm not trying to bring you trouble.

Speaking about something else I ain't trying to bring you. I ain't trying to start disrespecting you by feeling I can talk to you any ol' way I want. I know I'm from the streets, and you know the aspect I been around all these years, but even with all that, my Momma taught me to respect women, so I owe you an apology for talking to you the way I did on the phone. I was wound, yeah. Had some things, a lot of things on my mind, yeah. But nothing excuses me talking disrespectfully to my woman, so please forgive that.

Okay, so you asked me to spend some time with this thing. To be honest, the time I need to spend with it ain't nothing that I can share with you. This is work I gotta put in on myself, Baby, to make sure you don't have to worry about this or about me. But I'm gon' say this. You asked me to set it down, to put aside this anger I got over what your uncle did to you. My first reaction to that is 'Nah, she trying to tell me how to love her again,' but Audria, what your pops said to you in your dream is right. Love shouldn't make somebody feel anger.

Yeah, I want to protect you, and I'm gon' do that in every way I know how, but I can't say no to you. You asked me to set this down, so I'm setting it down, for you. I'm not trying to have my woman be afraid of me or think I'm reverting back to that bad boy I told you I left behind. What I do want is for you to know I'm here for you in any way you need me to be for you. If you decide you want to get ol' goat prosecuted, I'm by your side. And if you decide you want to just let it all go now you've talked about it, I'm still by your side. Got you, Babygirl. Not gon' let you fall, alright?

Okay, there's a lot more I want to say, but I'ma fallback right here. One last thing though. It's time, Babygirl. Come see me. On the next page, I'm attaching some information you need to send me in your next letter - drivers' license information etc., cuz I gotta get you cleared through prison administration before you can come, but I want to see you. It's time, Babygirl. So let's do this. We gon' say, tentatively, that you come see me the weekend of November 10th. You can come either the Friday, Saturday or Sunday. On Friday, visiting hours are 8 a.m.-6 p.m. and on Saturday and Sunday, it's from 2 p.m.-8:30 p.m. Weekend days are the busiest, but you decide. Damn, can't wait to see my babygirl, live and in person. Bring some smiles, alright? Okay Audria, talk to you soon.

Love,
Michael

P.S. I'm sending this letter today 'cuz I'm hoping it gets to you on October 10th or before. I know you said October 10th is the anniversary of your dad's death, so you might be feeling a little sad. So I'm on my job, Babygirl, coming to cheer you up a little bit, alright? Loving you.

thirty-eight
Gonna Follow My Heart

Audria was sitting at her computer working on her first novel. She wasn't really sure where she was going with this. She had never really attempted a full length novel before. In the past, she had focused on writing poetry and a few short stories here and there, but for the last few weeks, in between all her letters to Michael and thoughts of him, she had gotten an idea for a book.

It wasn't exactly about her life, but the story shared some similarities with hers. It was about a thirty-something year old woman who was finally facing up to abuses in her past that had caused her to have one failed relationship after the next. In her last letter to Michael, she had even mentioned it to him, explaining that he was the one who had given her just the right kind of encouragement she needed to get started. In most of his letters to her, he would ask her in some way or another, what she was doing to change the things in her life she didn't like, including her job situation.

Audria recognized that she was always going to hate the line of work she was in. Law firms came a dime a dozen in D.C. Some were the multi-state and international conglomerates that had a thousand or more lawyers, and others were mid-sized versions of the same that served as warehouses for Ivy School elitists that by virtue of the money they had laid out for law school, felt they were entitled to the world on a platter. Still others were the smaller boutique law firms that specialized in one area over a myriad of legal specialties. Most often, these firms got by on having a big name personality join the partnership that virtually guaranteed the steady flow of big bucks as long as his or her name was bandied about sufficiently.

As far as staff went, it didn't matter not in the least lil' bit what type of firm you worked at; they were all the same. They were designed to put the majority of the money in the pockets of the greedy partnership and operated on the trickle down effect for everybody else. Unfortunately, staff was at the bottom of the barrel, and really didn't count for much in the overall scheme of the partnership. So at the end of the day, you were lucky if you broke even with the federal government's cost of living increases.

Audria didn't know how some of her coworkers did it, especially the ones with young children. She knew many of them were a paycheck away from being homeless, but her bottom line was a little better than most. She didn't have any kids and, except for her mortgage, her bills were minimal, so she was getting by okay. But that didn't mean she liked the kind of work she did. Some days she felt like a modern version of a handkerchief on the head wearing Beulah on somebody's plantation. She wasn't trying to trip, but she was nobody's slave or fetch-it girl and it was time to start taking steps to move herself away from this kind of treatment.

So, she was working on her novel. It's not like she thought of herself as the next Terry McMillan or Octavia Butler, but she read a lot of books and judging from some of the stuff she saw out there by other African American female authors, she felt she had just as valid a voice as any of them, so she was gon' do exactly what her man had told her to do. She was gon' come with her coming and see where her coming took her.

Michael.

Audria found herself thinking more about him than she had ever thought about anyone else. There were times she still couldn't believe they had found each other. He seemed so positive most of the time, always encouraging her to be the best person she could be, and challenging her to discover who she really was. She didn't understand how he could be and stay as upbeat and optimistic as he seemed to her, especially living where he lived and being surrounded by so much misery, but she was so thankful for him.

It was hard for her to think about what her life had been like before him. Not that she lacked motivation. Her life was pretty full. She was always doing something or going someplace with her girlfriends or her Mom. She worked out as often as she could get her lazy ass motivated enough to do it, and she took the occasional course over at University of Maryland when she felt her mind needed challenging. But something had definitely changed for her since meeting this man. Everything seemed brighter, fresher, the world more alive for her, more vivid and brilliant, and for the first time, she was starting to allow herself to think about building a future, a *real* one, with someone she loved.

That was it exactly. Building a future. All the other men she had been with over the years, had been just that – men she could be with, pass the time with, for as long as that lasted, but she had never really considered having a future with any of them. Now all that had changed. She found herself thinking about living with Michael, waking up with and to him, cooking for him, doing his laundry, having them go grocery shopping together, take drives together. All the mundane things some people would consider boring or commonplace were exactly what she was looking forward to enjoying with him. And judging from what he had shared with her, he felt the same way. She smiled as she thought about one of his recent letters where he talked about wanting to dance with her, something he hadn't done in almost sixteen years. And he wasn't talking about going dancing at a nightclub either. He had written her a very descriptive letter where he talked about just wanting to dance with her for hours in a quiet space. Audria couldn't wait to give him his heart's desire.

And it wasn't just the little things either. Lately, she had found herself sharing things with him she had never felt comfortable sharing with any other man in her life; things like her annual salary, what she had paid for her house, and the overall state of her finances. It wasn't that she was trying to impress him or anything, 'cuz she didn't have all that much to be bragging about to anybody, but she didn't want to hide anything from him either.

Audria knew her mother would have a fit if she could read some of what they shared with each other in their letters, especially from Audria's end. It seemed ever since the love of her life had died, Viola felt one way and one way alone about men – she didn't trust them. Even the ones she had tried bringing around to set up her own daughter with were suspect. She was always in Audria's face going on about making sure she kept this thing private and the other thing private. And like Viola herself loved to say, the apple didn't fall far from the tree. Audria had pretty much always been the same way with the men she dated. Half the time, they didn't know what she did for a living, not really, and most of them never found out where she lived until six months down the road, if either of them could tolerate each other that long. If they didn't have a place of their own or couldn't afford to take her out to restaurants or other venues, she would cut them off. The last thing she was looking for was some brotha who didn't have a pot to piss in trying to move in with her just 'cuz she looked like she had it going on, with her own place and all. She preferred that when a man stepped to her, he had his own and would be bringing to the table just as much as she was, or more.

And it wasn't that she was such a proponent of the feminist movement that she had to have every little thing be equal straight down the middle like some of her girlfriends. Even Angela and her husband Ford, as long as they had been together, were like that. A few years back Audria had been surprised to learn they kept separate bank accounts and even did their taxes separately. When she asked Angela about it, her girlfriend tried shooing her off, but Audria insisted on finding out what was up with that. Eventually, Angela told her that when she met Ford, his credit was jacked and he had over six figures in debt from trying to live large like some buddy of his that played for the Washington Redskins. Angela's thing was that although she loved her husband and everything, she wasn't trying to have him mess up her A-1 credit, so they decided from jump street that they would keep their finances separate. After some years, Ford had gotten his stuff straight, but by then, they had already gotten used to keeping things separate, so they just kept on going the way they had been, not bothering to make any changes.

Audria had always thought she would be the same way if she ever got married, but meeting Michael had changed all that. She knew her man would need her support in many ways when he came home, financially and otherwise, but that knowledge didn't scare her. It wasn't like he was going to just lay around with his hand out while she had to struggle for both of them. He hadn't even said anything specific to her about what his plans were, but he didn't really need to. She knew he would be about his business, and she was fine placing her trust in him to do just that.

And she wasn't deluding herself either. Sometimes she watched those judge shows on t.v. – Judge Mathis, Judge Judy, and Judge Joe Brown, and if you paid attention, it was the general opinion of the courts that convicts were all the same. They met a woman who was hungry for love and looking for it in all the wrong places, preyed on her emotions, and started lining themselves up a nice place to stay when they got out and all the punani in the world they wanted. Most of them used the woman until she got sick and tired of them bleeding her dry, and then hauled ass to greener pastures. Audria knew she wasn't suffering from the ostrich syndrome. She didn't have her head buried in the sand when it came to recognizing how some people were, but her heart and soul told her she had found a man that was an exception to the rule, and she was going to follow her heart all the way.

thirty-nine
In Technicolor

OhGawdOhGawdOhGawdOhGawd.

Audria was here, finally here. She couldn't believe it. In just a few minutes, she would see her man for the first time. She felt like she was about to hyperventilate the way her heart was slamming around in her chest.

This was her first time ever visiting anyone in prison and her emotions were having a field day, scattered here, there, all over the place. One part of her was so anxious to see him, to feel his essence live and in technicolor that she could barely stand it. But another part of her was afraid that seeing him like this, in these surroundings, would maybe reduce him somehow in her eyes, and she didn't want that.

It was Friday morning bright and early. She had taken the day off from work, but had driven up from Maryland the night before so she would be fresh and not all worn out from the drive. Audria had arranged to stay the weekend with her girlfriend Rose who lived in Pittsburgh. They sat up until the wee hours playing catch up, with Audria telling her girl all about the man she had fallen in love with. Rose didn't have to say it. The skepticism in her eyes and the cautioning tone of her voice when she told Audria to watch her back, spoke volumes. Audria understood that's what she would be dealing with from most people, but she wasn't allowing it to faze her.

Wanting to spend the whole day with Michael, Audria woke around seven, waited until Rose left the house for work, and started getting ready. This had been one of the hardest things for her to decide on before leaving on the trip -- what to wear. She wasn't into clothes the way some women were; that was her mother's shtick. If Audria left it up to Viola, her wardrobe would have every designer label in it. Her mother was a clothes horse, always buying her stuff. Half the outfits she bought for her weren't really her style, but she didn't want to hurt her mother's feelings by saying no, so she took the gifts and played mix and match from the things she liked in an attempt to tone down Viola's expensive tastes. Now though, she wanted to look good for her man.

Audria's first thought had been to wear something sexy, kinda provocative, so Michael could see all of what was waiting for him, but then he had sent her the dress code for the facility's visiting room and that changed everything. She guessed it made sense for the prison to require women to dress appropriately. It would be beyond cruel and unusual punishment to tempt the inmates unnecessarily by allowing women to bust up in there wearing some hoochie momma stuff. So she spent some time looking through her closet in an effort to find something nice. She wanted to still offer a hint of the provocative while being tasteful, but needed her outfit to pass muster with the institution's guidelines.

It hadn't been easy, but she finally settled on four separate outfits, in case she decided to visit Michael more than once during the weekend. The outfit she was sporting now was a little risqué, but she thought it was classy enough to get by. She had decided on a baby blue silk chiffon cami gathered below the bust line with drawstring ties and featuring a racy v-neck cut. Over top of that, she had opted for a buttonless sky blue crushed velvet blazer. A Vivienne Tam 'Waterlily' chiffon skirt and a pair of Christian Dior dark blue suede boots rounded out her ensemble. At the last minute, she decided to pin a light pink and blue silk rose in her braids over her right ear. She threw herself a kiss in the mirror on her way out the door and pocketed the extra key Rose had given her so she could let herself back in. Audria knew she looked good for her man. She couldn't wait to see him.

Feeling a hundred paces past intense, she tried to take deep breaths to calm herself as she went through the inspection process at the prison. Michael had already written to her letting her know what to expect. Not only had her braids and purse been searched, but she'd had to consent to a body pat-down as well, and then was guided through a bank of metal detectors. She had to present her drivers license, the visitation form, and sign a release and the visitor's log so it could be checked against Michael's official visiting list. Finally, she was ushered into the visiting room by a bored looking guard, deposited at an empty table with four weathered-looking chairs around it, and told to wait.

Audria looked around nervously, feeling weird and out of her element. There were less than fifteen people in the room excluding the guards and she thought maybe it was because she was here as early as she was. Although excited to see Michael, she felt slightly embarrassed, like the guards posted at various spots around the room were making judgments of her without even knowing her story. She found herself thinking that she didn't want to be thought of as some convict's desperate girlfriend. After a beat though, Audria pushed away the negative thought and put a smile on her face. She wanted to make sure it was the first thing that greeted Michael when he laid eyes on her.

"Strong, Michael." Audria heard a guard's booming voice call the name and she looked up expectantly at the door opening on the far side of the room. A uniformed guard and a khaki-clad inmate were standing there talking. Her eyes quickly dismissed the guard and focused on the man next to him. *Her man.* He stood solid, his legs wide apart, looking like a block of bronzed granite breathing. Audria's eyes searched for Michael's and after a brief pan around the room, his found hers. That was enough to start her heart trip hammering around in her chest again.

She could see the guard's mouth moving, talking to Michael, and after a beat, Michael responded, tilting his head slightly in her direction. Although she couldn't hear what was being said, she could tell the guard respected Michael, just from his body language and the way he looked at him directly, man to man. After a minute or two, the officer made a staying motion to Michael and walked over to the two other guards in the room. Nodding almost imperceptibly at her, he said something to them, then walked away. He signaled for Michael to walk forward, gave him a light tap on the arm as he walked past, then turned away.

Her man's eyes were glued to her face as he began walking her way. She liked the way he moved, how relaxed he seemed in his skin, and found herself thinking of a lion or panther, some predatory beast moving lithely through a jungle. But there was nothing predatory about his eyes. They held nothing but love for her.

"Babygirl," he murmured, and Audria found herself on her feet, her arms involuntarily reaching for him, snaking their way around his neck as she leaned into him, feeling his strength, the supreme power of him, his manliness. The top of her head rested in a perfect fit just below his chin and she felt like her body had found an everlasting home.

"Michael," she breathed, inhaling deeply of his scent, some soapy freshness with a hint of body musk. She saw him give a quick look to his left where the guards were standing, but they had all turned away. His arms encircled her, going beneath her blazer like they were gravitating to the warmth of her flesh. Finding her waist, Michael's arms pulled her close. She could feel herself trembling violently on the inside, but had no idea whether that carried to the outside as well. They stood in each other's embrace for a short while, just holding each other. Audria could feel him breathing in her scent as well, felt him sniffing deeply from her hair, smelling the jasmine and aloe-scented oil she had rubbed on her braids before leaving the house.

"I can't believe I'm really here, that I'm really holding you," she whispered to him, feeling her eyes getting teary.

"Yeah, me too." He spoke softly back at her, his voice filled with emotion, a low rumble that she felt more than heard from his chest.

One of the guards suddenly cleared his throat, and Michael eased away from her. He laughed for only her ears to hear. "Lemme look at you, Babygirl. Lemme see what's mine."

Audria giggled and moved back from him another foot or two, and shook her waist in a little ta-da dance for him. "Here I is, Big Daddy. Now I'm here, whatchu gon' do?"

They laughed, then sat together at the table, Michael pulling his chair as close to hers as he could get it. She felt his knees touch hers beneath the table and felt a jolt of something shoot through her lower abdomen. From the look on his face, she could tell he had felt it too.

"I brought you some things," she said to him, trying to fill the silence. She didn't want it to get awkward between them.

He just looked at her, shook his head slowly, then shushed her. "Shhh Beautiful. Lemme just breathe you, breathe this moment, a'ight? I need to just drink you, Baby. Drink every drop of you right now."

Audria closed her eyes briefly, feeling the shiver return to the pit of her stomach, and focused on her man's voice. She reached across and touched his face, caressing the smoothness of his skin, her eyes on his, their pupils doing a sensuous dance. Her fingers found an uneven surface on his left cheek and she turned his face a little to the right so she could see what it was, tracing what was there.

"How'd you get this?"

"Old battle scar from the streets," he said, and a hand found hers beneath the table. Audria wasn't a little woman, but Michael's hand seemed to swallow hers and she once again found herself thinking that everything about her man was as his name – *strong*.

He again glanced over at the guards, and she asked him what that was about. "We ain't supposed to touch each other or be this close, but I asked for a return favor from dude," he said, tilting a chin at the guard he had been talking to originally. "Still gotta watch it, though."

He looked at her directly, his gaze unwavering, like he was really drinking in her features, storing every bit of their interaction for a slow rewind when their visit finally came to an end. Audria wanted to do the same.

"I so want to explore all of you, Michael. Want to learn your body the way I've learned your mind."

He pulled free a single braid, tugging on it gently between two fingers, while still looking at her, then released it. "It's coming, Audria. You just gotta hang in with me, Beautiful, but trust our day's coming. It's gon' be here before we know it. We just gotta be patient."

Audria smiled at him. "Got so much to tell you, Baby."

Michael leaned back in his chair, knees still lightly touching hers, but giving her a little room. It was almost like he had read her mind, had figured out that she was starting to feel like things were getting a little too intense between them. "We got all day, right?" he asked her, tilting his head up a bit."

She gave him a devilish look. "Actually, we've got all weekend," she corrected him.

He raised dark eyebrows at her. "All weekend?"

Audria nodded. "The whole weekend, Baby."

He shook his head, smiling. "There you go, Miss Speedy. Always ten steps ahead of your man. When you gon' learn to slow down?"

"Why you can't learn to speed up?" Audria teased with him.

She saw a momentary frown flit past his face. It was gone in less than a second, but she knew she had said something he didn't like.

"Does it really bother you that I'm so in love with you and can't help but move at my own pace?"

Michael looked at her, then shook his head slowly. "Bother me? Hell naw. Babygirl, the fact that you love me ain't the thing that's got me worried. That's the thing that keeps me going. What bothers me is how intense you get sometimes with it, you know? I'm not trying to disappoint you or do nothing to hurt you, a'ight? I know how long I still got behind these walls. Guess I want you to stop focusing so much on us getting somewhere together and start enjoying our journey, even this part of it, you know?"

"Why can't I be doing both?" Audria asked him, getting serious. "Is it so hard for you to understand that I'm enjoying the journey but that I'm still anxious to see certain things happen between us? Still anxious to have you come home to me?"

"Naw, I can get with that, but you gotta let this thing happen naturally between us, Audria. It ain't gon' do what it do with neither one of us forcing it in the direction we want it to go."

"I know, Michael," Audria assured him. "I know."

* * * * * *

Idyllic was the only word Audria could find to describe the day she'd had with Michael. She knew people would think she was crazy to say that, particularly in light of their surroundings, but surroundings was the last thing she thought about, being with him. And although Audria knew Michael didn't see it exactly the way she did, she knew she had allowed him an opportunity to come into her world, even if it was only for the ten hours they spent together.

She couldn't remember ever in her life just talking with someone continuously, communing the way they had the whole day. As people came and went, the room slowly filling up to capacity, they lost themselves in their own little world, talking about things they had covered before, likes, dislikes, even their spiritual beliefs. She was surprised to discover her man had a deep love for God and in the power of the Universe.

They talked about holistics, politics, youth programs, camping, sports, and so much more. Audria painted her man mental pictures of ballets she had attended, trips she had taken, and some museum tours she had gone on recently to the National Museum of Women in the Arts, the Old Stone House, and the Mary Mcleod Bethune Council House.

They shared with each other about books they had both read and liked – *The Miseducation of the Negro* by Carter Woodson, *Race Matters* by Dr. Cornel West, *Breaking The Chains of Psychological Slavery* by Na'im Akbar, and one of Audria's favorites – *From Niggas to Gods, Part I* by Akil. This was one Michael hadn't heard about and Audria explained to him that the book was written particularly for the younger generation who couldn't seem to grasp that they were still enslaved to a great degree, just not in the physical sense anymore. Their enslavement these days was insidiously psychological with subliminals that fostered their gravitation to the bling bling, expensive foot wear, and feeling their only options for success hinged on whether they could get shot ten times to one-up the nine bullet holes Fifty Cent sported so proudly.

She and Michael even wound up having a heated debate about the word Nigga. Audria was honest with him about her disdain for the word and told him she didn't like when he or any other brotha used it as a self-descriptive.

"Baby, don't you see? People can try to say that when we use that word it has a different meaning than when Whites use it, but what makes us think that the dirty taste the word leaves in our mouths and the aura it leaves behind in the air when we speak it makes its potency any less than when Massa So-and-So used it to spit in our faces back on the plantation?" She touched him gently. "It disrespected us then and it disrespects us now, no matter *who's* using it."

Their conversation took twists and turns, like they were on a grand high road taking a journey together, and Audria felt a deep longing inside her to have her man come home, so they could do the exact same thing, but out from under the watchful eye of guards and free of barbed wire fences.

Michael talked about what he sometimes did in his spare time – boxing, calisthenics, even the way some of the other younger inmates looked up to him and tried to get him to give them advice. They explored their mutual love of music, and Audria shared with him the artists she loved, people like Theolonius Monk, Miles Davis, Nina Simone, Ella, Aretha, Prince, Sade, India Arie and Jill Scott. Thinking ahead and wanting to do something special for her man, Audria had gotten advance permission from the prison to bring him an iPod Shuffle. Although she had to leave it at the visitor's desk, she was assured he would get it after she left. She had spent hours at home downloading all kinds of music for him. From R&B to funk to Pop to Reggae to Trance to Indie Rock, she filled up that bad boy with tunes that he would be listening to for months and months.

They shared new things as well. Michael told her about his son and the trouble the boy had gotten into recently. She felt trusted and special when he asked her opinion on how she would approach the situation if she were trying to parent from a distance, like he was. She could see the depth of his feeling as he explained to her that very often he found himself having to talk hard and street to his son to compensate for the lack of his physical presence. She shared her thoughts with him and loved him harder for listening as intently as he seemed to be to her advice.

Although Michael was a hard man, what most women would call a *manly man*, he didn't hide his emotions from her. She felt an openness from him as he talked to her, something that seemed missing from most of the men she had been with in the past. They spent so much time trying to impress somebody or trying to project some image they thought women wanted in a man that they forgot to just be real. Audria supposed that being isolated from the usual male-female interactions as Michael had been for so long, virtually guaranteed the absence of game-playing. She found his openness attractive, and told him so.

"You're amazing to me," she said, touching his arm furtively. "How do you do it? How can you be here where you are and still be this man, this person who feels so deeply and loves me the way you love me?"

He winked at her, smiling. "Don't you know?"

"Would I be asking you if I did?"

"You make it happen. You make all this possible. You and the love you bring me. So don't think it's all me, 'cuz it ain't." His fingers started a light caressing of her neck. To anyone watching, it would seem like his hand was casually draped on the back of her chair, but Audria could feel his hand stirring the hairs on her neck. He kept talking to her, his voice soft. "'Keep telling you I got my sides too, a'ight? You seen some not-so-cool sides to me, and you gon' probably see a whole lot more of that as we get deeper in this thing, but I'm banking on our love keeping the good sides face up to the sun and all that bad shit buried for much of the time, you know?"

Audria could barely concentrate on his words, feeling distracted by his light touch. She sat forward in her chair, trying to give herself a momentary escape.

"Would you quit that already?" she whispered at him. "I can't think when you do that."

"So why think?" Michael said, messing with her. "I thought you were all about feeling."

Audria smiled at him coquettishly, then reached into her purse for one of her journals. Two could play at this game, she thought. Crossing her legs and trying to ignore the things his touch had stirred within her, she asked him if he wanted to hear some of her work. For the next forty-five minutes, she read him pieces of her poetry she had brought along with her, stuff from the naughtier pages, steaming hot erotica she had never shared with another living soul. She loved watching him as he closed his eyes, listening to the mellow sound of her voice.

She had just finished reading him a piece she'd wrote especially for him called *When We Ride,* when she heard him make some sucking noise like he was cleaning food from between his teeth. He leaned back in his chair, the lower half of his body slouched low. Her eyes involuntarily went to his lap, and she was surprised to see he had an erection. Not wanting to stare, she averted her eyes and looked across the room at one of the guards standing in a far corner.

Michael laughed softly and brushed a muscled leg against her knee. "What? You gon' start playing coy with me now? Especially after what you just served me up?"

"I'm not playing coy," Audria protested softly, eyes still averted.

"Then why you can't look at me?"

"I can look at you," she said stubbornly, looking anywhere but at him.

He laughed again, softer this time, his voice smooth and taunting, but with an undercurrent of something that sounded dangerously delicious to it. "A'ight, I dare you. Look at me."

Audria turned, wanting to show him she wasn't afraid to meet his challenge. She looked him dead in his eyes. What she saw there took her breath away. He was looking at her with passion blazing in his eyes, undisguised. She wanted to look away, to break the connection, didn't feel like she could handle the intensity of his direct gaze right at that moment, but his eyes wouldn't release hers.

"Look at me, Woman. Can you feel it? You feel this thing between us?"

Audria nodded, not trusting herself to speak.

"When I tell you I got you, you think I'm playing?" he asked her softly. "I got you in every way you could possibly think of, Audria, even in *this* way." He looked down quickly at the word *this*, eyes taking hers to the erection that hadn't gone anywhere, making sure she got his meaning.

She felt her throat constrict and she just stared at him, not knowing what to say. Michael backed off a little, breaking their gaze. "Look, I'm not trying to disrespect you or nothing. You'd be surprised how many of these guys get their women to come up in here and pay the guards so they can play jerking johnsons under the table." Audria smiled at that, finding it funny how plain speaking he could be sometimes, but Michael kept going, wanting to finish his thought. "I'm not trying to disrespect my woman, you feel me? But I just want you to know that when the time comes, you ain't gon' have no worries on this score, a'ight? I'ma take care of my Babygirl."

She broke out in smiles, wanting to lighten the moment between them. "I know you gon' take care of me, but you better start taking your vitamins. I'ma need a whole lotta taking care of, you know."

"Oh yeah?" he said, back to teasing her.

"Most definitely, Sir."

"Then you better start practicing."

Audria frowned. "Practicing?"

"Yeah practicing," Michael came back.

"Practicing what?" Audria questioned.

"Practicing how to stay up for 'bout three days straight, Babygirl, 'cuz I will."

Audria popped him on his arm. "What you gon' try to do, kill me or sump'n?"

Michael looked at her, eyes back to his earlier intensity, and he caressed her face gently. "Naw Beautiful, I'm just gon' love you to death, or better yet, love you to life." Giving a quick glance around at the guards who were, once again, conveniently looking elsewhere, he pulled her face close to his and kissed her softly, a quick, sensual kiss that ignited liquid fire all through her veins.

"You think you can handle that, Miss Audria?" Michael asked her, mouth still on hers.

"I'm sure gon' try, Mister Strong," Audria teased back softly, then gave herself completely to his kiss.

forty
Let's Party

"CHICA! TIME TO GO SHAKE YOUR TAILFEATHER!"

Audria listened to Angela's loud ass banging on her front door, trying to sound like a Hispanic mamacita. Just look at one of the neighbors call the cops on them with all the ruckus she and Miss Ghetto Fabulous Vanessa were creating on her doorstep.

She threw open the door and they all screamed "Happy New Year's Eve" at each other, then broke out laughing. They started turning this way and that, checking out each other's outfits.

Audria was siced. They were headed to a New Year's Eve party at Yvonne's house; the same Yvonne that had thrown the adult toy party some months before. It was her first invitation to a themed New Year's Eve house party, and she was looking forward to the night. Yvonne had gone whole hog again and planned some elaborate party that her invitations had dubbed the Nasty-Not-Nice New Year's Eve Red Affair. Explicit instructions came with the invitation that required all guests to wear "elegant pajamas or boudoir lounge wear." There was a catch though -- you were only allowed to wear red or you weren't getting in. Audria thought it was fun, kinda like P. Diddy's all-White dress celebrity parties.

She had fun shopping around for *elegant* pajamas, but eventually decided to go in a different direction. She settled on a three-piece African lounging outfit in a vibrant sage red. Everything about her choice screamed comfort, but that's exactly what she was going for. The deep-pocketed pants were as loose and wide as Hammer pants, as was the top that came down to mid-thigh. To spice things up though, she unbuttoned the top almost to her waist to show off the red lace teddy she was wearing beneath it and the frilly red Victoria Secrets Bandeau bra she was also sporting. She had piled her braids up on top of her head in an elegant knot and wound the red matching African scarf in and through the bun. She purposely wore her makeup in monochromatic colors, giving the impression that she wasn't wearing any. Except for the bright, racy red lipstick lined with mocha brown liner painted on her full lips, Audria looked natural and fresh.

Angela spun her around and screamed. "Ya 'ho. Where'd you find that get-up? That is niiiiiiiiiiicccccceeeeee!"

Audria giggled and stepped back, checking out Angela and Vanessa's outfits too. Angela had gone classic, wearing a two-piece silk pajama pants suit, red of course, with a floor-length matching Kimono robe. And always true to form, Vanessa didn't surprise her, not in the least lil' bit. The woman had only two modes of dress – hoochie and hoochier. She was wearing a fiery red sheer lace-up babydoll teddy that hit her right below her backside. Red garters snaked down from her thonged nether regions hugging her muscular thighs, and snapped onto a pair of red fishnet stockings with fake rhinestone studs that formed a zigzagging line up the back of her legs. A pair of blindingly shiny, four-inch heeled patent leather boots rounded out the slutty ensemble. Audria just looked at her and shook her head. She couldn't believe Vanessa had actually stepped foot outside her house showing all her goodies the way she was.

"What?" Vanessa looked at her, raising her eyebrows confrontationally. "You got sump'n to say?"

"I ain't saying a word," Audria said, eyeing her friend sideways.

"You better not, 'cuz lemme tell you something..." Vanessa slammed a hand on her hip and started the neck rolling thing she did so well, doing a pretty decent impression of some round-da-way project girl. "You can be faithful all you want to your baby boy on lock, but I sure nuff intend to rock in my new year with something nice and hard, okay? And I ain't talking nothing artificial neither."

She and Angela high-fived and Audria looked at them, suppressing a pang of something that pierced her deep inside as Vanessa tactlessly reminded her of Michael's incarceration. She frowned, wondering if something had escaped her.

"Wait a minute. You want to fill me in on what I'm missing here? Weren't you just all hugged up with some dude named Jerome two weeks ago who was ready to give you the sun, moon and the stars?"

Whipping her neck around, Vanessa waved her off. "Sun, moon and stars? Girl, that broke bastard couldn't give me two nickels to rub against each other if somebody had a gun to his peanut head, with his fake wanna be Michael Jordan ass. That is sooooo yesterday."

"What happened?" Audria asked, hollering at her friend's craziness. "I thought he was *the one*."

"Yeah, the one to watch out for, okay?" They piled in Angela's truck and on the drive to the party, Vanessa had them all squealing and in stitches as she told them how boyfriend had been charging up dinners, shows, and all kinds of gifts and whatnots for her left and right. That is until the credit card companies finally caught up with his "trifling ass." Unfortunately, the catching up happened right after a $200 dinner at some Pan-Asian restaurant called TenPenh over on Pennsylvania Avenue.

"Y'all, why that Negro had the nerve to ask me to break him off wid' a lil' sump'n sump'n so he could cover the bill?"

Angela was hollering. "What'd you do, V?" she asked, reaching across to grab Vanessa's arm. "Don't tell me, I *know* you didn't."

"You damn skippy I did. Told Management they better call the cops, told boyfriend he better roll up his sleeves and commence to washing some dishes, and rolled the hell out."

Audria shook her head. "Vanessa, how could you do that to the man? Why would you embarrass the brotha like that?"

She thought Vanessa's head would blow right off her little body. "Me embarrass him? Me embarrass him? I ain't the dimwit who decided to take somebody out to dinner knowing good 'n damn well I'm broker than the Humpty Dumpty egg, okay? He embarrassed me."

Audria just shook her head again, but found herself for the umpteenth time wondering how Vanessa had become the woman she had. It was obvious she had been hurt badly by somebody in her past, and had erected a 20-foot high materialistic wall all around her to prevent it from ever happening again. She didn't understand that kind of thinking, but to each his own. Vanessa was her girl, whether she was a scheming, manipulative, purely hedonistic lil' thing or not. And it felt good to Audria knowing she didn't have to worry or wonder whether her girls had her back.

Even after the blowout argument she'd had with Angela over Christmas, they were able to move past it. Audria had been furious when her mother accidentally let it slip that Angela had been the one she called to get the skinny on Michael. They wound up having a knock-down, drag-out screaming match that turned the festive day into a disaster. But two days later they had made up and their relationship was just as solid as ever. Audria loved these women and knew they were destined to be lifelong friends.

"So how many people gon' be at this shindig?" she asked Angela. She was sure her girl would have the inside scoop.

"Girl, you see the way Yvonne roll, don't you? You know it's gon' be wall to wall people up in that joint. When I talked to her a coupla days ago, she said her guest list was over a hundred and fifty and she had already gotten more than a hundred RSVPs from people coming."

"Damn, a hundred and fifty people?" Vanessa screamed. "I'm damn sure getting me a balla tonight."

Audria shook her head and sat back, tuning out Vanessa's horny rambling, choosing instead to groove off the Peter White CD *Glow* playing softly in the background. Her thoughts turned to Michael. It amazed her that conversation between them continued to be as easy and stimulating as it was. Her man wasn't the most educated, but then she couldn't claim to be anybody's scholar either. What she loved was how real Michael kept it with her. He said what he meant and meant what he said. She didn't have to worry about him playing mind games with her or trying to confuse her with double talk. She loved how open he was too, even though his openness seemed like a contradiction sometimes. So many men thought they had to keep their feelings all bottled up inside in order to project some image of masculine manliness. As far as she was concerned, they could all line up to take lessons from her baby. He was the epitome of strength and masculinity to her. Sometimes she felt he even had her beat when it came to expressing his feelings. That made her love him with a fierceness that, in turn, made her feel like some ten foot Amazon warrior princess. That was *her* man.

"Daaaaaammmmmmnnnnnnnn!!!!" came an unexpected, high-pitched squeal from the front seat, and Audria's attention snapped back to her present surroundings. She leaned forward from the backseat to see what Vanessa was going on about now. "Ain't that Andre Brown, Macho Harris and Kareem Moore from the Washington Redskins?" Vanessa started flapping her hands all crazy, like she was some prehistoric bird trying to achieve lift off. "Angela, stop the car, stop the car and lemme out. Lemme out right this minute."

Angela sucked her teeth and cut her eyes at Vanessa like she had bumped her head. "Girl, you better get your horny lil' ass under control. I'm not stopping right here in the middle of the street. Don't you see the valet waving for us way up there?" She shook her head at Vanessa. "Would you act like you got a *little* bit of class about yourself? You think them brothers gon' give you the time of day if you go running up to them acting like some ghetto chickenhead who's pressed for a man?"

Audria rolled her own eyes in the backseat. Them two, always going at it. She thought if nothing else happened tonight, she was sure to be entertained by their antics. The night was off to a memorable start.

From the look of things, Yvonne had the entire block on lock, and some of the surrounding ones as well. Everywhere she looked,

Audria saw red-jacketed valets signaling frantically at people to keep the flow of traffic moving. They were hustling about to get the cars racked and stacked as quickly as they could. As they walked back up the block to the over-crowded driveway as people waited to get in, Audria saw two limos pull up back-to-back and uniformed chauffeurs hopped out to get the doors for their celebrity clients. Vanessa was craning her neck to catch a glimpse of who would get out. She and Angela each grabbed one of Miss Hoochie's arms simultaneously and dragged her along.

"Come on here, ya 'ho and put your tongue back in your head," Angela hissed at her. "You can wait 'til you get inside to see who they is."

After waiting almost twenty minutes in a long line that wrapped all the way around the corner, the three of them finally got inside. Audria looked around in awe at what Yvonne had done to the place. The house was decorated in a Winter wonderland motif, done all in white. Everywhere she looked, there were hanging snowflakes, fake snow, white pine trees, snowmen, and other symbols of Winter. There was even a life-size sled complete with a rosy-cheeked Santa Claus and his eight reindeer that had somehow been artfully mounted over top of one of the fireplaces. Santa looked like he was riding right out of the wall. The place looked divine, and judging from the amount of food and liquor scattered at various stations all over the place, Audria knew Yvonne had plunked down some serious loot to throw this bash.

She grabbed a glass of champagne from a waitress bunny dressed in an all-white ruffled mini maid uniform, and took a sip. Vanessa took a sip from her own glass and let out a squeal under her breath. "Y'all, I can tell when I'm drinking Cristal, okay, and *this* right here is definitely Cristal."

Audria rolled her eyes and walked away from Vanessa. She wasn't trying to listen to her materialistic mess all night long. Angela was right behind her, leaving Vanessa to start cozying up to some football player type who was trying too hard to look cool.

"Damn, she is so frigging shallow sometimes," Angela leaned into her, so Audria could hear above the noise in the room. "If it ain't the money, it's all about the male honey. She's crazy."

Audria looked over at Angela. "Weren't you the one high-fiving Miss Money 'n Honey Grubber earlier when she was talking all that nonsense? You just as bad as she is sometimes."

Angela waved her off. "Girl, I'm a happily married woman, okay? I ain't here looking for no man, and besides, Vanessa's grown. If she's cool with being a 'ho to the ballas, then that's on her. She's the one got to look at herself in the mirror, not me."

"Yeah, whatever," Audria responded, guzzling down some more of the champagne. It really was some good stuff.

They were both looking around, checking out the crowd. It was an interesting mix of people. Everywhere she looked, Audria saw men and women dressed to the nines, all sporting their versions of loungewear. Most of the men had played it safe, opting for velour lounge sets, some jogging wear, workout gear, and a variety of red silk lounging robes. The more risqué of the bunch, the pretty boys who had cut-up bodies, were sporting side-mesh sailor boxers and silk chiffon lounge pants with either nothing on top or silk knit tank tops that barely covered their chests. Audria had even spotted one guy who had obviously lost his fool mind, wearing a tiny red man thong with gold side clips. Boyfriend had a bumping body though and knew he had it going on as he strolled by just strutting.

Some of the women had gone way over-the-top with sparkling jewels and bling bling everywhere, reed-thin stiletto heels, and sporting lingerie that looked like it could either get them arrested or if they breathed too hard essential body parts would start popping out left and right. Most of the outfits left barely nothing to the imagination, and Audria felt like she was approaching spinsterhood when she compared what she had on with some of the get-ups. She almost choked on her second glass of champagne when some knot-faced sister went past her walking all slinky in a completely see-through red body stocking with nothing on underneath. Audria's jaw dropped open when she realized she was looking at the woman's heavily-dimpled backside wiggling on past.

"Did you see what that lunatic had on?" she whispered at Angela. "Don't make no kinda sense wid' these women."

The two of them drifted in and out of the crowd over the next few hours, sometimes hanging together and other times exchanging casual conversation with familiar faces. Audria would occasionally spot Vanessa making googly eyes at some man and would head in the opposite direction. She knew her girl well enough to know that Vanessa didn't like interruptions from other females when she was *working* a testosterone packed room. And speaking of testosterone? From the looks of things, Yvonne had obviously made sure to invite more men than women to the party. It looked like there were at least two men for every woman in the house.

"Girl, you need to quit knocking back all that bubbly and find you sump'n to eat." Angela yanked on her arm, popping up outta nowhere.

"I'm not hungry," Audria said, shrugging free and spinning around to watch some scrumptious male eye candy going by. "I'm having me a good time, girl."

"Yeah, you gon' be wishing you didn't have such a good time come tomorrow."

Swallowing another mouthful of champagne, Audria waved her off and started making her way across the room to say hello to Yvonne.

"Hi Yvonne," she said, tapping the woman on the back. Yvonne was lovely, in a flowing Korean Koshibo caftan that accentuated her figure and gave her an almost regal look. The woman turned around, smiled, and hugged her warmly.

"Audrey, right?"

"No, it's Audria," she said, correcting her hostess. "You look lovely."

"And you're a vision," Yvonne squeezed her arm. "And I don't need to ask you whether you're having a good time. That's kinda obvious."

Audria giggled. "Nope, no need to ask. I'm having a great time." She frowned a little bit, hearing a slight slur to her voice, like her words were starting to run together. Maybe Angela was right. She should probably go get some food after this.

Yvonne turned around momentarily, putting her arm around some man. She turned back to Audria, pulling the brotha she had collared with her. "Have you met my neighbor?" she asked.

Finishing another sip of bubbly, Audria looked up smiling, ready to say hello. The smile died on her lips as she saw who was standing there.

"You," she said, her voice dripping with something the opposite of enthusiasm. Al, the idiot who had almost run her down in his driveway, was standing there with a stupid grin on his face. Her eyes quickly took in the lace-up microfiber lounging pants he had on that showed entirely too much of a large, leaning bulge in the front, and the sleeveless tank tee that seemed welded to his chest.

Yvonne looked from Audria to Al, then back to Audria again. "You two know each other?" she asked in a puzzled voice.

"Kinda sorta," Audria mumbled, quickly thanked Yvonne for inviting her to the party, and started to move away.

"What is it with you?" she heard a voice from behind her, and knew he was following her. She ignored him and kept going, not even liking the sound of his voice. A moment later, his hand grabbed her arm, hard. "Would you stop walking away from me?"

Audria whipped around knowing this fool had lost his damn mind. "Get your freaking hands off me," she said, all loud, not giving two shits about the heads close by that started turning.

Al let go of her, slowly put his hands in the air, and took a step back. "Damn, somebody would think I'd robbed you blind, burned your house down, and killed your puppy the way you're acting," he said. "I was just trying to say hello to you and find out what's up with this attitude I keep getting from you." He looked at her, his eyes unreadable. "And by the way, you owe me six dollars and eighty-eight cents."

"I owe you *what*?" Audria spluttered at him, not even sure why he got under her skin as much as he did.

"You owe me six dollars and eighty-eight cents," he said again, speaking slowly like he thought she was mentally challenged. "That's the money I spent buying new hinges and nails for the door you broke. Remember? The same door I asked you not to slam?"

"I don't owe you jack," Audria gritted in his face and turned around in a huff to walk away. She hadn't gone two steps before she heard his voice behind her again.

"I just figured it out."

She wanted to ignore him, but slowly turned around, eyeing him warily. "Figured what out?"

"Why you keep acting the way you do."

She folded her arms, shook her head, and bit. "What?"

"You're scared," he said, nodding, then grinned at her with some weird glint in his eye.

"Scared?" Audria asked him, laughing sarcastically. "Scared? Of who? You? I'm supposed to be scared of you?"

He stepped closer in to her, closing the gap between them, and leaned his head down to her left ear. She could feel his breath on her neck. "You're not *supposed* to be," he spoke softly, "but that doesn't change the fact that you are."

"Negro, please," Audria said, stepping back. She made to walk away again, but apparently Al had something else in mind.

"I can prove it," he said, raising his voice again.

Audria looked back at him over her shoulder, then turned around slowly. "Oh really?" she asked, putting a hand on her hip. "And just how you gon' do that?"

He cocked his head to one side and she saw his pectoral muscles give an almost imperceptible twitch. "*I'm* not gon' do it. You have to." He smiled at her again, and Audria sensed what was coming even before he spoke the next words. "If you dare."

She folded her arms across her chest and looked him up and down. Something inside her was screaming at her to walk away, walk away now, but she ignored it. She walked back over to him. "What?" she asked, feeling a strange fluttering begin in the pit of her stomach.

"Dance with me," he said, still smiling.

"You want me to dance with you?" she asked him, exaggeratedly pointing a thumb then index finger from her chest to his.

He nodded.

Audria thought about it for a minute, then tilted her chin at him. "Okay, you're on."

The sentence was barely out her mouth, when he spoke again, almost over top her, adding, "At my house."

Audria rolled her eyes at him and spun on her heel to leave.

"Chicken," his voice mocked her departing back, unrepentantly.

Two minutes later, they were heading for the door.

* * * * * *

Oh Gawd, this feels so good. Feels soooooooo good.

Audria was shaking both on the inside and out. She knew what she was doing didn't make a bit of sense. She had a man who loved her, had pledged himself to her, had basically told her he would give his life for her. So what was she doing here in this man's living room feeling the things she was? A part of her didn't want this, wanted to will herself to behave, but she couldn't stop herself, couldn't think clearly.

"You know you want this," Al whispered in her ear, slowly sucking on her earlobe, pulling it between his lips. His mouth felt warm and wet and Audria moaned deep in her throat, feeling herself mimic his mouth.

This wasn't happening. Wasn't supposed to happen. Okay, so she was a little tipsy, and probably shouldn't have allowed him to goad her into accepting his dare, but she thought she was stronger than this. They were supposed to just have a dance. That's what she had agreed to. Not all this other stuff.

Audria couldn't even remember their walk over to Al's place. She vaguely remembered him turning on some music, something soft by Gary Taylor, crooning lyrics in his smooth, buttery soft tones, and the next thing she knew, she was encircled by strong arms that felt so good around her. She had closed her eyes, leaned her head against his chest and allowed her body to sway to the beat of the music.

After awhile, she found herself becoming more aware of his body. The feel of his chest against her breasts, the warmth of his breath on her skin, the strong arms holding her close, and the push of his pelvis into hers. Audria's eyes went wide over his shoulder as she realized the slow ballooning she was feeling pressing into her was a growing erection.

She pushed at his chest, knowing she had to stop this before she did something she would regret later.

"You don't understand. I can't do this. I can't. There's..."

Al cut her off. "I'm not asking you to *do* anything, Audria. Let me."

Audria frowned at him slightly, her head feeling far too swimmy and her vision seemed out of focus. "Let you? Let you do what?"

"Let me please you," he whispered to her, dipping his head low and sucking her earlobe into his mouth again. "You *need* this. I can feel it. You can feel it. So, let me."

Audria moaned again, thoughts all tumbled and jumbled around in her head, but giving in to her desire. A picture of Michael tried to surface, fighting its way up and to the forefront of her thoughts, but Al had already laid her down on the couch, had slowly removed her clothing, and was leaning in between her legs. His tongue found her warm, wet centerspot and moments later, pleasure was her only thought.

forty-one
I'm Human

A blinding white hot then blood red laser beam of light seared through partially opened eyelids and a loud knocking noise stabbed viciously through the temples then on into and out the back of her skull.

Audria jerked upright, feeling her stomach turn over at the sudden movement. Her head felt like it was at dead center of a radioactive mushroom cloud and her heart felt like it would bore a hole straight through her chest, it was beating so fast. She turned to get out of bed and stopped dead in her tracks as it dawned on her she was in a strange bed, naked. Then it all came flooding back to her and she screamed, reaching for rumpled bed sheets to cover herself.

Al was up and at her side in an instant, reaching for her, attempting to calm her down.

Audria batted his arms away, swatting at him with real loathing. She wanted to gouge his eyes out for daring to touch her.

"What did you make me do?" she screamed at him over and over again, real agony in her voice. "What did you make me do?"

Al tried again to hold her, not understanding, but feeling her distress, wanted to offer comfort if he could. "It's okay, Audria.

Whatever it is, it's okay. You didn't do anything you didn't *want* to do, and I didn't *make* you do anything."

Audria hated the sound of his voice, hated the defensiveness she heard creeping in, especially in that last sentence. Of course, it was him. It was all him. He had seduced her. He knew she was drunk and he had taken advantage of her, goaded her into coming to his house, and then had his way... made her... had his way with her. She hated him.

Her hand whipped out and slapped him hard across his face once, then again harder, and she screamed at him, spittle flying from between her lips. "WHY didn't you leave me alone? I didn't want this. I didn't want to do this. You made me. You made me break my..." She broke off into loud, braying sobs that made her shoulders shake uncontrollably, and collapsed down onto the bed, her heart aching at the thought of what she had done.

Hurtful images started racing through her mind, disjointed flashbacks from the night before. Al between her legs lapping at her softly like a kitten. Her body shuddering uncontrollably with need. Strong arms gathering her to a hard chest. Big hands grabbing her naked backside. Picking her up. Carrying her up some stairs. Placing her gently on a down comforter-covered bed. Her legs raised high, spread wide, lifted over massive shoulders. Her voice, laced with desire, begging, pleading, for long-delayed entry. Mingled moans as she's pierced by something ridiculously large but oh so filling.

Audria screamed again, quieter this time, but with no less anguish in her voice. She felt Al's weight shift beside her, and a moment later, he laid back, face turned her way. He spoke stiffly, his voice tight, and Audria could tell he was angry she had hit him, but she didn't care.

"Listen Audria, I don't know what this is about. We had a good time. You needed to be with somebody and so did I. What's the big deal? It's not like I'm asking you to marry me or something. It was just sex, right?"

She cried even harder, thinking about the absurdity of the situation and what he was saying. Of course to him it would be *just sex*. That was men. Always thinking with the little head. If they felt the urge, they gave in to the urge, and that was that. It meant nothing to them, other than relief. But that wasn't her. She wasn't some floozy like Vanessa who wasn't afraid to flaunt the fact that she chased dick all the live-long day. Sex meant something to her, always had, always would, and she wasn't the type of woman who gave in to casual booty calls or one-night stands just because she hadn't been with a man in some months.

And Michael.

Audria felt her body shudder as she considered her betrayal of him. She had just seen him a few weeks ago. At the end of their visit, in his raw, plain-speaking style, he had reminded her of her promise to be faithful to him, had explicitly told her he could handle a lot of shit, but couldn't handle the thought of her laying up with another man. And what did she turn around and do? The exact opposite of what he had asked.

Her head was pounding like an entire marching band had taken up residence behind her eyes, and her stomach started roiling like it was imitating a storm-tossed sea. Audria felt it coming and tried to sit up, but the movement made it worse, and she had just enough time to lean over the side of the bed before the retching began. It seemed to go on forever, great big splatters of sour smelling bile, vomitus and $500 guzzled-down Cristal spewing everywhere. She wanted to fight off Al, shrug away his over-sized hands that were holding her protectively from behind, but had no strength left in her.

When the retching finally tapered off, he let her go, got up, and came around to her side of the bed. She let him lift her up and carry her into his master bathroom, placing her under a too-warm shower stream. Once he'd gone away, leaving behind soap, washcloth and towels, Audria stood there and allowed the water to run over her body. She couldn't stop crying. Although her body wasn't being racked by the massive, gut-wrenching sobs from earlier, her heart felt like it was breaking, and she couldn't get it together.

She eventually began bathing herself slowly, letting her tears mingle with the now tepid water falling on her skin. Adjusting the temperature of the water even cooler, she allowed the stream to further soothe her overheated, over-stressed body, then stepped out after a few more minutes. Using some mouthwash she found in the mirrored medicine cabinet, Audria rinsed out her mouth, then dried herself off.

When she walked into the bedroom, Al was nowhere in sight and neither was the nasty mess she'd made. He had already cleaned it all up, had changed the sheets on the bed, and her clothes were in a neatly folded pile at the foot of the bed, along with her purse and shoes. She looked around at the neatness of the room, and found herself thinking a strange thought, wondering if Michael would be as neat in her house when he finally came home.

As she stepped into her panties, her mind gave her a vicious mental dig, reminding her what the very act meant, what she had done to warrant getting out of them in the first place, and the tears began flowing again. Audria sat on the edge of the bed, half-dressed, and cried her eyes out at the loss of the innocence of her relationship; a loss that she had caused. She felt weak and dirty and totally unworthy of Michael.

After awhile, she stood, finished dressing, then went back to the bathroom to wash her face. She looked at herself in the mirror and felt even more disgusted at the image staring back at her. Her face was red and puffy, especially around her nose and eyes, and she looked like a drunk who'd had one too many hangovers. Running some cold water, she soaked a washcloth and pressed it to her face, hoping it would help. Putting her shoes on afterward, she slowly made her way downstairs. She wanted to just leave, walk right out the door without saying a word, but she knew she had to face him, just like she would have to face the dirt she'd done.

Al was standing in the kitchen drinking a cup of something, and he turned as she walked in, holding out a cup to her.

"I made you some tea," he said. "It's chamomile with a little amaretto and brandy. It'll help with your headache."

Audria took the cup from him, careful to avoid touching his fingers, and sniffed at it. He pulled out a chair for her at the kitchen table and sat down, not waiting for her. Feeling uncomfortable, Audria sat, tucking a leg under her, and concentrated on sipping the hot liquid. It burned a little going down, but felt good, immediately warming her insides.

As soon as he started to talk, she felt the tears spring to her eyes again.

"Okay," he said, exhaling a puff of air and running a hand through his short, curly hair. "All this, you being this upset, can only mean one thing, right? You've got a man." He didn't say it like he was asking her, but as though he were stating a fact.

Audria nodded and immediately began to sob again. When Al leaned over to comfort her, the tears came even harder. He got up from his chair and pulled her to her feet, encircling her in his arms. "It's okay," he said softly, awkwardly trying to console her. "It's okay."

She shook her head against his shoulder and backed away, guilt twisting at her insides for even allowing herself some seconds in the comforting circle of his arms. "You don't understand. It's *not* okay. I promised. I made him a promise that I'd be faithful to him, and I couldn't even do that."

Al had never been comfortable around tears and didn't know whether to try to hold Audria again or leave her be. He opted for the latter, backing up, and jamming his hands into the front pockets of his faded jeans. He wasn't sure why he wanted this woman, still wanted her even now with her standing in front of him, defenses down and looking a mess, but he did.

He had always been a practical-minded kinda man. Women were important to him, but his focus had always been more on building a future for himself, through education, professional accomplishments, and meeting personal goals. He never thought he'd get to be forty-three and still find himself unmarried with no children and no prospects, but he had spent so much time in academia, then building his businesses, that by the time he started to think about it, most of his friends had already taken the marital plunge years before, and he felt way out of his element when he even considered wading into the dating pool.

His friend Gina, who he had met at Howard University, was always trying to set him up with friends of hers and had finally convinced him to come out to one of her barbecues to meet some woman. Although he had gone and met the sistah, there was no chemistry between them, so he was fine writing that off. What surprised him was the image that stayed in his head for weeks after the barbecue, remembering the naturally pretty, brown-skinned woman with nearly flawless skin who had sat with her eyes closed and hands thrown up, listening to a Patti Austin song, like that was the only music in the world. And when he took care of his need in the dark even months later, his own eyes closed, it was her face that always appeared before him.

Then there had been that weird chance encounter, when she walked out of nowhere right into his driveway. He had felt like he was dreaming seeing her again. He had enjoyed the feeling of bringing her into his home and the brief conversation they had. She seemed open and inquisitive, like she was genuinely paying attention as they talked and not just asking questions to make polite conversation.

Al didn't quite know why he goaded her the way he did. He knew he got under her skin, but it wasn't like he was really trying to. In fact, he wanted the exact opposite, but he always seemed to say the wrong things to her, pushed her buttons, and something about seeing the fire flash in her eyes when she got upset gave him a thrill.

It felt kinda lowdown how he had tricked her into coming to his place the night before. He knew he had mentally bullied her and that he shouldn't have. It wasn't like he hadn't been able to tell she was close to being blitzed, but when he saw her looking so fine in her pretty red, saw the swell of her breasts peeking out from beneath the bra and lace teddy, watched her mouth move as she told him to take his hands off her, he succumbed to a selfish moment, wanting to get her alone. He could smell the need coming off her, felt it in the air she left in her wake, and that made him know that if he could get her alone, he might have a chance, just once, to taste what it would be like to have a woman like this.

And he wasn't talking about some sex thing either. He might have said that to her earlier, his casually flung comment about it being just sex, but he didn't mean it. He just hadn't felt like complicating matters any more than they already were, by telling her what he was really feeling. She shook him. To his core. In a way no one else had ever done.

He really had *only* wanted to dance with her, but when he took her in his arms, he felt like he was home, like she was or could be a perfect fit for him as a woman. And when he began to feel her body shake, tiny temblors moving through her, he experienced a deep need, a longing within him to please her, to do whatever he could, no matter how small, to give her release.

It wasn't supposed to go any further than that. He had told himself that he wouldn't take this woman to bed. She was too special, too much of a lady for him to treat like some one-night stand. He wanted to please her orally though, show her how a man was supposed to and could worship a woman's body without expecting anything in return. And that should have been it. Except it wasn't.

Al had never been with someone who needed as much loving as Audria had commanded from him. She didn't command or demand with words, but her body spoke to him, and he listened. Unfortunately, he had just allowed himself to get caught up, imagining in his head for a few hours that she was his wife and he her husband. And when she began that low mewling thing she did in the back of her throat, begging him to go inside her, he ignored the restraint he had been trying to show up until that point, and took her to bed.

In the middle of the night, he woke, sat up and watched her still form sleeping. His penis immediately grew hard looking at her soft body and remembering how she had urged him on as he put her legs over his shoulders, raising her high to meet him. He started to wake her, but stopped as she rolled over, throwing an arm casually across his chest. She breathed a name in a muffled, half-snore, then rolled back the other way, turning away from him.

Hearing her speak a name that wasn't his only confirmed what Al already knew. She had a man. He had felt it before, back when she started to protest during their dance, but he didn't care. Her man was an idiot. And obviously didn't know and didn't appreciate what the hell he had. What man left a woman like this open to other brothas? What man left his woman in such a state of need that you could smell it coming off her like a stink? Whoever her man was obviously wasn't handling his business, and in Al's mind, that meant only one thing. He didn't deserve to have her.

He reached a decision in his mind, but put that thought aside. That was only for him right now. He stepped back to Audria and pulled her hands away from her face. "Alright, so you got a man," he said, stating the obvious. "And obviously you love him and feel bad about what we did, right?"

She nodded.

Al swallowed down some emotion trying to rise up in his throat. "Then this gotta be between you and me. It doesn't have to go anywhere but here. Nobody else has to know."

She shook her head. "But *I* know," she said to him, her voice sounding tortured. "And you know."

He shrugged his shoulders almost nonchalantly as she looked up at him, giving her the impression that their night together hadn't meant anything to him. He knew the truth though, that what he was leading her to believe was the exact opposite to how he really felt.

"Okay, so we know," he shrugged. "Big deal. I don't have to tell anyone, and you sure enough won't be telling anybody. So there, problem solved."

"It's not that easy," Audria countered. "I... I don't do... stuff like this. I don't just sleep around and..."

Al cut her off, feeling like he would lose her to another round of tears any minute. "Audria, I don't really know you, okay? But I know *enough* about you to know, *with certainty*, that you don't sleep around. Hell, the kind of need you had last night wouldn't have been there if you were the type of woman who sleeps around." He ran a hand through his hair. "You need to cut yourself some slack on this, alright?"

She looked at him like he had grown an extra head. "Cut myself some slack? Don't you understand that I broke one of the only promises he asked me to make him? He doesn't even believe in promises, but he still asked."

Al wasn't trying to go there. Wasn't trying to start listening to her talk about some faceless brotha he had no respect for in the first place, especially one who could have his woman in the state of desire that this one had been in. Suddenly though, his eyes narrowed as something dawned on him.

"Where's this *him*, Audria? Where's your man?" He made an effort to soften his voice a little. "I mean, is he like long distance or something? Overseas?"

She shook her head, but he'd had enough years reading people to recognize the veil that had just come down over her eyes. She was hiding something.

"It's complicated," Audria said, her voice barely above a whisper. "And I don't really want to get into it."

Al pretended nonchalance again. "That's cool. You don't have to. It's not really important, right?"

He turned around and started removing their cups from the table, taking them over to the sink to wash. Keeping his voice casual, he spoke to her over his shoulder. "Okay, so you made your man a promise. Far as I'm concerned, you can still keep your promise. Last night's history. I mean, it was nice and all, but it didn't mean nothing to either one of us, *especially* not to me." He purposely over-emphasized the 'especially', then added the thing he knew would send her over the edge, although it was the biggest lie he'd ever told. "I've had better."

He heard the quick intake of breath, then, as expected, she let him have it, both barrels blazing. "You arrogant, son-of-a-bitch. What? You think you're God's gift to the planet or something?..."

At the sink, with his back still turned to her, Al smiled a slow, stiff smile that didn't quite reach his eyes, and tamped down the hurt that felt like a knife thrust to his heart. Watching her lying in his bed the night before, he had accepted then the same truth that he was accepting now. He had fallen in love with her somewhere between the barbecue, the boo-boo, and the third or fourth mewling sound she made as he gave her what her body needed. He wanted her, ached to have her in every way a man could want and need a woman, but this wasn't the right time. So, he was giving her what she needed right this minute, a face to hate, an obnoxious personality to despise, to take her mind off the betrayal he knew was hot and ripe in her mind.

It didn't bother him that she thought she despised him right this minute. It was a brand new year, but it was only time, right? He didn't know what time would bring, and that was cool. But what he did know was that wherever her man was, the brotha was sleeping on the job, and he didn't know about anywhere else in the world, but right here in the good ol' U.S. of A? Whenever somebody got caught sleeping on the job, they lost their job. Al had already decided that if and when that happened, he would be the first one in line for the position.

forty-two
Saying Goodbye to Nothing

"You deaf or sump'n? You hear me talking to you? Where he at?"

"I done tol' you. He ain't heah."

"See that? You ain't listening. You already said he ain't here, but I ain't asking you that. What I'm asking you is where he at."

"I... ah... I... don' know where he at. I swear, I don' know."

"Okay, let's try another question. When he lef'?"

"I... I don't know. He wasn'... he didn' come home las' night."

"Oh, now he didn' come home? Nex' question. When he comin' back?"

"Wha... whatchu want me to tell you? If I don't know where he at, how I'm gon' tell you when he comin' back?"

"Bitch, is you tryin' to get smart wid' me? 'Cuz if you is, that ain't sump'n I recommend."

Trina was scared. More scared than she had ever been in her life. She felt her bladder let go and the burning hot stream of her own urine seeped out from between her pressed together thighs, soaking the heavily worn couch she sat on. The scent assaulted her nostrils and, oddly, jogged her memory back to the last time she had wet the bed as a little girl of four. Her mother had worn out her behind for messing up the sheets. As much as that had hurt, she wished she could will herself back there if only to get away from the thug standing in front of her, but he had already told her she wasn't going anywhere.

He pulled out a small silver .9 mil and started switching it from hand to hand, like he was playing with a toy. Suddenly, Trina felt a cold finger of something crawl rapidly up then down her spine, and she thought the sensation was what her mother had sometimes referred to as premonition goosestepping across somebody's grave. Something in her gut told her this wouldn't end well. She decided to try talking her way out of it though.

"I... I'm not tryin' to be smart, okay? But fo' real, he ain't heah an' I don' know when he comin' back." She wet her lips nervously, then raised a pleading hand to the stone-faced youngster standing in front of her. She pointed a shaky finger across the room to her purse sitting on the kitchen counter. "Look, I jus' got my check today an' stopped to the check cashin' place on the way home. It ain't a whole lotta money, but take it an' go. Please."

He looked at her, eyes cold and lifeless, missing the thing that connected most people -- humanity. "How much?"

"A lil' ovah nine hundred."

A corner of his lip curled up in a sneer, and he looked at her, eyes dead, but she could feel the disdain, ripe and potent in the air between them. "That ain't shit. Your lil' man got more'n twenty times that for me right now. What you think your lil' nine hunnerd dollars gon' do for me?"

Trina knew she had made a mistake, but didn't know what else she could say now. She looked down and her peripheral vision caught a glimpse of something to her right. She turned her head that way and focused on the picture of her two boys sitting on a side table. Lil' 8-year old Milty, short for Milton, and her oldest son, Michael, Jr.

Michael, Jr. She looked at the image, feeling a sadness move through her. He looked exactly like his father. So much so, that at various times during her life when she focused on this fact, she had found herself hating and loving him with just as much intensity as she loved and hated his father. But love him or hate him, he was her son, and he was obviously in some serious trouble if men like the one in front of her were looking for him. Her heart hurt for her boy.

She looked up as the thug started talking again. "Here's what's gon' happen."

Trina looked at him. She wanted to say something, but didn't want to interrupt. All she could do was will him to see the helpfulness in her eyes. She would do anything she could, *anything*, to keep this from ending badly.

"When tha' lil' mu'fucka geh' back, you gon' give him a message for me."

She nodded her head, thinking that maybe there was some hope after all. A moment later when he raised the gun, pointing it directly at her head, she realized he hadn't been talking about any verbal message. Trina's last thought before she saw the blinding flash erupting from the end of the gun was of *Michael*. Both her Michael's. Father and son. The men she had loved and hated for more than half her life. She wondered if either one would miss her.

* * * * * *

"Up, Strong. Let's go. Warden wants to see you."

Michael looked up from the book he was reading and frowned at the strange request. He put the book down and got up, automatically turning around to allow the guard entering his cell to shackle his hands together. In his thirteen year bid, he had only been to the warden's office a handful of times. It was never good news.

On the way, he suppressed an urge to question the guard about the visit, see if he knew what this was all about, but at the last minute, he decided to fall back on that. He had been in enough unexpected situations in his life to learn that patience was, undeniably, always a virtue. He kept his mouth shut and kept walking.

Minutes later, he sat across from the warden in an office easily four times the size of his cell, stunned. Trina dead? It didn't make sense. None of it made any sense.

The warden had just finished giving him the news straight, direct, no cut card, looking right at him with unreadable eyes that took his measure. Apparently, Trina's youngest son had been the unfortunate one to arrive home from school and find his mother, hours long dead, with a bullet hole in her head. The boy was being cared for by a psychiatric counselor at a facility in Queens, and would eventually go to stay with his grandmother, Trina's mother, when he was able. The police were still looking for Michael, Jr.

Scrubbing at his face with a hand that felt less than steady, Michael felt a tick-tock pulse begin at his left temple. He didn't know what to feel. Reached inside himself and *tried* to feel something, anything, but all he felt was a cool numbness, a detachment that he didn't understand. He had spent a little over five years of his life with Trina, long enough to father a son with her, but except for that, he wasn't proud about their time together. He had been a different man back then, decidedly selfish and far too often cruel with the kind of cruelty that should have been reserved for someone who didn't love him as much as Trina loved him. He suddenly felt ashamed that he couldn't have been a better man to her. And now she was dead, and his son missing.

"Eyes and ears. Anybody see anything, hear anything?" he asked the warden, thinking about the letter Trina had written him some months back that talked about Michael hanging with the wrong crowd. He was sure his son's choice of friends had ultimately caused his mother's death.

Warden Stevens shook her head slightly, adjusting her suit jacket behind the desk. She looked like she was waiting for Michael to ask her something, but he wasn't going to give her the satisfaction beyond what he'd already asked. Wasn't his style. She already knew the answers to the questions he wanted to ask, so he would let her give them without asking.

They stared each other down, engaged in a visual battle. Michael wasn't trying to be disrespectful. He recognized the warden's authority, actually respected her for her ability to oversee a facility the size of Blasenburg, but he needed her to recognize he wasn't gon' beg her for nothing.

Finally, she broke the charged silence between them with a raspy clearing of her throat. "She was your wife, so you'll be allowed to attend the funeral, of course, if you'd like to, but under full guard."

Michael nodded, waiting, as she went over the particulars. One part of his mind focused on the details the warden was sharing, but the other was on his son. He knew the boy was resourceful, but resourceful or not, he was only fifteen, and clearly in way over his head. He could feel his stomach starting to twist up in knots as he thought about Michael Jr. on the outside, on his own and running, alone and scared. He wanted and needed to help his son and felt a frustration that burrowed deep within him at the fact that he couldn't.

Warden Stevens wasn't a big woman, but she made up for her size with an imposing personality and with an uncanny ability to read people in a way that immediately cut past the walls erected. She made it her business to know everything she could about the men incarcerated at her facility. She knew the ones who were one-timers -- those who had made a mistake, got caught, were paying for that mistake, but would never be back once they left. Conversely, she also knew the hardened criminals, those career bad-boys whose crimes virtually guaranteed that prison was treated as a revolving door. They did long stretches, were released, but one could almost bet money in the bank they would be back.

Over her twenty-two year career in the industry, Stevens hadn't encountered too many inmates that she couldn't read. She considered that ability almost an essential for anyone in her line of work. But the man sitting in front of her was a rare exception, falling in the category of people she couldn't read. Although she was careful to treat all cases with impartiality and complete professionalism, she had lived long enough to be able to acknowledge a truth about herself. She was a pessimist and generally didn't have much faith in the ability of people to recreate themselves. Michael Strong, Prisoner #03579-212, had done the opposite of what she expected.

As the years passed, she had watched him systematically transform himself, moving away from the angry, incredibly violent, always brooding man who had walked through her gates thirteen years prior. The man in front of her had become a quietly introspective person who kept out of trouble, helped others when he could, and offered advice to younger inmates when they asked him for it. She didn't think he was an angel, actually felt that he struggled to keep a tight rein on his emotions most times, but she saw entry after positive entry in his file and knew that he participated in seminars that focused on personal and professional development and on successful reintegration into society. Stevens found herself, pessimistic nature and all, thinking that he would do well when he eventually left Blasenburg.

She knew he was waiting for her to bring up the business about his son, but also knew he wouldn't particularly like what she had to say. "I can *only* give you permission to attend your wife's funeral, Strong; nothing else. That means you travel under armed guard to the church, to the burial ground, and then you return here. Start to finish, a twelve-hour round robin."

Michael raised an eyebrow at her, feeling his emotion control slip a little. "And my son?"

She shook her head. "Nothing we can do there. If he comes to the funeral, I'll instruct the uniforms with you to give you a chance to talk to him, but beyond that, we let NYPD do their job."

"He ain't got nobody but me now. You understand that?" Michael asked her, voice tight, and jaw muscles working. He didn't want her to see how much this meant to him, but felt like he didn't have a choice at the moment.

"Yes, I understand that," Stevens responded, nodding her head slightly, "but you know the rules. We do what we can, when we can, but beyond that, nothing."

"A'ight," Michael said, knowing he had gotten all he would get out of her. As far as he was concerned, he was done here. He looked away, staring absently across the room, and waited for her to bring the meeting to a close.

After a beat, the warden tapped a manicured finger on the desk, pulling his attention back front and center. "Do I need to increase security detail for this trip?" she asked him, and Michael read between the lines. The warden was worried he would try to *do* something while on temporary release.

Although his face didn't change any outwardly, he smiled on the inside at how absurd a question that was. He might love his son, might feel desperate to offer him whatever protection he could now that the boy was in trouble, but he wasn't about to jeopardize the freedom that loomed closer with every passing day. He had too much to look forward to, like a brand new future with a woman that had provided him with the first real motivation he had felt in years. His Audria.

He looked Warden Stevens in the eye and slowly shook his head. "No worries on that," he assured her. "No worries at all."

* * * * * *

Michael was standing at the back of the gravesite in handcuffs and leg irons, three guards flanking him. He recognized they were just doing what they did, so he did what he was expected to do in an effort to keep everybody relaxed.

He knew looking at his face, one might think he was bored and emotionless, but on the inside, he was the exact opposite. As a matter of fact, Michael felt like he was experiencing some kind of emotional overload. Perhaps it was the combined experiences of being on the outside for the first time in thirteen years, the drive, the trip to the church for the funeral, and now here at the gravesite, that were all working conjointly to shake him up, but he felt shook to the core. He wanted to close his eyes, shut out all the stimuli, but he didn't want to chance missing his son.

His eyes had been constantly at work, especially in the church, seeking, searching, looking at every face, examining every dark corner where someone could have secreted themselves away to be an unseen party to the service. Nothing. There had been no sign of his son. Not at the church, and not here.

At the church, there was an awkward moment when Trina's mother had stopped in front of him after touching her daughter's closed casket. She hadn't cared for him back when he was with Trina, and by the look in her eye, she didn't care for him now.

He remembered with perfect clarity a conversation he'd had with her where she told him, voice low and gruff, to get the hell out of her house and never come back. She thought then, that if he kept going the way he was, he would get her daughter killed some day. Now, standing in front of him, her eyes were coolly accusatory and as she walked away, gathering Trina's youngest closer to her, she dropped words behind her, verbal grenades that pierced and wounded him deeply. "Like father, like son," he heard her mutter.

Michael wanted to shout at her, rage at her, tell her to shut the fuck up, that she didn't know what the hell she was talking about. He wasn't that man anymore. The one she used to hate. The one she felt wasn't and would never be worthy of her daughter's love. He knew he wasn't that person. He had worked hard to bury that angry, selfish, cruel dude, even though he tried to resurrect himself every so often. But he had put in work; long, hard years, to leave that bastard behind. People like this woman, though, would never know this. They would make their assumptions based on who he *used* to be and based on what his circumstances told them he was, ignoring the pure heart standing before them.

He couldn't do anything about the path his son had taken. He had done his best to share the mistakes he had made with the boy. Taken pains to be brutally honest and real with him, not hiding his own flaws and faults, but showing him that people always had choices in the paths they decided to take. Unfortunately, Michael had opted to go down the road he himself had walked so many years before, a road that maybe would ultimately lead his son to do time himself. There was nothing he could do to change that now. Still, his inability to change his son's course, didn't stop him from wanting to holler at Trina's mother and to the rest of the world, that things weren't always as they seemed, and that maybe, there were times when the saying *like father, like son* didn't always apply. But he kept his mouth closed and listened to the minister drone on.

Now, here he was standing on the lip of this six-foot deep hole, saying his final goodbyes to a woman who had loved him in her own way, and who had fathered him a son. He thought back to the letter he had written to Audria many months before when he thought he might have lost her. It made him feel guilty what he had said about Trina then. Although he had called her his wife, he had said that she was really his 'nothing.' It made him feel dirty and low for referring to her that way.

Yeah, he didn't love her, had never loved her, now found his heart gripped by love for the first time ever, but Trina was still a woman who had loved him, despite his being gone for thirteen years. She was still a woman who had been an active part of his life for half a decade, and an inactive part for almost two, and who had borne him a son. By virtue of all that, she deserved far more than he had been willing to give her. So now, here he stood, feeling something, while saying goodbye to his *nothing*. Michael lowered his head and a single tear rolled down a hardened cheek.

forty-three
Speaking Truth

"Momma, I did something really bad, and I'm not sure what to do about it now. I need your help."

Audria was sitting on a high-backed, wrought-iron, swivel bar chair, slumped over the Iridian granite countertop in her mother's kitchen. She wasn't sure whether it was a mistake to share what was on her mind with Viola, but she didn't know who else to talk to. She had already put off Angela and Vanessa with their twenty questions about where she had gone, who with, and how she had gotten home from the party. And it had taken her almost a whole week to stop the hysterical crying that would erupt when she least expected it. She had finally admitted that she needed to talk to somebody or go crazy, but when she tried to get a hold of Nadira, she hadn't been able to, so that left her mother.

"What you done gone and done now?" Viola asked her, turning away from the omelet she had just flipped, to eye her. She held the spatula in her hand like she was brandishing a weapon.

Audria held up a hand to stop her mother before she could get wound up. "Mother, I *need* you to be supportive of me on this, okay? That's why I'm sharing it. Please don't start off judging me. I don't think I could take that too on top of everything else."

She watched her mother's posture change, soften. Ever since they had talked at her dad's gravesite, Audria could tell that Viola was making an effort to listen more and say less, and was genuinely trying to improve their relationship. She no longer felt like her mother was *just* her mother; somebody who bought her expensive clothes, needled incessantly, and who dropped by at inopportune times to be a huge pain in the butt. For the first time, she felt like they were connecting on a much deeper level, and felt proud of their relationship. Sometimes, it even felt like what they had was something resembling friendship, which was something she had never been able to say or feel before about her mother.

Viola turned off the burner and removed the skillet from the fire, covering it. She came around, took Audria's hand, urging her down and off the stool. She lead the way over to the kitchen table, where they sat across from each other.

"Okay, you got my full attention. Tell me," she coaxed, patting Audria on her arm.

Audria could feel her eyes stinging and blinked rapidly to clear them. "I messed up, Ma. Broke a promise to my man, and I don't know what to do about it now." She looked up at her mother, waiting for her to say something, but Viola kept looking at her, like she was waiting for her to go on. Audria found herself telling her mother the whole story from start to finish. It felt strange talking to her mother about sex, especially admitting that she struggled with the passionate side of her often, but she closed her eyes in the places where she felt most uncomfortable, and bulled her way through.

When she was finished, she looked up at her mother, then spread her palms in a questioning gesture, waiting for Viola to say something. Her mother looked at her, then raised one eyebrow. "Audria, you think you the only woman in the history of women who done messed around on her man?" She waved a hand casually backward. "Women do it all the time, girlie. An' let's not talk 'bout how often the men got us beat when it comes to keepin' they lil' peckers in they pants."

Audria interrupted. "I know that people cheat, Mother. That's not really the heart of my issue, as much as the promise I broke that I made to Michael. It's not like he's asked me for much. You'd think I'd be able to keep one little promise to him, Momma."

Viola coughed like she had swallowed wrong. "One little promise? One lil' promise? Didn't you tell me this man gon' be in prison for four more years?"

"Well, it's actually more like three years and four months now."

Viola waved her off dismissively. "Three years, four years. Do it matter? Is still a helluva long time for a man to ask a woman to commit to something like what he done asked you. Is not like youse seventy years old and cobwebs hanging all off your stuff."

Audria's mouth dropped open in the face of her mother's bluntness. Recovering quickly though, she looked at Viola sideways. "Momma, now you got me confused. You sound almost like you're saying you don't believe in fidelity. But wasn't that the big issue you had with Daddy in the beginning of your marriage? Didn't *you* tell me that?"

"Unh unh," Viola said, shaking her head and wagging a finger back and forth at Audria. "In my mind, is a big dif'rence between a man layin' wid' somebody 'cuz he like to explode if he don't, an' one who hit the sheets jus' cuz some floozy say come do the humpa-romp."

"What?" Audria hollered at her mother, not wanting to laugh, but unable to stop herself.

"One scenario got to do wid' need, genuine need," explained Viola, holding up a finger like she was ticking off from a list. "And the otha' got to do wid' pure-d selfishness." I had issues wid' yo' daddy 'cuz he was bein' selfish. Ain't like he didn't have a woman at home who was ready, willin' 'n able. He jus' wanted to pull a fast one like mos' men do and think 'bout variety. Quantity 'stead a quality. An' that's when I had to set him straight."

"So what are you saying, Momma? That my need excuses what I did?" asked Audria, "'cuz the difference is that I have a man."

"Yeah, you got a man," Viola agreed, "an' although ain't no real excuse for what you did, he ain't here, is he? An' that fact ain't gon' change the need inside you from happenin' one way or the nex'."

Audria started to interrupt, but Viola cut her off. "Bottom line is this. Your man shouldn'ta asked you to make him that kinda promise. He shoulda jus' lef' it alone. From the minute he asked you not to feel what comes natural to humans to feel, women an' men alike, he was settin' you up to break that promise."

"And I did, Momma," Audria groaned. "Gawd, did I ever!"

Viola picked at something from between her teeth, then sucked loudly at it, eyeing Audria crossways. "It was that good, huh?"

Audria's head jerked up in surprise, and Viola cackled. "Girl, your Momma wasn't born yesterday. Everything you goin' through now, I done walked that road some years back." She started nodding her head. "You prob'ly feelin' as much guilt as you is 'cuz you enjoyed yo'self."

Audria kept quiet, but Viola wasn't ready to let it go just yet. "What this boy like? He nice? You feelin' sump'n for him too?"

"If you count disgust and revulsion," Audria muttered, wanting to say *ewwww* loudly at what her mother was implying. "It was just something physical that should never have happened, Momma. I can't stand the sight of him."

Viola looked at her daughter, eyes darkly penetrating. "Hmm," she said, getting up from the table, and heading back to her now cold omelet on the stove. "So what you done decided to do about all this?" she threw over her shoulder at Audria.

"I have to tell the truth," Audria said quietly, resuming her perch atop the bar chair, so she could watch her mother.

"An' you done gave this *how* much thought?" Viola asked her, getting the fire going again.

"A lot, Mother. I've given it a lot of thought."

Viola turned halfway around and peered at her, chin tucked down. "Ain't you nevah heard that what somebody don't know can't hurt them? You *sure* you want to bust your man's bubble like that?"

"I don't look at it like that, Momma. I just want to be honest with him. He's so big on that. Has been all along. And if I can't be honest with my man, then who can I be honest with?"

Viola turned back to her omelet, not trying to let her eggs burn. "So long as you're sure," she said, voice low and suddenly thoughtful. "But if you get a reaction you wasn' expectin', don't say I didn' warn you."

Behind her, Audria frowned slightly, then reassured herself, talking out loud. "That's just a chance I'm gonna have to take."

* * * * * *

> *Sun. 1/6- 6:38 p.m.*
>
> Hi Michael.
> I can hardly believe that it's my first time saying hello to you for the New Year. Other than the letter I wrote you on New Year's Eve morning, this is my first chance to say Happy New Year to you, Baby. So, HAPPY NEW YEAR!!! ☺ I'm not sure what it was like for you bringing in the New Year. That can't be easy, especially after all the years you've been there, but I hope it wasn't all bad, and that you thought about me, even if it was a little bit.
>
> Michael, there's something I need to share with you, but before I do, I have to tell you that I love you. Sometimes I love you so much that it seems to hurt me way down on the inside. But, of course, I remember our scripture in Corinthians, right? Love is not supposed to hurt, so I know that the ache I feel is probably what surfaces when I think about the possibility of ever losing you. I never want that to happen, Baby.
>
> It's hard for me sometimes to think about what my life would be like without you in it. And I've done that, you know. Maybe it's just the pessimistic side of me, that glass-half-empty Audria that sometimes thinks about the what-ifs. So I've found myself on a few occasions thinking about what my life was like before you came into it and what it is now. My life has meaning, Michael. Real meaning. For the first time, I feel like I have a strong sense of who I am as a woman. Especially when I think about being <u>your</u> woman. I'm excited and anxious to build a future with you, Baby, to create our own special little world that will make people jealous at what we have.
>
> It's like sometimes I think about how people are so quick to judge and haphazardly decide that you don't deserve a second chance at a good life, even a <u>great</u> life, just because of the things from your past and because of the person you used to be. I don't understand that. What's the point in using the word 'rehabilitate' if we're already counting out the people who are being rehabilitated before they even have a chance to re-enter society? It's so unfair and so judgmental, and it makes me furious that you'll even have to go through any of that and deal with narrow-minded people who don't understand the importance of forgiveness. Please know that I'm always on your side, Michael.

And Baby, speaking about forgiveness, this brings me to what I have to share with you. Michael, this is not easy for me, but I'm not running from it, okay? I need for you to understand that. In one of your letters some months ago, you talked to me about apologies. You explained how you feel about them and that they can sometimes make liars out of people, because we'll feel sorry and we'll make promises about not ever doing something again, and then when we turn around and do it anyway, it's now made a liar out of us because we weren't able to keep some impossible promise. You said to me in that letter that we would probably both mess up during this relationship, but that you wanted us to just put the issue on the table, deal with it and move on. So Michael, I need to put an issue on our table.

I messed up. Messed up pretty bad. I don't know where to begin, and I don't even know what I should tell you or shouldn't tell you, but I want and need to tell you the truth. First, I NEED to apologize to you. Yes, I'm doing the thing you said you don't believe in, but see, I believe in apologies. How else can we repair the damage we've done if we don't learn to say I'm sorry? And it's not that I'm saying 'I'm sorry, I'm not going to do this thing again', because I know you don't want to hear what you might consider false promises. It's just that because I love you and want to honor you and show you respect, I need to tell you how sorry I am for messing up.

Okay, I can keep going around and around in circles, or I can just get to it and tell you what I've done and what's in my heart. In my letter to you on New Year's Eve morning, I told you about a party that I was going to with my friends Angela and Vanessa. Remember? The one at that woman Yvonne's house? Well, we went to the party. It started out really nice, but Michael, it didn't end up nice. I got a little tipsy. Well, not a little tipsy, I got _a lot_ tipsy. There was this person, this guy there, and I was missing you so much and feeling so passionate, and with all the drinking I was doing and everything, things got out of hand and Michael, I went home with him. I'm sure you can guess the rest.

Baby, please know that I'm not trying to hurt you by telling you this, but you asked me to be truthful with you, always, and I don't want to keep any secrets from you. I love you too much to do that. Michael, I can blame this on too much alcohol, the festive mood of the party and all that, and yes, maybe some of those things played a part in what happened, but I have to take responsibility for my actions. This is the only thing I can remember you asking me to make you a promise about, and I wasn't able to keep my promise. I'm more sorry than I can tell you, Sweetheart, but I made a mistake. I'm asking you to understand how difficult it is for me sometimes with this side of me. I told you from the very beginning that I'm a needy somebody. It's hard for me to not have physical contact, even if it's just somebody to hold me for a little while.

> *I don't know what to say. I want to promise you that this won't ever happen again, because as needy as I am, I know I can be faithful to you. I want to be. But I know you probably don't want to hear me make you any promises, especially seeing as how I've just broken the only one I made you to begin with.*
>
> *Michael, please forgive me for this thing. I'd really like to talk to you about this, maybe come visit you again so we can address it face-to-face, okay? Baby, I know that this will hurt you. I'm not kidding myself about that, but I hope you'll be able to understand that I didn't intentionally set out to do this. I just lost control of myself for a bit and it happened. Baby, I'm sure you know that I'll be anxious to hear from you about all this, so please write or call me soon? And please remember I love you.*
> *Your Babygirl,*
> *Audria*

Audria read the letter over again, stuck it in an envelope, sealed it and put the stamps on. She had a sinking feeling in the pit of her stomach about it, wasn't sure if she was doing the right thing, but she wanted to be truthful with Michael. He had asked her to be, and she didn't want to get into some habit of keeping things from him, just because he wasn't in a position to know whether she was being totally honest or not. That's how relationships got in trouble all the time, with people hiding this little thing or the next little thing, and then pretty soon, the little things got to be big things, and before you knew it, the relationship was on a downward spiral. She had found herself doing that in other relationships, had actually been okay with that kind of interaction for most of her life, but Michael meant too much to her to do the same old thing she had always done. So, she didn't have to give this too much thought. She knew she wanted and needed to speak the truth to him. She would just have to bank on him being understanding enough to get them past this.

Audria took a sip from her wineglass, and found her mind, strangely, straying to Al. He was so weird and beyond infuriating. It had been hard for her to even sit next to him perched up high in the front seat of his Suburban truck on the drive home. She would have been more than happy taking a cab home, but he insisted on driving her, to the point of an argument, and Audria let him have his way since she didn't have the energy in her for another battle of wills.

He didn't say two words to her the entire time on the drive to her house. Just turned on a Jill Scott CD – *she had been surprised at that* – and headed out Suitland Parkway to Branch Avenue and then on into Waldorf. From there, she gave him blow-by-blow directions on where to turn right then left until he pulled into her driveway.

Once again, he had insisted on opening her door for her and then walked her up the few steps to her front door.

"You don't have to do this," she protested, not sure why it bugged yet pleased her that he was insisting.

"I know," he replied, his voice even and quiet, and that had been that. When she got the door open and turned around for a civil goodbye, his back was already turned and he was walking away to his truck. He backed out of her driveway without even the smallest glance at her standing in the doorway, and drove off in a cloud of dust. Audria slammed the door shut. And not just her front door either. If that was the last time she saw his ass it would be too soon. What an arrogant so-and-so, she thought, knowing that things would never have happened the way they had between them if it wasn't for all the champagne she had guzzled down. She had been all too happy then to put him out of her mind and focus on the *real* issue at hand – telling Michael the truth.

And speaking of Michael, she felt something else gnawing at her, an uneasy feeling that kept churning around in the pit of her stomach. Normally, she could feel him very strongly, felt his love for her, sometimes even felt when he was writing to her, but she hadn't been able to feel him like she would normally, in the last few days. She wasn't sure what the odd disconnect meant, but hoped her man was okay. This was the part that frustrated her the most – not being able to truly be there for him in every way that he could possibly need her. Audria pushed the thought out of her mind though. She would have to, for now. She would have to lay back and allow the mail to do its thing. Here she was, back to what she hated the most – waiting.

forty-four
Get The Hell On

Audria,

This ain't gon' take too long, so don't get all comfortable with your glass of wine, soft music, candles and all that shit. Got some things to say, so might as well just get to them and wrap this fast.

Not even sure where to begin, but since you like to paint pictures so much, let me paint you one. Had me a first in thirteen years this week. Want to know what? Got me my first taste of the outside, and I ain't talking about walking the yard neither. I mean, I actually got to leave from behind these walls. Want to know why? Had to go bury my wife, the mother of my son. This woman who ain't never hurt nobody in her whole life, but was just unlucky enough to find herself standing in the way of the bullet probably intended for my son. Yeah, my son, who's now missing. But ain't none of that no concern of yours. I'm just painting you a picture, right?

You want to know what's really jacked about that trip, Audria? It's that the <u>whole</u> time, with everything on my mind, weighing me down, all I could think about was you. Thinking that the man I used to be and everything I was into prevented me from being a good husband to my wife. So there I was tasting freedom for the first time in over a decade, and liking it. Liking the sweetness of it on my tongue, like some delicious candy. And there I was thinking that this is just a lil' bit of what it's gon' feel like when I walk free from these walls to come find my babygirl.

There I was sitting in that prison transport thanking God for giving me a second chance to do right by a woman, one *who I really loved this time around. Thanking him for sending me a true woman, one who got my back and ain't afraid to give the world her ass to kiss if they don't understand the love she got for me. One who I know been walking a hard road herself, but she been facing all that. One who I know it might be hard for, but she promised me, stood in front of me and let her lips form the words and made me a promise about the one and only thing I ever asked her for.*

And I'm feeling you. Feeling the love between us like I ain't never felt it. You asked me what I was doing on New Year's Day? You really want to know? Want me to paint you a picture? I was talking to God, Audria. Thanking him for bringing me a good woman who I can make a wife. Well, you know what? He can keep your ass 'cuz I ain't trying to turn no 'ho into a housewife.

Listen to me real careful like, Audria, 'cuz I don't believe in repeating myself most times. You said you sometimes find yourself thinking what your life would be like without me in it? Well, here's your chance to find out. Get the hell on and leave me the fuck alone. Don't want to know you.

Michael

<u>forty-five</u>
Grace

Audria felt like she was losing her mind. She had never cried so much in her entire life. It had been a little over three weeks since she received Michael's angry, dismissive letter that seemed to shatter her whole world. Despite her mother and friends rallying around her, she had been inconsolable.

This all felt surreal to her, like it was somebody else's life these events were unfolding in. Although she knew it was happening to her, there were times when she felt like she was standing outside herself looking at some stranger who could barely function. She was going through the motions, doing the things she was required to do, like showing up for work, paying her bills, and some domestic duties, but she didn't know how. It seemed like she had been in a fog for weeks, and she would cry at the oddest times and for the least little thing. If it wasn't for her mother constantly hounding her to make sure she ate, food would be the last thing she thought about.

And maybe she could stomach this strange existence she had come to know, but what she couldn't handle was not being able to *feel* Michael. When she reached mental fingers out to him like she had been doing since they met, all she felt returned was a cold, stony stillness that seemed devoid of any emotion. No love, no passion, not even anger. Just nothing there. That, more than anything else, was the thing that made Audria deathly afraid that she had lost forever the man she loved.

She didn't have energy for much of anything either. She went to work, came home, and crawled into bed, sometimes laying in bed for hours at a time, just staring at the walls. On the weekends, it was worse. She would stay in bed, her frame curled into a tight ball, allowing the pain she felt deep within to move through her like an emotional typhoon. She wanted to fight with her mother, argue with her to go the hell home and leave her alone with her suffering, but she didn't have the energy. And even if she did, Viola wasn't going anywhere. She would hover around like the queen bee she was, mothering Audria persistently. When it was obvious she couldn't coax her daughter out of bed, she brought what she needed to her there. Water, tea, food, smiles, warm hugs, and a calming presence that only a mother could bring.

And when she felt those things failing, felt Audria teetering on the brink of a place where she could never reach her, Viola climbed into bed with her, wrapping her limbs around her daughter's trembling body, and crooned comforting words in her ear.

"'S okay, Baby. Everything's gon' be okay, Audria. You just gotta give it time."

Audria's body shuddered against her mother's. "It's not okay, Mommy. It's never going to be okay again. I betrayed him and now he doesn't love me anymore."

Viola wasn't sure what to say to her daughter. She wanted to reassure her that wasn't the case, wanted to promise her that time healed all wounds, but she had read the curt letter Michael had written Audria. She had found it on the floor of her daughter's living room, in the very place where it was dropped after Audria read it. It cut her to the bone reading it, and if it hurt her as much as it did, Viola couldn't imagine what it had done to Audria. She understood the man's anger, knew her daughter had done him wrong, but a part of her hated him for so cruelly dismissing her child. She didn't want to extend some false hope in the face of so much pain, but she needed to offer Audria a lifeline, something that would make her think beyond the moment.

"Audria baby, sometimes people need time to work through they anger when is fresh and raw in they mind." She smoothed Audria's braids. "Your man's hurtin' right now, an' is obvious to me he sent you that letter in the middle of him hurtin'. You just gotta give him time to calm down and realize that youse human. Everybody makes mistakes. You ain't perfect and he ain't perfect. He gon' probably do things to hurt you down the road, and this ain't gon' be the last time you hurt him. Thas' just human nature."

Audria wailed out loud, her body wracked with sobs, and Viola knew she had said the wrong thing. She rubbed Audria's shoulders and back, waiting patiently for the new round of tears to subside.

"That's just it, Momma," Audria said after awhile, her voice sounding tortured. It's *not* my nature to hurt people, especially not somebody I love so much."

Viola gently tugged Audria's shoulders, turning her daughter's body around to face her. She wanted her to see the love she had for her in her eyes. "You ain't nevah heard the old saying that we hurt most the ones we love?" She raised an eyebrow at Audria. "You think thas' just old people blowin' smoke? Is true. Is jus' a part of human nature that everybody find theyself strugglin' wid' from time to time, including you. We jus' have to make a effort not to let it happen too often, but it's gon' happen, whether we want it to or no."

She wrapped her arms around Audria's shoulders and rocked her gently. She didn't like the way her daughter loved, this all consuming, too intense giving of herself. It was almost like Audria made the person she loved her entire world and if something happened to take that love away, her world crumbled at her feet. Viola didn't know where that kind of behavior came from, because it sure hadn't come from her. As much as she had loved her dead husband, she always made good 'n sure he understood that she could stand on her own two without him. But her daughter was different from her, more fragile when it came to matters of the heart. It worried her how Audria would react if this was her last time hearing from Michael.

"Did you write him back, Baby? Did you ask him to forgive you?"

Audria shook her head, sniffling. "Momma, what else can I say to him? I already told him how sorry I am when I wrote him to begin with. I don't know how else to make him understand the way I feel about this and about him. Momma, I can't think. I can't think." Audria covered her face with her hands and leaned into her mother's chest.

Viola gave her a few minutes of comfort, then pulled away slowly. She tucked a finger under Audria's chin and lifted her daughter's head. "Listen to me, Baby. You know I wasn' crazy 'bout you bein' wid' somebody in prison, but you done 'splained to me 'bout the way you feel and how it wasn' your choice to fall in love wid' this man, an' I believe you. We don' have no control over who we love. But I got to tell you this, Audria. If you love this man the way you say you do, then you got to fight for your love, Baby. Do everything you can to hold on to him. If you do that and he still don't come 'round, then you can rest easy knowin' you done did all you can."

Audria looked at her mother, her eyes red and puffy. "You really think I should write him again?"

Viola rolled her eyes up to the heavens, then tapped her knuckles against Audria's head lovingly. "Hello? 'Course you should write him again. What I jus' got done tellin' you? Sometimes people need time to get ovah they' anger, but then once they get past it, they ready to discuss things again. Write that man, tell him the way you feel about him, and ask him if y'all can work things out."

She swung her legs off the bed, preparing to get up, but looked back at Audria over her shoulder. "You ain't gon' fix what done gone wrong in your relationship layin' up in this heah bed cryin' your heart out. Whyn't you get up, go take yourself a nice, hot shower, put on some clean clothes and then sit down and write your man. I'ma go cook us some dinner in the meantime."

Viola smiled at her daughter, then headed for the kitchen. Behind her, Audria buried her head in her pillow for a few more minutes, then got up. Her mother could get under her skin sometimes, but she was glad she was here, and was helping her think things through. She knew Viola was right. If she wanted to save her relationship, it was up to her and no one else. She would do exactly what Viola had suggested. Although it was strange to think about writing him a letter like the one she had to, especially on a day like today, she was determined to take her mother's advice. She would get herself cleaned up, get comfortable, sit down and write to her man again.

* * * * * *

Thurs. 2/14 - 5:15 p.m.

Hello Michael. Baby, I know that maybe you might not want to hear from me, that maybe you're still angry with me and still hurt, but please just allow me to share with you what's on my heart. If after that happens and you don't feel any different, then okay, I'll try to understand and not bother you anymore, although that will hurt to do, but please just give me a chance to say some things.

First, although it might not be a happy day for you, I want to wish you a Happy Birthday. I know you told me birthdays aren't really a big deal for you, but in my family, they have always been special days, and since it's hard not to think of you as a part of my family, the day you were born is and always will be special to me. So, Happy Birthday, Baby. I've attached a birthday card for you, okay? Hope you like it.

The next thing I'd like to say to you from the heart is that I love you. I know you might not want to hear that from me, but I have to say it, Michael. I DO love you. Yes, I know I didn't keep my promise to you, and I know how important that was, not just to you but to me as well. If it wasn't important to me, Baby, I wouldn't feel like my insides were all tied up in knots the way they have been since all this happened. And I have to say this too. If the promise wasn't important to me, I wouldn't have bothered to tell you that I had broken it. You're in prison, Sweetheart, behind walls. I didn't have to tell you what happened. I could have just dealt with it, handled the guilt on my own, and gone on like nothing had happened, and there's no way you would ever have found out. But I love you and didn't want to compound breaking my promise by keeping it from you.

Please believe me when I tell you that I didn't tell you to hurt you or to try to bring drama to you or anything else. Keeping my word about something is important to me, especially a promise. And Baby, there are no words to express to you how deeply I regret what I've done, but I'm human, and don't all humans make mistakes?

Michael, the third thing I want to say is that you know me. Know me in a way that goes deeper than anyone else has ever known me. I wouldn't have shared me with you the way that I have if I didn't love you, and vice *versa. You wouldn't have opened up to me and shared all the things you have with me about your life if you didn't love me. I know you love me, Michael. I can't feel it right now, because you're hurt and angry and feel betrayed, and what you're feeling has taken you to a not so good place. I understand all that, but I know you love me.*

Baby, you yourself have shared with me about the kind of man you used to be. You were the kind of man who didn't allow yourself to feel things. You were selfish and awful and you hurt people without a second thought to their pain, but what did you do? You turned your life around. You recognized that you didn't want to do that anymore, that you didn't want to be that kind of man any longer. And although you ended up incarcerated for the things you did and are paying for those things, you're a far different man now than you were in the beginning. If you could turn your life around from being the kind of man you used to be, why is it so hard for you to forgive me for this one mistake and to trust me never to do it again?

I didn't mean to hurt you. I didn't set out to break my promise to you. I didn't just callously say I'm going to do what I feel like doing just because I felt like doing it. It was a mistake, a moment of human weakness, Michael. Please don't let that destroy everything we've been building. Please don't allow it to destroy our love.

Baby, I've been thinking about you so much and missing you more than I can say. Every time I think about you, it makes me think about how special you are to me and how special our love is. Sadé has a song that says 'hold on to your love.' That's what I'm trying with all my heart to do. I'm holding on to my love, because I know it's a once-in-a-lifetime kind of love that we have. I've never felt the way I feel about you for anyone else, ever, and I don't want to think about living my life without you and our special love. Please Michael, I'm asking you to forgive me. I know it's a lot and I know you might not want to, but if you can let your love for me guide you a little, then Baby, please extend me some grace.

Remember I love you and will be waiting to hear from you.

Your Audria

forty-six
Sight

Audria sighed deeply, inhaled then exhaled a slow, cleansing breath, and allowed herself to fully relax in the comforting circle of the woman's arms. She wasn't exactly sure how she had wound up in Nadira's bed, but it felt good to her and she recognized the need to be good to herself right now, so she was going with the flow.

Lately, it seemed that things had been spiraling quickly out of her control, and far too often for her comfort, Audria found herself feeling like she was in the passenger seat instead of the driver's. It was this same out-of-control feeling that had brought her here to begin with. Thinking to seek her friend's unique insight and guidance, she had called Nadira earlier in the day and asked to see her.

When the woman answered the door, Audria's mouth felt like it hit the floor. Nadira was standing there completely naked, but acting no different than if she was wearing a rack of clothes. Audria's eyes widened even more when the woman turned on her heel, her backside jiggling loosely.

"Close de door afta' you," she threw over her shoulder in her soft yet commanding sing-song, as she headed for some inner room. "Is time for you to know yo'self."

Audria could swear she stood there for a good three or four minutes more, trying to decide whether to haul ass for her car or what. Eventually, when she was sufficiently convinced her feet weren't about to cooperate enough for her to leave, she stepped across the threshold and closed the door behind her. She headed in the same direction Nadira had.

It was a small, odd-shaped sitting area situated just off the living room. The first thing Audria noticed when she entered the room was the huge difference between this space and the rest of the house. The foyer, living room, kitchen, and bathroom, all rooms she had spent time in during previous visits, were warm, homey, inviting spaces filled with African and Ethiopian art, loving expressions of Nadira's ethnocentricity. Here, the walls were stark white and bare in contrast, and there were only two pieces of furniture in the entire room. The first was a four foot wooden chest and Nadira was standing in front of the other, motioning her into the room.

"Come on now, Daughta'," she encouraged Audria. "Ain't nut'ing here can hurt you."

Stepping to one side, Nadira tilted her chin commandingly at Audria. "Take yo' clothes off. If you is to see yo'self fo' true, you not gon' need 'dem."

Audria hesitated. She wasn't particularly shy about showing her body to another woman, had done so at various times when she went clothes shopping, to the gym, spa, or the few times she had skinny-dipped with her girlfriends, but that was different from what Nadira was asking her to do. Every time she had undressed in the past, even with men, it had been for a specific purpose that she knew of and was reasonably comfortable with. This was sufficiently different to take her completely out of her comfort zone. She tried to verbalize what she was feeling to Nadira.

"I... I'm... not really sure..." That was as far as she got before Nadira cut her off.

"Queen, didn' you ask me to try to help you?"

Audria nodded.

"How come you ask me?" Nadira questioned, raising an eyebrow.

Audria frowned, not sure she understood the question. "What do you mean?"

Nadira looked at her with a direct gaze that felt like it penetrated the soul. "Alright, let me ask de question in anotha' way. When you ask somebody to do somet'ing for you, why you ask it?"

Audria frowned again, but thought about it for a second. "Because you want whatever it is you're asking for," she replied after a beat.

Nadira nodded slightly, but Audria could tell she wasn't satisfied. "Thas' right, but is anotha' perhaps more basic reason why we ask somebody to do somet'ing for us. What you t'ink it is?"

Audria started to shrug her shoulders, but Nadira's arms went up and out, gripping hers firmly. "Step outside yo' normal t'inking, Queen, and use yo' mind."

A long, silent moment passed between them, then Audria spoke hesitantly, her voice sounding like she was making a tentative guess on a quiz show. "Because we think the person has the ability to help?"

Nadira clapped her hands suddenly and laughed aloud, her voice echoing peculiarly in the near empty room. "You unda'standin' t'ings more every day, Daughta. See, 'fore we ask fo' help, we first have to believe in some way an' on some level 'dat who we askin' fo' 'dat help, have de power to render it. 'Dat little t'ing, Pretty Audria, is called faith an' trust." She reached out and pulled one of Audria's braids through her fingers. "So, you ready to show me yo' faith, an' trust me lil' bit?"

Audria nodded, her mouth feeling arid, like all the spittle had permanently dried up.

Nadira made a motioning backward gesture at her with a forefinger. "Go on now. Take off yo' clothes."

Audria slowly stepped out of her slacks, then unbuttoned the pale yellow cashmere sweater top she was wearing. She stood self-consciously, arms at her sides, in tangerine colored matching underwear.

Nadira took her clothes from her, folded them neatly and set them atop the wooden chest. She cleared her throat softly, encouraging Audria to finish.

Audria removed her underthings and stood completely naked, feeling diminutive and painfully vulnerable. Nadira stepped behind her, placing her hands on her shoulders, and turning her to the only other object in the room – a full-length antique mirror. She reached around and Audria could feel the woman's breasts graze her back and shoulder blades. Nadira cupped Audria's chin and cheekbones in her hands and tilted her head directly at the mirror, forcing her to focus on her reflection.

"Open yo' eyes, Queen Audria," she whispered softly, the breath from her mouth stirring the baby fine hairs on the side of Audria's neck. "To see yo'self is to know yo'self, Daughta. Now, let's begin."

If someone had tried to prepare her for what came next, it would have been difficult for Audria to comprehend. Nadira painstakingly covered every inch of her body, piece by piece, her fingers lightly touching whatever part she happened to be focusing on at that particular time. She was relentless with her questioning.

"What is 'dis, Queen Audria?"

"That is my left breast."

"And what purpose does yo' lef' breast serve?"

"It compliments my right breast and serves to balance the way I look."

"What else?"

"It can provide milk for a child if I had one and wanted to nurture it in that way."

"What else?"

"It provides a soft place for someone to lay their head for comfort."

"What else?"

"It is one of a woman's many attributes that attracts the opposite sex."

"We not talkin' 'bout a woman. We talkin' 'bout you, Daughta. Audria. Now, how you feel 'bout yo' lef' breast?"

"I... I... I don't know what you mean. How I feel about it?"

Impatiently. "Yes, how you feel 'bout yo' lef' breast."

"I guess I feel fine about it. It's okay."

"What you would change 'bout it if you could change somet'ing?"

"Maybe I would make it a little smaller."

"Smaller? Why smaller?"

"Because I don't like when men talk to my chest instead of talking to me."

"Mm hmm. Let's continue."

And so they went, from one body part to the next, Nadira's fingers lightly touching, her voice softly questioning, but insistent, and Audria responding as best she could.

She had never experienced anything so singularly scrutinizing. She felt as though all of her, her entire self, had been placed under a microscope, and she was being picked apart molecule by molecule. What intensified the feeling was that this wasn't just a physical examination, but an emotional one as well. She was never sure why Nadira chose to focus intently on one part of her body over another. Although not a single piece was missed, there were areas that Nadira would only ask three or four questions about, and then others that she lingered on for a half hour or more.

Audria felt emotionally and physically drained by the time they had gotten to her belly button, and said so. Nadira looked at her curiously like she was trying to figure out what Audria was saying, but then smiled. "Forgive me, Queen. Sometimes me forget 'dat not everybody can go same pace. Come. Lemme make us some ginger tea an' you can talk to me 'bout what brought you here today."

Audria let Nadira take her arm, drawing her out of the room, down a short hall, and into another room.

"Is this your bedroom?" she asked, no longer as self conscious about her nudity.

For the first time in anyone's presence, she wasn't thinking about sucking in her stomach to hide the bulge, or keeping her arms close to her breasts in an effort to push them closer together and slightly upward to disguise the imagined beginning effects of pre-middle age sag.

Nadira shook her head. "No one visits my bedroom 'cept for my lover, and since I don' happen to have one of 'dose jus' now, 'dat door is only fo' me. 'Dis room is what I call de halfway point. Is where we can rest togetha', talk, cry, share love an' anyt'ing else."

She motioned Audria to a frameless feather down mattress sitting atop mahogany wood planks on the floor. Audria sat down, then immediately laid back, allowing the softness of the bed to envelop her. She thought she heard Nadira say something about putting on the tea, but felt herself drifting away. She was too exhausted to fight it and allowed sleep to take her.

Sometime later, Audria drifted awake, slowly becoming aware that her head was nestled against the softness of a woman's breasts. She felt slightly uncomfortable, but didn't want to move, which would signal she was awake. Nadira was perceptive enough to figure it out though.

"So, you back wid' me finally, Pretty Audria?" she asked, her chest rising and falling slightly as she spoke.

"Yes," Audria answered, keeping her voice as intimately soft as Nadira's. She started to move away.

"Stay," Nadira urged her. "You wanted to talk, so let's talk."

Audria poured out her heart to the woman, telling her the whole story about the New Year's Eve party and of breaking her promise to Michael. She allowed the tears to come in some places and enjoyed the tender, comforting touch of her uniquely perceptive friend.

"You finish now?" Nadira asked her, after a lengthy silence had passed between them. Audria answered yes, then waited. Nadira didn't disappoint her.

"Until you face yo' Monster, Audria, you gon' always have problems wid' yo' flesh." Nadira looked down at Audria, who herself was looking up at her friend intently, waiting for the rest. Nadira shifted her weight slightly, then continued. "I bet you real money that you done had experiences wid' the darker side of eroticism. Things like bondage and pain." She said it as though stating a fact and smiled when Audria's eyes got wide. "When somebody introduce us to evil, hurt us, do us bad, 'dey have a power ovah us 'til we choose to break 'dey power. Yo' monster gon' always control you from yo' waist down, if you don' break his power ovah you."

"How am I supposed to do that?" Audria asked, genuinely confused.

"You got to face 'dat monster, Daughta. Face him and take back de power he tief' from you. Until you do 'dat, you can make yo' man all de promises you want, but yo' gon' break every one a' 'dem promises 'cuz somebody else got power ovah you."

Audria started to interrupt, anxious to know more, but Nadira shushed her. "Latah for 'dat. We got more work to do. Wais' down 'til we finish de body, yes?"

Audria sighed but knew it was pointless to argue. She nodded and moved to get up. Nadira gripped her from behind though, pulling her back into her warm embrace. Audria felt an electric shiver move through her as she felt the woman's arms encircle her, but tried to ignore it, remembering the words Nadira had just spoken. The last thing she needed was to further complicate things by succumbing to some physical desire to be with this woman. She closed her eyes and tried to relax. After a moment, Nadira began rubbing her shoulders in a halfway circular motion. When she spoke, her voice was back to a whisper and seemed contemplative.

"Yo' evah hear of sight that ain't sight wid' de natural eye?"

Still feeling somewhat uncomfortable pulled back against the woman the way she was, Audria frowned at the unexpected question. She nodded after a beat though. "Yes, I have."

"You undastan' what it mean?" Nadira asked her.

"I think so," Audria answered. "It's when somebody has the ability to see something that's going to happen?"

"Thas' part of it," Nadira agreed, and Audria could feel the woman smile although she wasn't looking at her.

"Do you have sight, Nadira?"

"What you t'ink?" Nadira replied, answering Audria's question with one of her own, and her voice taking on a lilting, teasing quality.

Audria wasn't playing with this though. She felt like it was important. "Yes," she answered. "I think you have sight."

Nadira said nothing for a beat, then spoke quietly. "I see some t'ings 'bout you, Queen."

Audria twisted her body around quickly. "You do? What do you see? Please tell me."

Nadira shook her head. "Thas' not how 'dis work. I can't jus' tell you what I see, you undastan'? But what I have to tell you is you need to get yo'self ready. Yo' life 'bout to change in ways thas' beyond anyt'ing you can expect."

Audria felt an uneasy fluttering begin in her chest, that out-of-control, runaway feeling from before. "Is it good, Nadira, or is it bad?"

The woman eyed her with unreadable, darkly penetrating eyes. "Only you can answer 'dat question," she said, "but howevah you answer it, yo' need to get yo'self ready."

* * * * * *

Audria threw her car keys on the kitchen counter, kicked off the new Ferragamo mules her mother had bought her a few days before, and went to the refrigerator to pour herself some iced tea. She took a long, refreshing swallow from the glass and plopped down on the nearest kitchen chair.

She was exhausted, mentally and physically drained from everything that had happened at Nadira's. When she'd called her friend asking to talk, she would never have expected things to go the way they had, but she was glad she had been open enough to allow Nadira to help her.

Audria took another sip of her tea and started replaying things in her mind. She thought about how strange her friend was. The kind of help Nadira offered certainly couldn't be called traditional, but just from spending the day there, Audria felt far stronger than she had ever felt. She had never considered the importance of connecting her physical self with her emotional self and working to fully integrate and accept the two. Now though, after the work she had done with Nadira, she felt like she was on her way to embracing a new and improved Audria. She was good and tired though. Nadira's relentlessness had worn her out, but she knew the hours had been hours well spent.

Audria got up, stretched her back muscles, and reached for the phone to check caller i.d. and her voicemail. She found herself hoping not to see the familiar 202- number that would mean another call from Al. He had called her for the first time a few days after their *thing*. Not recognizing who A. Hunter was, the name showing up on the caller i.d., Audria had answered the phone, still in a fog of anguish and was surprised to hear his voice on the other end of the line.

"Hi Audria. It's Al," he said, his voice hesitant.

"Yes?" she questioned, not bothering to hide her displeasure at hearing from him. It felt like a vicious reminder of her betrayal of Michael.

"I uh... I got your number from Gina," he spoke again, still sounding hesitant. "Hope you don't mind."

She didn't respond, couldn't bring herself to show him any kindness, and after a protracted silence, he got the hint. "Listen, I just wanted to check on you, find out how you've been doing considering..." His voice tapered off and although she could feel his discomfort, Audria felt a bitterness well up in her throat. She felt like she could and *would* do him real bodily harm if he was standing in front of her.

"I'm fine," she said in a flat, lifeless voice. "Please don't call again." She dropped the phone receiver in its cradle and lay back across her bed, hating the man intensely for what he had made her do.

She had thought then that it was the last time she would hear from him, but she had seen his number pop up again on the caller i.d. the next day, and the day after that. Every time she saw it was him calling, she ignored the phone, stubbornly refusing to entertain any further discussion with him. He had already proven he couldn't be trusted, and Audria wasn't about to test herself to see whether she could be trusted either. It was better to avoid temptation altogether by simply staying the hell away from it and from him.

Now, though, knowing herself in a much deeper way than she had before, she felt a prick of conscience that she had cruelly dismissed him the way she had. It had been far easier to hate him and blame him for making her break her promise, but Audria recognized she needed to own up to her role in how things had unfolded too. It certainly wasn't all Al's fault, so whether she disliked him intensely or not, she was wrong to treat him the way she had. She wasn't sure why he kept calling, and she really didn't feel up to it, but she made herself a promise that the next time he called, she would talk to him.

She started going through her voicemail and giggled as she listened to two back-to-back messages from Angela and Vanessa. In one of the messages, Vanessa gave her a blow by blow description of her latest beau and Audria shook her head. It never ceased to amaze her how easily Vanessa found man after man so stuck on the idea of having a beautiful woman on their arm, that they were willing to practically buy her. She hung up the phone, still smiling, then went to check her mailbox. A minute later, she was racing back inside holding a letter pressed to her chest and feeling like she had just won the lottery. *Michael.* Her man had written her back.

* * * * * *

Sun. 2/24

Peace Audria. Off the bat I got to tell you I don't really know what to say to you. Honestly, don't even know why I'm writing. Been holding on to your letter more than a week now and keep finding myself reading it over and over again. Not really sure why. It's not like I'm going to get some different meaning from it the tenth time I read it over the first. The words ain't changed. To be honest, when I first got it, I was all set to trash it and keep rolling, but to do that would be too much like stepping back to the punk ass I used to be, and I already put in too much work over all the years of my bid trying to move away from that dude. It's bad enough I stepped back to him long enough to write you my last letter, but on the real, that's enough stepping back for me. That ain't who I am, at least that's not who I'm trying to be, and every time I go back there, it's like I undo some of the positive work and progress I'm making.

Look Audria, I can tell you all day long for the next four years how sorry I am and make promises to you that I'm never gon' talk to you the way I did. I can even tell you I'm gon' forget about the broken promise that got us to this place to begin with. But the bottom line is I'd be flat out lying if I said any of that. It's harder for me to admit this than you know, but I told you from the beginning that I don't run from nothing, even if that means me facing the sides of me that ain't cool. In this case, I'm talking about the angry, dirty-mouth dude that disrespected you and then shut down just 'cuz you made a mistake.

Hell, that's one of the parts of your letter I kept coming back to over and over. You made a mistake. When I stack that up against all the shit I've done, I can't judge you. All my life, I been big on trying never to make the same mistake twice. If you remember, some months back I was lecturing you about getting your anger in check, when that's really my issue more than yours. This is the second time I let that rule me with you. Don't like losing control like that. But Audria, this love thing ain't easy. It's like what I feel for you is so strong, it starts making me go a little crazy inside my head to think about losing that or thinking about some other dude stepping to what's mine. I guess finding out I'm jealous, a emotion I ain't used to, is hard to swallow. I'm trying though. The old me would just walk away from all this, even with feeling you like I feel you, cause I don't like emotions I can't control, but I'm not running. I just gotta put in more work at fixing some of the things in my personality I don't like.

I can't lie to you. Yeah, I want my woman to be faithful to me. I feel like I can't handle the idea of you being with somebody else, but even with all that, I recognize it was selfish to put that kinda pressure on you, so it's off. I'm not telling you I'm cool with you doing what you did again, but I can't ask you to make me any promises when I'm having problems keeping some I made myself.

Don't know why I love you and don't know why I love you as much as I love you. And honestly, I ain't losing a whole lot of sleep over either one. It is what it is, right? Let's just try to love each other, move on from here, and slowly rebuild the trust between us. If you're game to try, then count me in, Babygirl. I'm with you.

Your Man, Michael

P.S. Need to see you soon. Come visit me.

forty-seven
Facing Goliath

A bone chilling wind whipped fiercely through her braids, flinging individual strands of hair against her face and neck. Her heart was pounding a rapid staccato beat in her chest, her palms were sweaty, and she felt feverish and emotionally raw. She stopped moving for a minute and found herself wondering if this was the way all would-be murderers felt.

Nothing much had changed in the twenty-six years since she had been here. The yard was still jacked, the grass brown and withered, growing in uneven patches that appeared in completely random spots over the tiny landscape. The old rusted-out John Deere tractor still sat in the same spot it always had, tall runaway weeds poking up through the engine block and all over tires that had deflated long years before. The house was the same drab gray color she remembered, with paint peeling in huge paper-thin chunks that fluttered lightly every time the wind blew.

As she walked slowly up the five broke-down steps leading to the rickety porch, they creaked betrayingly beneath her weight and she felt a nervous flutter begin in the bottom of her belly. The worn rocking chair stood still, its frame resembling an angular-bodied wooden dinosaur relic crouched in wait of prey. As she passed by it, reaching a shaky hand for the doorknob, she imagined she smelled a stink coming off the chair, an old mustiness that made her shudder. It made her think of urine, blood and semen all at the same time. She clutched the item she was holding even tighter, trying to find a small degree of courage from it, and pushed the door open.

The inside of the house smelled far mustier than the porch and it was dark and dreary looking. She took a moment to let her eyes get accustomed to the dim light, then moved cautiously across the room.

He was sitting in a ratty recliner, head thrown back in a slobbering sleep, the muted light of the television flashing eerily across his face. He looked almost half the size she remembered him being, not as big, tall and imposing as he had continued to live on in her mind. She was tempted to make some noise to jar him awake, so he would see it was her and know what was coming. But instead she moved stealthily and positioned herself directly behind him.

When she was satisfied she was standing in the best possible position, she leaned in closer, fighting the gag reflex beginning at the back of her throat. He stunk. A sour stench of unwashed body parts, sweat, old age and some other undefined thing rolled off him in a foul wave that assaulted her senses. She knew she needed to hurry up and do what she had come here to do or she would lose her nerve.

Holding her breath so as not to smell any more of his stink, she gripped the handle of the knife firmly, feeling the hardness of the wooden handle dig painfully into the soft flesh of her palm. She brought the blade up and over her head, seeing a reflection of her eyes momentarily flash back at her in the room's half light. She steeled her nerves and brought it down quickly, slashing over and over again into her monster's chest, watching his gushing blood coat her hands with every thrust.

Die. Die. Die. DIE. DIE.

Audria kept saying the words over and over again, voice hoarse, barking them out into the room and allowing them to fuel every downward slash. Suddenly, she felt a piercing pain move up through her fingers, through her wrist, and up into her hand and arm. She jerked backward and came awake in her car, breathing fast, realizing she had just cracked her knuckles hard against the steering wheel.

She looked around, confusion in her eyes, trying to get her bearings, then remembered. She was sitting half a block up the street from her uncle's house, trying to work up enough nerve to do what she had come all this way to do. It was time for her to face her monster.

Making an effort to slow her breathing, she took a big, gulping mouthful of air and leaned her head back against the seat rest. This had seemed like such a good idea when it first popped into her head. She had been on such a high since receiving Michael's letter some weeks before. She felt so optimistic about their relationship and about rebuilding the trust between them, but she didn't want to forget the things Nadira had said to her. As difficult as it was and as scary a prospect, she knew her friend and mentor was telling the truth. If she didn't face this thing, it would find a way to keep coming up and eventually wreck everything she treasured.

Nadira had been clear. Because of what he had done, her uncle would always maintain a power over her. It was up to her to face her fears, face him, and take back what he had stolen so many years before. Audria knew she needed to do this not just for her own sanity but if she wanted to preserve the future she was trying to build with her man, it was important.

She loved Michael and couldn't take the chance that she would wind up in another compromising position. In his letter, he had talked about not asking her to make him any more promises, but whether he did or not, Audria wanted and needed to be able to keep the promise of fidelity she had made to herself. And if that was going to happen, then she needed to face her uncle. Now that she was here though, she had no idea how to begin.

It had been much easier *deciding* to do something than actually doing it. Even committing to the more than four-hour drive to Rocky Mount had been okay, but for some reason, she hadn't allowed herself to think about what would come later once she got here. Audria thought about how impulsive she could be sometimes. Viola was always lecturing her about how it would get her in trouble some day, but that's just who she was.

Earlier that morning, she had bounced out of bed after waking up from some crazy nightmare that involved Michael busting out of prison. Sitting at her kitchen table, drinking a steaming cup of hot chocolate, she started thinking about wanting to go visit her man, but realized she didn't want to see him until she had confronted her demons. An hour later, she was showered, dressed, grabbing the keys to her Pilot, and on her way. Now that she was finally here though, she wasn't sure how to take the next step.

Audria glanced at the dashboard clock. The digital readout said 2:46 p.m. She had gotten here long before noon, had been sitting here the whole time trying to work up enough nerve to get out the car. She knew she needed to get her head right too, because entertaining thoughts about committing some bloody murder like she had been earlier, was not the way she needed to be thinking. It was just hard to think real straight now that she was so close to *him*.

She scrubbed at her face, took some moments to breathe a silent prayer, and reached across the passenger seat for her purse. It was now or never. Either she was gonna do this or concede failure, turn tail and run back home. And she was nobody's quitter. Damn it, she was Audria Hope and she believed she was strong enough to face all her fears. Even this one.

Pushing the car door open, she got out and started walking down the street to her monster's house.

* * * * * *

Audria didn't know what she had expected to find, but this wasn't it.

Every time she had thought about seeing her uncle again, she imagined he would look like some burned out husk of a man that resembled the grizzled old Danny Glover in *The Color Purple* after the love of his life left him and he was reduced to living in squalor among the pigs and the chickens on his rundown farm.

The man standing in front of her wasn't the big, strong, imposing figure she remembered from twenty-five years before, but neither was he some decrepit, feeble thing she felt would keel over if a strong wind blew by. He looked steadily at her with the same piercing, beady eyes she remembered, the dirty screen door the only thing separating them.

"Whatchu want?" he asked, his voice scratchy like steel wool on a rusty sink, sounding far more feeble than he looked. "I ain't buyin' nothin'."

Audria looked at him like he was crazy, then realized he was serious. Obviously, he didn't recognize her.

She could barely stand to look at him, but knew the sooner she got talking, the quicker she could deal with all this and leave. "I'm not selling anything. It's me, Audria," she said, her voice clipped and tight to her ears. "Viola's Audria," she added, not sure why she felt the need to say that. It wasn't like he had a bunch of Audria's showing up on his doorstep every day.

He just stood there peering at her through the screen like he hadn't heard what she said. Audria was getting ready to repeat herself when she saw his mouth open and close in surprise forming an 'o', and he raised a gnarled, arthritic-looking hand to his face as though he were wiping away cobwebs from his eyes. He pushed open the screen door in a non-verbal gesture for her to enter. She felt like laughing in his face. There was no way in hell she was stepping foot in that house ever again.

"You come out here," she gritted at him. "I got some questions for you and I'm not coming in there." She turned away and leaned against the dusty porch railing, folding her arms tightly across her chest. She felt defensive and angry, scared too, but she'd be damned if she showed him any sign of fear.

She tried to calm herself, watching as he hesitated in the doorway, the beady eyes shifting here and there like a cornered rat. She still wasn't sure exactly what to say to him, but she was already committed to this, so God would just have to bless her with divine inspiration. She started saying silent prayers to Him again, over and over in her mind, asking for the strength necessary to face this.

"Viola know you heah?" he asked her as he pushed the screen door all the way open and walked out onto the porch. He stood awkwardly in front of the ancient rocking chair, hooking his thumbs through dirty suspenders and looking like he was trying to decide whether to sit or stand. He must have decided he needed all the advantage he could get, because after a beat, he seemed to make up his mind to keep standing.

Audria purposely ignored his question, not wanting to admit she had been foolish enough to come all this way without telling anyone where she was headed, especially her mother.

"Look, let's get something straight," she said to him, making her voice as harsh as she could. "This is not a social visit where you ask me how I've been and I pretend I care about you. We both know why I'm here."

Audria forced herself to look him dead in his eyes, trying to ignore the raised hairs on the back of her neck and the goose pimples that were popping up all over her arms. He stared back at her, his beady eyes unreadable, and she wished she could pull a genie eye blink and head nod and automatically see what was in that dirty mind.

He cleared his throat like he was ready to say something, but she didn't want to give him any opportunity to distract her.

"You know why I'm here," she repeated flatly.

He looked at her and shook his head slowly. Audria pretended not to see the ticking pulse that started throbbing an in and out beat at his temple and the glassy glint of mist in his eyes.

"You owe me," she said, grinding her teeth hard as she bit off the words at him. "It's time for you to give me some answers."

He shook his head again and Audria saw him fumbling behind him for a handle of the rocking chair. She guessed he had decided to sit after all. Something about that infuriated her, and her leg shot out and kicked the chair hard, sending it scooting out from behind him and clear across the porch. She didn't want him pretending to be weak. At the very least, she wanted him to stand up and face her like a man. Audria ignored his stumbling backward steps and the harsh exhale of air as he banged into the wall.

"Why did you do it?" she ground out. "Why did you *rape* me?"

She made herself say the word, although it sounded vile on her tongue, but she needed him to hear her say it as much as she needed to hear herself say it. It was time for her to stop using safe words like *hurt* and *violate*. Yeah, he had done those things as well, but the days of sugar-coating what had been done to her were a thing of the past. She had been brutally raped at thirteen by her own uncle, this piece of inhuman garbage standing in front of her, and she wasn't leaving this place until he gave her some answers about why.

* * * * * *

"You don't know why? You don't know why? That's all you have to say to me?" Audria glared at him fiercely with fire in her eyes and resurfaced thoughts of murder on her mind. "That's the best answer you can come up with after all this time?" She couldn't believe this shit.

"Whatchu want from me, chile? I don' know whatchu want from me." He was holding his big head between gnarled, oversized hands, and Audria felt a shudder move through her body as she thought about those hands touching her.

"I'm not a child, okay? And what I *want* from you is for you to tell me why you did what you did."

He was just standing there bent over, still holding his head, but not saying a word, and Audria felt her blood start to boil again. She didn't want to start some loud scene out in the open that the neighbors might hear, but she hadn't driven over four hundred miles and worked up the courage to face her fears only to have him try to weasel out of talking to her.

"Look, I don't know what you think, but I'm not going to just go away. And for real, you don't want me to go away, 'cuz trust me, if I leave here without you making an effort to give me some answers, you're not gon' like who comes talk to you next."

That seemed to get his attention. He peered at her then slowly put his hands down. They dangled at his sides uselessly and Audria couldn't help but think of the way an ape's oversized limbs sometimes hung down in much the same way. She stared at him coldly as he opened and closed his mouth repeatedly trying to

319

say something. Finally, he got his tongue to cooperate with his brain.

"I done spent mos' these years tryin' to figure what it wuz that made me do it... made me do what I done to you." He swallowed hard and Audria saw the pulse begin again at his temple. She wondered what would happen if it was the precursor to a blood vessel exploding in his head. Would she help him or would she walk away leaving him to rot.

When she looked at him, she felt four distinct parts of her warring for attention. The little girl in her shook with terror at being in such close proximity to the man who had brutalized her.

Then there was the angry grown Audria who wanted to lop off his head and shit down the jagged hole left in his neck, that's how mad she was.

There was also a part of her that felt detached, almost clinical, like she wanted to pin him to a glass slide and put him under a microscope. Put him under a microscope like some alien bug and dissect him to try to figure out what made him different from every other man who lived their whole life without succumbing to the urge to rape a little girl.

Then the last part of her that she was trying hard to ignore was some sympathetic side that kept wanting to feel sorry for him. This side of her kept trying to remind her of the giddy feeling she used to have when he would pick her up as a child, those good times before he transformed into a monster. She pushed those memories away and refocused her attention on him. He didn't deserve any sympathy, and especially not from her.

"Tell me how it happened," she demanded.

He stared at her with a confused look in his eyes. "Whatchu mean how. You know how."

"I know *what* happened," Audria corrected him, putting emphasis on the word *what*. "That's etched into my memory forever. What I don't understand is *how* it happened. How did you allow it to happen? What were you thinking that would make you do something so awful? Had you done something like that before with somebody else? Did I do something to lead you on?" Audria's voice kept getting louder and louder with each question and by the time she got to the last one, she felt like she would start hyperventilating any second.

She wasn't expecting to see Carl crumble the way he did, all at once. One minute he was leaning back against the porch wall, and the next his knees were buckling and he was down in front of her groveling at her feet.

"Oh gawd, oh gawd, forgive me. You wuz jus' a lil' gal. You didn' do nuthin'. Seem like one minute I wuz watchin' you play, an' the nex' I wuz watchin' you wipe the bloody floor wid' the kitchen towel. 'Til I seen you nekkid, I didn' understan' what I done."

His sniveling made Audria lose it. She didn't remember how her purse got off her shoulder, but the next thing she knew, she was clutching the straps fiercely and pounding him in his head with the bag. Then she reversed things and started slamming the leather strap against his neck and shoulders, raining lashes down on him like a mother punishing a truant child.

"You. Were. The. Adult.

"I. Was. The. Child.

"I was a child, God damn you.

"It was your responsibility to protect me, to love me and keep me safe, not hurt me."

She was sobbing loudly, tears streaming rivers down her face and her breath kept hitching in her throat making her feel like she couldn't breathe. She whipped down even harder, angry she had lost control and that he was seeing her cry.

He tried to touch her feet, his clubby fingers grabbing at her ankles, and Audria hopped away, feeling a shudder of revulsion pulsate through her. "Don't touch me," she shrieked at him. "You can't *ever* touch me again." She turned away from him, buried her face in her hands, and gave in to the flood that she could no longer hold back.

* * * * * *

Audria was sitting on the stoop, feeling a surreal sense of time. She knew she was now an adult, but it felt so familiar to her to sit here this way. Almost like she had stepped back across the years and crept back into the body of the little girl who had sat in this exact same place summer after summer playing with her dolls.

She grabbed her knees pulling them close to her body and watched a mangy-looking stray dog go slinking by. Its head hung so low that any lower and its jaw would be dragging in the dirt. It looked like it had been whipped into submission over many years. Something about it made her think back to the groveling picture her uncle had presented down on his knees, trying to grab at her ankles. That had been at least an hour before. She was grateful things had calmed down a bit. She still felt like a train wreck on the inside but at least she had stopped bawling.

He was sitting next to her on the stoop. She could tell he was being extra careful not to touch her, but he wasn't going anywhere either. They had talked a little, in short sporadic bursts that sometimes left her feeling kinda panicky in the pit of her stomach when she realized he was as much in the dark about what he had done as she was. But at least he had answered all her questions, or tried to where he could. And although from time to time Audria smelled fear on him, worry about his future, he seemed to want to help her get the answers she needed.

After another long silence, he cleared his throat in a half cough-half snort and looked over at her briefly. "You done tol' your mother what I done?"

"She knows," Audria answered him, not feeling much like explaining the way Viola had found out. Out of the corner of her eye, she saw him getting ready to ask another question, but wasn't ready to grant him absolution just yet.

"Did you ever think about trying to make things right with me?" she asked him. "Did you wonder how I would handle it? What it would do to me growing up with the knowledge of what you did?"

He nodded slowly and passed a hand across his eyes. "I cain't tell you 'bout all the times I done wished I could go back an' live ovah that day, but much as I pray God for that, ain't no goin' back. I want you to know ain't a single day goes by when I don' think 'bout what I done and pray forgiveness for it."

As much as she hated to, Audria looked at him. She knew he was telling the truth. But whether he was or not, it didn't really matter in this instance. The forgiveness he was seeking would have to come directly from whatever God he felt he was praying to, which in her mind, could never be the same God she loved and believed in. And as far as her forgiving him, she hoped he wasn't waiting for her to give him that, because it would be a much longer wait than he had years to live.

Some minutes before, a word had popped up in her head out of nowhere. *Closure.* Her psychologist friend Gina was always throwing that around saying how important closure was. Maybe on some level she had started believing that by coming here closure would be something she would automatically get, but Audria now understood that if a person had enough self love, it was within their own power to gift themselves with closure.

She reached behind her for the pocketbook that was still sitting in the same place she had dropped it, stood up slowly and dusted off the seat of her corduroys. She wasn't sure what to say. It's not like she could say the usual things people said when they parted company, like 'see you next time,' 'take care of yourself,' or 'love you.' None of that applied here and she wasn't about to turn herself into a hypocrite.

She thought briefly about thanking him for talking to her, but that seemed too much like telling him she was now okay with what he had done. In the end, she decided on the simple truth.

"I'm leaving now," she said, swiping at a stray braid and pushing it behind her ear. "I won't be back." She emphasized that last and looked at him pointedly, making sure he got the message.

Audria felt she could never bring herself to tell him. Tell him this was as far as she would go with exacting any payment from him for what he had done. She might be willing to move on with her life knowing she had finally faced her monster, but to *tell* him that's what she was doing, to actually say the words out loud? Wasn't happening.

Without any preamble, she simply walked away from him, from the house, and from the scared little thirteen-year old girl whose life had been forever changed in this place. As she walked up the street heading for her car, she felt a lightness in her spirit that she had never felt before. It was something indescribable and so freeing that in that moment, Audria knew exactly what David must have felt after winning his battle with Goliath. She smiled a beautifully deep smile that seemed to emanate from the depths of her soul and did a little skip. She couldn't wait to get home.

<u>forty-eight</u>
Dead Weight

Audria was perched on two cushions, sitting low at Viola's feet, enjoying the feel of her mother's hands in her hair. Although she was worn out from the back and forth drive to North Carolina and the emotional strain of facing her uncle, she hadn't felt like being alone when she got back. She had come straight here.

It continued to amaze her how close she and her mother were getting. Although Viola still got under her skin from time to time, and in ways nobody else could, she felt like their relationship had changed sufficiently to where both of them genuinely enjoyed each other's company. Even something as simple as having her mother grease her scalp and braids made Audria feel so much closer to Viola.

She wiggled her backside a bit to get more comfortable and leaned her head back into her mother's lap.

"Would you stop all that squirmin' 'round," Viola fussed at her, sectioning off another chunk of braids. She dipped a finger into the jar of coconut oil and tea tree hair food sitting on the nightstand near her and twisted Audria's head to one side. "Whatchu been doin' all day? I been by your place 'nuff times lookin' for you. Me an' Sylvia was goin' out to Nordstrom's an' I wanted you to go wid' us."

Audria let her mother ramble on telling her about the shopping trip with her friend Sylvia and all the great deals they had stumbled on. It gave her a chance to get her thoughts together and to figure out how to tell Viola what was on her mind. She waited until her mother came up for air and then turned around so Viola would pay attention.

"I went to see Uncle Carl today."

"You did WHAT?" Viola asked, raising her voice. Audria could see her gearing up to get all loud and didn't want to give her a chance to get started.

She held up a hand. "Mother, would you just listen to me for a minute?" she said, looking at Viola hard. "I *need* you to hear me."

Viola's mouth slammed shut and she folded her arms tightly across her midsection. It was killing her not to be able to interrupt, to ask even one of the hundreds of questions flitting through her mind, but she kept quiet, realizing her daughter needed to unload. She allowed Audria to tell her story.

When Audria finally finished, Viola reached out and pulled her close, cradling her head and shoulders in her lap. She didn't understand why God had seen fit to make her child suffer so much. It didn't seem fair for one person to have to bear all this, but Viola wasn't trying to second guess God's plan. She would just have to do whatever she could to ease things for Audria, but before all that, she had to speak her mind.

"You know I gotta tell you I think you was crazy to go talk to Carl by yourself like that. Anything coulda happened to you." She shook her head. "I can't believe you was so reckless."

"You're right, Momma, but I needed to face him and try to get some answers from him about what he did."

Viola nodded, but put a restraining hand on Audria's shoulder. "I understand what you sayin', but I don't know what the big rush was. You coulda asked me or one of your girlfriends to go wid' you. It don't make no kinda sense that you went down there by yourself."

Audria felt herself starting to get frustrated with her mother, and took a deep breath. "Mom, it was important for me to do it for a few reasons. First, it happened to me, not to anyone else, and it's been affecting *my* life, not anybody else's. I know it was impulsive for me to go down there like that, but it just hit me all at once that if I didn't face up to it, this thing would always be hanging over my head and interfering with my relationships and my life."

She reached out and took hold of her mother's hand. "You know what I've shared with you about Michael and how important he is to me. I've already screwed up with him once and hurt him. And although I can't exactly prove it, I believe that happened because I never got real with myself about my past."

"You think you cheated on your man 'cuz of what Carl did to you?"

Audria nodded.

"Why you think that?" Viola asked, sounding puzzled.

"It's a combination of things," Audria said, shrugging her shoulders. "But all my life, I've had problems with men. It's either I'd be too needy, clinging to them like they're supposed to be some lifeline for me, or when they would get into me and really start showing me genuine affection, I'd get scared and freeze up and not show any emotion at all. I didn't want to keep going like that, especially since I finally found me a good man."

Viola made a low *hmm* deep in her throat, then peered over her glasses at Audria. "Baby, I ain't gon' pretend like I understand what you sayin'. Now I ain't sayin' what that dog Carl done to you didn' have some lasting effects, but you soundin' to me like some a' these people who blame all the mess they get into in they' adult life on bad parents or on they' Momma not breastfeedin' them long enough."

Audria looked at her mother, then realized her jaw had fallen open. "What? Are you trying to say you think I'm not being responsible or something?"

Viola held up a hand again, trying to calm things down. "I think you misunderstandin' what I'm sayin'. 'Course you bein' responsible, but you can't decide to be responsible 'bout some things and then when it's more convenient, you blame the rest on something from your childhood. That sound like what you yourself always callin' white folks' psychobabble."

Audria scrambled to one side and got on her feet fast. "I don't believe you," she said, slamming her hands on her hips and raising her voice at her mother. "I'm not picking and choosing when to be responsible. Do you know how much I've learned about myself just in this last year? The way things were before, I'd just live my life trying to pretend that my uncle hadn't raped me, but that's not something you forget, no matter how hard you try to. And it would find a way of coming up over and over again and mess things up for me. Now that I finally get tired of having that happen, get tired of being some kind of victim, and decide to confront it, you're going to sit there and lecture me about using it as an excuse?"

She was beyond hot, felt her blood boiling. "Do you have *any* idea how difficult it was for me to do what I did? If you think it was easy, well let me enlighten you, Mother, it wasn't."

Viola stood up slowly, putting her own hands on her hips. She was getting ready to give Audria a piece of her mind, opened her mouth to do exactly that, but felt a sharp, paralyzing pain slam into her neck and on down the left side of her body. She put a hand out to balance herself, tried sucking in a breath, but felt a strange pressure seize the center of her chest like an iron fist. As her knees buckled and she began to fall, Viola heard her daughter start screaming. She tried to turn her head to say something reassuring to calm her baby, but her vision blurred then went dark and she tumbled over like dead weight, flat on her face.

forty-nine
Miracles

Alright, was time to walk the line.

Michael shifted his eyes left without turning his head and waited for the verbal dance to begin.

People like him who had ten or more years in were considered old heads. As such, he had walked the line enough times in the last thirteen years to know what to expect.

A heavy hand fell on his shoulder from behind and he smiled on the inside, enjoying the moment. This always made him think back to the kind of man he used to be. Back then, the first time a correctional officer, or CO, had put hands on him like this resulted in dude walking away with two broken fingers and a penalty of six months in the hole for him. A year plus two months had been added to his sentence for that bit of ignorance. Although he was a different person now, with that incident twelve years past, the word had gotten 'round. No one touched him without asking first. No one except Ramirez, and Michael just barely tolerated that. It was cool though since it only happened on days like today.

"Good luck, Man," came the low growl at his side.

"Luck ain't got shit to do with this."

"True that, true that," came the voice again.

Michael waited, warming to their exchange.

"So what's the game plan?" Ramirez asked. "Same as always?"

Michael heard the jovial, half-mocking tone behind the question, but wasn't fooled by it. He knew Ramirez genuinely wished him well, but the gratitude he saw in the man's eyes made him uncomfortable. As a matter of fact, he made a point when he could to avoid the older man's eyes or just avoid him altogether. Some years back, he had stopped another inmate from knifing the guard in a fight gone bad. Since then Ramirez always went out his way to help Michael however and whenever he could.

This wasn't exactly kosher with Michael. He knew the nature of people enough to understand that prolonged gratitude occasionally bred resentment, but he would be a jackass to think that a man in his position couldn't benefit from the kind of alliance that had developed between him and Ramirez. He was careful never to take advantage of it though, especially around other inmates. Wasn't always good for a man's health to get the reputation of being too pally with the people holding gate keys.

They began walking down the hall together, Michael's hands handcuffed in back and shackled to waist chains at his sides. The cold steel of the cuffs felt like arctic fire against his skin, and although both he and Ramirez knew this wasn't necessary, they were following the facility's procedures.

This day got some inmates all discombobulated, the whole going before the board thing, but not him. He could face a bunch of skeptics any day, but being cuffed and shackled made him *feel* like a criminal, and that was no longer the way he defined himself. Although this happened once a year, it still felt weird to him.

In the state of Pennsylvania, as well as some other jurisdictions, if an inmate got sentenced to twenty years, they were eligible for parole in four and a half years, roughly a quarter of their sentence. Every year on the anniversary date of your processing into the facility, you went before the parole board for evaluation.

Michael knew most people didn't understand the system and how it worked. It had taken him more than a minute to comprehend all of it, but as an inmate, he had learned long ago that if you didn't show interest and get pro-active about your own situation, nobody else would give a damn.

It still surprised him how many inmates didn't understand the difference between parole and probation, especially since it was so easy to follow. Basically, it boiled down to this. Parole was defined as a conditional release from imprisonment that entitled the person to serve the remainder of their sentence outside the prison as long as they complied with the terms of their release.

Because of widespread corruption and abuse of powers by various state parole boards, a bill was introduced in 1994 providing for the abolition of parole. The legislation stipulated that, going forward, parole would be eliminated for any offense committed on or after July 1, 1996.

This meant that for Michael and other old heads who had committed offenses prior to July '96, their cases were still overseen under the former system of parole and their cases were reviewed by the PBPP -- the Pennsylvania Board of Probation and Parole. In direct opposition, young boys new to the system dealt only with probation, which was generally handled by a sentencing judge and then an assigned probation officer.

An important difference between parole and probation was if a released person violated probation, they could receive up to three warnings by their probation officer or even the sentencing judge without serious consequences.

If you violated on parole, was no playing baseball. You got yanked the hell back in front of the Parole Board and more than likely you'd be required to do the rest of your time on lock.

He had done his research on the PBPP. Comprised of nine members appointed by the Governor and confirmed by the state senate, it was the Board's responsibility to make decisions on parole and other such matters. They operated in two-person panels that traveled to various state prisons to interview inmates. They considered such factors like an inmate's behavior and attitude, present custody level, drug status, notes in an inmate's file about his character and background, and they took recommendations from the sentencing judge, prosecuting attorney and even the warden or superintendent of the inmate's assigned facility.

This was Michael's seventh time coming up for review before the Board. He had done three years in before the first review came up and back then, he was still young, buck wild and so full of anger and of himself that nobody could tell him a damn thing. The two board members might as well have laughed in his face, the way they sayonaraed his ass out of that first meeting, with him cussin' both of them on the way out.

The next few hearings weren't much better. It was only after his third or fourth time that he had gained enough perspective and control of himself to be able to participate in the interview process like he had some sense. But although his attitude improved, there was an odd sense of resignation that made him go through the motions, just saying whatever he felt like at the time, depending on his mood, or what he thought the board members wanted to hear him say. Now, he felt like an old pro at this. He knew he had never regarded the process with the respect it deserved, but he already knew today would be different. He had too much riding on this meeting to be blasé about it and he intended to fight for all of it like a heavyweight champion with titles on the line.

"Well," Ramirez prompted him again, "what's the game plan?"

"Truth is my game plan to the grave," Michael answered, smiling slightly. He turned in the direction of the security door at the end of the hall. The one that would take them through to the adjoining building where his fate would once again be decided by strangers with familiar faces. When they stopped outside the closed door, Michael waiting for the cuffs and shackles to be removed, Ramirez stepped directly in front of him, forcing eye contact between them.

"So you gon' do what you do then, Big Man?" he asked, bending slightly to remove the restraints.

"Every time," Michael responded, touching his knuckled fist to the guard's in a dap.

He knew the man would be sending up prayers for him and that was a good thing. He could use all the help he could get right about now, but it was gon' be what it was. He would have to allow fate to run its course and the man upstairs to do his thing. He opened the closed door and walked through.

* * * * * *

He walked into the meeting room, hesitated briefly to give the two board members a chance to get used to his imposing size, then said good morning. They both nodded at him but gave no verbal response.

He moved slowly, deliberately to the chair designated for him. It was positioned in the center of the room, eight feet away from the six foot long table that created a barrier panel for the board members.

He sat. Planted his feet flat on the floor, legs apart, back straight, keeping his hands loose in his lap, his posture as non-threatening as he could make it.

He took measure of the two that had been sent this time. He hadn't yet figured out the cycle the board relied on to rotate its visiting members. This was hard for him, always was, surrendering to the idea that these people held the power to decide his immediate future. Not his life. That was up to him and God, but they damn sure could decide to commute his sentence and send him home early, and he was dead set on helping them do exactly that.

He had done the math. The way it worked was if his sentence was computed, he would be required to do two months and two weeks for every remaining year. He had a little over three years left to stay in. If he could successfully convince the board to commute his sentence, he would be looking at eight months or less before he could go home.

Alright, just like he had hit the streets with a vengeance, strapping up and slanging like wasn't none better at it before or after him, he would approach this the same way. It was time to roll and he was ready to talk his way through it.

He looked up at them again. The designated talker, a thinning haired old fart who always managed to look constipated, cleared his throat and started things off.

"Well Mr. Strong, how have *we* been? How's *our* time going?"

These questions, the same ones he had been hearing for too many years, set him on edge like they always did. He wanted to ask the two-hair-strands fart what he knew about doing time. These types always included themselves in the equation as if they were grinding años with the natives. He wanted to put his foot up his ass and wipe that smug, self-satisfied smirk off the wrinkled face, but he tamped down the aggression and tried to be chilly.

He reached up and lightly patted his pocket, taking reassurance from the two photos there. His woman and his son. They were his motivation to get through this and to go home. He let himself relax and thought of the sound of Audria's voice the last time he had talked to her. He smiled.

"I'm doing well, Sir. Better than ever."

Michael kept his thoughts light, breezy and started talking, letting the words come naturally, rolling off his tongue like the ebb and flow of ocean waves spinning at high tide. He talked about the classes he had recently started taking to finish his degree, about the various certifications in life skills and society reintegration he had received over the years. He answered question after question, invasive darts thrown with force at his psyche, but he didn't buckle. He was a soldier, was gon' be that till the day he stopped breathing, and he was handling things like soldiers everywhere handled their business. Sucked up the emotion, put his game face on, and talked the talk.

And not that talking the talk meant he was lying. Untruths wasn't his thing, but he instinctively understood when it was time to slather the lather.

Over the years, this was one of the many lessons he had tried to teach his son. You could be the biggest, most cut-up buck in the yard, whether your yard was inside or out. You could earn the respect and reputation as dude most likely to beat the brakes off another John Doe for looking at you cross-eyed, but if you didn't have your awareness up and understand the importance of knowing when to set the testosterone aside and resort to your brain power and negotiation skills, all you would ever be was a big, cut-up mufucka stuck on stupid and laid up in the same place a decade down the line, whether that place had to do with geography or mentals. And he sure as shit wasn't gon' be that dude. He knew what was ahead of him, and most of it wasn't gon' be no cakewalk, but he was about as ready for it as anybody could be.

He was waiting on *the* question to come, the one they invariably got around to sooner or later. They took turns asking it every time they met with him. This time it was the feisty little redhead sitting next to thinning hair. She kept glancing at her Lady Rolex every three minutes like she had somewhere more important to be, and he felt himself wanting to smile as she gave a dainty little clearing of her throat and started talking.

"So Mr. Strong, what has changed for you since we saw you last?"

Michael knew this was institution double-speak for the question they really wanted to ask. *Why should we let you out?* His old gangster mentality that he sometimes thought would always be with him, made him want to write both of them a fuck you post-it note and staple it raw to their foreheads, but he was sure that would be received as a less than positive gesture, so he pushed aside the thought, put things important front and center, and answered the question. This was ride or die time and he wasn't ready to fight the black-robed, blade grasping freak just yet. Was time to saddle up instead.

He didn't really like people all up in his business, was protective of his own, but this wasn't the time to get overly paranoid with people who could help him. He laid it on the line for the two of them and by the time he got done, they had a clear picture of what he was facing.

He spoke low, humbly, sharing with them much more intimately and personally than he had ever done. He told them about Trina's murder, attending her funeral, and even talked about how that had made him feel. He talked about his son, his blood, his hope, the way the boy was fighting to find himself, warring with doing right but constantly getting caught up in bullshit and bad company.

He didn't have to fake the emotion he felt, didn't even have to reach too deep for it, 'cuz it was right there on the surface. He was afraid for his child and said so, made them understand that he was all Michael Jr. had, and he wasn't about to lay back and abandon his boy to the fates. He made certain they understood this, and his willingness to do anything and everything in his power to prevent his son from walking the same road he had.

Michael stopped talking abruptly, something inside him telling him to fall back. He had said everything that needed saying. Was out his hands now. They were gon' do their thing one way or the next, with or without him flapping gums.

He forced back a desire to crack his neck muscles, knowing it might be construed as too aggressive a stance, and started the quiet down process inside himself that made it easier to listen and read the body language and vibe in the room. He didn't think much had changed from the year before. Of the nine total on the board, he knew the four who were on his side, had been with him solid for the last three years, and the five who weren't. These two were part of that five, so obviously they were his main concentration. All he needed was to swing one his way, just one, and freedom would be something far closer than a dream.

Although he knew how important this was, he suddenly felt dog tired in his spirit. He was tired of society wanting to hang their shit on him, blaming him for their failures. From the parents who failed their children by not being there enough, to the children who allowed weak character to lead them to make bad choices. Yeah, he used to sling narcotics, but he never put a gun to nobody's head and force them to rock the rock. He had done what he did, and had more than paid for it, was still paying for it, but people like these two and others like them would always see him as the slanger. He knew he wasn't that man any longer, but they didn't know that and most didn't care.

Ignoring another clearing of the throat from the thinning-haired fart, signaling the man was getting ready to say something, he started talking again, feeling a desperation in the pit of his stomach that he had never felt before.

"I don't know you, neither of you. I mean, other than seeing you in this room every couple years over the last ten, I don't know you. And that's cool. I'm not supposed to know you. But it's your *job* to know me. You're supposed to look at me and my file, evaluate, then make a decision about whether I been sufficiently rehabilitated to go home.

"I don't know what other people come in here and say. I can only talk for myself. Anybody who knows me will tell you one thing about me. I'm a man whose word is bond. I don't give it unless I know I can deliver. And on this thing, I'm two hundred percent sure I can deliver. Give me a chance to prove to the Board, to society and anyone else who might doubt it, that I'm a different man than the one who walked through these gates thirteen years ago."

He thought about his Audria, their love for each other, and kept going.

"Somebody important to me just wrote me a letter not long ago and she said something I agree with. She said that our world is as beautiful as it is because of the constancy of change. I'm a result of change. You can choose to believe that or not. I really want you to, but I'm *never* gon' beg you to."

He sat back in his chair, looked at them both directly, then closed his eyes. A minute later, Hausman, the thinning-haired dude, asked him to leave the room. Michael left, unsure of what would come in fifteen when he returned.

Twenty minutes later, he was on his way back to his cell, feeling something he hadn't felt in a long time. Surprise. And when Ramirez questioned him about what had happened behind the closed conference room door, Michael could only answer with two words.

"A miracle."

fifty
Change

"How many of you in this room are ready for change?

"'Going to know what to do with it when it comes knocking on your door?

"Are you ready for it?

"Well if you are, let me hear you say the word!"

Audria shouted the word *CHANGE* into the air, her voice just as strong or stronger than the enthusiastic hundreds crowded all around her. These people were strangers to her, she wouldn't be able to pick out nary a one of them from anybody else on the street come tomorrow, but at this particular moment, she felt an affinity and kinship with them that came from their collective belief in the same thing – their ability to bring about change in their lives.

It was standing room only in the beautifully posh, 21,000 square foot ballroom at the L'Enfant Plaza Hotel, and there were people crammed in that joint to the max, on every side of her. It wasn't noon yet but her dogs were already barking tired from the four-inch Dior mules she had put on that morning. Obviously, she must have bumped her head hard when she decided to pull those out of the closet, but it was too late now to be overly concerned with footwear. Besides, she was way siced. She was getting to hear her favorite author turned motivational speaker for the first time.

Madame Zoe Questia Truth was this five foot two fiery ball of energy from Burkina Faso in West Africa who had a whole lot to say and demanded an attentive audience. Madame had gained an international reputation through the telling of her personal story of survival. The woman had seen the underbelly of hell and lived to talk about it. She was a survivor of female circumcision, an awful practice that she had been subjected to as a little girl.

Then at the age of thirteen, she was kidnapped from her home by rebels from the Ivory Coast, a neighboring country. Ripped away from the only family she knew, she had been raped repeatedly, then sold into a child prostitution ring where she spent the next five years enduring horrors most people only read about. With the help of a friend, she managed to escape on her nineteenth birthday, stole passage on board a freighter headed for France. From there, she eventually made her way to the United States. Her autobiography, *The Changing Breath I Breathe*, was on the New York Times bestsellers list and was expected to stay there for more than a minute.

It was plain to see that despite going through all of what she had, Madame Truth had a lust for life that ran deep. As she shared the awful events in her life through her book and talks, she was able to galvanize and inspire thousands of people to accept personal hurts for what they were but to eventually move past them. After seeing a copy of Madame Truth's book at Nadira's house, Audria picked up a copy and felt an instant bond with the woman. So as soon as she'd seen posting of the upcoming talk in the Weekender, she knew she had to be in there.

Trying to ignore the shooting pains in the arch of her feet, and the sweaty-armpits smell coming from the too-damn-natural sistah next to her, she refocused her attention on Madame.

"If you have eyes, you can see past the barriers in your way.

"If you have ears, you can hear the call of success and personal fulfillment.

"If you have feet, you can run, not walk, away from the hurts of yesterday and move swiftly to claim your greatness."

For the umpteenth time, she joined in with the applauding crowds and the room thundered with sounds of their admiration for this blessed sistah and all her wisdom.

Audria looked at the tiny woman bouncing around the slightly raised platform at the front of the room. It was easy to picture this person with all her bubbly energy effecting change in her life, but she found herself thinking about her own situation, and wondering if anyone could ever really prepare themselves for change. You might be able to roll with the punches when they came at you, but was it really possible to get your mind ready in advance of change? To hear Madame tell it, your very existence depended on how ready you made yourself for the various changes that would inevitably come.

So much crazy shit had been happening in her life lately that she had trouble remembering her own damn name most days. Seemed like Viola's heart attack had just been a nasty appetizer to the banquet of misery laid out in front of her. It was one thing after the next.

Wasn't more than a month ago that her mother had keeled over right in front of her in the middle of their argument. Audria blessed the day two years ago that she had decided to take the six-week course offered by her firm on CPR and First Aid. All the training from the Saturday morning classes came rushing back and it didn't take her long to figure out her mother was having a massive heart attack.

She hauled ass to the phone, dialed 9-1-1, then immediately began mouth-to-mouth to keep a steady flow of oxygen to her mother's brain, heart and the rest of her body. By the time the ambulance got to the house, Viola had started coming around and Audria gave her an aspirin to chew on. That was something else she remembered from the CPR class. The instructor told them that it had been proven aspirin reduced the fatality in heart attack victims by as much as 25%. The man explained that it works to thin the blood and lets more oxygen-rich blood get through the narrow or blocked artery to the heart.

The bad news didn't stop there though. When they got Viola to the hospital, and once the ER doctors got started with their tests -

- an EKG and an echocardio-something or other, and all kinds of lab work, they came hustling out to tell Audria that Viola needed emergency bypass surgery. She had barely finished filling out the stack of consent forms and other paperwork and settled in for the long wait, when her cell phone started chirping. More bad news. It was Vanessa calling her all frantic to say that three knuckleheads from Berry Farms had carjacked Angela at gunpoint, pistol-whipped her, and took the brand new Mercedes Benz SUV her husband had just got her for her birthday.

"Them Niggahs done fucked our girl up," Vanessa kept hollering in the phone over and over, just blabbing 'til Audria had to holler back just as loud to get her to shut the hell up and tell the story from the beginning. By the time it all came out, it was obvious Angela had just been unlucky enough to be in the wrong place at the wrong time.

Apparently, she and 'Nessa had gone to an aerobics dance class earlier in the day, then stopped at Ben's Chili Bowl for chili dogs, *just like them to go work out and then go stuff their faces right after.* After they left The Bowl, Angela had dropped Vanessa off at home and was on her way in too. The last thing V remembered her saying was that she was running low on gas and needed to stop at the Exxon before jumping on 495. Hours later when Vanessa called the house to ask Angela about the next week's Sunday brunch, she still hadn't made it home. And twenty minutes later her husband Ford was calling back to say DCPD had just called to notify him about the carjacking.

"What hospital she at?" Audria asked, trying to keep Vanessa from breaking off into another loud, confused rambling tangent.

"Ford say they was tryin' to take her to that triflin' ass Hospital Center, but he made them take her to Georgetown. Thas' where her doctor office be at."

Audria gritted her teeth. Even in the middle of all this crisis, she wanted to correct Vanessa's English. It didn't make a bit of sense the mess that came out the woman's mouth, especially with her being college-educated and all. It was one thing to lapse into occasional Ebonics, but you had to know when to turn that shit off. She bit her tongue though.

"You say they're at Georgetown? That's where I'm at now."

"You at Georgetown?" Vanessa bellowed in her ear. "Why come? Whatchu doin' there?"

Audria didn't much feel like explaining everything to Miss Noisy over the phone, including the fact that she, just like Ford, had insisted the ambulance driver bypass Southern Maryland Hospital, which was the main health facility that serviced the Waldorf area, and take her mother directly to Georgetown. She ignored the question.

"I'll tell you when you get here. I'ma go try to find Ange, or at least find Ford or somebody else who can give me some information. Get moving and call me back on my cell when you get here."

She pushed the end button, left a message at the nurses station for Viola's doctor with her cell phone number in case they came looking for her, then went in search of her friend. Forty-five minutes later, with loud ass Vanessa in tow, they finally found Angela and Ford in one of the tiny examining rooms in the Emergency Room triage.

Audria was shocked at the way Angela looked, and knew Vanessa must be too, but before she could caution Miss Loud Ass not to say anything, Vanessa busted out with a loud bawling in the narrow room.

"Oh Gawd Angela, look what they done done to your face."

Audria rammed an elbow in her side and pushed her out of the way, looking pointedly at Ford. "Why don't you take a break Ford, and maybe get us all some water or something." She hugged him, then prodded Vanessa. "Whyn't you go help him?"

When they were gone, she sat on the edge of the cot and hugged her friend. She could barely recognize Angela, her face was so beat up. Both her eyes were black and blue and swollen, and there was a gash under the right one that had closed it even further. Cotton was stuffed up both nostrils, so Audria guessed her nose must've gotten busted or broken. There was a cut on her lip and another huge slash that ran from just below her right temple to her chin that had been stitched up. Audria knew that would leave a scar. She wanted to scream out loud at what had been done to her friend, but she smiled instead.

"You gon' be alright, Precious. This ain't nothing but a minor setback. You gon' be as right as rain. Hell, you gon' be as right as Rush Limbaugh, Karl Rove and the whole Bush clan put together in no time." She giggled. "Well, maybe not as right as all that, but you gon' be alright."

Audria giggled again, hoping to get a rise out of Angela, but her friend just shook her head and started crying softly. Audria reached for her and sat for some minutes just holding her.

"They hurt me," Angela cried softly, and Audria could tell it was painful for her to talk. "I didn't fight. I didn't argue. I was gon' give them the car, and still they hurt me."

Audria shushed her and rocked her gently back and forth. "You know how these young guys are these days, Baby. They don't value their own lives, so we can't expect them to value other people's."

They talked some more, and Audria let Angela take her time telling her how things had gone down. She had stopped at an Exxon to get gas before heading home, pulled up to the pump and went to get out when a raggedy ass Cadillac backed in fast in front of her and a pick-up truck smashed up close right behind. By the time she realized what was happening, the guy from the Cadillac was up and out the car, mask on, hammer pulled and beating her upside the head with it. Then somebody else jumped in her truck and they all sped off.

"They took everything, Audria. My wedding ring, my purse, my credit cards, checkbook, keys to the house, everything." She started to cry again, but when Audria went to hold her, she pushed away and strained to sit up in the bed.

"You got to promise me you gon' keep a eye on Ford. He talkin' crazy 'bout gettin' some guys together to go down to the Farms to look for them punks." Angela gripped Audria's fingers in her hand. "I've lost enough today, okay? I'm not tryin' to lose my husband too. Promise me you gon' look out for him?"

Audria knew she already had her plate full with everything happening with her mother, plus she knew how men got when their powers of protection were called into play and the testosterone got to pumping. But this was her girl, her ace, and she wasn't about to let her down.

She nodded. "I'll talk to him," she promised, then hugged Angela. "You get some rest, 'kay? I'll be back to see you soon."

The next few hours were hectic. She kept going back and forth between the surgical floor to see if there was any news about her Mother, then back down to the ER to check on Angela. During one of her trips, she pulled Ford aside, sat him down and talked some sense into him, eventually getting him to promise that he would let the police do their jobs. She even had a chance to school Vanessa on what was appropriate and inappropriate to say to their friend about her present appearance, then filled her in on what had happened to Viola.

It seemed like a never-ending six hours, but finally the cardiovascular surgeon and her mother's regular doctor came to find her. The bypass surgery had gone okay and Viola was in recovery. They were expecting to move her into ICU within the next two hours where she would remain for probably a week or two before she could be released for home.

"Your mother is a very lucky lady," the surgeon said, giving Audria a grave look. "Going forward, she will need to begin a whole new chapter on how she takes care of herself. Healthy eating, exercise, and *absolutely no stress* of any kind."

Audria nodded, knowing that all sounded a whole lot easier than what it would probably be. She knew how stubborn Viola was when it came to doing as she damn well pleased.

"Do you live together?" the surgeon was asking, and Audria snapped back from her thoughts.

"No, we don't. We have separate residences."

The words were barely out her mouth when she knew what was coming.

"You'll need to make arrangements for her then. Someone will need to take care of her for the next few months."

Audria nodded again, already one hundred percent sure that the *someone* who would be taking care of Viola would be her.

Wasn't no stranger gonna take care of her flesh and blood. It was her responsibility and no one else's.

It hadn't been easy, but she had done it. Once again, she had to throw herself on the mercy of the higher-ups at her firm, explaining the situation about her mother. They agreed for her to take an extended leave of absence from work and Audria moved into one of Viola's guest rooms. She had entertained the thought of bringing Viola to her place for a hot minute, but she knew her mother well enough to know that she would welcome the familiarity and the comforts of her own home. That proved to be the best decision she could have made, 'cuz Viola wasn't no picnic. She was two hands full on a good day and a barrel of diseased hands on her bad days.

She finally got a routine going though, splitting her time between caring for her mother and visiting with Angela almost every day. Although the physical wounds were starting to heal, it was obvious her friend would wear the emotional scars from the carjacking for a long time to come. The police had finally retrieved the SUV, but the inside of it had been so badly wrecked that the insurance company declared it a total loss.

Angela didn't seem to care though. She was far too obsessed with making sure the police found the lil' wanna-be gangstas responsible for jacking her. And she seemed to have developed some weird side effect that was probably a result of post traumatic stress. Audria knew she wasn't a doctor, but Angela was acting like somebody with OCD -- obsessive compulsive disorder. The woman was taking a shower every hour *exactly* on the hour, even setting her alarm clock to wake her up in the middle of the night, and washing her hands ten times before leaving out the bathroom. That behavior just didn't seem normal to her. But any mention of seeing a psychiatrist or counselor sent Angela into such a panic that Ford would have to give her a painkiller to knock her ass out. They all learned real quick that mental health therapy was a taboo subject in that household.

Then going into week two of her new routine, the third serving of bad news arrived. She answered Viola's phone one morning and got a shock when a man on the other end announced that he was a police detective calling from Rocky Mount, North Carolina. Her uncle Carl had been found in his favorite easy chair, sitting in a stinking puddle of his own piss, shit and blood, with his throat cut from ear to ear in a deader-than-dead man's grin.

Although there was an 'I'm sorry' note and the bloody knife within reach of one of Carl's ape-like hands, things wasn't adding up in the detective's head. Now he was calling next-of-kin to try to piece things together as best he could.

Her mind in a jumble, Audria explained her mother's condition to him, gave vague answers to his inquiries, and got the hell off the phone in a hurry.

Uncle Carl, dead? She felt a cold chilliness wrap itself like a snaky fog all up, through and around her bones, and her teeth started a loud chattering in her head. On some level she was physically reacting to the news - *teeth didn't chatter all by themselves for nothing-* but deep down inside where she was *supposed* to feel something, there was an emptiness there that suggested a side to her existed that was icy cold, reptilian-even in its detachment. That, more than the news about Uncle Carl, bothered the hell out of her.

Then she wasn't sure why a picture of her man suddenly flashed up in front her face, *her man who she hadn't heard a peep out of in almost a month, although she had been writing him constantly every spare moment she got.* She wondered too why her heart had started slamming around in her chest thinking about what an awkward way that was for someone to commit suicide. Was it even physically possible for somebody to slit their own throat?

Eventually she quieted herself enough to where she could start going over things in her mind, picking the whole mess apart. Okay, only five people on the planet knew about Carl and what he had done to her. Her mother, her man, her best friends Angela and Vanessa, and her new friend Nadira. Of the five, only four of them were passionate enough about it to want to take some kind of action – Viola, Michael, Angela and Vanessa. Angela was still messed up, besides this OCD thing was kicking her ass. And Vanessa was Angela's shadow, the two of them practically joined at the hip. If Angela wasn't up to something like that, Vanessa wasn't rolling alone. She also knew her mother was accounted for. She had been laid up for weeks in the hospital and now at home, right under her nose. That left Michael.

Audria thought about it for some minutes, then realized she was losing it. What was she thinking? The man was locked up. How could he possibly have anything... Wait a minute. Wait just one damn minute. Audria stopped herself short. Michael *did* have all the information he would need to find her uncle or have someone find him. She hadn't hid anything from him. As a matter of fact, she had even written to him about the weird waking daydream she'd had about slitting the old man's throat. Maybe he... NO! She dismissed the thought before it could take further shape in her mind. NO! Her man didn't have a thing to do with this. He had promised her he would set down his anger. This was simply an old coot grown tired of living day-to-day with the guilt of what he had done. Carl had finally decided to do her and the world a favor and put himself out of his misery.

What's done is done, Audria told herself, refusing to listen to some part of her clamoring loudly for attention. It is what it is and that would be the end of that. It was time she put Carl and that awful thing in her past to rest forever.

* * * * * *

Thinking about the past made Audria remember it was way past the time she had promised Viola she would be back. It didn't matter that her mother was constantly trying to shoo her out the house and telling her to go have some fun somewhere. It was her responsibility to take care of her own and she needed to be about that right now. Besides, she could feel the crowd getting fidgety. Them folks would be stampeding the buffet line in short order. It was about time she made her exit.

She started bulling her way through the throng, moving in the direction of the double doors on the far side of the room. She was ten feet away when she spotted a familiar face directly in her path. Just freaking great. Audria let out a groan under her breath. She would have to run into *him*.

She was just about to start searching for a way to back up and go around to avoid him, when she saw him start scanning the room like he was looking for somebody. A couple seconds later he turned and their eyes met. She looked at him coolly, keeping her face emotionless, but started moving in the direction of the doors again. She would be damned if she let him think she was so affected by him that she had to find an alternate route out of the room.

She was all set to just smile and nod and brush right on past him, but she should have known better. Pest that he was, he certainly wasn't going to allow that. As she went to pass behind him, he took a step back blocking her path, then had the audacity to reach for one of her hands.

"I've been looking all over this place for you."

Audria snatched her hand away. "I don't see how you could possibly be looking for me when you wouldn't even know I was in here."

Somebody off to their left shushed them, pointing at the platform to show that the closing prayer was about to begin.

Audria figured God would understand, but she had to get the hell away from this man. Mumbling hushed 'excuse me's' as she went, and trying not to step on too many feet, she finally got to and through the door. And of course, he was right behind her. Before she could even turn to cuss him out and tell him to leave her alone, he grabbed ahold of her arm and spun her around.

"What is it with you, huh Woman? What? You up for nastiest person of the year award or something? You tryin' to make sure you get it?" He shook her arm slightly, then seemed to regret that move, 'cuz he instantly let go of her and dropped his hands to his side.

Audria just looked at him in disbelief that he had actually laid hands on her. She started to steam, could feel the hairs rise up on the back of her neck and her upper lip start sweatin'. He stunned her into silence before she could blow though.

"Gina's sick, a'ight?" He ran a hand through his short wavy hair. "I didn't want to tell you like this, but you wouldn't answer your phone, and Silas been pressing me on this, 'cuz Gina's been asking for you."

Audria looked at Al, confused, her anger forgotten.

"My Gina? Whatchu mean sick? How sick? What's going on?" Audria's mouth was suddenly dry. She thought bad news was supposed to come in threes, but this news was taking her past her quota, wasn't it? She stared at Al, the question still in her eyes.

"She has stage four lung cancer," he said softly. "The doctors can't do anything more for her." He looked miserable, but his eyes didn't waver. "She doesn't have long, Audria."

She felt the sting of tears hitting the back of her eyes. Bubbly Gina, dying? It didn't seem possible, didn't seem right. What would happen to Silas? To little Isaiah? *Oh my God, Isaiah.*

Her head snapped up. "What about Isaiah? Is he okay? Does he know what's going on?"

Al shook his head. "He doesn't understand what's happening, just that his Moms not around right now. I think that's one of the reasons Silas' been asking for you. You're real good with lil' man."

Focused only on her friend and the devastating news, Audria started heading for the hotel lobby to go get her car from valet parking, then realized she was being rude. She turned around.

"Thanks for coming to find me Al. I really appreciate it." Then it dawned on her what she was really saying. He had come to find her. "Matter of fact, how *did* you find me? Other than my Mom, nobody knows I'm here."

Al nodded. "Yeah, she told me."

"My mother did *what*? You talked to my mother?"

Audria looked at him confused, but before she could say anything else, he started in her direction. "Look, I know you're probably parked in hotel valet. Do you want to leave your car here and I give you a ride to the hospital? I'll bring you back."

She started to say no, then thought it over. Too much was being thrown at her all at once and her head was swimming. She was in no shape to go racing off anywhere. She nodded, then allowed Al to lead her to his truck sitting out front. When he touched the small of her back to help her in, she felt a shiver race up her spine. It felt like fire and it took everything inside her not to jerk away, but she couldn't let him see what she was ashamed to even admit. He still had this crazy effect on her. Audria closed her eyes and took a breath. She knew she was going to have to address this madness between them sooner or later, but now wasn't the time. All she could think about was her friend Gina.

<u>fifty-one</u>
Promise Me

"You want me to do *WHAT*?"

Audria's mouth was hanging open by the jaw hinges, and she couldn't help looking at her friend like she had lost her damn mind.

"I want you to have joint guardianship of Isaiah."

"Joint guardianship? What do you mean, Gina?" Audria was confused and more than a lil' bit flabbergasted. "I can't do that. That's your little Precious."

If her head had been swimming earlier, it was ready to explode clean off her shoulders any second. This wasn't happening. Her friend wasn't lying in this bed in front of her trying to get her to agree to be responsible for her 3-year old son.

She shook her head, trying to clear it, and made an effort to get her thoughts together, but her tongue refused to work. On top of that, she could clearly recognize the set-in-stone look on Gina's face, the way she always looked when she was about to be real unruly and seriously stubborn about something she wanted.

"Audria, this isn't something I'm pulling out of the air. I'm dying, okay? As hard as that is for me and everybody else to swallow, the doctors aren't lying. They're not playing some April Fool's joke on me. This is for real. Now, I've given this a lot of thought and you're the only logical choice, so I'm asking you. Would you please agree to joint guardianship of Isaiah?"

Audria wanted to give in to the denial that kept flaring up inside her like a freshly struck match, but this wasn't the time for it. Nor was it the time for her to try to wrap her mind around the fact that Gina's days were seriously numbered. It was obvious her friend wasn't doing well. She was lying in front of her hooked up to a whole bunch of noisy, beeping machines with an oxygen mask over her face and backup tanks nearby. She knew this wasn't about her and her feelings right now. This was about whatever she could do to set Gina's mind at ease.

"I'll do what I can, Gina," she said, slowly nodding her head.

Gina struggled to sit up and Audria reached down to help her up, feeling a sense of dejavu as she thought how similar this was to her visit with Angela recently at Georgetown. Although some people had their doubts about Howard University hospital, Gina wouldn't let a single soul touch her except the doctors at HUH.

Gina grabbed hold of her arm.

"No Audria, this isn't about you '*doing what you can*'. It's about you making me a promise to watch out for my son like he was your own." She inhaled deeply, struggling to draw air and fogging up the oxygen mask with the effort. "You have to promise me right here and now that you're going to take care of Isaiah." Obviously exhausted, Gina fell back in the bed, but her eyes stayed steady on Audria's face, waiting for an answer.

"I promise," Audria whispered, feeling like a freight train was just around the corner getting ready to run her ass over. "I promise, Gina."

An hour later, she felt like the train had bucked the corner in all its locomotive fury and had flattened her into the tracks like a steamroller running over Wile E. Coyote. Gina had shared so much information with her about her plans that her head was reeling. And it was more than obvious to Audria that the woman hadn't been playing when she said she had given the whole thing a lot of thought. Every question she thought to ask, Gina had the answer ready and waiting for her, like she had anticipated every last one of them.

"Are you sure about this? Is this even legal? I thought you had to be one-half of a couple to be able to share custody? What about Silas?"

Taking her time, Gina explained the difference between custody and guardianship. As Zi's sole remaining parent, Silas would have custody of him, but under the legal arrangement Gina was proposing, Audria and another person would share joint guardianship. This meant they would pick up the slack for Silas, help out wherever they were needed, and would play an active role in making decisions affecting Isaiah's future and such.

Audria was just opening her mouth to bring up a part of this she was dreading when Gina beat her to it, obviously anticipating this question too.

"If you're wondering or worrying about how much this is gon' cost you, don't. This is not about money. Isaiah's financial needs are not an issue, okay? I've taken care of that, Audria, so don't worry. I just want to make sure my boy gets raised right."

Audria sighed on the inside, wishing this conversation wasn't happening, but she let Gina keep talking.

"Now, as far as Al sharing joint guardianship, I know that..."

"WHOOOOOAAAAAA," Audria threw up her hands and hopped back a step. "What you mean? What you saying? He's a part of this?"

Gina reached for her again and Audria tried her best to calm down, although she was back to feeling all panicky in her chest area.

"Look babygirl, you know my husband. Silas is probably the sweetest man that ever walked this planet, but he's also a simple, down home, country boy with simple, down home, country boy tastes, and you know his background. He grew up rough. Not that I'm saying he doesn't have valuable lessons to teach Isaiah, but I want my son to have the best of both worlds. I need him to be exposed to things that Silas won't know about, cultural things like art, history, social graces, politics."

"But *why* does it have to be *HIM*?" Audria pressed, feeling her stomach balling up in knots.

Gina just looked at her, eyes weak yet fierce at the same time. Not wanting to seem argumentative over something that should really not matter to her, Audria nodded her head so Gina could see she was okay with things, although she really wasn't.

As a shift nurse came bustling in, obviously ready to begin the shooing out process, she picked up her purse and slung it over a shoulder. When she looked up, Gina's eyes were on hers.

"When you slow your mind down long enough, maybe you'll figure out what it is you're so afraid of with Al."

Audria started to shake her head, but Gina squeezed her fingers lightly, cutting her off.

"Al's a good man, Audria. Maybe if you gave him half a chance, you would realize that and stop chasing after the unattainable."

That cut her, hurt her deeply, 'cuz it was obvious Gina thought her relationship with Michael was something outside her reach or not meant for her. The way she felt right now for real, if it wasn't for the circumstances, she would probably cuss out Gina and walk out, but how could she, not knowing if this would be the last time she laid eyes on her friend. She bit her tongue, gently squeezed Gina's fingers in return and bent over, kissing her on the forehead.

"I love you," she whispered softly in her ear, feeling the words move through her powerfully, her anger temporarily forgotten. When she drew away, Gina's eyes were already closed in sleep.

* * * * * *

Al was nervous. It wasn't something he felt too often, but with this woman, and how unpredictably crazy she was, he didn't know what to expect, and that made him nervous.

He had waited for her in the hospital lobby and they were walking back to his truck together. He knew she must be going crazy with all the information Gina had laid on her. He had felt the same way when he got asked to be a joint guardian to Isaiah. He started to say no but probably anticipating his answer, Gina quietly told him who else she was going to ask. *Audria.*

On some level, he hated the fact that his feelings for Audria were so readily apparent, that he was so transparent to her and that she knew which of his buttons to lean on, but Gina was a shrink after all and was up there with the best of them in the art of manipulation. The mention of Audria's name made him shut his mouth and listen to what she was proposing, and pretty soon, he was agreeing to it.

It's not that he didn't care about Isaiah and want the best for the boy. As a matter of fact, he loved little Zi and they got along real good, but he wanted children of his own and didn't want to confuse the two issues, using his relationship with Isaiah as some weak substitute for what his heart now longed for. But the chance to share something this important with Audria was not an opportunity he was about to pass up.

So, he allowed Gina to manipulate him to get what she wanted, but not before using some manipulation of his own. He wanted information about Audria and who best to provide it than one of her closest friends. By the time he left Gina's bedside, he had all the information he needed. He knew Audria was on an extended leave of absence from work to take care of her sick mother, and that she had temporarily moved into her mother's house to make things easier. He even got the address and phone number too. He found out about her friend Angela who was having a tough time recovering from a carjacking. And Gina even told him about the novel Audria was working on and how she was hoping to get published some day soon.

Most importantly though, he got the real deal on the *man* she felt so strongly about. Al was surprised to find out the brotha was in prison. She didn't strike him as the kind of woman who would get caught up with some locked-away loser, gangster type who had nothing to offer her. Not that he knew all that much about her, but she seemed like a classy kinda woman to him, and women of her caliber were careful about who they gave their hearts to.

But honestly, that piece of information just made him feel even stronger about what he had already decided to do. He wasn't nobody's fool and didn't much like the idea of having his love spit on, but he was gon' fight for this woman. Skittish or not, emotionally over-the-top or not, he wanted her as his, and would do whatever he could to get her.

He was blown though and even more surprised when Gina read him. It was obvious she had his number and he didn't like it. They had known each other for years, enjoyed a level of comfort in conversation, as much as anybody could talking to somebody whose profession involved picking people apart, but there had always been this thing between them, an unspoken barrier that Gina knew not to breach. She broke down the wall with what came out her mouth though.

"Why don't you just tell the woman the way you feel about her? You're not gon' stand a chance if you don't at least give it a try."

Al looked at her, surprise showing in his eyes, and just stood there blinking.

"Yeah, I'm talking to you," Gina stared back at him. "Lawd, why is it men can be so dense sometimes?" she asked to no one in particular, then patted the bed next to her, encouraging him to sit.

"Look Al, I love Audria to death. She's one of the nicest, smartest, funniest women I know. She's the genuine article, the kind of woman that's not pretentious or a game player or any of that other mess so many women seem to be about. She's just real. But with all that, I think when it comes to love, she's as clueless as they come."

She looked at Al, who knew when to be quiet and listen. "Now, for whatever reason, she's got it in her head that this jailhouse clown is her soulmate. Don't ask me why, 'cuz I don't understand it, but as far as you're concerned, it's not even important. I know you got it bad for her. I saw the effect she had on you the first time you met her, and I've been knowing you long enough to know that you don't casually ask questions about no woman unless you're way the hell interested. So all I'm telling you is to quit asking your questions and start doing something with the answers, unless you want to wait 'til lockdown lover comes home and you gotta compete with all that testosterone."

Al didn't know why that last comment got under his skin, but he felt his lip curling up in distaste at the thought. It made him think about some greased down freak with muscles bulging climbing on top that beautiful, caramel colored, soft-skinned body. If he had anything to do with it, *that* was never gonna happen.

He sighed on the inside remembering his conversation with Gina, then tried to steel himself for the hurricane. He turned to Audria, keeping it light.

"Hey, you feel like having a drink or grabbing a quick bite to eat with me?" he asked her, then added quickly. "I was thinking maybe we could talk about this whole guardianship thing."

He looked over at her, trying to keep his expression neutral, but felt something drop inside him at the look of mistrust instantly on her face. He had wanted them to go somewhere nice where he could have a quietly civil conversation with her, but alright then, if it had to be like this, then he would just have to let it be what it was. He stopped walking and turned to her, purposely backing her up against a column in the underground parking lot.

"Okay look, we need to get something straight right here and right now," he started in, making himself ignore the fire he could already see flashing in her eyes. "I refuse to let you keep blaming me for something beautiful that happened between us, you hear me? You had a need and I was there for you... we were there for each other... I mean, it happened. We didn't plan it, it just happened, but I didn't force you, so stop telling yourself that lie to justify the outcome of a choice you made, a'ight?"

She looked at him, eyes piercing into him like red hot fiery darts, then unleashed a flood of emotion that got his juices stirring in a way they hadn't been stirred since the night he had laid with her. He knew this was not the time but he felt the mushrooming bulge in his crotch area even as she let him have it both barrels blasting.

"*SOMETHING BEAUTIFUL?* SOMETHING BEAUTIFUL? You call what happened between me and you something beautiful?" A harsh sound barely recognizable as a scornful laugh came out of her. "*That* was nothing beautiful. It was dirty and ugly, sordid and cheap, and it left me feeling no better than a two dollar 'ho walking somebody's strip. And every time I look at you, it reminds me of how weak I was to let it happen."

She advanced on him, her face a contorted mask of anger. "And you have the *nerve* to speak of outcomes? You want to know the outcome? You nearly cost me everything. You nearly made me lose the respect and love of the only man on the face of this planet who loves ME."

She was practically screaming at him now, but Al was past the point of caring, especially because of what had just come out her mouth. It was his turn to back her up.

"Oh, so you think because somebody writes you a few letters and strokes your ego and tells you all the things you've ever wanted to hear from a man, that this magically makes that person the only person who loves you?" He grabbed both her arms in the spot right above the elbows locking her in and pulled her against him hard. "I LOVE YOU, you stupid, stubborn woman. I love you."

She tried to pull away from him, brown eyes going wide in alarm, but he wasn't letting go. Al pulled her even closer, an arm still pinning one of her elbows and the other holding tight to the spot just below the small of her back. He could feel her struggling against him, her breasts heaving up and down with the effort, and that excited him even more. He lowered his head and clamped down on her mouth, covering hers with his, his tongue forcing its way between her lips, reaching, seeking, wanting to taste every drop of her.

He pushed her back into the column, forcing her upwards against the concrete, somehow wrapping her legs around his waist, and planting himself solidly in between. She was still fighting him, but he could feel the fight losing steam, could feel her wanting to give in. He kissed her harder, sucking her tongue into his mouth and felt his body shake as he tasted the sweetness of her saliva.

Hearing what he thought was a moan, he reached up and grasped one of her breasts and, in one motion, pulled it free from the bra and shirt she was wearing. The nipple was enlarged and puckered hard, and he licked at it gently, then sucked the entire breast into his mouth, feeling like he could stay here forever.

Some part of him recognized that he was taking advantage of her, trying to force her to submit, but he felt that if she just gave him half a chance, she would see how good things could be between them.

He began stroking her face, a hand reaching up to touch her braids. And in between licking and sucking on her nipple, he tried talking to her. It's not like he hadn't already put it out there, the way he felt about her, so he might as well keep going.

"I'm here, woman... I'm here... Flesh and blood man... right in front of you... Holding you... Wanting you... Loving you.... You don't have to wait for me... like you're waiting... for this man... I'm right here... And I'm not... feeding you lines... that I've learned... over the years... 'cuz all I have is... nothing but time... to learn them... That's him... That's not me..."

Audria suddenly wrenched away from him violently, so violently that he lost the grip he had on her and she fell hard to the dusty concrete floor. He could tell the wind was knocked out of her, so he started to reach down to help her, but she scrambled away from him, high heels clacking against the uneven surface and shot up on her feet.

"SHUT UP. You shut the fuck up and get away from me. *How dare you* touch me like this and then talk about him. You don't know what's in his heart for me or what we've shared with each other. You don't know him and you don't know me."

Al started to say something, but she screamed at him even louder, cutting him off. "If you knew the littlest thing about me, you would know not to do what you just did. You would know not to attack me, not to force me, because it makes you no better than that motherfucking bastard of an uncle of mine who did the exact same thing to me when I was JUST A LITTLE GIRL."

Al stopped dead in his tracks, still. He felt like something massive was weighing down on him, crushing him. "What? What? I didn't know, Audria... I didn't know that..."

She just sat down where she was, abruptly, legs going wide on the concrete, splayed out like a wooden doll's. He expected tears but when he looked down at her, he was shocked to find her mouth open in a silent scream, and she started doubling over at the waist like she was in pain.

Al got down on his knees next to her, not sure what to do, but reaching for her just the same.

She batted his hands away repeatedly, not allowing him any closer and they went through the same exercise for several minutes. He felt like a complete shit. It was now obvious that what he had thought was a passionate moan was instead a groan. Whether out of disgust, fear, or something else, it didn't matter right now. All he knew was that he had messed up big time. He didn't know what to say but knew he had to say something.

"Audria, sweetheart, I didn't know, okay? I would never force myself on you or on anybody. That's not who I am." He hesitated for a bit, then kept going, refusing to back off anymore. "Here's the thing though. I don't know you because you won't let me in. You won't let me get to know you. You're so afraid of..."

Audria cut him off, nodding her head and laughing a harsh, bitter laugh as she struggled to her feet. He stood up as well. "You're right. I'm afraid, okay? I'm afraid. But not the kind of afraid you think. I'm afraid that this..." she waved a hand back and forth between them while dusting off her clothes... "this nonsense will make me lose my man and I'd rather die first before I let that happen again."

That shut him up momentarily. How could he argue in the face of that kind of blind devotion? Al could see they were going nowhere in this conversation and he didn't want things to escalate again all the way around. He took a deep breath, deciding to try to diffuse things a bit. He made sure to keep his voice as low as possible.

"Look Audria, what I started to say is that you're so afraid to let anyone else get next to you that you're limiting your options. Okay, so I don't know you that well... hell, after what just happened, it's obvious I don't know you at all, but the little I do know about you tells me that a woman like you *should* have options. You should have the best. Not that I'm saying I'm the best either, but I'm damn sure better than some convict."

He pressed on before she could open her mouth again. "Why do you think so many people close to you want to see you give something or someone else a try? It's not because they're trying to run your life, Audria. It's because they love you and know your worth. They know you deserve the best, and waiting indefinitely for some man who's locked up isn't the best you can do."

Al tried to ignore the knot in his throat and the gigantic thing that felt like a stone lodged in the pit of his stomach. From the look in her eyes, he knew this was a battle he wasn't going to win, not today. But what he felt for her made him keep going. He smiled at her, trying to lighten things up even more.

"Audria, you ever just knew before you did something that you would be good at it?" He waited a beat for her to agree or disagree with him, but she just stared at him coldly, so he went on. "I've felt that way about a few things in my life. I knew I would be good at track before I even tried out in junior high. And I knew before I ever got behind the wheel of a car that I would know how to drive my ass off. Same thing with Tae kwon do. Same thing with anything involving architecture or real estate, which is my business focus."

He looked at her, refusing to let her coldness get under his skin. "It's the same thing with what I feel here, what I feel for you. I *KNOW* that I can be everything you need a man to be to you, if you let me. But only if you let me."

He stepped back, waiting, hoping she would say something, anything, but she kept looking at him like he was some alien bug she wanted to step on. Even in the face of her anger and her coldness though, Al wanted nothing more than to take her in his arms, hold her and just love her, but he could tell she would never allow it. He didn't want to admit it, but he recognized he would need to let this go a little bit or the intensity of what he was feeling would eat him up. He wasn't sure of what else he could say or how to end the conversation, so he just spoke from the heart.

"Alright then. I can see from your face that you're not trying to hear me or give me the chance I'm asking for, so I'm gonna let you go."

She started to turn away from him, but Al reached out a hand to her. "I didn't mean literally, Audria. I can still give you a ride back to your car."

She shook her head at him. "I'd rather walk," she said, coldly, her voice flat. "I don't want anything from you."

That felt like a giant foot slamming a kick into his chest, but he ignored it and still managed a half smile at her. "Okay, if that's how you feel." He started to turn away as well, but turned back almost immediately. He found himself talking to her back as she walked away, but he didn't care.

"Audria, I love you and I'm here for you. If you ever change your mind, I'll be here waiting for you."

She didn't turn around, not once, and as he pulled his truck out of the garage into the fading evening light heading for home, he saw her standing on the corner hailing a cab, her face still a stubborn mask of anger.

fifty-two
What You Want?

"Why yo' askin' me to try to help you figure out somet'ing *you* feelin? Dese is your feelin's, Queen. I couldn' help you make sense a' what's runnin' through you no more'n a body can make sense outta the bobblehead dummy that rules the waves of Talk Radio."

Audria was sitting naked on a Navajo Indian throw rug in Nadira's living room. This was how she would inevitably wind up every time she visited her friend, the both of them sitting butterball naked facing each other on the floor. Nadira believed this was the only way she could get people to keep things real.

"No clothes, no walls. No walls, no lies. No lies, no nonsense."

Although Audria had mostly gotten used to Nadira's eccentric behavior, she sometimes found herself wondering if Nadira preferred men or women. They had been knowing each other for months now and she still didn't have a clue about that.

The woman suddenly snapped a finger right in front her face. "Listen now, who I lick on an' who I let lick on me don' have nothin' to do wid' dis t'ing you tryin' to figure out."

Audria sat back a bit, startled. Nadira was doing it again. This wasn't the first time she had seemed to crawl right inside her head and snatch some thought she'd just had. It was scary weird and always left her feeling unsettled, but that was Nadira. Scary, weird, all that.

She had been sitting here for a good twenty minutes trying to be as honest with herself as she could be, only to have Nadira mockingly tell her she was fooling herself.

"You playin' games o' what? You t'ink I have time to waste while you keep lyin' to yo'self?"

"I'm not lying to myself, Nadira. It's just that I'm confused about this guy and especially about the effect he has on me."

"You said dat already. Tell me somet'ing you haven't tole me before."

Audria took a deep breath and tried to think what to say. She had already told Nadira the entire story about what had gone down between her and Al in the parking lot, so she knew that Nadira wasn't fishing for more details. Before she could open her mouth to come up with something, Nadira was in her face again.

"Look here, Queen. What it is 'bout dis bwoy... what's his name? Al?" Audria nodded. "What it is 'bout Al thas troublin' you so bad? You had one drunken fling wid' 'im an' somehow yo' keep lettin' dat indiscre'shun interfere wid' how yo' move 'roun' him. Why dat is?"

Audria threw up her hands. "If I had the answer to that, I wouldn't be here asking you, Nadira."

Nadira waved her off with a look of impatience on her face. "Okay, we gon' figure out dis t'ing. I got some questions fo' you." She tucked a leg firmly under her backside. "Now when yo' talk 'bout de effect dis Al got on you, what kind of effect yo' talkin' 'bout? Tell me what you mean."

Audria thought about it for a little while. "It's like this... this energy that's always there between us."

"Yo' talkin' 'bout sexual energy?"

"Yes, and it bugs the hell outta me, but that's not the only thing about him that gets under my skin. There's this vibe there that I'm afraid of."

"First of all, you don' have hell inside yo', so it can't get bugged outta yo'. And second, what otha vibe you speakin' 'bout?

Is a good vibe? Bad vibe? What?"

"It's not a bad vibe, exactly," Audria said softly, almost thinking out loud.

"Then is a good vibe, right? 'Cuz a body usually only 'fraid of bad vibes, and you say is not a bad vibe." Nadira was relentless, just kept pounding away with the questions.

"Look, I'm not sure, okay?" Audria started feeling huffy and bothered. She felt like Nadira was pushing her in some direction that she either didn't want to go in or wasn't ready to go in.

A long silence grew between them, and she started getting uncomfortable with Nadira just eyeing her. "What?" she finally asked, getting a little too loud for the intimate setting.

Her friend made a harrumphing sound deep in her throat and reached to light another Tibetan incense cone. "Queen, what's de problem wid' what you feelin'?"

Audria looked at Nadira like she had just swallowed a whole bottle of stupid pills. "What do you mean 'what's the problem'?"

"I didn't t'ink I was talkin' in a foreign tongue. I asked you what's de problem wid' what you feelin'?"

"Well, for one thing, I'm not supposed to be feeling sexual energy with anyone other than my man."

Nadira snorted then threw her head back in a loud, long laugh. When her noisy cackling had gone on for way too long in Audria's estimation, she cleared her throat loudly, suppressing an urge to roll her eyes. "I don't see what's so funny."

"You're de funny, Queen," Nadira answered, stifling another laugh. "Beautiful, you t'ink that jus' 'cuz you foun' yo' soulmate dat mean you never gon' feel attraction to, an' sexual energy wid anotha'? It don' mean nothin' other than you breathin', Pretty Audria. It don' mean you have to act on what you feel. We already covered 'dis before, an' you tole me 'bout de promise you made to yo'self an' how strong you feel 'bout it since you faced your demon. Now, all you got is a feelin'. You don' have to do nuthin' wid' it. You feel it, you recognize you feelin' it, an' you let it pass through you like water through a sieve. What is fo' you will be fo' you, an' what isn't fo' you, then let it gwon 'bout it bizness."

Audria couldn't help smiling at Nadira. It was strange the way this woman could simplify the most difficult seeming things, just break them down into nothingness until you felt good 'n stupid for worrying about whatever it was to begin with.

"So, it's that simple, huh?" she asked, still smiling at Nadira.

Nadira looked at her curiously, then countered with a question of her own.

"Lemme ask you somet'ing, Queen. You believe dat dere can be more than one soulmate to a body?"

Audria frowned as she thought about it, also wondering why Nadira had this weird knack for asking some of the most difficult questions.

"I'm not sure," she said, "but if I had to give an absolute answer, I'd say no, I don't think there can be more than one soulmate for each of us."

"Why you think that?" Nadira asked her, cocking her head to one side.

Audria thought about it for another moment and then committed herself to the answer. "Well, I think that for whatever reason, God or the Universe or the fates, whatever, they decide to converge at certain points in time and they bring two people together who were just meant for each other. Those people were always meant to be together but for whatever reason, it wasn't their time yet, but then these forces make it happen for them when the time is right, and although their individual lives might have been rich and full and promising before that moment, all of a sudden, it's like they've found the other half of themselves. It's a unique and special experience, so that's why I think there's only one for each of us."

Nadira looked at her, her eyes hard.

"Oh, so you t'ink you can define love and limit love? You t'ink that jus' 'cuz o' what you feelin' for yo' man Michael that such a feelin' is so unique and special that it can't be duplicated?"

Audria frowned again, not sure what Nadira was getting at but not liking her tone.

"Yes, I happen to think that what Michael and I share is a one of a kind feeling. Not that I'm saying other people can't find love too, but the feelings he and I have for each other can't be duplicated."

"So when dis man Al spoke his words of love to you, what yo' t'ink? He was lyin'? You don' believe him? You t'ink dat what he feelin' is dif'rent from what you feelin' for Michael?"

Audria snorted, then quickly wished she hadn't at the sharp look Nadira shot her way, but this was a point she had to make. "Of course what he feels is different, 'cuz everybody's feelings are unique, and what a couple shares is unique. But that's not the only reason why I think his feelings are different. What he's feeling is sexual. It's all over him and all up between us. Plus he barely knows me, so how can he love me?"

Nadira laughed again, throwing her head back and waving a hand in the air like some old church lady throwing up praises to the heavens. When her laughter tapered off, she reached a hand out, tucking fingers under Audria's chin. "Princess, there you go again t'inkin' you can define an' limit love. You can't do neitha one, so you need to stop tryin'. Who you to set a time limit on love? Is only in dis Western society we live in dat people always tryin' to dictate how long you got to know a body 'fore you can love dat body. You need to open yo' mind more, Daughta. Expand yo' t'inkin', then maybe you'll undastan' bettah the vibe you feel when you 'roun' dis man Al."

Audria was past confused. "What are you saying, Nadira? That you want me to forget about the love I share with Michael and give this man a chance?"

"I didn' say no such t'ing," Nadira countered, giving her another hard look.

"Well, what are you saying?" Audria asked, growing even more frustrated.

Nadira got up abruptly, walking away from her and heading for the kitchen. As she went, she looked back at Audria over her shoulder.

"Precious daughta, I happen to believe dif'rent from you. I t'ink dat we can have many soulmates in dif'rent lifetimes. And Queen Audria, a life force strong like yo' own can have two, three, four, maybe even ten soul mates in the course of a lifetime."

She laughed again as Audria jumped to her feet, mouth open, then reached an arm out to her.

"Come, let's take some ginger spice tea and talk 'bout t'ings, Princess. You have much to learn 'bout dis t'ing we call love, an' I got some otha information to share wid' you."

* * * * * *

"MOMMA. Momma where you at? I got news!"

Audria hustled through the front door, banging it behind her and went racing from room to room, looking for Viola.

"Girl, how many times I done tole you not to be slamming my front door closed like you ain't got no sense."

She followed Viola's scratchy voice straight through to the kitchen and found her mother sitting at the table getting ready to throw down on a huge bowl of fried ice-cream. It was ridiculous. The thing had caramel chocolate topping, hazelnuts, fudge shavings, marshmallows, and a mountain of whipcream. She snatched up the bowl from in front of her just before the spoon swooped down.

"Momma, *how* many times I gotta tell you you're not supposed to be eating this stuff? For Chrissake, you just had a heart attack. You want to end up back in the hospital?"

Viola looked at her and rolled her eyes. "I knew I shoulda hurried up and had my frycream 'fore you got back in here. Why you all the time botherin' me 'bout what I want to put in my mouth? You think my life s'posed to be over so far as good food eatin' go jus' cuz I had a lil' chest pain?"

Audria plopped the bowl down on the kitchen counter, folded her arms and looked at Viola with fire in her eyes.

"Oh, so that's what you're calling your heart attack now, a little chest pain? May I remind you that your little chest pain almost resulted in you checking outta here permanently?"

Audria was beyond frustrated with Viola.

"Momma, you gotta do better with your diet, and if I bug you, it's not 'cuz I don't want you to eat foods you like and that taste good, it's because I want you around for fifty more years, hell, a hundred if I can bribe God, so would you please please please not make this more difficult than it has to be?"

Viola sucked her teeth, folded her arms, and started pouting like a little kid. Audria wondered for the millionth time why her mother had to be as stubborn as she was. She sighed, then turned back to the counter, grabbed two much smaller bowls off the draining board and scooped a small portion of the fried ice-cream into both, then plopped down next to Viola.

"Okay, you can have a little bit, but that's all the dessert you're having this week," she lectured, handing her mother the bowl. Viola snatched it greedily out her hand, scooped up a big chunk of the Mexican delicacy she had perfected making over the years and chucked the spoon in her mouth.

"Lawd, thas' some good," she said, smacking her gums loudly and licking the front and back of the spoon. "I been cravin' me some fry cream for weeks now an' finally got you out the house long enough so's I could make me some." She looked at Audria sideways, spooned another chunk out the bowl, then questioned. "So, what's this news you got? That fella Al found you over to the book signin'?"

Audria looked at her mother, her eyes widening. "So *that's* what he was talking about when he said you told him where I was." Audria slammed a hand on her hip. "What are you doing giving out my whereabouts to people?"

Viola eyed her and took her time chewing on another piece of the ice cream. When she was good and done, she set her spoon down slowly. "First off, I'se your mother an' I'm grown. Them two things 'title me to do what the hell I want. And second, wasn't no harm tellin' that nice Al where you was at. He was real polite, very gentlemanly, an' he 'splained to me that yo' friend Gina is sick an' been askin' to see you an' nobody could get a hold a you, so she or her man up an' gave him my phone number 'cuz you wasn't answerin' your cell. Once he tole me his business, I didn' see nothing wrong tellin' him how to find you."

Audria decided to just let it go. It wasn't worth arguing over, plus she knew there was no convincing Viola not to give out information about her if that's what her mother was hell bent on doing. She was gonna do exactly what she wanted to do all the live long day, whether you had objections or not.

"Okay, okay, never mind," she said, waving a hand in the air. It really doesn't matter. What I got to tell you is..."

An hour later, they were still going at it, just talking and talking and talking. Audria told Viola about the promise she had made to Gina to assume joint guardianship of Isaiah. She suffered through a whole round of eye-rolling with that one and had to listen to her mother lecture her on the stupidity of making someone use a guilt trip to force you into agreeing to something you would normally reply to with a resounding "Hell to the Naw."

"Okay, I understand what you sayin' 'bout her being close to death an' all, but why it got to be you? You mean to tell me wid' all them high-falutin' folks she know over to that University, she couldn' ask not nary one a them to sign up for this guardianship thing? What? She tryin' to get money outta you?"

Now it was Audria's turn to roll her eyes. "Momma, what'd I tell you? Gina and Silas are loaded, okay? They don't need my lil' bit of money, and besides, this isn't about money anyway. She picked me because she knows I get along well with Isaiah. That's something hard to find with just anybody."

"Hell, damn a get along," Viola fired back, waving a hand dismissively in the air. "The boy is three, Audria. Ain't but so much getting along he gon' be doin' anyway, and once he fed, clothed, schooled, got a roof over his head, he good, ain't he? And last time I checked, anybody wid' a checkbook can provide all that. Why it gotta be you?"

They went back and forth with that until Audria's patience ran out and she decided to change the subject just to get Viola to hush up about it. Her mother was like a pit-bull sometimes. Once she got hold of something, was no letting go. Didn't make no kinda sense. She had other news to share anyway.

"I've got some other news, Momma," she said, barely able to contain herself.

"What? What?" Viola asked her, somehow catching her excitement. "You gon' tell me 'fore I get some more gray hair?"

Audria waved away her mother's nonsense. "Remember I've been telling you about the novel I'm writing, right?"

Viola nodded.

"Well, guess what?"

"So now I have to guess?"

Audria ignored Viola, rolled her eyes and kept going. "My friend Nadira found me a book agent that wants to take a look at it soon as I can get a draft to her. If she likes it, she's gonna find me a publisher."

Audria reached over and hugged her mother. "Momma, this is like a dream come true for me. I can hardly believe it."

Viola hugged her right back, then eased off slightly from their embrace. She looked at her daughter, feeling proud, but knew she had to ask what was on her mind.

"What you want, Audria?"

When she saw the beginning of a frown creeping into her child's eyebrows, she reached a staying hand out to touch her face. "It ain't a trick question, Chile. Whatchu want?"

"I want a lot of things, Mommy, but mostly, I want my life to be good, to mean something. I guess I just want to be happy."

"And you think you deserve it?" Viola held her breath on the inside, hoping a specific answer would fall from her child's lips. Sometimes she could scarcely believe she had given birth to and raised such a beautiful, poised woman. She knew her daughter had gone through some things that would and could easily break somebody else, destroy a lesser person's spirit, but she had walked through her fire, was ready to walk through more, and was *still* standing. What she needed to know, though, was whether Audria was ready to set aside all the bad that had seemed to stalk her almost all her life, and wrap herself up in her good.

She waited, her old raggedy heart beating strong and steady in her chest, despite all her doctor's fussing.

Audria looked at her mother, smiled a small but beautiful self-possessed kinda smile, and reached up to squeeze Viola's fingers caressing her face.

"I don't *think* I deserve it, Momma. I *know* I do."

"Amen to that," Viola nodded, smiling back at her child, then handed her the empty bowl. "Now, go get me some more fry cream."

fifty-three
Emancipation

Hell, not forty-eight hours on the outside, and he was already breaking the law. Didn't have no choice though. Was do or die time, and he'd already decided he had too much to live for. Wasn't no dying happening, so was time to do.

Michael was sitting across the street from a dirty, bombed out mess of a tenement building, stooped in the shadows but keeping a careful watch on the comings and goings. There was a whole lot of activity, too much to suit him really, but in this neighborhood, it was what it was. This was ghetto trading at its highest, people dropping, people copping, but shit kept moving at all costs. The activity didn't surprise him, but a few other things did.

The age of the young'uns was the first thing that got his attention. Back when he was on the streets slanging, this kinda business was best left to men. Young, greedy, and confused, but men just the same. What he was looking at was barely-past-similac age wankstas playing at being gangstas. That bothered him, 'cuz contrary to what mainstream thought, there was a code of honor among the type of men he slung coke with back in the day. He wondered how the thirteen and fourteen year olds he was looking at had learned that code. Then it came to him. Simple, a no-brainer. They wouldn't know it. And you didn't know the code, you couldn't honor it. And if you weren't honoring the code, you were capable of damn near anything. That meant shit was a hundred times as dangerous for him right now.

Another thing that bugged him was their lack of awareness. He had been watching now for almost a half hour, and in his first five minutes squatting, he had already scoped the jump out squad all hunched down in a parked gypsy cab three blocks up and peeping the building through a pair of night vision 'nocs. That's why he was keeping his movements to a minimum until he was ready to make his move. It didn't make sense to him though, that nobody across the street seemed particularly concerned with looking out for the boys in blue. That was on them though. He knew what was up, and all he wanted to do was get to his boy, get him away from all this, and be gone before shit started jumping off.

He raised up slowly from his crouch, stretched his legs and back in place, patted his waist briefly, then started a slow, circuitous zigzag across the street, working his way to the building's entrance. He was careful to keep his face turned downwind, away from the jakes up the street. Back in the day, the way he would deal with cops was to never be out of their sight. Long as they were looking, he was looking. They could see him, he could see them. But that was back in the day. Now, he didn't need that kind of attention, not for this.

He walked up some crumbling steps littered with bits of yellowed paper and a discarded KFC chicken box, stepping over a barely conscious body all lit up off the boat. As he pushed through the dirty, iron-barred front door and out of sight of prying cop eyes, he immediately dropped the slow shamble and started walking purposefully to the first row of narrow stairs.

"Yo, who you Niggah?" came a reed-thin voice from behind him and he looked over his shoulder to find a tall, skinny boy not a day past sixteen stepping out from the shadows under the stairs.

Michael wasn't surprised. He was expecting a challenge. He tipped his head at Slim slightly, but ignored the question, instead asking one of his own. "You know Strong? Michael? 'Bout sixteen? 'Bout tall as you, but bigger? My complexion?"

Michael saw the dude's eyes flicker and knew he knew his son, but he also recognized this wasn't gon' be easy. But he had to speed things up too, even if it meant flat out lying. He didn't know when the dicks up the street would decide to make their move.

"Look, he know me. I just hit him on his cell. I'm copping."

Skinny looked him up and down, like he was detecting bullshit, but wasn't sure of it, then suddenly pulled a phone off his waist clip, pressed a button and chirped. "Yo Strong, some niggah here sayin' he 'posed to cop from you. You got his shit?"

Michael started reaching a hand under his jacket before the answer chirped back. "Ain't nobody called me, Niggah. I ain't got shit."

Before he could wrap his fingers evenly around either of the hammers he had stuck in the waist of his jeans, thinking to bus' on Skinny, there was movement off to his left that he hadn't anticipated, and he felt cold steel pressed up against his temple.

"Don't move Mufucka, or is your last time breathing."

Michael slowly let his hand fall and turned to look at who had got the jump on him.

It was like looking into a mirror twenty-five years back in time. Holding the Ruger .45 like his hand was permanently glued to it, his son was staring back at him.

* * * * * *

This was odd. Standing here in the same broke down Mott Haven neighborhood he had grown up in, the same stomping grounds where he had once slung Black rock, yayo or shwag to losers who couldn't shake the drug monkey, where once he had gotten the jump on too-slow, bo janglin' mufuckas who let their guard down, even for a second. And now, he was the too-slow mufucka who had let his guard down, and his son was the one sucking his flavor, holding a piece on him. The one thought that had been repeating in his head for the last couple months surfaced again. *Things were moving entirely too fast.*

Michael had barely had time to let it sink in that he was a free man. From the time the parole board surprised him by recommending his release, things had been moving fast, sometimes too damn fast for him. It wasn't that he didn't want to be free, hell, that's all he had been dreaming about for years, but suddenly, confronted with the idea of walking free of walls that had held him for over a decade, knowing he would have people depending on him, people he cared about like his woman and his son, made him start feeling like he needed to slow shit way the hell down.

He was all set to say exactly that to Warden Stevens the next time he saw her, when it hit him that he might be falling victim to the IN disease. Hell, over the years, he had laughed at some of the old-timers his damn self when they would be back on the pound after just weeks or a couple months of being gone. He and everybody else would welcome them home and laugh harder when they got the finger or a 'fuck you' in reply. Now though, he realized, he was playing at the same shit, and damn it, he would prove everybody wrong. He was not institutionalized. Once he walked free, he would stay free. Didn't have to tell him twice to be gone.

As it got closer and closer to his new release date, he tried to get himself mentally prepared for being on the outside, but soon gave that up. It was too exhausting thinking about how he would adjust from the kind of confinement he had gotten used to over the years to wide open spaces all over again. On top of that, Audria was writing him almost constantly, the tone of her letters shifting from questioning to confused to angry, because she wasn't hearing from him.

He wasn't exactly sure why he had decided not to write her to tell her the good news. It wasn't like he wasn't excited about it and didn't want to share, because he was. When he thought about it, the closest he could come to an explanation was that he didn't want to jinx the shit. He knew his fear was probably baseless, but some part of him kept saying to lay back on this, so he wasn't trying to talk about it with her until he was all the way free. She would just have to trust his judgment when she found out later.

But apprehension or no, things kept moving at lightning speed. Before he knew it, he was having this meeting and that meeting with the Warden and with his case counselor to discuss transitioning him to street life. He got information on the halfway house he would be staying in for at least 30 days after his release, information on what was expected of him as a parolee, and contact numbers for the parole officer he would have to see who would help settle him into life on the street.

Warden Stevens kept talking to him in a matter-of-fact way about beginning his life again in New York, but Michael tuned most of that out. He had already decided that was one of the first things he would need to cover with his parole officer. Wasn't no going back to Mott Haven and The Bronx. Much as he loved the Boogie Down, it was time to say goodbye to it.

That was the thing he never got about the system and how it worked. You could take a bad ass off the streets, stick him in prison and supposedly rehabilitate him, but if you let him out and put him right back in the same environment he just left, chances were he was gon' revert right back to SOS status. Same old shit.

Michael already knew the deck would be stacked against him enough, walking out with nothing really to show for the past fourteen years but time served and a new attitude. He wasn't trying to stack it some more by stepping back to temptation.

The thing he had never shared with his woman, hell, with nobody really, was that he enjoyed what he used to do. Enjoyed the shit out of it. Not only did he like counting his money, feeling all that green in his hands, but wasn't nothing like staying up forty-eight or seventy-two hours straight, walking or driving the hood, strapped up, feeling comforted by steel on his hip, leather on his back, and slanging product.

And he wasn't confined to one 'hood like most slangers. He went where he felt when he felt like it. The Mott, Morrisania, East Tremont, Castle Hill, Parkchester, didn't matter. Being a Bronx cat especially doing what he was doing and strapped like he was, meant he lived without fear. And if somebody challenged him 'cuz he was on their block or even looked at him funny, he didn't have to worry about a conscience getting in the way to stop him from knocking their noodles loose. He traveled in lanes he knew well 'cuz when it was all said and done, he wanted to leave his mark in the game.

Sometimes, if he went at it real hard, he could clear as much as ten pianos in one weekend, so yeah, he loved the shit outta what he did. But that no-conscience-having, poor excuse for a man he used to be wasn't who he was today. He had too much to live for now, so it was either he step all the way away from the man he used to be or why bother. That's why he had his own agenda. Somehow, he would have to figure out a way to get his parole officer to work with him so he could get to his son and eventually change his home state to Maryland.

When his release date finally rolled around, he was nervous and pacing the whole day, wanting the entire mess to be done and over with. Every second of the two and a half hours he spent in Processing felt like a prolonged agony. He kept feeling like somebody was gonna April Fool his ass, come busting in and haul him back to his cell, hollering *PSYCHE* the whole way. When they finally told him he was free and clear, he dapped some brothers for the final time, then walked out in a pair of heavy-stitched, stiff-ass denims that felt like sandpaper on his skin, a regular ol' button-up shirt on his back, and some sneaks. Under one hand was a cardboard box filled with his mail -- letters from Audria and from his son, pictures of both, and his release papers, everything that meant anything to him.

He got dropped at a Pittsburgh bus station by a prison transport, swapped his $25 release voucher with the bored pit-faced heeb at the counter and was on a bus headed to New York in another couple of hours. Technically, he was a free man.

He had spent five thousand, nine hundred and ninety-six days in hell. That was equivalent to thirteen years, eleven months and sixteen days, walking a tightrope, living with his guard constantly up, always watching his own back and sleeping with one eye open. He had a little over sixty grand on his books that the Feds were supposed to mail him by Priority in the next couple weeks. That, along with what he had stashed on the outside before going in, would guarantee some things. First, that he could get himself on the right track, start doing things legally. Second, he would be able to show his woman that he could handle his business, take care of her. And third, he could get his son situated.

Now, here he was, staring down the butt of a Ruger with his boy's eyes fast on his. Shit wasn't looking kosher at all. Not in the least lil' bit.

* * * * * *

"You got three seconds to start talking an' you better make it believable, or I'ma slump yo' ass."

Michael didn't doubt for a second his son was serious, but he wasn't having it. First, they didn't have time for this nonsense with the jump out squad getting ready to do what they did best – jump out. And second, he would be damned if he let any young'un, son or no, put a gun in his face. It wasn't happening.

In a move that surprised even him with its quickness, 'specially since he'd been away from the game for as long as he had, he stepped away from the barrel, whipped out one of his snub-nose babies, a .357 mag, and slammed it hard upside Skinny's jaw bone. The lil' dude was out on the floor in spit's time, which was exactly where Michael wanted him. He needed to handle business with his son, and he needed to do it without distraction. He turned to face his blood.

"Is me. Strong. Your pops," he said, wasting no time gettin' to it. "Put that down." He could tell his son was on the edge with an itch in his gun finger, and he needed to calm things down, but he wasn't talking to his child with a gun in his face.

Michael Jr. looked at him with distrust in his eyes, still clutching the .45 and pointing it dead at him. "You ain't my Pops. He in the Feds."

"Until two days ago," Michael answered him, keeping one eye on his boy's face and another on the piece. "Couple months back, Parole Board decided was time to let me out, so I'm out. Here. Come to get you. Now, I ain't sayin' this again, put that shit down or I'ma put it down for you."

Junior lowered the weapon to his side, but his finger never left the trigger, and he was still looking at Michael suspiciously. He was opening his mouth to talk, but Michael cut him off.

"Look, I know we got a lot to talk about. Know you got a lot to ask me, and I got some things I got to ask you too, but not here."

His son must've sensed something in his voice, 'cuz he was on that right away, questioning. "Why, what's up? You seen sump'n comin' in? There's this dude lookin' for me, say I owe him and..."

"Well, he ain't the only one lookin' for your ass right now," Michael interrupted. "Jump out squad up the block lookin' to make a move. Is time to bounce." Minutes later they were haulin' ass out a first floor window in back of the building and Michael felt right for the first time that day. He was leading his son to safety, saneness and hopefully, a new life together.

* * * * * *

El Valle Restaurant was this rice and beans Mexican joint in the heart of the South Bronx. Didn't look like much of nothing from the outside, and didn't look like much of nothing from the inside either, but damn, them Amigos could *burn* in the kitchen.

Michael was sitting in front of a massive plate of falling-off-the-bone roasted chicken with yellow rice, black beans, corn and platanos, *Spanish for plantains,* heavily seasoned with ground chile, cilantro and poblano pepper, and a huge hunk of almond flan on the side. Now, *this* is what food was supposed to be about. The chicken was crispy but still juicy, the rice fluffy but not soggy in his mouth, and the spicy flavors were exploding on his tongue soon as his fork landed.

Junior was sitting across from him, watching him with a mixture of wariness and distrust but with an aloof interest, a detached curiosity about the man in front of him claiming to be his father. In the last month being on the run with the Juice man after him, he had found himself more'n a lil' bit wishing he could seek his father's counsel. His old man had to be the wisest dude he knew. He wasn't just some schlump stupid enough to get busted and wasting 24-7s on lock. This was his father, and sure as he was that didn't nobody else give a fuck about him, he felt in his gut that his Pops was his only real ally in the world.

He had already tried to start conversation between them twice, but with no results. Each time he went there, Michael shut him down. He was so frustrated the second time that he slammed a hand on the table and got loud.

"Look, you actin' like eatin's more important to you 'n this, me an' you. You jus' grubbin' like this yo' first food or sump'n since you been out."

"Yeah, matter of fact, it is," Michael waved a half eaten drumstick at him. "So shut the fuck up and lemme enjoy it. We gon' get to you 'n me soon enough."

Junior laid back then, taking an occasional sip of the weak coffee he had ordered and watched his father eat. It was hard to believe his old man was actually here and had cared enough to come looking for him before even getting something to eat. It made him feel loved in a way he hadn't felt before, and proud that this man was his father.

He wasn't feeling this waiting thing though. He was trying to be patient but it wasn't easy. Hell, he had Niggaz looking for him and wasn't for no polite conversation neither. He knew what Juice was plannin' for him was ten times worse than what he'd done to his mother. Shit, every time he thought about Trina, he felt the hole inside him grow more massive. Okay, so he didn't put the hammer to her head, cock and pull, but he might as well had. Sure as he was breathin' he was just as responsible for killing his mother as Juice. That was always gon' be with him.

His father interrupted his dark thoughts unexpectedly, shoving his plates aside and taking a long swig of his beer.

"A'ight, let's get to this thing. We got a lot to cover and we only got 'bout an hour more 'fore I gotta be counted for, so let's get crackin'."

Michael Junior sat up a little taller in the booth figurin' he would start things off, but it was obvious he would have to get used to his old man's straight and direct approach.

"Three questions. I got three questions for you and I expect truth, hear me?"

Junior nodded.

"First, how much paper you owe an' to who? And keep shit simple, a'ight? Cut to the crash." Michael looked at his son, eyes daring him to come with even the smallest white lie. Junior thought his Pops would fuck him all the way up if he detected anything other than the truth.

"I owe sump'n like twenty-four Gs to this dude named Juice from over East Tre. He the one that…"

His father held up a hand, stopping him. "Is twenty-four Gs or *something like* twenty-four Gs?"

"Is twenty-four Gs," Junior confirmed.

"Second question," Michael counted off, holding up two fingers. "You usin' what you slanging?"

Junior shook his head, then realized his father was still waiting, apparently wanting an audible response.

"Naw, I'm not usin' a'ight? Smoke some blunts every now an' then, but nothing else."

Michael nodded. "Ok, home stretch. Last question. You know this cat was lookin' for you before or after he found your mother?"

He was unprepared for his son's reaction. He saw him inhale deeply a few times, then Junior put his head on the table and his shoulders started shaking. In a bone-weary voice and in stops and starts, he told his father the truth.

"I known he was lookin' for me from the jump, a'ight, but I didn't think he would get family involved, 'specially not Moms. I just figured if I stayed gone from 'round the house, she would be cool. Expected him to just keep looking for me. Didn't think he would hurt her, let alone off her."

Michael stood up abruptly, put a twenty and a fiver down on the table, then lightly tapped his son on the arm. "Come, let's walk."

They took off down the block and walked a bit in silence until Junior pulled out a Black from his pocket and lit up, taking some deep drags on the cigar. He offered the smoke to his father who looked at it strangely, took a hit, then handed it back. They walked on. When Michael felt it was time, he stopped and turned to his son.

"Look, I can tell you a lot of shit here. I can tell you I'm disappointed in you that you still managed to get caught up in the same life I warned you off of. I can tell you how stupid I think you was to steal from the hand supplying you. I can tell you what a fucking coward I think you was for runnin' and leavin' your mother to pay for your shit, to pay with her life."

Michael looked at him hard.

"But even if I waste air sayin' all that, it ain't changing nothing. What we got to focus on is the down-the-road scene, future days an' all that. Ain't no traveling back in time to fix the shit that's already broke, but we can set things in motion now so we not loop de loopin' all over the place and making the same mistakes when the future gets here."

Michael turned and walked over to the side of the road, copping a squat on a short, broken down half wall. Junior followed him and sat too. They sat together quietly for a long while, then Michael looked over at Junior.

"Son, my future is here, and I'm not talking place, I'm talking time. Now, much as I love you, I ain't fucking my future up for you. It's this simple. I can help you, and we're never gon' do details with that, but I can make all this shit you facing go away. I just need one thing from you."

"What?" Junior asked him after a bit.

"You gotta walk away from it and start fresh with me somewhere else."

"Somewhere else? Somewhere like where?"

Michael looked at him hard in the dim night light. "That shouldn't matter none to you. Make a choice. This madness, 'cuz that's what it is, or a new life with me somewhere else."

It wasn't hard for Junior to decide. Word on the street was Juice was lookin' to make an example out of him. Even if he managed to come up with the money on his own, which was damn near impossible, it wouldn't be enough to buy his life when somebody like Juice thought his rep was on the line. And he wasn't ready to clock out just yet. Maybe this new life with his Pops wouldn't be all bad. Maybe it could work.

He looked over at his father, happy to be able to give up control even in the short term, to someone he knew would always have his back.

He nodded, then stood up.

His father was on his feet next to him, immediately dwarfing him in size, he was so big.

Michael looked at him, then dapped his son for the first time, careful to give the moment its proper significance.

"Solid."

fifty-four
See You Later

Do not sit here and weep.
I am not here, I do not sleep.
I am the thousand winds that blow,
I am the diamond glint on snow.
I am the sunlight on ripened grain,
I am the gentle autumn rain,
I am the shining star at night,
When you awake to the morning light.
My time has come, I am at rest.
I am the sunset in the west,
I am the clouds that race above,
Where I watch over those I love.
Do not sit here and cry,
I am not here, I do not die,
So hear these words that now I say,
I am the love that guides your way.
                    - Author Unknown

    Audria finished reading the poem, walked a few feet to the mound of dirt piled high and partially enclosed by a short, purple-colored curtain, and stopped. Determined to hold it together, she bent, placing a single white rose on a clear patch of earth in between several dozen extravagant wreaths and exquisite floral arrangements.

Although the poetic words weren't hers, she had felt them just as deeply reading them as if they were birthed from the depths of her soul.

"This ain't goodbye, Precious," she whispered, blinking back her tears. "This is a 'see you later,' 'cuz we *gon'* see each other again, believe that." She stood up, stepped to one side, and closed her eyes along with the rest of the crowd to say The Our Father.

Forty-two years old, in the prime of her life with a husband who worshipped her, a love child too young to understand, and a rack of friends and colleagues who adored her. Great career, well respected by her peers and in her field, financially independent, awesome home, beautiful human being, not a care in the world. And just gone at forty-two. The dreaded C word bulled its way in, did its damage, ravaged the body and left a hollowed out shell of a woman who barely no one recognized towards the end.

For the umpteenth time, Audria found herself thinking how cruel and unfair this was, but like Nadira was all the time telling her, hadn't "nobody swore on a pack of bibles that life wouldn't smack you upside the head like a dry coconut fallin' out a tree." She felt good 'n smacked too, the noggin bruised like it had never been. And if she was feeling the pain of Gina's death so deeply, she couldn't begin to imagine what it must be like for Silas.

She looked across at him and winced at the devastated look on his face. He had been inconsolable, simply beside himself with grief since Gina died. It almost felt like he had stopped functioning. Some of their friends felt his judgment was seriously impaired too, and Audria had to wonder if they weren't right. The man had chosen to bring a 3-year old to a funeral for Chrissakes. It didn't make a bit of sense.

It was bad enough Isaiah had been crying for his mother almost non-stop, but to subject him to all this grief just didn't seem the wisest thing. If she'd had even the slightest hint Silas would have done this, she could've arranged for her Mom or one of her girlfriends to watch the little guy until this whole thing was over. But to have him here? Just wasn't right.

Soon as the minister finished with the closing prayer, she made her way over to them, and waited patiently while the steady procession of well wishers stopped past to shake hands. It seemed like almost half of HU's faculty had come out, including several deans, the general counsel, and the President of the University himself. It was obvious they had all loved Gina and would miss her.

Suddenly, she felt a tiny hand grasp hers and she looked down to find Isaiah's teary eyes looking up at her, obviously reaching out to something familiar, since his father was far from it these days. Immediately, she scooped him up into her arms and held him close, soothing his sobs and feeling his heart beats up close, right next to hers. It made her know *exactly* what she had to do. She handed Zi off to Silas, made sure he had a firm grip on him, then stepped forward, holding up her hands.

"Folks, thank y'all so much for coming out to Gina's homegoing, but we need to get the family, especially the little one here, back to the house and situated for the Repast." She thought about it and wondered if Silas had even given a second thought to the need for one. Hell, too late now. She took a quick look at her watch. "For those of you who plan on stopping by, we'll start around 4:30. Thanks again for all your love and support. See you in a few hours."

With that, she hustled Silas, still holding Isaiah, to the waiting limousine, saw him seated, then scooped Zi out of his arms as soon as he started reaching for her.

"Here, let me take him," she offered to Silas, then leaned over to give the driver instructions, making sure he understood his destination. She asked Silas a couple questions, not wanting to overwhelm him anymore than he already was, then hopped into her Pilot, buckled in Isaiah, and headed out after them.

On the drive, she was on her cell phone the whole way, calling everyone she knew until she found a reasonable soul-food caterer who could handle all the food arrangements on such short notice. Then it was one thing after the next. She was running around like a chicken without a head, putting out fire after fire at the house.

First, it was getting Isaiah situated in his room in front of the TV with his favorite Blues Clues tape, a PB&J sandwich in hand

and milk in his sippy cup. Next it was getting out extra seating for the guests coming and arranging all that. Then she had to go find Silas who had wandered off to the garage and was sitting on a milk crate, still in his black suit, guzzling on moonshine and staring at album pictures of Gina. She swallowed the lump in her throat as she glimpsed the beautiful pictures of her friend, but took charge of the situation like she was taking charge of everything else. She gathered up the albums, set them aside, then shooed Silas inside, putting him to work. Then it was on to the next thing until the guests started arriving.

Somewhere in the middle of all the frenzy, she saw Al come in, nodded to him and signaled upstairs. She breathed a sigh of relief as she saw him head up in the direction of Isaiah's room. That was one less thing she would need to worry about.

It was hours later after the last guests had left and she had cleaned up the mess, before she was able to really surface for air. By then, Silas was all the way drunk and had passed out in a stupor back in the garage. Obviously, he had found another stash of moonshine from somewhere. She headed upstairs, keeping her fingers crossed Al was still around.

She headed in the direction of Isaiah's bedroom but stopped short at the door. They had both fallen asleep, Al's long legs hanging off the bed and Isaiah curled up next to him, a little arm thrown back across his buddy's neck. She couldn't help but smile as she watched them, and was suddenly glad Gina had picked somebody like Al to be a joint guardian to her son. If nothing else, this boy would be cared for by people who loved him and who would do everything in their power to keep him out of harm's way.

All at once she realized she wasn't the only one watching. Somewhere in between her random thoughts, Al had wakened and was looking at her.

"That's the first time I've seen you smile like that," he said softly, obviously trying not to wake Isaiah. "You should do it more often. It suits you."

Audria looked away from whatever emotion she could see starting to fill his eyes and cleared her throat awkwardly. She wasn't going there with him.

"Listen, I need your help. Silas is passed out cold down in the garage. I want to get him up here and to bed."

"What about Zi?" Al asked, still whispering, and it dawned on her she hadn't even thought that far ahead.

"I guess I'm gonna have to take him with me. I mean, I was planning on giving Silas a break by keeping him for awhile, but I was gonna take him starting in a couple days, but I might as well pack his things and take him with me from tonight."

She watched him slowly extricate himself from Isaiah's tiny arm, and stand up cautiously, still trying to be quiet. Then they headed downstairs to find Silas. On the way down, it was almost like she knew he was getting ready to say something before he even opened his mouth.

"Audria, I've been wanting to call you," he said, his voice still almost a whisper. "I've been thinking about you, about our last time together, and wanted to apologize again. I hope you believe me when I said I would never force myself on you or on anybody."

Thinking about Nadira's advice, she made an effort to really listen to what he was saying and not allow herself to start getting all emotional. She nodded, letting him know she was listening.

"But what I said to you about the way I feel hasn't changed. I..."

"I know," Audria cut him off, not wanting to hear him say the words out loud again. It bothered her that he felt the way he did about her. Bothered her that she had something to do with causing him to fall for her, and that she would never be in a position to return his feelings.

"Let's get Silas and then we can talk for a little while, okay?"

Between the two of them, they struggled and strained and half carried, half dragged Silas' dead weight up to the master bedroom. Audria took off his shirt, socks and shoes, and rolled his drunk behind under the covers. She left two bottles of Evian on the nightstand next to him, rummaged in the bathroom medicine cabinet until she found some Extra Strength Tylenol, and left that out in plain sight too. Then she wrote him a note telling him she had Isaiah and would be keeping him for a few weeks while he sorted things out, and to give her a call when he felt up to it. Then she headed downstairs to look for Al.

She found him in the kitchen waiting with a cup of tea for her, and felt a twinge of something run through her as she remembered the last time he had made tea for her like this. It had been the morning after...

She cut that thought off soon as it surfaced, and pulled out a chair. Wasn't like she was expecting this to take too long. Taking a sip of the steaming hot tea, she set the cup down then forced herself to look at Al directly. She needed him to see the truth in her eyes.

"Al, I need to say some things to you."

He looked at her, waiting.

"First, I want to apologize for the way I've been treating you. I think you're a nice guy, I really do, and you haven't done anything to deserve me kirking out on you like I've been. So, I apologize."

He just looked at her and nodded. For some reason, she had this feeling that he wanted to reach across and hold her hand, but he kept still, his hands remaining in place.

"The next thing I want to tell you is this," she said, grabbing a braid and flicking it back. "I fucked up, okay? I was so in need of comfort and wanted to be with somebody so bad that night... the night we were together... that I allowed myself to just give in, instead of fighting something I knew wasn't supposed to happen."

She stopped, getting her thoughts together, and forced herself to slow down, taking another sip of tea. "Here's the thing, Al. What's done is done. Neither one of us can undo it..."

"I don't want to undo it," he interrupted her. "It was beautiful. You're beautiful."

Audria squirmed a little in her seat and ignored that. She wasn't going there with him.

"Please let me finish," she said softly, then went on when there was no further interruption. "The thing is, Al, that for me, *all* it was... was giving in to what I was feeling at the time, that need, but there was nothing else to it. There wasn't then, and there isn't now."

She looked him square dead in the face and kept going.

"Although I feel something every time I see you, I finally understand that all I feel is nothing but sexual attraction. I don't feel what you feel and my heart is for someone else, Al. I don't want to hurt you saying any of this, but I have to be honest. I *need* for you to understand that and for you to leave me be."

She stopped again and took a breath.

"Now, for whatever reason, Gina decided to kinda throw us together in this joint guardianship of Zi. I don't think she ever really believed in the love I have with my man, so maybe this was her way of trying to break that up, I don't know. But that's *not* going to happen. So I just want you to respect that Al. Please."

Audria sat there looking at him, waiting for him to say something.

He just stared at her for a long time, then finally got to his feet. She stood up as well.

"You know what Audria? I'm *always* going to love you. Whether it's today, tomorrow, next year or fifty years from now, I'm *always* going to love you." He stopped and Audria could see him struggling with his emotions. "But that love, Beautiful, by itself and without any interference from me, makes me *have to* respect your wishes."

He smiled a sad but genuine smile, then reached out to her. "Can I get a hug?"

Audria hesitated, but realized she was being silly. She knew Al would never hurt her. She sighed then walked into his arms, letting him hold her. She even rested her head on his shoulder for a little while.

"I'll always be here whenever you need me, whether it's for Zi or for you," he whispered softly to her, lightly stroking her back. But because she was already beginning to feel something fiery stirring in the pit of her stomach at being so close to him, she pretended not to hear what he said and stepped away.

Hours later, glad to finally be kicked back and relaxed in the warm comfort of her own home, she smiled, remembering how brave she had been facing Al and saying the things she said to him. It wasn't that she had ever lacked confidence or considered herself shy, because neither was true, but in days gone past, it would have been damn near impossible for her to be as open as she had been with him about what she really felt.

And to admit to a man she wasn't planning on getting with that she felt sexual attraction to him? That right there was a miracle all by itself. But when she really laid back and thought about it, she knew this was part of the new Audria that she was really beginning to appreciate, the one that had surfaced after facing her demon.

So much had happened in her life in the last year and a half and she was still getting used to all the changes and new emotions, but she was embracing every bit of it too. Nadira sure nuff hadn't been lying when she told her to get ready for change. Talk about your prophesying, 'cuz it had been change after change after change that kept coming her way.

Sipping on a glass of Chardonnay, she started going over all of it in her mind like a projector reel shuttering back through an old black and white film. Finding Michael. Falling in love. Messing up and sleeping with Al. Facing her dark past. Confronting her uncle. His brutal death. Her Momma's heart attack, then moving in with her for some months to take care of her. That whole mess with Angela and the carjacking. Gina's battle with cancer and then her passing. Her book project. This joint guardianship of Isaiah. It was so much, almost too much at times, but she was still here daggone it, and she felt bold and strong in her spirit that if she had faced all those things and was still standing, then she could face anything.

Audria set her wine glass down then walked into the guest bedroom already set up for Isaiah. She sat on the edge of the bed, and watched his tiny, sleeping form and felt her heart swell with love looking at the little life laying there. This wasn't the first time she had experienced this deep maternal tug in the pit of her being that she was feeling. A tug that told her she wanted this, wanted it permanently. She didn't want to make Michael feel guilty about not being able to grant her this particular wish, but she knew she had to start trying to find out how he felt about children. She wanted to be a mother. Wanted to be mother to *his* child. Maybe even to more than one child.

She had even talked about it with Viola and it was just like her Momma to point out the practical way of looking at things.

"You bettah hurry up an' ask your Michael how he feel 'bout havin' rugrats then. All you need is to find out he can't stand kids an' think they nothin' but a nuisance, when you all set to plop one out."

As much as Audria hated to agree with her mother, she knew she was telling the truth. This was the number two reason why couples broke up, the number one being money. If one half of a couple wanted children and the other didn't, that could throw the whole relationship into a tailspin that was hard to recover from. It would make more sense if people took the time to discuss something so basic beforehand, but that was people for you. Folks were always jumping into shit before knowing what they were jumping into. She would make sure she did things different with Michael. Just as soon as she could find him.

Audria tucked the covers up around Zi's chin, kissed him for the umpteenth time, then turned off the lights, and headed for her room. The first place she looked when she walked in was at the nightstand and the framed picture of Michael that was the only one she had of him. She frowned. It was bothering her like crazy that she hadn't heard back from him. She didn't understand it. Was he pissed about something? Hurt? In the hole? On punishment? What? It didn't make a bit of sense that he wasn't responding to her letters and she had been writing him constantly.

The one thing she knew though was that he was still *with* her. She had tried several times to explain this feeling she had to her Momma and to her girlfriends, but they always looked at her like she was more'n a little nutty. It was just that she *felt* Michael's love almost like a physical blanket covering her. It had been that way between them for months now, and the one thing that made her know she wasn't loopy was that he had told her the same thing about *feeling* her.

She sat on the edge of the bed, kicked her heels off and started massaging a foot, still looking at his picture. She smiled at him. "Boy, I'm gon' rock your world when you come home to me, you hear me?" She busted out giggling just as the phone started chirping next to her.

She picked up. "Hello?

"Oh, it's you, Momma." And they were off and blabbin', Audria answering all Viola's nosy questions about the funeral, who was wearing what, who looked tore up from the floor up, and who was eyeing who. In the middle of all that, the doorbell rang and she snatched a twenty out her purse and headed for the front door to pay for her food. Didn't make no kinda sense that she hadn't gotten a scrap of all that good soul food the caterers had delivered to the Repast. She was some kinda hungry and had ordered Chinese soon as she got in the house.

"Momma, hold on. It's my food delivery," she said, snatching the door open, ready to hand over money. But it wasn't the cute Asian guy standing there who normally brought her food. When she saw who it was instead, she slammed the door closed and put her back to it, scared out of her mind. What she was seeing just wasn't possible.

fifty-five
What's Mine

All the air was sucked clean out his chest when she slammed the door closed in his face. He understood what she had to be feeling, but wasn't about to give her too much time to process nothing. She might lock the door or something, and he hadn't come all this way to get shut out. He turned the knob and very slowly pushed the door open.

When he stepped inside, she was standing there staring at him like she was seeing a ghost, her mouth opening and closing like she was trying to say something but couldn't figure out what.

"Hey Babygirl," he said, drinking her in with his eyes.

She just kept standing there staring at him, and the more he looked at her, the more he wondered whether surprising her hadn't been a bad idea. She seemed scared out her mind, and she looked like she was shaking, standing there in her pretty stockinged feet.

He started feeling uncomfortable, but nipped that quick as he felt it. This was all he had been dreaming about for more than a solid year. Now that he was here, he wasn't about to second-guess nothing. He stepped to her, then realized she was holding a phone. He could hear squawking coming from that direction and pointed at it. She seemed to gather herself then, looked at the phone strangely, then put it to her ear.

"Momma, I gotta call you back," she said, after listening for awhile. He heard some more squawking, then, "No, everything's fine. I'll call you back." She carefully set the phone down on a nearby table and then moved like lightning. She slammed into him with a speed and force he wasn't expecting, almost knocking him off his feet, but he held firm.

"Ohmigawd Michael. It's really you. Here. Standing here. How's this possible? Ohmigawd... ohmigawd... OHMIGAWD!" She kept repeating the same thing over and over, but all the while her hands were on his body touching him, exploring, verifying for herself that he was really standing there. She was all over him. His chest, shoulders, abs, arms, neck, face.

"Yeah, is me, Babygirl," he assured her, holding her still. "Your man's here." Then he scooped her up, holding her tight, as close as he could get her without crushing her. He could feel her shaking almost violently in his arms, her body wracked, and she wound her arms around his neck like she planned on keeping them there forever.

He stood that way holding her, smelling her exotic scent, from the oils in her hair to some earthy perfume she was wearing. And he could feel her heart beat, like a steady gallop in her chest. He walked with her across the room and set her down gently on a chaise lounge right next to a fireplace. As much as he felt like never letting go, he pushed away from her after awhile and stood back a bit.

"Lemme look at you Sweetheart. I need to see what's mine."

She was sitting there, thick and phat, nice big ass thighs, just as fine as she wanted to be. She was dressed up in stockings, no shoes, and a little black sleeveless dress that showed off her toned arms. Her caramel-colored skin was radiant, beautiful, and looked soft, flawless. It was hard to believe he was finally here.

She looked up at him, a tilt to her beautiful, oval-shaped face, her big brown eyes soft, blazing with life and with love for him. That look made him want to sign his soul over to her forever.

He smiled at her, experiencing what felt like pure joy to him, for the first time in his life. Her eyes started tearing up, and she reached up for him. He stooped down in front of her, feeling her arms encircle his neck again. He felt like he would never ever take this woman's touch for granted, it was *that* sweet. He could feel their connection in the deepest part of his being.

"Oh baby, you just don't know. To have you here today of all days? God, thank you so much for sending him to me just when I need him most. You're so good to me."

Michael pulled back from her, surprised and a little confused at what she was saying. At the question in his eyes, she explained. "I buried my friend Gina today. Remember I wrote you about her having cancer? Well, she passed this past Wednesday." He nodded, simultaneously tightening his arms around her, instinctively wanting to shield her from anything else that could hurt her.

She looked up at him. "She was soooo young, Michael. This shouldn't have happened to her."

"As opposed to somebody else?" he asked her gently. "Baby girl, can't none of us second guess the man upstairs, a'ight? When it's your go, is your go, and if we behind try to say it ain't fair when somebody we love goes, that's like telling God He don't know what He doin'." He tipped her chin up with a finger. "I know you miss your friend, Audria, but ain't it better she not sufferin' no more? You said she was, right?"

She nodded, and he moved to sit next to her, cradling her closer. "What about your friend's son? Didn't she have a little one? And her husband? They a'ight?"

Audria instinctively looked to the back bedroom, thinking of Isaiah, then shook her head. "Silas is so messed up, Baby. That's Gina's husband. He's not handling this well at all, and poor little Isaiah doesn't understand what the heck is going on. I brought him home with me. Just didn't think it was a good idea for him to be staying with his father right now."

"You did good," he said, rubbing her neck.

She sighed, laying her head against his broad shoulders. She was so tired she could barely think straight. She knew she needed to be peppering him with questions right now, asking him where the hell he'd been, why he hadn't responded to any of her letters, and how come it was possible he was even standing in her living room. But she was physically and emotionally drained. She was trying to shake the tiredness away to say something, but he shushed her.

"I know you got a lotta questions you need me to answer for you, and I promise you it's gon' happen, but right now I need you to trust me, a'ight?"

It was like watching a storm cloud come rolling in across her face, temporarily obliterating his sun.

"No, that's not gon' work," she said, shaking her head and moving away from him. "Far as I knew, the last time I heard from you, you were in prison. Now you just show up on my doorstep telling me I gotta trust you? You need to give me more than that, Michael."

He was seeing another side of her for the first time, and he found it sexy as all back round, but she didn't have to know that. He stared at her for a long while, then put a frown on his face. He was gon' have some fun with this. He stood up, keeping his body language tight and making his face dead serious.

"A'ight, you ain't gon' trust me? Cool." He started heading for the door. "You want me to go? 'Cuz I didn't come here for this."

She was on her feet and in front of him in a flash. "Oh God, are you crazy? I don't want you to go anywhere, Michael. I'm… I'm sorry. It's just that…" Her voice tapered off and she stopped talking when she realized he was messing with her.

"You not right," she hollered at him, raising a balled-up fist in the air. "I'm gon' get you." Then she launched herself at him like a missile, but he grabbed her, spinning her around so her back was to him and wrapped her up in the circle of massive arms.

"Ain't no gettin', Audie. You got me," he whispered in her ear, encircling her waist and pulling her back against his body, letting her feel all of him. The moment felt strange to him, surreal-like. This was all he had been thinking about and dreaming about, coming home to this woman, but in lock-up, because of the element he was around 24-7, he lived most days in an emotional void, denying himself the full strength of *any* emotion, except for anger really. Anger served him well on the pound, kept his awareness up, kept him alive. Now though, he was feeling so much emotion coursing through him, it almost felt like *too* much. But like with everything else involving this woman, he wasn't running from it.

He turned her around, touching her shoulders gently and looked deep in her eyes. "I'm here, Baby girl. Let me *feel* you." He didn't have to tell her that he wasn't just referring to a physical touch, that he wanted to *feel* her love wash over him like a passionate rain. He knew she would understand without him saying another word.

They came together hard, fast, strong, emotions bare. He kissed her deep, tasting the sweetness of her mouth, drinking her. He could feel her tasting him too, drinking greedily from his mouth, and that made him want her even more.

A part of him wanted to rush this, to speed through it so he could be inside her, giving her what he could feel her wanting, needing, but the other side of him needed this to be long, never-ending, so he could savor every little moment and enjoy each one separately, giving her the same.

He picked her up, hands sinking into the curvy, round sweetness of her phat ass, feeling her legs automatically wrap around his muscular thighs. She started to shake in his arms again, and when he pulled away to look at her face, the tears were flowing freely.

"Whas' wrong, Baby girl? Talk to me."

"Michael, I love you *so* much. I've been dreaming about this, about you coming home to me. Having the opportunity to touch you, feel you, taste you, share *all* of me with you, and I just can't believe you're here, standing here, and my dreams have come alive, you know? They're really real, but it still feels so strange."

"Yeah, I know what you mean," he nodded. "I feel it too. But you know what's good? We got the power to decide how we want this to go."

She slid down off him, then reached up and touched his face, tracing his features with her fingertips, and following them with her mouth, giving him sweet, butter soft kisses. When she got to his mouth, he took over, mashing his lips to hers and sucking her tongue into his mouth. She ground her body into him, and he could feel the ripe fullness of her breasts punching into his chest, and the curvy hips with pelvis thrown forward, straining to feel him.

She started a low pitched moaning deep in her throat that sounded so full of need that it instantly made him hard. He grabbed her ass pulling her closer, grinding her thick hips into his groin. She was breathing hard, her chest moving up and down rapidly, and she kept nipping at his lips, giving him tiny love bites that made him want to lay her down where she stood.

"I need you, Michael," she told him hoarsely, her voice thick, barely above a whisper. "Need you bad."

He took one of her hands in his and slid it down the length of him, letting her feel his thickness. "You not alone, Baby girl. I need you too." He kissed her again hard, sucking her tongue into his mouth and letting her need and desire wash over him, fueling his own even more.

He started getting that surreal feeling again. The closest he had come to touching a woman in the last fourteen years was in his dreams. To go from dreams and the occasional beat off to holding a flesh and blood woman, to actually feel her heart beating and to hear her moan passionately for him, because of him, that shit felt other worldly, like it shouldn't be happening. In some weird way, he almost felt like he was sneaking a guilty pleasure. That bothered him some, 'cuz this was his woman, no one else's, and who else was supposed to touch her but him.

He began caressing the nape of her neck, ready to lay her back on the chaise, when the doorbell rang, interrupting the moment.

"That's my food," she said, about to go around him, but he held her in place. "I'll get it, Baby girl. Just wait."

Audria watched him walk away from her, watched him move, how lithe and beautiful he was like some big, black jungle cat, a combination Vin Diesel, Morris Chestnut, The Rock and Training Day Denzel all rolled into one. Although darker than her, his skin was smooth and unblemished, his bald head shining. She remembered Vanessa talking about that penitentiary glow brothers got and how they would keep it sometimes up to four, five months after they got out. She guessed that's what she was looking at.

Her man was fine with a capital F. He had on some Tommy jeans, a white wife beater, and a plain black unbuttoned shirt. Everywhere she looked there were muscles bulging, especially in his chest area. And he smelled delicious too. She couldn't wait to feel his naked body next to her. She watched him pay for the Chinese, take the bag, and walk back in.

"Come," he said, taking her arm. "You gotta be hungry. Where's the kitchen?"

As much as he wanted to give in to everything he was feeling and take her to bed, there were things they had to cover. He had already decided never to put his woman in a position of having to ask. Not about the important shit anyway. It wasn't fair to make her wait for answers. 'Sides, he needed to slow things down, and he was hungry too, so they might as well eat.

She showed him into the kitchen and sat when he pulled out a chair for her. She was loving his style. He walked around finding stuff on his own without asking. Bowls, plates, forks and knives. She was surprised at how comfortable he seemed in a brand new environment, but she was glad. This was exactly how he needed to be if they were going to live together. Damn, that was another question she needed an answer to. She decided to ask.

"Baby, you seem so relaxed and comfortable, although you've never been here before."

He turned around and smiled at her. "I'm comfortable anywhere I'm breathing, Beautiful. Always comfortable in my skin. Everything else is just geography."

He set her plate down in front of her, dished out some of the Kung Pao chicken, Lo Mein and steamed spinach for both of them, then sat next to her. They ate in a charged silence, both of them feeling the weight of unspoken questions and answers between them and the still lingering effect of their passion. He knew she was antsy but Michael had to make her understand from the jump that he was a different kinda cat who walked a different kinda way. It was either she get comfortable with that now and learn to trust him, or was no use. 'Cuz that side of him wasn't up for negotiation or change. He was who he was and there was gon' be no more apologies to no damn body for the way he rolled.

He could feel Audria's eyes on him every move he made. When he couldn't stand it anymore, he looked over at her. What he saw in her eyes, the unguarded love and raw desire, made him forget the food in front of him. He was suddenly hungry for something else, ravenous, and all this delaying wasn't moving him any closer to it.

"Okay, let's get this thing poppin'. Got some things for you, Baby girl." He pulled some papers from his pocket. He handed Audria a picture.

"That's my blood, my son Michael Jr. He's sixteen and a half and done got into some things that ain't for him, but I'm handling all that."

He spent a quick moment wondering whether to give his woman details on exactly *how* he was handling things for Junior, but something told him to fall back on that. Much as he was determined to walk the line now, he was equally sure situations would jump off every now and then that called for him to buck back to the old him, just for a taste. He didn't think Audria would be comfortable with knowing that right now, so he left it alone, choosing instead to talk about his boy.

"Here's the thing Audria. It's a package deal. Love me, love my son. From here out, he's with me."

Audria started to say something but he put a hand up and shook his head. "We'll talk about it." He passed her something else. She scanned the official looking form with the Pennsylvania state seal on it, then looked at him questioningly.

"Thas' my release papers. It basically says the state parole board decided to let me go home early. Not sure why exactly, but I ain't never been one to question God. He had to do this for me, for us. Couldna happened otherwise. The thing with this early release is that since 2015 was my official release date, I'm gon' be on papers til' then."

"What does that mean, Baby?" Audria asked.

"It means I still gotta walk the line, watch my step and all that 'til I'm off papers. I gotta see a p.o., that's a parole officer, once a month. Gotta demonstrate to him I can be trusted. Gotta show him I can keep a job, drop clean urines, stay outta trouble, show up on time for meetings and sh... stuff. Then, if he gets comfortable with what I'm showing and after he gets good 'n ready, he might decide to move our meetings to once every three months. Basically Baby girl, this just says I ain't all the way free, not yet."

He looked at her. "Plus, I'm released back to New York, my home state. Much as I want to be here with you, gotta stay there awhile, work, prove myself to this dude, and then we can put in for a state-to-state transfer after awhile. Right now, I'm stayin' in a halfway house, but I'm tryin' to get some rooms for me and Junior, just until we can state transfer."

He could see the look on her face as she asked the obvious. "How long you gotta stay in New York, Michael?"

"At least three months, maybe four," he answered her, not wanting to sugarcoat nothing. It was best he kept it all the way real with her.

He reached into his pocket for another piece of paper and again handed it to Audria. She looked at it and her eyes widened when she saw what it was.

"Thas' a check for thirty-four thousand and some change. Thas' what I got from the Feds for my time in. They took out for fines, penalties, and my restitutions. This what's left. Want you to have this. This for us. Put it in the bank, whatever, but this for us."

Audria looked at him. She felt a little dumbfounded. "You sure, Baby?"

"Never more," he nodded at her. "Look, I know some of this is new to you, but I'm old school, Baby. I ain't one of these kinda dudes that believe things gotta be separate in a relationship. I think what's mine is yours and what's yours is mine."

He caressed her cheek and pushed a braid back out her face. "But that's the way I think. I know you might need me to prove myself to you before you get comfortable thinking the same way, but it's cool. We'll just go with the what's mine is yours part for now, a'ight?"

He handed her a final piece of paper. She took it from him, looked at it, then looked at it again closer. She felt tears welling in her eyes. It's like he had thought about everything she needed to ease her mind.

"Oh baby, you didn't have to do this," she said, but he shushed her, standing and pulling her to her feet. She kept holding the slip of paper. It was dated two days earlier, and was from a clinic in the Bronx. It was proof he had been tested and was HIV-Negative. "You really didn't have to do this, Michael."

He shushed her again. "Yeah, I did. This is so you never have to worry. I can't offer you a lot Audria, but I'm gon' show you my word is my bond. Promise you that sooner or later when I say something to you, anything, you gon' rest easy knowin' it's *always* gon' be truth."

He stepped off, and she watched him take their plates, wash the dishes, then dry his hands. Then he started moving around finding light switches and turning them off. He came back and held a hand out to her. She looked up at him.

"Can I take you to bed now, Wife?" he asked her, his voice a low growl, deep, husky but soft. He looked down at her with love in his eyes. Then he invaded her space, slipping an arm tightly around her waist and pulling her close. Audria didn't mind though. She wanted him all up in her space and so much more.

"Yes Husband," she answered him, liking the feel of that word on her tongue. She held her man's hand, feeling the power of their love wash over her when he held hers in return.

"Let's go to bed."

epilogue
My Future

Audria was in the kitchen whipping up some good ol' fashioned, down home, Southern-style cooking. Fried chicken. Baked chicken. Collards. Dressing. Mac and cheese. String beans. Corn on the cob. Corn pudding. Baked beans. Mashed potatoes, from scratch. Turkey barbecue. Corn bread. And her specialty, a double decker sweet potato pie with almonds.

She hardly ever cooked this way anymore, especially since this stuff always went straight to her thighs and since Viola was on such a strict diet, but hell, this was a special occasion. Her man was home. At least for a few days, anyway. He had already told her he hadn't gotten permission to visit her, and as much as she wanted him to stay, neither one of them wanted him in trouble. They only had two more days together until he had to go back to New York, so she was determined to make it all count.

She peeked around the corner at him sitting on the living room floor with Isaiah. Zi was showing him one of his picture books and Michael was reading from it, pointing out pictures to the little guy. Her heart ached with the love she felt for this man. He was so natural with people. Just like she had come to understand over the many months communicating with him, there wasn't a pretentious bone in his body. He was simple in his thinking and the way he expressed himself, real as anybody could get. And when he chose to, he could be as open as the gates of heaven. Hell, he was charming the socks off a 3-year old kid who usually went screaming in the opposite direction if anybody new even tried to say hey to him. *That* was her man.

She went back to her cooking, tasting the peanut and giblet gravy she was making to go with the mashed potatoes. As she reached across the stove, she felt the soreness between her legs and smiled. Lawd, the man had some serious skills in the bedroom. He was like some insatiable beast that kept coming back for more, and even when she was good and exhausted, feeling like she had run eight miles followed up by a three-hour Zumba workout, she just couldn't say no to him.

As big as he was, she was surprised at how versatile a lover he was. It's like he instinctively knew when to be slow, almost agonizingly so with her, to where she had to beg him over and over to stop. And then when both their need reached its peak, fiery hot desire that felt like it would consume them, he entered her fast, pounding rough and hard, filling her up with a fullness she had never experienced before, raking her back walls and eliciting multiple orgasms that washed over her in waves of pleasure.

"I need this, Audie. Need you," he whispered fiercely to her, as he covered her with his massive body. "Gimme your juice, Baby girl. Lemme have it. Gotta have it." Audria loved it, loved the feel of him handling her so effortlessly, turning her this way and that in one position after the next, as he found new ways to bring her even more pleasure. She loved him talking dirty to her too, something that got her fired up even more. Every time she felt like she was starting to get used to his style, thinking ahead to what was next, he would come with something new and blow her mind all over again.

In the beginning, she hadn't really thought she would be up for making love. She felt so drained from the long day and the emotional rollercoaster that all she wanted to do was lay her body down. They took a shower together, and it was obvious he was the exact opposite to her. She felt self conscious about some of her body's flaws and having him see them, but he acted like he had been undressing in front of her for years. When his clothes were off, she understood why. His body was flawless perfection. She had never seen anything like it, except for maybe in bodybuilding magazines, but he seemed oblivious to the effect he had on her. She couldn't keep her eyes off him. It made her hungry to watch.

In the shower, she washed his back and as much of his body as he would allow her to, then he bathed her body slowly, taking his time, running the soapy washcloth over every surface and through every crevice. By the time he was through, she was shaking so violently with need that her knees felt like they would buckle if he wasn't holding her up. They stood together under the showerhead, kissing passionately, letting the water rain down on them. Then he took her to bed.

He laid next to her, the king sized bed easily handling his weight. Slipping an arm around her shoulders, he pulled her close, cradling her head against his neck. She began lightly, almost absentmindedly caressing his chest, feeling the bulging smoothness of it beneath her fingers. Beside her, he stirred, turning his body slightly to face her.

"Okay, you gon' have to help me out a lil' bit here. I got will power like the next man, but I'm trying to keep my hands off you 'cuz I know you gotta be tired. Ain't gon' happen though if you keep touching me like you doing."

Audria rolled over and purposely pushed her bare breasts up against him, then she deliberately reached for him, caressing the rock hard thickness between his muscular legs. "I don't recall asking you to keep your hands off me. Why don't you forget all about whatever willpower you're trying to have?" She didn't have to tell him twice. It was on from there. He surprised her by how long he lasted his first time. She thought men who hadn't had sex in a long time usually couldn't go very long before coming, but he disproved that theory, lasting almost forty-five minutes their first time. He got more and more longwinded each time after that until she had to demand sleep.

They both drifted off, but not an hour later, she was reaching for him and he was right there, ready for her in every way. After one of their hotter sessions, he rolled over from between her legs, then sat up, propping pillows up behind him and leaning against the headboard. She sat facing him, cross-legged Native style, reached over to wipe his face, then fanned herself a little.

"What?" she asked him, seeing he obviously had something on his mind.

"I'm just thinking about my boy," he answered. "You a'ight with the idea of him being here when the transfer comes through?"

"Of course," Audria assured him, not even needing to think about it. "As long as he's not gonna get into trouble here, and you think you can handle him, I'm okay with it."

"Oh, I can handle him," he promised her. "Ain't nothin'. That's the last thing you need to worry about, Baby girl. Nothing's changed. I still got you."

She smiled at him, then got quiet. She was trying to figure out a way to bring up her desire to have a baby, but couldn't quite decide on the best approach. She was ready to just blurt something out, when he surprised her first.

"How you feel about us having a baby?"

Audria's head jerked up and she gave him an intense look. "Are you serious?" she asked him.

"If you don't want to, it's cool, but I was thinking it would be something to see what you look like pregnant. Think you would make one helluva sexy momma."

He smiled at her and Audria smiled back. "We'll talk about it," she said, trying to be cool, but feeling like doing a cartwheel on the inside. Things just seemed to be falling in place for them.

"You know we gotta get married first, right? Our baby's gon' be all the way legal."

She gave him a weird look. "Are you asking me to marry you, Michael?"

"Woman, what I gotta ask you for. You already my wife. We just gotta make the thing official, on paper and before God."

She folded her arms and started pouting. "Well damn, how totally unromantic is that. I want to be asked."

"Yeah, a'ight," he said, his voice mocking, then he reached out and poked her in the ribs. "You gotta let me do me. It's gon' come. Just wait for it."

She huffed out loud, then laid back, turning on her side and burying her toes under his.

"I'm not changing my name, hope you know that," she said, play pouting.

"Oh yes you are. Gotta be Strong. Like your man."

"Unh unh, Big Poppa. I like my name. I'm keeping it."

"What? You don't like Strong?"

"I like Hope better."

"Okay, what about if you do Audria Hope Strong?"

"Nah, how 'bout I do Audria Strong Hope?" Audria countered. "Or, what if you do Michael Hope Strong and I do Audria Strong Hope? We'll keep people good and confused and guessing 'bout our names."

"Don't care 'bout people. Just care 'bout us, 'bout you."

She tickled the bottom of his feet with her toe. "You care about me? For real?"

"Yeah," he growled at her, pushing her toe away.

She put it back, tickling him some more. "For real, for real? You care about me?"

He pushed her toe away but started tickling her with his own. "Fo' sho'."

She rolled over, opening her legs, making sure he got a good, long look. "Come show me how much."

"Bet," he answered, and was on her in much less than a New York minute.

In the morning, she woke up to find him gone. She was about to panic when she heard voices in the kitchen. Pulling on a robe, she walked out to find him and Zi sitting together at the counter eating out of a big bowl of cereal. She kissed both her men good morning, grabbed a spoon, and joined in.

They talked softly, enjoying something so simple as having their first breakfast together, and Michael told her his plans and how long he could stay. Then he got a kinda strange look on his face that Audria couldn't read.

"What Sweetheart? What is it?"

"Just thought about something I want to do today, if that's cool."

"What?" she asked, expecting something strange.

"Wanna go grocery shopping."

"Grocery shopping?" she asked him, her voice full of surprise. "Why grocery shopping?"

"Baby girl, when you've spent almost fourteen years having somebody else decide what to feed you and you have no say over what you put in your stomach, then grocery shopping is one of the first things you want to do. It's options, Audie. Options I ain't had in way too long."

She reached across and caressed his face, suddenly making up her mind about what else she wanted to do with their day.

"I want to cook for you, Baby," she told him, feeling energized and the most happy she had ever been. "I want to get in that kitchen when we come home from shopping and burn for hours, you hear me?"

"Do you then, Momma," he patted his rock hard mid-section. "It's 'bout time I had me some food that loved me."

She shooed them out the kitchen, showed Michael where the guest bathroom was, and handed him towels and washcloth. Then she washed up Lil Zi, dressed him, and propped him up with a book in the living room. She took a quick shower herself, threw on some jeans shorts, a tank top, and some slippers, and they were out. In less than two hours, they were back with a whole rack of groceries, and she was in front the stove ready to burn.

She liked the fact that in a short while, she would be able to cook for her man every day if that's what she felt like. She was determined to make every day for him as happy and idyllic a day as she could make it. He was a good man and deserved nothing less. Yeah, he had made some mistakes, but didn't everybody? And he had done his time. Obviously too, they wouldn't have let him out early if somebody somewhere wasn't convinced he had changed.

It surprised her that she wasn't the least bit worried, had no trepidation at all about him or the prospect of them living together, even having his son come live with them. It felt like the most natural thing in the world to be with Michael, and she was going to follow her heart until her feet fell off.

She took another peek round the corner at him sitting on the floor, just as comfortable as he wanted to be, playing with Isaiah. They had so much to talk about, but she had no doubt that the things that needed to happen, would happen.

He would have to find a job, although she wasn't sure what he would do. They would have to get his son situated, make him feel welcome, and get him into a good high school. She would have to take care of Zi until Silas was in better shape and ready to take him. And then there was Viola. Lawd, she didn't even want to begin to imagine the arguments she knew were coming when her Momma realized she was moving a man into her house, but it was what it was. Viola would loudly voice her objections, Audria would listen to her and they would argue, but in the end she was gon' do exactly what she wanted to do. It was time she stopped living to please other people, her Momma included.

On her own front, it was time she decided some things once and for all. Nadira had already told her point blank she needed to get rid of the barriers in her life that were keeping her from success. And although she hated to admit it because it paid the bills, she knew her job was one of those barriers. So, she would have to decide to step out on faith and let it go. If she had the will, God would have to make a way. She had to believe in the power of her writing. It's what she had always wanted to do with her life, and it was time to embrace it all the way or leave it alone.

There was so much to think about, so many preparations she needed to make to begin their life together, but she wasn't afraid. Hell, she was excited about all of it, couldn't wait to get started. She looked at him and he suddenly raised his head, meeting her eyes. This was her man, her husband-to-be, her rock, her everything. She was looking at her future.

She crossed her eyes, stuck her tongue out at him, giggled, and went back to her cooking.

THE END

… for now!

AUTHOR'S NOTE

This project has been years in its coming, but I thank God for giving me the strength and courage to see it through to the very end. There are a great many people who deserve thank-you's and I'd be remiss if I didn't single them out by name here.

To the Unnamed... here. I still think of you from time to time and marvel at what almost was. Thank you for being who you are and for ultimately showing me the way to always speak truth.

To my Family. Love to each and every one of you. From Mommy right on down the line. Your support is constant.

To Dennis. My heart is yours. I'm thankful to our Higher Power for doing His work in us and allowing us to find each other, even though it felt like a gazillion katrillion years in the coming. I dream about the day when I'm finally your Mrs.

To my Girlz. The ones who read this book years before the masses and who were so open and honest with your feedback, suggestions, criticisms, and of course, love. Regina "Gina" Hill. Angela Robinson. Tonya Richardson. Stacey Sauter. Every one of you believed in me and I thank you for it. And to my soul sistah at work -- Audrey Morris. Your spirit never fails to inspire.

To My Readers. Although the great majority of this book is fiction and should be treated as such, I do however, believe that there are some very real 'teachable' moments that can be found in this book on how to move oneself past personal tragedies to a place of inner peace, healing and self-love. If even one person comes away with some lesson learned by turning these pages, then I've done my job.

Light & Love!

Olivia

QUESTIONS FOR BOOK CLUB DISCUSSION

1) What do you think about a love affair between an inmate and a "free" person? Would you "go there"? Under what circumstances?

2) Were there particular situations and/or characters you identified with in the book? If so, how? And why?

3) Audria decides to tell Michael about her infidelity with Al. What did you think about that decision? Do you think it was necessary? If you were in a similar situation, would you tell?

4) The relationship between Audria and her "girlz" appears solid, even though they are all three very different people. Do you think those differences help or hurt the forging of such a strong bond between them? Why or why not?

5) Can you equate the side of Audria that made her want to dabble in S&M and the dark side of eroticism, to the abuse that she had experienced in her early life?

6) What did you think about Nadira and her 'work' with Audria at having her get to know her physical self more intimately? Do you think it was necessary for her to merge her physical self with her emotional self? Would you yourself have been open to that kind of 'bare-all' intense scrutiny?

7) Did you agree with Viola and her initial belief that Audria's relationship with an inmate would bring her nothing but heartache? What did you think about their mother/daughter relationship?

8) Did you think that Audria's 400-mile drive to confront her uncle and her past was necessary? Could she have done it in some other way? If so, what were some other alternatives?

9) Do you think that Audria's uncle was murdered or did he simply kill himself in an unusual way? And if you do think he was murdered, who do you think murdered him?

10) Do you think an inmate involved in a relationship with a 'free' person should have the right to ask that person to be faithful? How long is 'too long' to wait for someone in prison to be released?

11) What did you think of the character Al? Do you believe he's really in love with Audria? Could you see a relationship developing between them?

12) The issue of guardianship is a tough one. Would you say yes to the kind of request Gina made of Audria, particularly under the same circumstances?

13) At what point in the book did you decide if you liked it or not? And was there a particular thing or situation that helped you make that decision?

14) Name your favorite thing overall about the book. Your least favorite.

15) Would you read a sequel to this book?

The author resides in the Washington, DC Metropolitan area and is available to attend book club events to read excerpted portions of the book and to answer your questions. Email your requests and/or questions to: olivia_scotland@yahoo.com. All inquiries will be responded to. Thanks for reading!

Olivia Scotland, a/ka Lady O is, by self-definition, a spiritually driven creative expressionist who is most alive when putting pen to paper. Originally from the Caribbean, she has been writing since childhood. She has self-published six mini books of poetry and has directed and starred in a one-woman production called "Windows to my Soul" produced by Phoenix Theatre D.C. She resides in the Washington, DC Metropolitan area, and is presently at work on the sequel to *Hearts On Lock*.